THE CHOSEN'S CALLING

GAILA KLINE-HOBSON

Words of encouragement from my wonderful editor, Jennifer Rees, editor of the *Hunger Games* and many other books:

Thank you so much for sharing *THE CHOSEN'S CALLING* with me. It is such an absorbing and terrific read. I deeply admire the idea behind this book (even from the beginning from your brief!) and love how Dina, Jo, and Gabe, our beloved warrior angels, are trained to battle evil and learn a lot about themselves in the process. I also really love how you work with the idea that there are many commonalities among faiths, and that, as you say, we are more alike than different. The inclusion of quotes and ideas that you are introducing to readers are all fantastic.

World building. You do a wonderful job with this. You create an entire world that is so inviting and interesting. I loved the freshness here as well—what their Heaven is like, how it works, what they find there—it's all very well done and I think readers will think this is all super cool and really get into the imagination of it.

PREFACE

I pondered this story long before I began writing it. I felt driven, almost compelled at first, then guided as I figured out how to develop the characters and the story. It is fiction and not intended to be viewed as theological, though I have to admit some of my own beliefs underscore the plot. I did my best to avoid preaching and to make it universally appealing to all faiths. My intent is to draw upon and honor great spiritual leaders' words of wisdom, regardless of the faith they practiced. I hope I illustrated how different faiths believe many of the same things, that we are truly more alike than different.

I've often been told I'm a detail person. I guess it's true because I constructed this story with attention to details in everything, from the characters' names and the names' meanings, to embedded symbolism and searching for quotes to add scaffolding to the story. Most things in this story are intentional.

The characters are fictional, people created by me. They're not based on any individual, but are composites of kids, adults, cats, and dogs I have known over the years, fully imbued with many fictional touches. The characters evolved as the story developed. If you've been a part of my life directly and recognize some traits you believe might be based on you, know that I carry every student and colleague in my mind and heart. You touched me more than you probably realize and linger with me way beyond our years together.

I'm the mother of three sons and I taught elementary school for forty years, both in the regular classroom and as a special educator. I loved my days spent with young people. Both at home and at school, I loved reading with them and talking about books we read. Read aloud at home and school were favorite parts of each day. As the years rolled on, I noticed more and more books for youths focus on dystopian societies and kids surviving on their own, or being overpowered and controlled by evil adults or forces. Crude language and rude behavior became commonplace, just a reflection of kids today, some would say. However, that's not a reflection of most kids I have known. Young people embrace good stories and good characters when they find them. They want to feel as if they know the characters and look forward to getting together with them when they return to that book. Most enjoy themes that are not so dark. They understand dark things happen in life and plots, but they want more than that.

We've all heard the expression "only the good die young." It's become a platitude to explain the passing of a young person or soothe those who have lost a young person in their lives. Everyone's heard it, yet it doesn't really do the job of soothing or explaining, does it? Just more empty words people offer when they don't know what to say, but feel they should say something of comfort to the parent who has lost a child, or the sibling who has lost a beloved brother or sister, or the child who has lost a young parent.

I was only four, and my sister was five, when our dad died. One of the things I clearly remember from that time was people saying over and over to my grieving mother, "Only the good die young." I remember hearing it and being afraid of what it meant. If you were good you would die young? If you didn't die young, did that mean you weren't good? It was all very confusing for little girls who found themselves surrounded by tears and sadness peppered with good intentions.

I didn't grow up in a religious household. Far from it. When I'd ask my mom what religion we were, she'd only say, "Protestant." I had no idea what that meant, except we weren't Catholic. She'd tell my sister and me that we could walk to Sunday School at the church a few doors away from our house if we wanted to, but she wouldn't go. With the advantage of hindsight and decades of living, I'm pretty sure that was because she couldn't grasp why God would let her be widowed at age 26 with two little girls she had to support and rear alone. As I grew, I'd ask to go with friends to their churches because my family didn't go anywhere. It was a good way to experience different faiths, though I never really felt like I belonged anywhere. I was always a guest. I loved going to church with my aunt and uncle when we spent weeks on the farm with them. I attended church with my boyfriend's family from the time I was a senior in high school. I was seeking answers as far back as I can remember, maybe because of losing my dad at such an early age. I wanted to understand things no one could explain.

I was baptized when I was twenty-eight. I was the mother of two sons by that time and had been teaching for seven years. I never had a child in my classroom who'd lost a parent in those first seven years. After I dedicated my life to the Lord, I had at least one child in my classroom every single year who'd lost a parent to death. Several were students in my class when their mother or father died. Thirty-three consecutive years brought children who had lost a parent into my classroom! I'm certain that was not mere chance.

Nothing is harder on a child than losing a parent, just as nothing is harder on parents than losing their child. I believe the Lord used me to comfort or guide some children on their journeys. The loss I felt as a child was part of my shaping to help others later. I didn't understand it as a kid, but I do understand it as an adult. All things in the universe are connected, if we are open to seeing the connectedness and growing from what we learn.

This story is my attempt to address why some people die young. It's a topic I've never read a fictional story based upon, probably because it's hard to think about, let alone talk about or write about. But, only by wading into the bog of confusion can our faith help us find the way to clearer water.

This story is dedicated to the parents who struggle the rest of their days on Earth to go on after losing a beloved child. I know you will never be the same. Part of you died, too, when your child died. I know the hole in your heart is beyond repair. I hope, however, you find some comfort in this story and a speck of joy as you wonder what your child is doing to fight evil and serve his or her greater purpose. I hope every one of you see their signs and hear their messages. I pray you can somehow accept that they are chosen ones, instruments of providence, and that you were an integral part of making that possible, even though their loss leaves you broken. They were chosen for good. You were chosen to bear it. I know your experience is shaping you for your everlasting mission, too. Comfort be yours.

CONTENTS

CHOOSING...

The honeycombed walls flashed and whirled, ever-changing scenes playing as the council evaluated needs and supply. Red and yellow sparks melded into a lava flow of desperation. The cost was high. The need even higher.

"Looking only at Earth, nowhere else in the universe, birth rates are over double death rates, yet more and more cells flash red. Evil plays offense. We must defend. We must have more warriors. It's always difficult to call the young, but we must do it. It is the only way, we all know it to be true," a voice rang from the dais. "Azrael is ready to fragment and escort all that we call. Let the Choosing begin."

"Let's focus on the ten-to-thirty-year-olds first. They master warrior training quickest, if we choose the fittest individuals and those who have suffered on Earth with trauma, disease, or disability."

The walls shifted, revealing thousands of images of young people going about their regular lives on Earth. Some suffered in hospital beds or rundown huts, but most were busy doing everyday activities. None knew a new Choosing had begun.

"Cluster those souls contemplating suicide away from the others," the prophet's voice boomed. "If they succeed in their own plans of self-destruction, they will enter the lowest rank, messengers and guardians. Warriors must be chosen by us. We must have those who can carry the whole armor of God and be able to stand against the Dark One and his minions."

Shuffling images showcased young people, all believing their whole lives stretched ahead of them, endless reams of blank paper as they wrote their unique life stories. They had no idea theirs were to be short stories, not epics or even novels.

"Are the comforting angels ready to dispatch? They will begin training those who will join them when lessons are learned. For now, they must bring dignity, care, and comfort to those left behind. Many lives are about to turn difficult corners."

"Merge life stories so those who must learn lessons from guilt and obsession are aligned with those who may become warriors. Accidents and homicides will bring us most of our new candidates. Drownings, road injuries, disease, and starvation will bring others to us. Arrange methods of death."

Golden edges framed thousands of cells. Pulsing gray wove around these cells. The prophets silently examined each pairing of golden- and gray-edged cells. Earnest faces scanned the chamber. Heads bowed, they confirmed their agreement.

Hundreds of hands raised at the same time as the prophets and those on the dais cried, "So be it!"

Anguish permeated the chamber as the Choosing concluded. Many new young recruits would arrive imminently. The Prophetic Council had fulfilled their somber duty, plucking lives of promise for an even greater purpose. Imposing years of grief on those left behind.

NOW...

avreel, who was responsible for forging new teams of warrior angels, watched silently as new arrivals transitioned with their escorting angels. One of her newest recruits would arrive shortly, a particularly strong candidate for a warrior team. As a guide for transition adjustment and training, Gavreel understood every newcomer had much to learn. This one would be no different. Gavreel knew she'd learn a great deal by talking with her directly and feeling her essence. A brief time spent individually with all new arrivals told her as much as reviewing their life stories.

Azrael and a tall girl appeared. "Here is your newest charge," Azrael announced, smiling. "It was a smooth transition. Now if you'll excuse me, I have another mission. The next one has been lingering, but the time is imminent."

"Thank you, Azrael. I'll take over now."

Azrael vanished as Gavreel turned to the girl. "I'm Gavreel, your counselor here. I can answer your questions and help you adjust to your new life. Walk with me. Tell me a bit about yourself as I take you to your new home."

The pair walked down a beautiful street but saw no one else.

The girl spoke timidly, clearly overwhelmed by her new surroundings. "I-I am thirteen years old. D-Dina Lerner is my name. Or at least it was. I don't know if it is any more. I always liked my name, Dina. I hope it's still my name."

Gavreel smiled. Her soothing and familiar presence helped put Dina at ease. "It is. You're still Dina here, but we have little need for surnames."

"So, I'm just Dina?"

Gavreel nodded, "For the time being, that's all you need. Go on, tell me your perception of where you think you are and how you happen to be here now."

"I think, I hope, I'm in Heaven. I was killed by a truck. Well, I guess I should say I was killed by the truck's driver. It happened really fast. I could smell alcohol on him. I remember everything so clearly."

Gavreel closed her eyes for a moment, then looked at Dina. "It was his third DUI, but he hadn't killed anyone until now. You're supposed to remember. It's part of your training and integral to your family's training to remember, but not part of his training. He has to learn his lessons without clear memories to help him. You *are* in Heaven, your true home."

"I saw my family after I died. They were so upset. Everything was so confusing until that angel came for me. I guess I'm still feeling pretty confused, but now I'm here."

"Yes, now you're here, where you're destined to be. This is your new home, Dina." Gavreel gestured to an adorable cottage surrounded by trees and flowers. "You'll be very comfortable here. You'll get less confused the longer you're here. Your lessons have begun. There's much to learn. Call my name if you need anything and I'll be right here."

Gavreel turned the knob so the door swung open before she disappeared.

Dina was amazed as she explored. "Heaven is this cool little cottage filled with things I love?" she wondered aloud.

Dina marveled at everything she discovered. Out of habit, or perhaps loneliness and longing, she started sharing her discoveries by talking to her little dog left behind.

"Yodels, my new house is so awesome. One room is filled with all kinds of art supplies, even things I had no idea what they were or what they were for until I took them in my hands. Then they drew me to the paper or canvas to create the images in my mind.

Remember how you always liked to lay by me while I was drawing? You'd love the art studio. It's so bright and sunny. You could stretch out in the sunshine and enjoy the warmth."

Dina smiled, thinking about talking to her dog. "I guess it's kind of silly that I'm talking to you, Yodels, because you're not here with me, but I want you to know where I am and what it's like. A soccer goal in the backyard captures my balls and sends them back to me. I can shoot goal after goal. My aim is perfect. Music I love fills my house whenever I want it. All I have to do is think about the music and it comes to me. If I want to have it quiet so I can hear the voices from below, I just think about quiet and it becomes quiet.

"If I lie down on the floor of my new house, Yodels, tiny cracks open. I can look through them and see what's happening with people I've known. Peering through the fissure in my bedroom floor, I see our house. I can hear everything happening there. If I lie down on the floor of my living room, I can peer through the crack and see my school. Somehow, all parts of the school and campus are visible from this portal. If I move to the kitchen, I see the soccer field where I always played. The art studio shows my friends' houses. That crack is like tree branches. If I look through different sections, I see different friends' homes. Sometimes that's good. Sometimes it's really hard. I had no idea what goes on in some people's homes until I observed from here.

"I can watch the family all the time, Yodels. I see you whenever I want to see you, boy. At first watching was really, really hard, with everyone crying all the time. It's so hard seeing everyone you love being heartbroken. I want to reach out and hug Mom and Dad and the boys. I want to tell them it's all right, that I'm right there with them. But, they can't hear me. They can't see me. They can't feel my presence. They just feel the emptiness and pain. I feel it too, Yodels, but it's different for me. I also have great joy and peace. I'm starting to feel like I'm Home, where I'm supposed to be, beginning the next phase of my life.

"I'm getting kind of obsessed with watching, Yodels. I think I've only spent a few minutes of my time watching below, but I know it's been days where I watched because it went from daylight to darkness several times. Time is very different here than it is there, boy. I need to go do something else."

Dina decided to wander outside. As soon as she stepped from the yard onto the sidewalk, Gavreel, the woman she'd met when she arrived, greeted her. Gavreel said she'd see Dina soon, when she was ready to grow. Dina hadn't called her nor thought about her since being home. She'd been too busy shooting goals, drawing, and watching. Now, though, Dina was glad to see her.

"Gavreel, you remind me of my mom," Dina blurted. "I mean that in a good way. I miss my mom and the rest of my family." Gavreel looked as if she was in her thirties, with a kind face and radiant smile. Having someone nearby who was sort of like her mom was part of Dina's Heaven, something she still needed.

"Why, thank you, Dina," Gavreel beamed. "I hope you'll always be comfortable with me and know you can come to me when you need anything. Look all around as we walk together. Observe carefully."

The air was crisp and clear, the perfect temperature, as Gavreel and Dina strolled down a lovely lane, under a canopy of leaves formed by huge trees growing along the sides of the road. Their leaves gaily waved, beckoning the pair. Surrounded by every kind of blooming thing imaginable, the two walkers reveled in the glorious colors and scents that filled the air. It wasn't overpowering though, just pleasant. There were all kinds of homes lining the street. Every house was different, but each was beautiful in its own way. Dina noticed so much more than she did when Gavreel had first escorted her at her arrival.

After a couple of minutes, Gavreel asked, "So what have you learned since you've arrived?"

"I'm not sure what you mean. I don't know that I've learned

anything. I've just stayed home, practicing soccer shooting, drawing, painting, and watching what was happening below." The question puzzled Dina because she hadn't gone anywhere except her home. She hadn't met anyone new except this woman. She hadn't read a book. She hadn't done anything but practice hobbies and lie on the floor, watching the people in her prior life.

Gavreel raised her eyebrows. "There are things to be learned everywhere. Your lessons have begun. Think. Tell me what you learned from playing and watching."

"I learned I'm a lot better athlete and artist here than I was there," Dina offered with a grin.

"Why do you suppose that is?" Gavreel prodded. Dina felt as if she were back at school.

"I'm just guessing, but maybe Heaven allows me be the best at what I love? I was sent to Earth with certain skills inside me, but I had to find them and practice them," Dina suggested. "I mean, I was good at soccer and art there, but things here seem to enhance my skills when I practice. Is that right?"

"It's part of it," Gavreel confirmed, "but you have more to discover. What else?"

"Well, I learned how much my family loves me. I always knew they loved me, but watching them since I died has been really hard. My mom sobs all the time. No one and nothing has been able to comfort her. I tried calling to her, to tell her I was still with her, but she couldn't hear me. My dad tries not to cry, but then he breaks down, too. He couldn't hear me either when I called out to him. Even my brothers have been crying, and they always try to act so cool and tough. Grandma and Grandpa arrived the day after I passed. They try to be strong for Mom and Dad and help with things, but then they go in another room and they cry, too. Even my dog, Yodels, sits on my bed and whines. Sometimes he seems to hear me when I talk to him. Sometimes he stretches out on the bed and looks up, pawing the air like he always did when he wanted me to rub his belly."

"Your earthly family is grieving. They are crying to relieve some of the pain. They're broken right now. What does that teach you, Dina?" Gavreel asked.

"I'm not sure what you want me to say, Gavreel. I mean, I know my family really loves me, and they miss me being with them. I know crying is part of grief, but I don't know what else it means."

"You have to observe closely and think outside the box, as some like to say. What about your grandparents? Think about them."

"They came right away when they got the phone call. They're so sad and miss me, but they're worried about the rest of my family. They're trying to help even though they're hurting, too. Maybe they feel as if they aren't really helping, but I could see that they were. They take Yodels out and give him lots of attention. They fix food for everyone and try to see that Mom and Dad take a few bites. They brought things to share at my memorial service. They're there, being part of the family. Family is what matters, being there for one another?"

Gavreel smiled, "That's a lesson well-learned. Now keep reflecting on what you saw. Reach further."

"I'm pretty sure my dog senses I'm near. He really seems to know, which sounds strange, but I think it's true. Sometimes he acts like he hears me when I talk to him."

"Go on," Gavreel prompted.

"I also think my grandparents might feel guilty because I died so young and they've lived to be old. I heard my grandma say she wished she could trade places with me. I could tell she meant it, too. I wish she didn't feel that way, because I can tell she's supposed to be there to help the family."

Gavreel clapped her hands gleefully. "You're starting to see things more clearly. You need to keep pushing yourself to make connections and figure out what each of them means. There's so much to learn and so much to do. We'll soon talk more about things you observe, but now I want you to meet someone."

Dina and Gavreel rounded the corner. A structure resembling a modern school loomed before them. Kids milled everywhere on the grounds surrounding the sparkling building. A girl saw Gavreel and waved. Gavreel's radiant smile erupted as she waved back. In a split second, the girl stood next to Gavreel and Dina.

"Girls, you're my newest recruits. I envision you working together from this day forward. I believe you have the makings of a strong team, but you need to get to know one another. Jophiel, this is Dina. Dina, this is Jophiel. I will leave you to get acquainted. Walk on one of the paths. You'll discover much."

The girls exchanged quizzical glances as they watched Gavreel glide away toward a group of boys who were laughing and talking loudly near the fence surrounding sports fields.

"You have done well, gentlemen!" she announced as she approached them. She raised her arms and they all vanished.

NEW FRIENDS...

Both girls stood staring where the cluster of boys had just been. "Well, that was interesting. Weird, but interesting. I wonder what they did well and where they went. By the way, I go by Jo, not Jophiel. That's my real name, but everyone calls me Jo."

"Dina's my full name. I've never gone by anything else."

"Gavreel told us to walk on a path and get to know one another," Jo said. "Do you care where we start?"

"Not really. I'm guessing we'll have to walk on all of these paths at some point. Do you want to start on the closest one that begins by the end of the building or try one of those?" Dina asked as she pointed to trails winding up hills behind the school building.

"Let's go to that one with the pinkish clouds floating above it. It isn't sunrise or sunset, so maybe those clouds mean something special. They look like globs of cotton candy hanging above that trail. I want to see what's there."

"Pink clouds it is," Dina replied as she turned to cross the soccer field and make her way toward the chosen path. "Come on, Jo."

As the girls made their way across the lush grassy field, the blades packed so tightly they could see only shades of green, they became aware of a whispering all around them. "The circle of caring must never end. The circle of caring must never end." A sideways glance between them confirmed they were both hearing the whispering, not imagining it.

When they neared the path, a small sign became visible. It was intricately carved with beautiful flowers and small creatures, painted with shades of pink and a palette of other colors. Part of a giant tree edged one side of the sign and formed a leaf awning protecting the detailed carvings of flowers, dragonflies, butterflies, and hummingbirds. Ornate gold letters read ***The Circle of Caring Trail of Discovery***. The girls exchanged another quizzical look as they glanced from the sign to the path before them.

The winding track shimmered and became soft mauve with dense flowers lining both sides as far as they could see. Each blossom, a work of art, danced with such joy and hospitality that the girls took their first step into this new world without hesitation.

The kaleidoscope of colors, patterns, and textures were ever-changing around them. The transcendence into this realm of beauty and peace was true medicine for the soul. They took a few steps on the rose-colored path, gaping at everything they saw. The girls clutched one another's hands and exclaimed, "We really are in Heaven!"

Gavreel appeared before them. "Excellent, girls! You chose a marvelous place to begin your journey. You're now unified in purpose and direction. Learn to read one another and become a team so you'll be successful on the missions ahead. Understand one another as you've never understood anyone before. Successful missions depend on strong teams. Yes, things happen faster and more easily here, but you need to observe closely and be open to changes. Be willing to merge thoughts and actions with your teammates. Work hard to grow and develop your skills. Your thoughts are synching already. Learn, learn, learn! Learn about one another and the things you see and hear as you stroll or sit among the majestic creations of this path. You must understand much before you can visit." As suddenly as she'd appeared, Gavreel waved her arms and vanished again.

"This is getting weirder by the minute!" both girls exclaimed simultaneously. "Weird, but fascinating."

Dina and Jo sidled up to the edge of the path. They bent to look at a swaying, bouncing cluster of flaming yellow and orange. The flowers appeared to hop up and down and side to side, bolstered by some strange wind the girls couldn't feel. They were incredulous as they peered at each bloom, discovering each posy was actually a young bunny, with floppy ears that swirled and gave the illusion of many petals rather than two ears surrounding each face. Their black eyes gazed lovingly at the girls who came so close. No longer needing to scan for predators, the eyes stared straight into the hearts of those who came. The cluster of flowers erupted into a throng, unrolling as far as Dina and Jo could see in every direction. They became a buoyant crowd happily greeting these new visitors.

With gentle fingers, the girls stroked the most divine softness either of them had ever felt. With the girls' touch, ethereal music began, music like none they had ever heard. Everything about the atmosphere was soft and soothing. They slid to the ground among these creations, stroking the petal heads and ears, as one might do with a beloved pet. Tranquility filled them.

After a time, the girls withdrew their hands. The majestic music stopped. The bunny-flower choir crooned, "Always be gentle. Gentle is always the best way. Fear can be conquered with gentleness. Pain can be conquered with gentleness. Gentleness can bridge chasms."

A pink cloud floated above the bobbing bunny blossoms, showering them with a pink mist, stilling them, and shrinking the rolling field of creatures back to the original cluster. It also dropped a flat stone at the girls' feet.

Jo picked up the stone and examined it. The sparkling pink pebble was engraved with the mantra the bunny-flowers had just chanted. When she turned the stone over, the flip side had a small button in the center. When she pushed it, the button opened like a bud bursting into full bloom. Each petal had words on them which she read aloud:

Gautama Buddha:
"In our interactions with others, gentleness, kindness, and respect are the source of harmony."

Mahatma Gandi:
"In a gentle way, you can shake the world."

Aisha reported: Muhammad, the Messenger of Allah (peace be upon him) said:
"Allah is gentle and He loves gentleness. He rewards for gentleness what is not granted for harshness and He does not reward anything else like it."

Philippians 4:5
"Let your gentle spirit be known to all men. The Lord is near."

The Book of Mormon, Alma 7:23
"And now I would that ye be humble, and be submissive and gentle; easy to be entreated; full of patience and long-suffering; being temperate in all things…"

When she'd read each one, she pushed the button and the petals slipped back together, somehow hidden in the stone. "One side has messages from different faiths about gentleness. The other side says exactly what the bunny-flowers declared before the pink mist showered them. Gentleness must be the lesson we're supposed to learn and remember!"

Dina's head shake indicated that their thoughts were indeed beginning to synch.

MOVING FORWARD...

The girls zigzagged from one side of the plush pink route to the other, often stooping to examine beautiful flowers or other colorful objects they spotted. They were astounded when they realized some of the flowers smelled like cookies baking and others smelled like cinnamon rolls. A grove of small trees with bright purple bark smelled like someone was grilling food for a barbecue.

Rocks of all colors splattered the path and nestled among the flowers. When the girls lifted one stone, its oval shape shifted into a musical note and emitted a pure tone, capturing their attention. They picked up several rocks, all of which shifted into musical notes and sounded different tones. As they tossed the handful of stones in the air at the same time, the heavens were filled with music. They did this several times, totally enthralled with the mini-symphonies they created by tossing different pebbles in the air.

Enchanted by everything around them, they hadn't even noticed the boy who watched them.

He stepped toward them, clearing his throat. For some reason, both girls felt he'd been watching them for quite a while. He approached somewhat hesitantly. As he got closer, they could tell he looked upset. Was he sad or dejected? Yet, his face also suggested a smirk. It wasn't the face of someone who'd been stroking bunny flowers, sniffing incredibly scented flowers, or creating symphonic arrangements by tossing magical rocks in the air.

"This part of the path is pretty cool," he announced. "You have no idea what's ahead of you though."

"And you do?" both girls chimed.

"I do. I did it already."

"You did it already?"

"Gavreel told me that I should join the next team on the path. I guess that's you two," the lanky boy muttered. "I'm Gabe. I started on this path with some other guys, but they left the path at the top of the hill. Gavreel said I hadn't learned enough to proceed. I guess some things never change no matter where I go. Anyway, Gavreel said I had to try again. She told me to join a new team and gain new perspectives with that team. As soon as she announced that, I was somehow transported back to this section of the trail. I've been waiting for someone to show up."

"I'm Dina and this is Jo. Gavreel didn't tell us to go with anyone else. She just told us to get to know one another and learn a lot so we'd become a team."

"Well, she told me to join the next team on the path. That's you two. I'll go with you and help you. I aced the next part. I'm sure you girls are going to need some help with it." The sad-looking boy sounded cocky and sarcastic.

"Thanks for the offer, but we should just go on by ourselves like Gavreel told us to do," Jo asserted.

The girls linked arms and walked away briskly, headed toward a curve they couldn't see around. Gabe followed, staying just a few paces behind them.

"Be careful as you go around there," he called.

They rounded the bend and saw a gigantic speckled boulder blocking the path. Tall trees flanked both sides of the boulder, nearly touching it. The spaces between rock and trees were much too narrow to squeeze through. Stepping off the path by one of the trees, the girls tried to go around the trunk. Branches grabbed the girls and swept them back onto the path. They tried to go around several times and were captured and deposited on the path every time. There was no going around the sides of the tree sentries.

As they studied the barrier, they noticed indentations near the center of the boulder and evenly spaced bulges of rock near each indentation. The bulges looked like hand-holds for climbing. Was this some kind of ladder to the flattened top? Looking up, they noticed the far edge of the flattened top featured a thin wall, about three feet taller than the rest of the top.

Near the boulder's steps, a scrolling electronic sign flashed messages in many languages. Each language popped up in a different color and stayed on the screen for only a few seconds, not nearly long enough to read.

"What do you think we're supposed to do next?" Jo asked.

"Maybe we have to figure out how to read this sign for directions," Dina suggested.

"It's scrolling so fast. I can't read it, even if I knew any of those languages," Jo declared.

"Me, either," Dina agreed.

"I told you you'd need my help," the boy named Gabe called out in a sing-song voice. He was standing next to one of the trees gloating over their dilemma. "I'm telling you, you won't make it past this point without me."

The girls' eye rolls were almost audible. They didn't know what to do about this guy who was tagging along, a guy who looked sad and vulnerable, but who sounded obnoxious. He seemed intent on joining them, but Gavreel hadn't mentioned anyone else. She hadn't given them any instructions except to get to know one another, to become comfortable synchronizing their thoughts and actions, and to learn as much as they could along the path. She hadn't mentioned anything about this boy, or anyone else, joining them.

"We told you, Gabe," Dina reiterated, "we're going to try to figure this out together. We're trying to do what Gavreel told us to do. She didn't say anything about joining up with some arrogant guy who believes he's better than us. So, if you'll excuse us, we have some work to do."

The girls turned to one another and whined, "Why do boys always have to act like that? I'm so *not* impressed." Their grins at saying the exact same words simultaneously melted away the feelings of irritation this boy had brought.

"Suit yourselves. I'll just wait right here and watch. Let me know when you're ready for my help." Gabe plopped down on the plush path and leaned self-assuredly against the tree. He sat cross-legged, resting his elbows on his knees and his chin on his hands. He didn't take his eyes off the girls.

"Maybe we should climb to the top and look over to see what is on the other side," Jo suggested.

Gabe smirked but said nothing. They thought they saw a slight shake of his head, but he remained silent.

The girls climbed the uneven stairs to the top. They stepped to the short wall on the far edge and stared over. They saw only a blanket of blackness, nothing except total darkness.

"Well, I guess this didn't work. We can't see anything past this stupid rock," Dina grumbled.

They climbed down and went to the tree on the far side of the path. Both of them tried reaching between the tree trunk and the boulder. The gap was just big enough for a hand to fit there, but nothing else.

"Maybe there's a hidden button or lever. If we find it, maybe the rock will open up, or move, or something," Dina speculated. "Let's try rubbing our hands on as much of the boulder's surface as we can reach and see if we feel something that might open a passageway."

Jo nodded in agreement.

"Since we're supposed to be a team, let's start on opposite edges of the boulder and work our way to the middle from both sides, running our hands over the rock at ground level. We'll see if we feel anything like a bump or rough edge," Jo suggested. "If we don't feel anything unusual on that strip of rock, we can work our way back to the outside edge a few inches higher. We can keep going back and forth a few inches higher each time until we have touched the entire surface as far up as we can reach on this side of the rock."

"Sounds like a plan," Dina agreed.

Gabe scooted over a bit as Jo approached the edge of the rock near him. She bent over and pressed her hands along the bottom edge of the stony blockade, sidestepping toward the center. Dina did the same thing from the opposite side. They met in the middle, feeling nothing but the smooth surface of the barricade. They raised their hands a few inches and worked their way back to the outside edges. They shook their heads no and worked their way back to the center. They repeated the in-and-out motion of the surface, scanning with their hands until they had reached up as far as they could stretch.

"Maybe we should go back up to the top and try feeling all around up there. That wall or the mesa top may have some kind of trigger to open or move this boulder," Jo suggested.

The girls climbed the rungs to the top and crawled around, rubbing their hands on the entire surface. They felt nothing but the smooth cool surface of the colorful slab which blocked their forward progress.

"I guess there's no secret tunnel through this enormous hunk of rock," Dina muttered. "We're back where we started."

The girls climbed down and stood back a few feet. They were staring at the barrier and the scrolling sign when Gabe clucked, "So far, this is a fail for you! Looks like you might need some help. I'm just the man for the job."

"No thanks," Dina and Jo barked. The girls looked at one another and whispered, "He thinks he's the man!"

Gabe offered, "Well, if you don't want me to help you get past this point, how about if I just give you a hint to get you going the right way? You spent a long time massaging that rock and you're no further ahead. I mean, if we're a team now, you should let me help you, even if it's just a little hint. Trust me. I know the way."

"We're only a team in your mind," the girls chimed. They snickered because they were clearly thinking and saying the same thing more and more often.

"I'm telling you, I can help," Gabe announced. "I know you're like everyone else, believing I can't do anything right, but I've been here and done this before. Did Gavreel tell you that you had to do everything alone? Did she tell you that you couldn't talk to others or get help? That doesn't sound like a way to build a team."

"No, she didn't say we had to do everything alone. But, someone telling us what to do seems like cheating," Jo declared. "She told us to work together and learn all that we could as we traveled on this path."

"It's not cheating. You still have to do it. I can just help you do it faster and easier. You still have to learn the lessons."

Dina sighed, "Fine. Maybe one hint to get us started. Jo, how about we get one hint and then try to figure out the rest?"

"I'm really not sure what to do," Jo admitted. "I do know we're supposed to get to the end of the trail and learn the lessons along the way. We can't learn the lessons or get to the end if we're stuck here staring at this thing."

"Okay, Gabe. We'll let you tell us one hint to get us started, but we want to figure out the rest on our own. Can you accept that?" Dina asked.

He nodded and offered eagerly, "You're right about the sign. It's the starting point. Hold one another's hands. With each of your free hands, both of you touch the top or sides of the sign. You need to touch one another and the sign at the same time. Make sure you can see the sign when you're touching it."

Dina and Jo joined hands and walked to the scrolling placard. It was still flashing symbols in varying colors and languages as they approached. "Here we go," they blurted as they reached for the top of the sign.

To their amazement, the screen erupted in bursts resembling fireworks. After a few seconds of brilliant colors exploding, the riot of colors on the screen shifted to bright turquoise bursts on a field of gray. As they watched, the bursts shifted into letters and the letters shifted into words. They were words they could read. They were printed in English! The top of the sign read:

Your combined auras indicate you are English speakers from Earth. The directions for this task are now being presented in English. Read the message carefully and make sure you discuss and understand what you must do before you begin. Once you begin, you must finish. There is no bypass of this task. You must trust one another in each role to be successful. Choose your roles carefully.

Just below that message, the girls read:

To pass this task and forward tread,
one partner must be blindly led.

The one above will see the way.
The one below must hear and obey.

The one up high will describe the route,
clear directions are the only way out.

The one below will not speak or see,
and must trust their partner to set them free.

An incorrect step, no matter when,
sends the partner back to start again.

Choose carefully who makes the run
because there's no end till the task is done.

Remember gentleness is always best,
even when facing a daunting test.

Partners must be patient and strong.
The challenge of trust is hard and long.

The girls read the message aloud several times, trying to process the directions and understand their next step.

"So, apparently, one of us is supposed to go back up on top of the boulder and look down to direct the other one who is on the ground. The 'one above' would be at the top of this barricade looking over that wall. Maybe that wall of blackness goes away once we start," Dina suggested.

"You're right about the 'one above' being up there," Jo agreed, "and the 'one below' being on the ground. So we have to decide who goes up there to give directions and who stays down here to follow the directions and try to get past this thing. I guess if we get something wrong, we get to start over. I don't know what it means about being 'blindly led' and being 'set free' though."

"Yeah, I don't really get those parts, either. It sounds kind of scary."

Gabe interrupted, "I'm telling you again, you should let me help you get through this part. Seriously, I can get you through."

"Gabe, we're glad you gave us the hint to read the message, but we told you we want to try to do this on our own. We have to try," Jo retorted.

"Okay, have it your way for now," Gabe said, "but I wish you'd get going. Something tells me we're going to be here for a very long time."

"You're free to go wherever you want. We didn't ask you to come here with us and you certainly don't have to be here a very long time on our account. Do whatever you want, just stop bugging us," Jo snapped.

"I'll wait. I wait a lot better than I used to," Gabe commented. "That's a good thing because this is going to be awhile. By the way, you're not sounding very gentle."

Jo turned back to Dina. "Do you want to climb up there and give the directions or stay down here and follow them? Either way, we both get to get away from him."

"Well, I guess it doesn't matter. Neither of us can go on until we figure out how to do this task together. We just need to get started."

"I'll climb up there and call out directions then," Jo declared, "if that's all right with you."

"That's fine, I guess, but the directions say the 'one below' won't be able to see or speak. So I won't be able to tell you if I don't understand what to do. We need a gesture that lets you know if I don't understand your directions. How about if I pat my head several times? If you see me do that, you'll know I'm confused and you can give me the directions again, maybe in a different way that I might understand better. Will that help us communicate better?" Dina asked.

"A gesture like that is brilliant, Dina. I guess I'll climb up there again so we can get started."

As soon as Jo reached the top of the miniature plateau, she heard Dina squeak. She looked down and saw her new friend now wore a shiny black blindfold and black tape over her mouth. Dina clawed at the blindfold and the mouth covering. Neither budged. The girls now understood what being "blindly led" meant. Dina could not see or speak. She was totally dependent on Jo and her other senses to get past this challenge.

TRUST...

"Stay calm, Dina," Jo soothed. "Don't claw at your face. From the looks of it, you can't take that blindfold or gag off until we finish. Hang on while I look over the wall again to see what's on the other side. "

Jo peered over the wall and still saw infinite blackness. She scanned both directions and noticed a flashing red arrow pointing to the space between one tree and the boulder. "That has to be the starting point," she murmured.

"Okay, Dina, I have the start figured out. You have to go back to the little gap between the boulder and the tree. Take three steps to your right and feel the stone. That's good. Now keep your hand on the rock and walk forward. It will be about ten steps. When you get to the edge of the boulder, put your hand back in that space between the tree trunk and the rock."

Dina dragged her hand along the stone until she reached the edge. She stuck her hand in the tight space. Nothing happened.

"Try running your hand up and down the edge of the stone," Jo called. "Maybe you have to touch something on the edge to go further." Nothing happened.

The arrow still flashed above Dina's head. "Try doing the same thing on the tree. Run your hand up and down the trunk. Maybe that will open up a passageway." Still nothing happened.

"Remember, to get the sign to work, we both had to touch it at the same time to activate the message? Try touching the boulder and the tree at the same time to activate the opening."

Dina placed her right hand on the stone and her left hand on the tree trunk. To Jo's amazement, the tree began to sway. It looked as if it was leaning out, away from the boulder creating a big gap. Choreographed by some unseen force, the branches danced, gaining speed and momentum with each sway. A sturdy vine unfurled from the limbs and looped around Dina's middle. It lifted her several feet above the ground, turning her into a pendulum in the tree.

Dina would've been screaming if the tape hadn't sealed her mouth. Her strangled screams hurt her throat. She frantically clutched the vine that held her.

"Don't panic, Dina. The tree is swinging you. It's going to move you to the next place. Just breathe and try to enjoy the ride. You're safe. The tree is the key to moving forward. Relax your body and see what happens."

Dina tried to relax, but that's easier said than done when one is blind and mute. It's even more difficult when one is tied up and being swung like a rag doll by some strange tree. Mentally she was repeating, "Stay calm, stay calm..." She remembered what Coach had told at them every practice: *Take deep breaths and visualize your goal.* She focused on slow deep breaths and visualized herself freed from the tree. After several more swings, the vine snapped out like a bungee cord and set her on something that felt springy.

A light shone on Dina. "Most excellent, Dina! You made it past the first task! I see a bright light on you and the boulder now. You're facing the boulder and standing on something that looks kind of like a trampoline, but it's a long rectangle and not too wide. Try bouncing on it. Can you bounce a couple of times and see what happens?" Jo called.

Dina bounced several times and got higher on each bounce, but nothing else happened.

Jo cried, "Stop bouncing a minute, Dina. Catch your breath and let me think." She noticed two glowing dots about the size of ping pong balls on the boulder, about three feet apart and about six feet above Dina's head.

"How high above your head can you reach?" Jo asked.

Dina stretched her arms above her head, but they were still several feet below the dots.

"Can you smack the wall with your hands each time you bounce, Dina?"

Dina showed that she could.

"Okay, now try reaching above your head and smacking the wall when you're at the top of the bounce," Jo told her.

Dina did as she was told. Nothing happened.

"There are two dots about the size of ping pong balls on the wall. They're about a yard to your right and about six feet above your head. You may have to bounce that high and hit one of them, or both of them, to get through this part. Sidestep over to your right slowly and I'll tell you when you're lined up under them."

Dina sashayed sideways until Jo cried, "Stop. Right there. You're directly beneath the dots now. Jump once with your hands above your head and I'll see how close you come to touching them."

Dina jumped once and slapped the wall with both hands.

"Your hands were about a foot below the dots, so you have to bounce higher. Those dots are about three feet apart, so keep your arms about that wide when you hit the stone."

Dina jumped and struck the wall several times, but missed her target every time.

"Keep trying, Dina. You're really, really close. The last time you were a little above them, but your hands were exactly the right width apart."

On the next bounce, Dina's right hand struck a dot. It felt warmer than the rest of the stone.

The next thing she knew, she was on the ground, standing next to the scrolling sign.

Jo announced, "You hit one of the dots, Dina, and you were put back here at the beginning. You're right next to the scrolling sign. We have to start again, but it's okay. Now we know you have to hit both dots at the same time to move on. Come on, you can do this.

You know how to get through the first part, so it should go fast. You'll get the second part pretty fast too, if you can hit both spots at the same time. Move to your right until you touch the stone again, Dina, and follow it to the edge."

Dina complied and quickly found herself wrapped with a vine and swinging faster and faster. It wasn't scary at all. It was exhilarating, more fun than anything she'd ever done before. Her taped mouth didn't stifle screams this time. She wished she could see herself dangling from the tree, gaining momentum as she swung back and forth.

Jo grinned from the boulder top, realizing how easy the first task was for Dina this time. Gabe watched from the path, nodding ever so slightly.

"You're doing great this time!" Jo shouted. "You're about to be tossed onto that trampoline thing again. I'll tell you how to move so you're lined up under the targets. Remember, hitting one dot sent you back to the beginning so try to hit them both at the same time."

The vine lurched several more times and stretched. Dina was once again deposited gently on the bouncing contraption. The vine spun her several times as it unwound itself from her middle.

"You're facing away from the stone, Dina. Turn around so you're facing the other way. That's right. Now take a couple of steps forward and reach out to touch the boulder. All right! Slide your feet to the left. I'll tell you when to stop."

Dina took several sideways steps to her left, stopping when Jo called, "You're right under them now."

Dina jumped with her hands above her head and smacked the wall over and over. Her legs and arms ached with exhaustion. Her hands stung from the repeated impacts. Jo kept calling that she was close, sometimes a little too high, sometimes a little too low, sometimes off to one side or the other. She didn't know how much longer she could do this. Frustration and fatigue mounted. How could she put an end to this ridiculous jumping-slapping routine? There must be some way.

As exasperation overtook her, Dina jumped and body slammed against the wall.

Dina found herself back on solid ground. She fell over and curled into a ball, her quivering body slipping into motionlessness. She lay in a heap at the starting line of this bizarre obstacle course.

"Dina!" Jo screamed as she headed down the rungs.

"Stop, Jo! You can't come down here. You can't touch her. The task isn't complete. Trust me, I'm telling you the truth. Stay on the top. I'll help her. I know you don't want me, but I know I'm supposed to be on this team. Trust me, and I'll help."

Gabe ran toward Dina, calling softly, "It's all right. You tried really hard, but there are some things no one can do alone. I'll help. We'll get through together."

He continued, "Jo, you're going to have to tell us clearly what you see. You'll have to tell us the shapes and colors of things you see. We'll need to know if the symbols are moving or staying in one place. Every marker means something. We have to work as a team to finish. As soon as I touch Dina, I won't be able to see or speak either. We'll both be depending on you to see the markers and describe clearly what they look like and where they are."

"Dina, I won't be able to talk in a minute, so listen carefully. If I tap your arm over and over quickly, it means we have to go as fast as we can together so you need to run with me. If I trace circles on your arm, it means we have to spin together. If I jerk your arm up, it means we have to jump together. If I hold both of your hands or hold you around the waist, you need to let me lead you without resisting. I know what to do. I really do, but you have to go with me and do it all too. We'll have to start over together every time we get it wrong. Do you understand?"

Dina nodded, tired but unbowed.

"Well, let's get this show on the road then." Gabe reached down and grabbed Dina's hand. He pulled her to her feet. Instantaneously, his mouth and eyes were shrouded exactly like Dina's. His right arm was bound to her left arm with the same shiny black material as their blindfolds.

A shocked Jo stammered, "Dina, he's blindfolded and gagged just like you now. Your arms are tied together with the same black cloth as the blindfolds. You're going to have to do everything together. Lord, help us. We can't do this without you."

The pair edged their way to the tree.

Dina and Gabe reached the starting point. Together they pushed on the giant rock and tree trunk. The tree began the leaning swagger. Soon the vine erupted from the center of the tree and wrapped itself around the pair, snatching them up. Jo heard muffled laughter. She watched as Gabe and Dina swung back and forth like the metronome her music teacher used to have in class. In a flash, the vine snapped out from the tree and plopped the pair on the springy surface.

"All right, guys, you're about ten feet from the white spots. You're facing the boulder though. You need to move right about ten feet. You're farther from the dots this time, Dina, but not too far. I'll tell you when to stop. Step to your right. Keep going, keep going. That's it. You're almost there. Stop! Dina, you're right below one of them and Gabe is below the other one. They're about six feet above your heads. Your bounces will need to take you up about four feet to reach them with your arms above your heads."

Jo watched as Gabe took Dina's unbound hand and moved it so the back of her hand touched her face, then moved it straight ahead so the palm of her hand touched the boulder directly in front of her face. He moved her hand back to her face, then back to the wall again. He repeated the motion with her hand several times.

Jo proclaimed, "I've got it! Gabe wants you to keep your hand on the boulder as you jump, Dina. He's lining your hand up with your head when he moves it. He wants you to drag your hand along the surface with every jump." Gabe shook his head in affirmation. He then placed his own free hand on the boulder in front of his face and raised his bound arm, lifting Dina's at the same time.

The pair began synchronized bobbing. It only took a few bounces until both of their hands skimmed over their targets.

"You did it! The white dots are changing now. They're getting bigger and you weren't brought back to the beginning. I don't know what's happening, but the white dots are getting huge and starting to move around. Keep bouncing, but I don't think you have to touch anything. You already activated the change in the dots."

The dots expanded to the size of toboggans and zipped behind the bouncing pair.

Jo cried, "Those dots have turned into something you can ride, like those round sleds. They're behind you. They're hovering right behind your butts. It looks like they want you to sit down on them."

Gabe squatted and the flying disc settled right under him, letting his legs dangle as it adjusted and raised up slightly to keep the rhythm with Dina's bounces.

"Dina, Gabe squatted and the white disc slid under him. He's sitting on it with his legs dangling over the side. Squat down and sit on the other disc so you guys can move to the next part."

Dina crouched down and felt the warm disc slide under her. It was very comfortable and she felt soothed by the warmth and rhythmic motion. She knew it wouldn't last long. She squeezed Gabe's hand and he squeezed back.

Jo marveled, "Wow! I've never seen anything like this. It's awesome! Brightly colored laser beams are flashing all around you, like you're in some kind of light matrix. The white discs are flashing, too. The discs are starting to move!" She watched as the discs carrying Dina and Gabe zoomed in all directions, up and down, diagonally, in circles, gliding together perfectly, like figure skaters on the ice.

All the neon beams converged on one point on the boulder. The discs circled and zoomed at the point where all the light beams met. As they hit that point, a giant hole opened and the discs flew through.

Jo was fascinated. Where she had seen total blackness when she looked over the boulder before, she now saw a scene that seemed to be inside the boulder.

"Guys, those things carrying you just broke through the side of the boulder. All the laser beams came together and marked the spot. When you hit the spot where all the lines met, a huge hole opened up. You're inside the rock now! A hole opened so I can see inside, too. I can't explain how, but somehow I can see you even though you're now inside."

Jo had no sooner finished saying they were inside the rock than the discs lowered Dina and Gabe near the floor of a cave-like room. They tilted slightly so the pair slid to their feet. The discs zipped away and disappeared.

"This place is spectacular, guys. It's lit better than the place with the trampoline, so there's no spotlight shining on you," Jo proclaimed. "The walls are shimmering with beautiful colors. Maybe they're gems or something. I don't know, but every surface is covered with sparkling colors and formations. Some look like icebergs hanging from the ceiling and coming out of the floor, but some look like statues. I don't know what the statues are, but light comes out of them. There's a long wide-open space in the middle. It looks like a hallway between the lighted figures, whatever they are."

Gabe raised his hands near his shoulders with his palms up, a gesture of confusion or questioning.

Jo observed, "I don't know what you're supposed to do here, but it's beautiful. Maybe that long open space is for running or something, but I don't know." She scanned the chamber, her eyes landing on what looked like a bright pink pulsing spiral at the far end of the enormous room.

"Oh, it looks like there's something different at the far end of the room. It's a long way away from you. I'd estimate it's about a couple of hundred yards from where you're standing. It's bright pink and looks like a spiral, like a giant spring for something. It's dark behind it. I can't see anything else past it, so it might be the far end of this room."

Gabe shook his head and pointed.

"No, not that way. You'll bump into one of the rock things if you go that way. You and Dina need to rotate to line up with the open space. Both of you turn a little to your right. A little more. That's pretty good. Now step sideways a few steps to your right so you're centered in the open space. That looks like you're in the middle. You're both facing the spiral now. It's straight ahead of you."

Gabe took Dina's arm and tapped quickly several times, drew circles on her arm, then wrapped his unbound arm around her waist. He repeated the pattern several times: tap, tap, tap, circles, hug. She understood his message. She moved his hand so it touched her head and shook her head up and down several times.

Jo called, "I understand. You're going to run toward the spiral, start spinning when you get close to it, and spin into the spiral."

Dina and Gabe flashed a thumbs-up sign with each of their free hands.

"Okay. You're lined up well with the spiral. I'll tell you when to go so you start running at the same time. I'll let you know when you're close to the spiral so you can start your spin. Good luck, guys. I hope this works."

Dina and Gabe took deep breaths and listened closely as Jo shouted, "Ready, set, go!"

The pair raced forward, matching strides even though they couldn't see one another. "You're about halfway there! Wow! You're so fast. You're about ten feet away. Spin!"

Gabe grabbed Dina around the waist and scooped her up as he started his leaping spin. He had done two full rotations when their bodies collided with the pulsing spiral. It sucked them inside, their beings becoming part of the swirl. As if inside a tornado, spinning and spinning, Dina and Gabe became part of the whorl. Suddenly Jo was inside the spiral with them, grabbing them as they whirled around. It seemed the three were being mixed up together to make a whole new being. The three clung to one another in the whirlwind as the dizzying gyrations gained speed and the blindfolds, gags, and arm binding disappeared. Pink flashes surrounded them.

The trio found themselves sprawled on the plush pink path next to the boulder. They saw no steps nor flashing sign. They grinned at one another and shrieked, "We did it! We got past the boulder! We're on the other side!"

The pink spiral stretched out straight, wriggled, and maneuvered to form the words: "Trust is a choice. Trust is crucial." The message flashed several times and the words flickered, disappearing in a rosy cloud.

A rose-gold charm, shaped like a four-leaf clover, fell from the cloud, landing at Dina's feet. Printed on one side were the words, "Trust is a choice. Trust is crucial." Small hinges appeared on the edge of each clover leaf. She turned it over and saw that the sections were like lockets that opened. She flipped one open. Words poured from the section and filled the air before them. She read:

Proverbs 3:5
"Trust in the Lord with all your heart, and do not lean on your own understanding."

Proverbs 28:26
"Those who trust in themselves are fools, but those who walk in wisdom are kept safe."

She closed that section and opened the next one. When she flipped open the second section of the clover these words were projected before them:

Buddha says trust is the best relative.

The Jataka says: "One who is worthy of your trust and who trusts you in return, who listens to you and is patient with you, follow him wherever he goes."

The third section contained the message:

al-Anfaal 8:27
"Verily! Allah commands that you should render back the trusts to those, to whom they are due."

The last section of the clover contained these words:

2 Corinthians 8:22
"We have sent them our brother, whom we have often tested and found diligent in many things, but even now more diligent because of great confidence in you."

"I read about shamrocks and four-leafed clovers for a report I did on Ireland," Dina shared. "They're not the same thing. A shamrock has only three leaves. Some say they stand for faith, hope, and love. The fourth leaf is rare, so some say it stands for luck. Maybe we have four leaves because Gabe joined us. You're our luck, Gabe!"

The boy's face no longer looked sad, but radiated joy.

The trio walked a few minutes in silence, basking in their success at completing such an arduous challenge. They marveled at the shimmering rose-colored path and its surroundings.

As they rounded a curve, they saw an ornate U-shaped bench filled with posh colorful pillows, beckoning them. Behind the bench, heavy navy blue drapes hung from the boughs of the two biggest trees they'd ever seen. The trees looked as if they were holding hands as well as holding the velvety curtains.

The air was alive with butterflies, dragonflies, and hummingbirds. The small colorful creatures filled the branches and the sky. Their beating wings and the trees' rustling leaves created soothing sounds, like beach sounds back in the place they used to call home.

Without even thinking about it, the girls headed to the bench and settled comfortably on the cushions. Gabe dragged himself behind them and slumped on a cushion.

Dina and Jo studied the trees from the bench, amazed that one tree seemed to be male and the other female. Above their heads, the umbrella of branches and leaves melded into one tree, like many hands reaching to infinity. Near the top of the trunks, where the limbs began growing outward and upward, each tree had a face, one decidedly masculine and the other feminine. The tree faces studied the girls as intently as the girls studied the trees; the trees' eyes were full of concern, but slight smiles tugged at their lips as they waited for something they knew was coming.

Gabe just sat there, looking down at the ground, his joy erased.

Magnificent butterflies, like fairies in painted silk, fluttered all around the bench. Finally a monarch, sunset orange with ebony lines, landed on Dina's arm. It slowly opened and closed its wings a few times, as if reassuring her that all was well. Mesmerized, Dina watched the pulsing wings perched on her arm.

Dina redirected her gaze from the winged beauty to her companions. Hesitantly she suggested, "Gavreel said we're supposed to get to know one another. For some reason, I believe we're supposed to share from this bench."

Still, Gabe just sat staring at the ground, his face proclaiming sadness the girls didn't understand.

Jo shook her head in agreement. "You go first, Dina. I had to do all the talking on that last part."

DINA...

"I'm not sure what to say, but I guess I should tell you my full name on Earth was Dina Maia Lerner. I was thirteen when I died. I lived with my dad, mom, and two brothers. My older brother is sixteen and my younger brother is ten. Yep, I was the middle child and the only girl. I always loved animals, especially my little dog, Yodels. I got him for my fifth birthday. I loved playing soccer and running. I also loved art—looking at art, reading about the great artists, and creating my own art. I could always imagine fanciful places and loved drawing the places I pictured in my mind. My favorite color has always been silver. I don't know why. Lots of people have told me that it's a strange choice, but anything silver is just beautiful to me."

The trees' smiles broadened and they exchanged a knowing glance. The draperies parted. A gigantic breathtaking portrait of Dina framed in ornate silver filled the space where the drapes had been. A wondrous light emanated from the portrait, glowing all around it and from the image of the girl.

"That... that's me, I think," Dina stammered, "but I've never looked that beautiful."

"Yes, you have. Every single moment since your creation," the butterfly on Dina's arm whispered. Dina looked closely and saw the face of her great-grandmother who'd passed two years ago, but this woman looked younger than Dina ever remembered. "Yes, it's me. I wasn't always as old as when you knew me," she chuckled. Then, more seriously, Granny whispered, "You must do this. "It will be fine. You'll see." With those words she flew from Dina's arm to Dina's portrait and landed on the top of the frame.

Dina was dumbfounded, but knew there was no stopping now.

The luminous portrait faded and was replaced by a slide-show, starting with a squalling baby covered in some kind of goop. Everyone in the room chattered delightedly. She saw her young-looking parents and knew this must be the delivery room when she was born. Everyone was busy, but she focused on her parents' faces as they beamed at the newborn nestled on her mother's chest. Her mom and dad kept saying, "Welcome, baby girl. We love you. We love you. Welcome to our family. You're our baby girl. We love you so much." Pure joy filled the screen.

It filled the bench too, as the youths beamed at one another, knowing the loving start Dina's earthly life had had.

In quick succession, the prismatic images showcased every event of Dina's life. Big events and small flashed on the screen, carrying with each image a full understanding of the event and how it formed the person Dina had become. Images showed Dina at home with her family, with her friends, at parties, playing soccer, creating artwork, doing chores, at school. Things she remembered and things she'd forgotten flashed before her. New understanding dawned as she watched the tapestry of her life and how everything was connected. The screen faded to black, as if waiting for something.

Dina stared at the screen and finally whispered, "This thing knows everything. I didn't even remember a lot of these things, but my whole life is recorded."

The Board of Insights roared to life again, spewing brilliant flashes and more scenes from Dina's life. In this collage of images, Dina helped an old lady, brushing her hair and gently applying lotion. Dina read to her and did puzzles with her. They created art together. They talked and laughed in every scene. They clearly loved being together. Next came images of the old lady slumping out of her chair, paramedics coming, and a funeral. Everyone knew her grandma had died. The family was sad, but also joyful. Dina's great-grandmother had lived a long and happy life.

The honeycomb of images slowed and stopped on one. The screen went to a full-sized image of that cell. Dina looked to be about eleven or twelve in the image. She looked far from beautiful. That Dina looked angry, with an ugliness of expression that filled Dina on the bench with sadness. "Oh, no!" she cried. "This is the time I was really mean to my brother. I said some awful things. Oh, guys, you're going to hate me..." The scene played before their eyes.

Dina sat cross legged on a footstool, engrossed in adding details to the magical scene she'd created in her sketch pad. Her little brother appeared to be about eight. His eyes sparkled with mischief as he sneaked up behind Dina, shouting, "Boo!" as he poked her in the back. Her pencil streaked across the page, leaving a long black line over the image she had worked on for hours.

Startled, she fell from her perch, landing on her beloved dog, Yodels. His yelping bolt from the side of the footstool crashed into the end table, knocking the lamp to the floor. It was not just any lamp, but Great-Grandma's Tiffany lamp, the one Mom had gotten when she passed. Glass shards covered the floor.

Dina jumped to her feet and grabbed her little brother. Shaking him ferociously, she shouted, "I hate you! You're such a brat! Our family was so much better before you were born! All you do is cause trouble. I hate you so much!"

He squirmed loose and ran from the room as she continued shouting, "Get back here, you little brat! This is all your fault!"

The scene shifted, showing Dina's brother sobbing into his pillow and a little dog licking his face. "I don't mean to be bad, Yodels. Really, I don't. I just wanted to make Dina laugh. I thought she'd jump a little and laugh. She was so upset when she got home because her friend teased her about her drawing. I didn't mean to make her mad or make her hate me. The family probably would be better off without me. I should run away and make Dina happy, maybe make everyone happy."

The screen returned to a prism of colors, shifting and swirling as Dina sat staring. "Oh, my God. I was so mean to him. I never apologized. I never did anything to tell him I didn't really mean the things I said. Oh, forgive me. I'm so sorry."

Her pleading eyes darted from the shifting colors to her new friends' eyes. "He ran away a few days later. We thought he'd gotten upset at school. Mom and Dad were frantic. We all were. Now I know it was me. I caused him to run away. How could I have done that to my little brother?"

Jo softly uttered, "We were studying Matthew in my Sunday school class. We had to memorize this scripture: 'Matthew 12:36: And I say to you, that every idle word that men may speak, they shall give for it a reckoning in a day of judgment.' I... I think *this* is a reckoning. Maybe we have to see and experience the bad things we did during our lives on Earth. None of us can change what we did, but we can change the way we see them. We have to see our faults and ask for forgiveness. I'm just guessing, but that's what I think. I have a feeling this is going to get worse before it gets better."

"You're right about that," Gabe whispered. "The Board of Insights is supposed to make you think. Another reason I'm sure we're supposed to be together is because I was really mean to my brother, too, Dina. Maybe we have that in common." He sat looking down, waiting for the girls to say something.

They stared at one another. No one ventured anything for a few minutes. Butterflies and dragonflies swarmed the bench and path, swirling around the teenagers who were locked in silent immobility. The creatures' wings created soothing ocean sounds once more.

Dina finally broke the awkward silence. "Well, Gabe, if you're part of our team, you have to learn more about us. Gavreel told us we had to learn all about one another. You need to learn about us and we need to learn about you. This is some embarrassing stuff. I'm not sure I'm ready for more, but I suppose more is coming whether I'm ready or not."

The girls smiled at one another and the awkward boy. He

turned and faced the projection board. He knew what to do.

The gyrating spectrum inside the ornate frame stopped and a new scene began. This time Dina was in uniform on the soccer field, dribbling the ball. Absorbed in her moves and drive to the goal, she didn't see her opponent approach stealthily from behind. The girl stole the ball and turned it around. A shocked and angry Dina pursued her opponent who had the ball. Dina was known for being a fast runner. She was well-conditioned and could keep up with the boys when they ran, even her big brother. It didn't take long for her to pass the girl with the ball. Rather than trying to kick the ball away from her, Dina stopped directly in front of the girl, causing a collision with her and another girl. The girl fell hard, bellowing as she hit the ground. Tears erupted as she tried to push up. Her hand dangled in an odd position. Whistles blew, people shouted, and adults rushed toward the girl on the ground. Dina smirked as she backed away whispering, "That's what you get for stealing *my* ball, you crybaby loser."

Horror filled Dina's face as she saw the scene as others might have seen it that day and heard the words she'd whispered as she moved away. "Oh, God, what did I do?" A tear rolled down her cheek as she bleated, "I'm sorry. I'm so sorry."

Jo and Gabe sat silently, feeling very sorry for Dina and what she was facing. Dread filled them too, knowing their pasts would also be bared.

More everyday scenes from Dina's life played on the board. They watched her race with her brothers. Day after day she played with and walked her dog. She read, drew, and did soccer drills just about every day. The parade of ordinary activities and ordinary days filled the screen and increased everyone's understanding of Dina.

The screen darkened, flashed, and displayed a full screen view of Dina sitting at a desk in a classroom, everyone busily writing on their papers. Dina discreetly studied the backside of her left arm before writing on her paper.

"Oh, gee. This is the multiplication facts test I had to pass before my parents would let me go to a soccer tournament. My folks always insisted schoolwork and my grades came first. I had a really hard time memorizing the times table. I'd already taken the test a couple of times and didn't pass it with 90%, the score we had to get before we could move on. I really, really wanted to go to that soccer tournament. So, I came up with a plan. I designed this intricate picture. I drew it on the inside of my arm, like a temporary tattoo. I used colorful felt tips and hid the times facts I couldn't remember in the design. Sometimes I was able to hide the actual numbers in the design so they weren't obvious and sometimes I used symbols like dots and lines that were really secret codes for the facts I couldn't remember. I put a few more pictures on other parts of my arms too, but they were just decoy pictures in case anyone examined my arm. It worked, too. I passed the multiplication test with 100% the third time I took it. I didn't think anyone ever knew about it."

Dina squirmed on her cushion, staring at her arm. Though nothing was there, she looked at it a long time before speaking. "I know I cheated. I didn't really pass that test. I was actually lying to my teacher and my parents. I guess I was lying to myself, too, because I was really proud of myself for pulling it off. I never should've done it. I was wrong. I'm so sorry. I hope you don't hate me for being a cheater."

"We don't hate you," Gabe and Jo both declared. They smiled at one another, acknowledging their synchronized thought.

"Most kids cheat some time or other. It isn't right or honest, but it's one of those things many kids do," Gabe comforted. "If you know it was wrong and you're truly sorry, I imagine it's one of those things that's easily forgiven."

"I hope so," Dina whispered. "The thing is, making the design and figuring out how to hide the math facts in the design actually helped me learn them. I only glanced at my picture a couple of times to reassure myself I was putting down the right answers. I actually do know all the facts now. I have ever since that day. But, I shouldn't have sneaked the facts in for the test. I could've made the design on paper and visualized it in my mind rather than looking at it on my arm. Cheating was wrong. I know that."

The screen's flashing colors faded to darkness and another scene began. This time, Dina was home, in her room, sprawled on her bed scrolling through her social media accounts. She came to a less-than-flattering picture of herself with a less-than-complimentary comment, which she had not posted. She was shocked and hurt. Incredulous that anyone would do such a thing to her, her first reaction was to figure out who'd posted it and get even by posting something even worse about them. Last week's sermon, "Love Your Neighbor," flashed in her mind.

Dina typed a comment under her picture:

I don't know who posted this and I really don't want to know, but I do want you to know I forgive you. You must be going through something really bad in your own life right now to do this to me. I'm sorry about that and anything I might have done or said that added to your pain. I forgive you for this and I hope you'll forgive me for whatever I did that offended you.

Before she could contemplate any more, she hit send. Her comment flashed into the comment section. A few minutes later, the post disappeared.

The board returned to its kaleidoscopic state, with beautiful colors and shapes continuously changing.

"I remember that so clearly," Dina recalled. "It was just a few days before the accident. I suppose I handled that one okay. I thought mean thoughts when I first saw it, but I didn't act on them. I even considered whatever was happening with the other person. I was starting to do that more and more as I got older. It's really hard to do, but it's part of becoming an adult."

The pulsating screen shifted to black once more. Another scene began, showing Dina in her soccer uniform holding a backpack. She stood on a corner next to a light pole watching cars pass by. "Where is he? He knows practice is over at 5:30. Mom's going to kill us if we're late for dinner again."

"Oh, no!" Dina gulped. "This is the end. My end. I was waiting at the corner of the school grounds for my brother to pick me up. He was about ten minutes late and I was getting worried. I was digging in my backpack for my phone to call him."

The screen showed a careening truck coming too fast, weaving all over the road. Dina didn't see it coming from behind. She was still searching in her bag when the truck hit her. The driver slammed on the brakes and the truck spun several times, plowing into Dina sideways. The truck pinned her to the lamppost where she'd been leaning and wrapped itself around her, trapping the driver in the cab just inches from her. Intense pain throttled her body. She saw the man's shocked face for just a second before everything went dark, then bright.

Dina floated near the top of the lamppost, looking down on the scene. She saw her blood-soaked body and the expression of horror on her face. She saw the trapped driver in the pick-up T-boned around her and the post. She heard his whimpers and smelled the stench of whiskey. She knew he was drunk. This man smelled just like her friend's dad did when he staggered onto the soccer field and made a scene with the referee. This guy was driving drunk and he'd hit her. He had blood running down his face, but he was alive. He whimpered and moaned.

People came from every direction. Cars stopped on the road and drivers ran to the carnage. The custodian and a couple of teachers bounded across school grounds to the corner. So many people had cell phones out calling 911 and snapping pictures. She heard sirens wailing in the background and people shouting. In only about a minute, the corner was filled with people who wanted to help her, but who were helpless.

Her brother drove up slowly, trying to figure out what was going on, why all these cars and people were gathered at this corner. He spotted the truck and lamppost. He threw his car in park and bolted over. The night janitor recognized him and tried to block his view of Dina pinned in her gruesome death pose. No one who loves you should ever see you like that. It's not a memory anyone should carry.

They jumped as a sound, like none the watchers had ever heard, blared from the screen. It was a sixteen-year-old boy's shrieks, his keening of agony, as he tried to get to his little sister, her lifeless body a magnet pulling him to her.

The janitor and others held him as he cried, "No, no, no! Oh, Dina, no! Oh, God, please. Please, God." He thrashed and pulled, trying to break free of the grip the men had on him. Heart-wrenching does not begin to describe it.

Police, firefighters, and paramedics flocked around the truck. One felt her neck and shook his head no. The first responders all looked sad, but knew what they had to do. They had to move the crowd back, get people behind the tape line they'd strung.

Two officers escorted Dina's brother, wailing and sobbing, to their police car.

Lots of equipment arrived as the first responders worked to free the driver from the crushed armor his truck had become. They got him out, wearing a cervical collar and loaded on a backboard, and rushed him to the waiting ambulance. It sped away, siren roaring.

Firefighters attached heavy chains to the truck. A fire truck pulled the pick-up back, inches at a time. Dina's body crumpled to the ground. Paramedics examined her and gently lifted her body to a gurney. They covered her with a sheet, pulling it over her head. The howl from the back of the squad car told them her brother had seen. Dina hovered above as they rolled her body to a vehicle and loaded it in the back. The side of this van featured bold lettering: Coroner's Office.

Dina's parents' car pulled up behind her brother's. They leapt out and headed toward the scene marked by bright yellow tape, calling Dina's name. A police officer stopped them at the tape line, his burly body blocking them from crossing. "You can't go over there. It's an active accident scene. We can't let any evidence be disturbed during the investigation."

"Our son called us and said he was here and we needed to come to our daughter's school. We couldn't understand a lot of what he was saying, but we knew we needed to come. Please, officer, we're just trying to get to our kids. Our son is sixteen. Our daughter is thirteen. That's our son's car over there. He was picking up his sister from soccer practice here at the school. Maybe she fell or something and is hurt. They have to be here. He called us." Dina's dad was trying to stay calm, but everyone could tell his worry was ballooning.

"Stay here just a minute, sir. I'll get someone to help you." The officer strode over to the squad car where Dina's brother sat. He talked with the cops and pointed to the couple standing nervously behind the crime scene tape line. One got out of the car and walked back to the perimeter.

"Mr. and Mrs. Lerner, if you'd come with me over to my car, I can explain what's going on here. Your son is already there."

The police chaplain stood next to the cruiser and opened the back door. Dina's brother hurtled from the seat and into his parents' arms. He blubbered, "Dina's gone. She's gone. Oh, God, she's gone."

Mom sputtered, "Gone? Somebody kidnapped her? From soccer practice?"

"No, not kidnapped."

The police chaplain stepped up saying, "Let me explain. There was an accident, a fatal accident. I am very sorry, but your daughter, Dina, was hit by a truck. She was already dead when the emergency workers arrived. There was nothing anyone could do."

Dina's mother, father, and brother clung to one another as if another one of them would be lost if they let go. The screams and sobs were almost unbearable to witness.

Dina tried to hug her family and comfort them, but they didn't know she was there. The police chaplain prayed over them, asking for God's mercy.

Dina's mom stared at what was left of the pick-up. It was being hoisted on the back of the flatbed tow truck. "Is... is th-that the vehicle that took our baby g-girl?"

The police officer nodded.

"Where's the driver?" she demanded.

"He's been taken to the hospital. He'll be treated for his injuries and tested for drugs or alcohol. We'll determine his level of impairment from that test."

"Level of impairment? He was drunk or high? Is that what you're telling us?" her dad inquired, his anger rising.

"We have to wait for the test results to be certain, but, yes, we surmise he was driving under the influence. Officers could smell alcohol when they removed him from the vehicle. Our investigation is just beginning. We are so very sorry for your loss. Officers will help you get your vehicles and yourselves home."

"Where's our daughter?"

"She's been taken to the morgue. One of you will have to identify the body. The coroner will do a thorough examination before her remains are released to you. Here's a card with their contact information. They'll be able to tell you when their part of the investigation is done and they can release her body to you. Again, we are so very sorry for your loss. Let these officers drive you and your vehicles home. None of you should try to drive at the moment."

Three young officers stepped forward. One of them urged, "If you would give us your car keys or fobs, we'll drive your cars home for you and transport you home in this police car."

A scene seemed to play in slow motion, showing Dina's family loaded into the police car, leaving the place of her death. Dina had never seen any of them look so bad.

Dina hovered above the scene as measurements and pictures were taken and glass and metal fragments swept up. Slowly, the crowd thinned and officers left. All that was left was a blood-stained lamppost and fluttering crime scene tape. Dina was all alone when a voice announced, "It is time."

The screen went black, the frame disappeared, and the heavy drapes closed.

Dina, Jo, and Gabe sat silently, no one sure what to say.

Finally Gabe broke the silence. "Well, that was intense. It reminds me of something my old neighbor used to say. For some reason, he was fond of a saying by Confucius: 'What can anyone know about their end? There is nothing for it but to patiently wait and see what will happen.' Now we know what happened to you, Dina. You had a quick death. You literally didn't know what hit you."

Both girls grinned and groaned. Dina tossed a pillow at Gabe who caught it and gushed, "Made you laugh!"

"Yeah, I guess you did. So, what do you think this little show of my life and death really means?"

Jo speculated, "I believe *you're* supposed to ponder what you saw and tell us. I mean, it was *your* life, *your* reckoning, *your* death. What do *you* feel it all means?"

Gabe interjected, "Yeah, when I did this part before with the guys, I was the only one who didn't have much to say after my life story. I was embarrassed. I'm pretty sure that's why I'm here again. I have to face things and figure them out in order to move on, wherever that may be. So, Dina, you tell us what you think."

Dina admitted, "Yeah, you're probably right. I think I was a pretty good person for the most part. Not perfect, but pretty good."

Her friends nodded agreement.

"But, I made some big mistakes that I should've apologized for and asked forgiveness for, like when I was so mean to my little brother and the girl on the soccer field. I was really, really wrong. I was really wrong about cheating too. I feel bad about the things I did wrong. I can't undo what I did, but I guess I can learn from those mistakes and ask God to forgive me. Perhaps we're supposed to learn that we have to forgive others, forgive ourselves, and accept God's forgiveness. Maybe we're supposed to help others learn those truths."

The leafy marquee rustled and the tree faces smiled like proud parents. Dina's butterfly returned to her arm. She was sure she saw her grandmother wink. A lovely blue morpho butterfly landed on Jo's knee.

JO...

Jo gasped when she looked at the butterfly closely. "Oh, Daddy! Is that really you? I can't believe it!"

"Well, you're going to have to start believing it, Pumpkin," a voice much too deep and resonant to be emanating from a tiny butterfly body boomed. "You know what's coming. You'll get through this. There's no other route up the hill, so you must trudge through this. You'll make it. There's no time like the present to get started. Put on that brave face you wear so well, and let's get this thing behind us."

Jo, Dina, and Gabe watched the sapphire wings flap a couple of times as the butterfly took to the sky. They watched in fascination as he circled the bench, brushed against Jo's cheek as if giving her a tender kiss, then flew back and forth by the drapes. He drifted from one side to the other as his audience watched from the bench, transfixed.

The overhead leaves rustled their now-familiar beachy sounds.

Jo jumped and stuttered, "I... I think that's my c-cue."

The others nodded as she began, "My name is, er, was... I'm not sure which one is right. My name on Earth was Jophiel Grace Moore, and I was the baby of my family. I lived with my mom and my sister when I died. We used to live with my dad too, but he was killed in action when I was eight. My family never got over losing him."

She cleared her throat and continued, "Life was hard after Dad died. Mom had to work so much and my sister and I were home alone after school and sometimes on the weekends. Mom got some money from the government because Dad died in the line of duty, but she used that to pay off their bills and Dad's truck. She put some of the money in a fund for my sister and me that she vowed never to touch until we needed it for college. Everyone cried so much and our life was never the same. For a long time, we all forgot how to laugh.

"We were only allowed to stay in our base housing for one year after Dad died. We had to move by the 365th day. That meant we had to change schools, too.

"It's really hard being the new kid in a school, especially when you're a kid who's sad and mopey. Most kids don't want to be friends with someone who's sad all the time. I didn't have any friends, just my sister. We moved into a two-bedroom apartment. It didn't feel like home, but I heard Mom tell Grandma that it was all she could afford since her survivor's benefit was less than a third of what Dad's salary had been. She was working full-time now, not just part-time like she had before, but money was always tight.

"Not long after we moved into the apartment, my sister and I found a stray cat, or maybe she found us. She was really skinny, but still beautiful. She was a calico, with patches of white, orange and black splattered all over her body. She was so sweet and rubbed against us and purred the whole time we were petting her. We took her into our apartment and gave her a bowl of milk and a can of tuna. She was starved! Mom walked in and found us sitting together on the couch, playing with a long piece of yarn and this skinny cat. We were both laughing at her antics as she tried to capture the end of the yarn. We were laughing! Before long, Mom was laughing, too. That's when we knew Mom would let us keep her. She brought laughter back to all of us. We named her Joy. She's the best cat in the world.

"As far as other things about me, I guess you should know I love to sing. My dad was a singer, too. We used to sing together all the time. I sang in church a lot. Everyone told me I had a beautiful voice. I sang in my school's talent show for three years.

"I loved to run like you, Dina, but we couldn't afford any sports or lessons. My sister and I would run to and from school and around our neighborhood. We liked to race one another.

"Also, I've always loved the color blue; even when every other girl my age loved pink or purple, I loved blue. Maybe it was because we were a military family and red, white, and blue were a part of who we were, but blue has always been beautiful to me."

The draperies parted once more and the blue morpho landed on top of a glistening frame mosaic made of sapphires and aquamarine stones forming intricate patterns. The black screen suddenly sprang to life. Light emanated from a dazzling portrait of Jo.

A grin crossed her face as she gazed at the alluring image of herself. "Seriously? I look like that?"

"You do," Dina and Gabe chimed in unison as they looked from Jo on the bench to Jo in the portrait. "It looks exactly like you!"

The portrait flashed and the expected psychedelic patterns of bright colors filled the board. In seconds, the scene shifted to the face of a woman who was obviously in pain and a man standing by her head telling her to breathe. She seemed to huff out breaths in a rhythm as he said, "That's right, Baby, that's right. Take a cleansing breath. Breathe till the next contraction."

Someone nearby soothed, "It's almost time to push again. Here we go! Push, push, push!"

Squalling filled the air and the doctor crooned, "It's a girl! You have a fine baby girl. She's so beautiful!"

Moments later, the squirming infant was laid in her father's arms. "Here's your daughter, Sergeant."

He leaned over, with the baby cradled in his arm, next to the woman who no longer looked like she was in pain. Both parents beamed as tiny baby hands circled each of their fingers. Her crying stopped as her parents' love and gentle coos surrounded her. "She's gorgeous! Feel that grip? She's so strong already. And what a set of lungs! Baby girl, we love you. Yes, we do. We love you."

As the portrait board faded to black, the three teens grinned at one another and chorused, "What a great beginning!" They erupted in laughter as they realized they'd vocalized the exact same words at the exact same time. Their thoughts and words were indeed becoming synchronized.

The board flickered and burst into twinkling colors that swam in every direction. Another quick succession of scenes flared across the board. Each image showed Jo as she lived her earthly life and provided understanding of the event and how it had chiseled Jo into the young woman she'd become.

They watched Jo at home, laughing with her parents and sister, doing chores, doing homework. They sat hypnotized as they watched her sing songs with her dad. From the time she was about three, Jo and her dad sang together when he was home. It didn't matter if it was "Row, Row, Row Your Boat," "Jesus Loves Me," or a song on the radio, when they sang together, they sounded as good as anyone Dina or Gabe had ever heard. Even as a young child, Jo had a voice of someone much older.

"You can really sing!" the pair exclaimed. They exchanged a here-we-go-again look and giggled. "You sound unbelievable." The giggling turned into full force-belly laughs.

More scenes flashed across the screen: Jo at school, at church, visiting her grandparents' houses, enjoying family celebrations and outings. Jo playing with her sister and friends. Jo and her sister running with their dad or with one another. Jo at the commissary with her family.

The rapid succession of scenes stopped here. "Oh, no!" Jo cried. "This is so embarrassing."

A commissary scene played. A much younger Jo whined and begged for candy. Her mother kept telling her no, but she kept begging. Finally, her frazzled mother whisper-growled, "If you don't stop begging for candy, you're getting a spanking when we get home. I said enough and I mean enough!"

Jo shouted at her mother, "I hate you! You're so mean. I bet

Daddy would get me a candy bar. Daddy loves me and I love him."

Her mother stared at her for a moment, then turned to the shelf and grabbed the next item on her list, quietly wiping the tear that trickled from her eye.

Jo kicked the cart and yelled, "I hate you!"

Her mother pushed the cart forward, trying to avoid the stares of the other shoppers. "Come on, Jo, we have to check out and get home." Everyone who'd stopped nearby moved on.

Jo snatched a candy bar from the shelf and stuffed it in her pocket.

The screen faded to black as the trio sat in awkward silence. Gabe broke the tension and the silence this time. "So, was that your favorite kind of candy, or would anything do?" That goofy grin was plastered on his face again.

Both girls snickered and Jo found her voice. "That was awful. I was awful. Watching it now that I'm older, I know I broke two commandments. Oh, how could I do that? How? I'm so sorry. I can't believe I said I hated my mother. I don't hate her. I love her. I love you, Mom. I do." The anguished words poured from her. "I didn't honor my mother and I stole! Please, forgive me. Please."

Dina reached over and wiped the tears running down Jo's cheeks. She took her friend's hands in her own. "You were very young. I know your mom knows you didn't mean it. Kids make lots of mistakes. If we learn from our mistakes and if we don't keep making the same ones, we're forgiven. I'm sure your mom forgave you. She looks like a really great mom. Somehow, moms always believe in their kids. They forgive the bad things their kids say and do as they're growing up and learning how to fit into the world. As far as stealing the candy bar, did you do it again? Did you turn into a kleptomaniac?"

Jo shook her head no. "It fell from my pocket when I bent over to take off my shoes as we came in the door. Daddy asked me how I conned Mom into getting me candy.

"Mom told him, 'I didn't get her candy.' She told Dad about the whole scene in the commissary. It didn't take them long to figure out that I hadn't paid for that candy."

Jo took a deep breath and continued, "Dad ordered me to put my shoes back on and go get the five-dollar bill I'd saved in my piggy bank. I did as he ordered. Before I knew it, I was back in the car. This time I was with my very angry father who lectured me about right and wrong, stealing, how to treat my mother, and endangering his job by such an act on a military base. When he parked near the commissary, he announced that we were going back in to talk to the manager. He told me I had to tell the manager what I'd done, give him my $5 to pay for the candy, and apologize. He told me that I couldn't accept change and to tell him that they could use the money any way it would help the store or the people who worked there. On the way out, he made me throw the candy in the trash can by the door."

Jo proceeded, "I never stole anything ever again. I never talked to my mom like that ever again either. I guess I learned a lesson. I know I did wrong. I feel so bad about it."

Glancing at the butterfly perched on her portrait, Jo continued. "I guess I was pretty lucky in the parent department. Watching that scene in my life now, I don't know how they could've handled that any better. They made me face my mistakes and try to make things right. They still loved me after I acted so bad and embarrassed them. I know they forgave me too, because they never brought it up again after that day. I really am very sorry it happened, but I know I have to forgive myself, like my parents forgave me."

The tree sentries rattled their leaves once more, filling the air with the relaxing sound of waves washing ashore. The trees exchanged that proud parent look Jo had seen her own parents exchange when she or her sister had done something well.

Momentarily, the shimmering colors of the board began again, and more scenes from Jo's life played, each filling the trio with appreciation for what the events meant in forming Jo. As expected, it soon slowed and stopped on another momentous event in the landscape of Jo's life.

The scene showed Jo's family saying goodbye to her father, dressed in camouflage and carrying a duffle bag. They were on a tarmac, a hundred yards or so from a huge plane, surrounded by other families embracing one another and murmuring farewells. Jo's father scooped her up, kissed her cheek, and commented, "I love you, Pumpkin. Be good and help your mother. I'll be back before you know it."

"You wouldn't leave us if you loved us," a tearful Jo squeaked. "You say you love us, but you're going away again. You won't even be here for my birthday next week. If you loved me, you'd be here."

"I do love you. You, your sister, and your mother mean the world to me, but this country and the freedoms we have mean the world to me, too. I have been called. I have to go. It's my job and my duty. Someday, I pray you understand all of this." He kissed her on top of the head, hugged her tightly one last time, and set her down. He marched toward the plane, turning twice to wave at his little family and throw kisses. He climbed a ramp and disappeared into the belly of the plane.

Jo hadn't seen the agonized look on his face when he left his family, but she saw it now as the scene played out before her.

"I did it again. This time I didn't honor my father. It was so hard for him to leave us and I made it harder. I was so selfish. I'm so sorry, Daddy. I'm truly sorry. I hope there's enough forgiveness in your heart to still love me after the way I treated you. You didn't deserve that."

Gabe consoled, "He forgave you and he loves you. You have to know that. He came to you as that blue morpho butterfly, knowing you had to face your entire life on the Board of Insights. Sometimes you can't say or do anything to help another person facing something difficult, but you can be there. You can be there beside them as they face whatever they have to face. He's here. Look up. He's right there on your portrait frame watching you face your entire life."

With that, a new projection began on the screen. Scenes passed in a flurry, displaying Jo, her mother, and her sister going on with daily life without her dad. They cleaned the house, shopped, had meals, played games, watched TV, read together, went to school and work. From time to time they went out to eat or to a movie. They went to Sunday school and church every week. Jo sang for the congregation several times. Jo's version of "Amazing Grace" left everyone spellbound.

The family shared letters from Dad and reveled in the occasional calls with him. Those were the only time the family seemed truly happy, laughing and joking until the call ended or the letter was tucked back in its envelope.

Days slipped into weeks, and weeks slipped into months. The slideshow slowed and stopped once more, filling Jo with horror. "I don't know if I can go on with this," she choked as the screen's burst of radiating colors quickly rolled to a new full-screen view of Jo's family.

The Moore ladies were settled at their kitchen table playing Trouble, sharing a plate of cookies they'd just made together. A knock on their door sent Jo scurrying to answer it.

Jo flung open the door and saw two soldiers in dress uniforms. One officer held an envelope and asked if Mrs. Moore was home. As she approached her daughter's side, she saw the men in uniform. "No, no, no!" she cried as she stumbled into Jo.

The men were on each side of her in an instant, gently grabbing her arms and guiding her to the sofa, where they eased her down onto the end cushion. They were kind and gentle, but everyone knew what had happened before the officer intoned, "We regret to inform you that your husband, Sergeant Major Michael Moore, was killed in service to our nation. He died honorably, saving several men in his unit. His body will be flown back to the base and is scheduled to arrive tomorrow. We will pick you up at 1400 hours to meet the plane at the hangar. The chaplain will come by to talk with you, as well as the wives' group that help in times like these. We are very sorry for your loss. He was a hero in battle." They handed her the envelope, saluted, turned, and left.

The girls pounced on their mother, who sat in stunned silence. They leaned against her, wrapping their arms around her and one another, melting into one another. The flood of tears began.

Many scenes and their meanings again rushed around the screen. People came to talk and brought food. The chaplain and their minister came and helped plan the service. The family sorted through family photos to share at the service. They saw the flag draped coffin unloaded from the plane by the military escort. The family, who loved him and were now trying to figure out how to go on without him, met the coffin on the same tarmac where they'd exchanged goodbyes. So many scenes of crying scrolled past. They viewed the memorial service and burial with full military honors, the honor guard firing three volleys in salute to the fallen hero, and the presentation of the folded flag that had shrouded him until his coffin was lowered into the ground. The screen went black again.

Dina and Gabe were instantly at Jo's sides, comforting her and wiping away the tears that streamed down her face. It didn't seem right or fair that any child should have to experience losing the same parent twice, yet that's what was happening to Jo right before their eyes. The trauma of eight-year-old Jo was now the trauma of thirteen-year-old Jo. They had to do something to help her as the scab of her grief was ripped away.

"Oh, Jo. I know this is so awful for you. That was hard for us to watch, so I can't even imagine what it was like for you, but you've made it this far. I know you can keep going. You have to. We're a team now, maybe even like a new family. We have to keep going forward together. We'll face whatever's coming together, but you have to stop clutching this part of your past so tightly that you can't embrace the future," Dina soothed.

Gabe added, "Besides, I want to hear you sing some more. I bet there's more music ahead if we can just get that thing to fast forward to some tunes. I guess I could sing, though music was never my strong suit." He belted out, "Fa, la, la, la, la, la, la, la, la."

The girls chuckled and groaned, "Stop! Your assessment of your singing is so correct. It's not your strong suit." They giggled the way only thirteen year old girls can giggle because the same words had poured from their mouths at the same time. Again.

Gabe shrugged. "Not the first time my music wasn't appreciated." He smiled that smile that seemed to light their way. They settled back on the cushions, now ready to move on together.

The swishing leaves filled the air with comforting seaside sounds again, but this time the waves seemed to be slapping out, "How great thou art, how great thou art…" The blue morpho swayed on top of the sapphire frame. He seemed to want to sing or say something, but knew he wasn't supposed to make a sound. So he just swayed from his post atop Jo's frame.

Three years of Jo's life illuminated the board in a swirl of images. They saw the weeks after the funeral when lots of people came by and the family trying to get back to their routines of school and work, all the everyday things. They observed sad looks on so many faces and heard the nighttime sobs of a heartbroken woman and two little girls as the grief overtook them again. They watched the family move to the little apartment that became their home when their base housing ended. They studied Jo's struggle to help her mom when nothing eased the pain, not even singing to her. They saw the girls find the stray cat by the dumpster behind their building. They heard the loud purring as she caressed their legs with her silky body and wheedled her way into their hearts. Everyone smiled as they watched the girls take the cat home, feed her, play with her, and convince their mother that they should keep the cat they'd already named Joy.

More scenes played, showing recovering girls and their mother. The girls made some friends and improved in school. Their mother got a better job so she didn't have to work three part-time jobs to pay the rent and put food on the table. The girls ran together, racing everywhere they went. Jo was singing again.

The next few scenes showed Jo suffering. She looked thin and had frequent nosebleeds. She was often tired and out of breath, even after a short run. She hurt all over.

Jo's family still got free medical care at the base hospital so her mom took her to the clinic. The doctor noted swollen lymph glands. He ordered blood tests, so they went downstairs to the lab. Jo was eleven now, so she tried to be brave. The lab technician told her mom the doctor should get the results in two or three days and that he'd contact her with the results.

"The blood test shows an abnormal white cell count," the doctor declared when he called her mother. "Jo will need more tests, the sooner the better." He wanted her to bring Jo to the hospital the next morning at 8:00 to do a bone marrow test, making sure she hadn't eaten or drunk anything after midnight. He explained they'd take a sample of her bone marrow from her hip bone. They'd know much more when they had the results. This didn't sound good, but they knew they had to find out.

The biopsy confirmed everyone's worst fear: leukemia. Jo had leukemia, childhood acute myeloid leukemia.

Shifting scenes showed Jo undergoing one medical procedure after another, with her mother at her side through them all. She was often in the hospital undergoing chemotherapy. She sang with her favorite nurses until her voice was too raspy and weak. She had a birthday cake for her thirteenth birthday, but she didn't have enough breath to blow out the candles. No matter what they tried, she didn't get better. She was deteriorating before their eyes. That Jo didn't look much like the Jo who sat on the bench with them now.

The screen froze on Jo lying in a hospital bed, hooked up to monitors and an IV. She looked ashen with only little wisps of hair, a shadow of her former self. She tried to keep her eyes open, but they kept drooping closed. Her mother, sister, and both sets of grandparents surrounded her bed, talking and smiling at her, each of them resting a hand on her arms or legs or head, reassuring her that they loved her and God loved her. Joy was curled up in the crook of her arm, purring and rubbing her head on Jo's arm as she cuddled the cat she so dearly loved.

Jo lifted her arms as if to reach out to someone and smiled. She slumped back, her eyes closed. The monitor's alarm sounded and the nurse came running. Her mother and Joy both shrieked as Jo left them. The last thing Jo saw was her mother collapsing on top of her body in a spasm of sobs, her grandparents and sister holding on to her and each other. A new cycle of grief had begun for her family.

The screen went blank, the jeweled frame disappeared, and the drapes closed once more.

The stillness surrounding them was uncomfortable, but no words came to any of their minds. Words simply escaped all of them. The silence was all there was as they tried to recover from Jo's passing.

After what seemed like hours, but really wasn't, Gabe blurted, "Well, this is just like the time my mom gave me 'the talk.' You want to talk about something that will leave you speechless. That'll do it."

A nervous titter soon evolved into a guffaw that lasted longer than the silence had. The friends were soon wiping their eyes, but these were happy tears among friends who shared a moment of unbridled mirth. Gabe brought them the gift of laughter.

Dina turned to Jo, "Just as you told me, this is your life story and your reckoning. You have to ponder everything we just shared and tell us what it means."

Jo nodded. "I know you're right, but I don't know if I can express what it all means. I had a lot of suffering and grief in my life. I had joys, too, but we spent so much time being sad. I guess I feel lost when I try to figure out why, and what it all means."

Dina coaxed her. "It's okay to be lost for a while. You don't have to have all the answers right now, but maybe you can examine just one thing. How about that time in the commissary? What does that scene in your life mean?"

"Well, I was pretty young when that happened, about five. I knew stealing was wrong, and I knew having temper tantrums was wrong, but sometimes young kids just can't stop themselves. They need adults to help them do right. That's what my parents did. My mom didn't make me feel bad about the way I treated her, even though I hurt her badly. She was mature and loved me in spite of my bad behavior. My dad made me face my mistakes and try to make them right. He showed me that anger is a genuine emotion and everyone gets angry sometimes, but you have to control the anger and not let it control you. He was angry when he lectured me in the car and when we were in the commissary, but he never lost control of his anger like I had. He loved me in spite of what I'd done. He showed me we could go on after we messed up. Seems that's like God. God expects us to mess up sometimes, but we've been taught we must admit our mistakes and try to make them right. Our sins are forgiven, but we have to really try to improve and learn from those mistakes. I never stole anything again and I never treated Mom that way again either, so I did learn my lesson. Because I learned, God forgave me like my parents did."

The trees winked at one another. They shook their leaves in an affirming way. The blue morpho drifted back and forth among the low hanging branches, circling but never landing.

Gabe remarked, "Hey, you're right! The trees and your butterfly agree with you, but they're waiting for more. You're going to have to dig deeper in some other parts of your life, not just this one thing that happened when you were little."

Jo took a deep breath. "I suffered a lot as a kid, which still doesn't seem fair to me. I was mad at my dad for leaving when he was deployed. I was mad at my dad when he died. I was mad that we had to move. I was mad that I had to change schools. I was mad at my mom because she was gone so much at her jobs. I was especially mad when I got sick and my whole life turned into one medical procedure after another. I was mad that I had leukemia and hurt all the time. I was mad that nothing helped me and I knew I was dying. I kept praying for God to cure me and it didn't happen. Mom and my sister kept praying too, but they could tell I was getting worse. I was mad when I saw the sad faces on everyone around me. It seemed like God just didn't care about me and I was mad at God, too. I'm not sure why I had to be so angry."

Dina mused, "Maybe God has a purpose for that anger. As you said earlier, it's a genuine emotion, and you learned to control it. I mean, you had a lot to be angry about, but you didn't go around hurting others, or committing crimes, or anything. On the other hand, you had to forgive a lot, too. I mean you had to forgive doctors and nurses who hurt you when they tried to treat you. You had to forgive yourself for getting weaker and knowing what your sickness was doing to your family."

Jo's eyes widened as she nodded. "For a long time, I did blame myself for getting sick. I wanted to help my mom and sister, because I knew what we'd all been through already, but I couldn't do anything and I had to forgive myself for that. I know this sounds horrible, but I felt I even had to forgive God for not curing me. Or maybe it wasn't me forgiving God, just figuring out that I had to forgive myself again for expecting God to cure me, rather than being open to God's will and God's plan. I needed forgiveness for my self-centeredness. Maybe those experiences on Earth that made me angry were just training for something yet to come. I did learn to control my anger most of the time. Dad was a great warrior and he controlled his anger. He taught me that I must control mine. Maybe the trials and suffering were also gifts because they helped me to grow in ways I wouldn't have otherwise. Is that possible?"

Dina and Gabe shook their heads to the sound of surf as the blue morpho landed on Jo's shoulder.

A yellow swallowtail circled Gabe and landed tentatively on his hand. "Here we go again," he muttered sadly. The grimace on his face told the girls how much he was dreading seeing his life story again.

GABE...

Gabe stared at the lemony wings of the butterfly perched on his hand as they gently opened and closed. He was paralyzed, locked in motionlessness by his dread.

Finally, the winged beauty whispered, "You know you have to do this. You faced it before. You know what's coming, but you must seek clearer insights about your life. You can't ignore things or hide from them. You have to delve and ponder. It's the only way to move forward. You've helped these young ladies get through theirs. I have a strong feeling they'll help you get through yours. You need to begin telling about yourself from your perspective to get this started."

"Yes, Uncle." Gabe croaked, "Please, don't hate me."

The swallowtail hovered near Gabe's face for a moment, seeming to sympathize with its gaze. It flew back and forth between the tree faces, as if pacing.

After another short pause, Gabe continued, "You know me as Gabe. My given name was Aslan Gabriel Burakgazi. My father's family emigrated from their homeland when he was very young. He grew up in the U.S. and married my mother, who was from a different culture and religion. My mother told me neither side of the family approved of their marriage, but they were young and in love, so they went ahead and got married.

"As the man of the house, my dad wanted everything to be traditional, mirroring the way he'd been raised. My mom tried, but many of his ways were foreign to her. He demanded much and she tried to please him, but soon love wasn't enough in their relationship. I'm not sure they even loved each other after some years had passed, but they had my brother and me by that time, so they didn't divorce. Neither was happy though, so our home was rarely a happy place.

"Bruno, my dog, always made me happy. He's such a good boy and a good friend. I really love that dog and he loves me.

"I was diagnosed with ADHD, attention deficit hyperactivity disorder, not long after I started school. I was impulsive and got into lots of trouble. Most of the time, I was an embarrassment to my whole family. My dad insisted that no son of his was going to take drugs, no matter what they were supposed to do. He declared he'd teach me to behave the old-fashioned way; he'd train me the way fathers should train their sons. That meant no pills, but heavy doses of the belt. My mom tried to stop him sometimes, but then he'd turn the strap on her. Black became my favorite color because it was my mood most of the time."

The now-familiar action of the draperies parting drew the girls' eyes from Gabe to his portrait. The frame, inlaid with onyx, was stunningly lacquered with tiny flecks of silver and gold peppering the shiny lacquered surface. The young man in the portrait looked like a god himself, so handsome with sparkling eyes and a gleaming smile. The swallowtail perched upon the frame.

The screen slid into a colorful prism, replacing the handsome face of the portrait. The shards of color shifted to reveal Gabe's birth. This time there were no happy faces or excited parents in the scene. The woman on the table was asleep with a mask over her face and light blue cloth draping her from the neck to mid abdomen. Doctors and nurses scurried around the delivery room getting things ready for something. A monitor made an awful noise. The doctor next to Gabe's mother blurted, "I have to go. I have to go now if we're going to save this baby!"

The flurry of his hands with the scalpel and the rapid commands he barked alerted everyone to the emergency. In a matter of minutes, he lifted a baby above the woman on the table. The baby was bluish and didn't cry. A nurse, or maybe another doctor, whisked the baby boy to the side of the room and began cleaning him, starting with his nose and mouth. In a few seconds, the bellowing first cry of a newborn filled the delivery room. Jubilation erupted as the medical staff rejoiced in the new life they'd just saved.

"His color is improving quickly. Listen to that lusty cry!" the woman attending the infant called. When he was clean and still bawling at the top of his lungs, he was weighed and measured. "Eight pounds, six ounces, and 21 inches long. Good sized baby boy!" The nurse diapered him, put on a tiny shirt and cap, swaddled him in a striped blanket, and placed him in a clear plastic basinet. She rolled him from the delivery room to a bright room with huge windows.

The nursery was filled with other babies. He was with so many and yet so alone the first hours of his life. No one held him or talked to him. No one cooed over him or kissed him. He lay in his basinet, drifting between sleepless minutes filled with longing for the mother he'd been taken from and fitful sleep. His sleep constantly interrupted by the cacophony of equipment, voices, and other crying infants.

The staff at the delivery table worked on Gabe's mother, closing and bandaging her incision. They lifted her from the operating table to a gurney and rolled her from the room before the screen faded to black.

The trio on the bench glanced at one another and tried to figure out what to say.

Dina quipped, "I always heard C-section babies were prettier than those born the regular way because their heads don't get smashed in birth. I'm not sure that's a true statement anymore."

This time Gabe tossed a pillow at her as his face broke into that winning smile. "But look what I turned into!"

Laughter rocked the bench as the friends cleared the first hurdle in The Gabe Show together.

Predictably, the rapid shifting of images showed Gabe's day-to-day life, conveying the intrinsic meaning of each one. He was a very active little boy. He climbed anything he came to, so effortlessly he seemed more agile animal than human. Rarely still, he ran and ran and ran, as if propelled by some super fuel. He reveled in risky behavior. They watched as he jumped from the roof of his house. They saw him grab a huge kitchen knife, pretending to be a swashbuckling pirate. The prism showed many examples of a toddler and young boy doing things that would put any child at risk of serious injury.

His parents tried valiantly to keep up with him and keep him safe the first few years of his life, but they were exhausted by the time his little brother arrived four years into Gabe's life.

His parents were exhausted with one another, too. The slideshow went from one fight to another, with much yelling and things smashing, Gabe in the background watching it all. Anger and hurt filled day after day. Gabe's dad grew more and more enraged about everything. At first, he only hit Gabe with his hand, yelling, demeaning, and cursing at him.

The pulsating prism of life scenes flashed and a full-screen image stalled on the screen. They knew they were about to witness one of the black letter days of Gabe's life.

The screen showed five- or six-year-old Gabe in a kindergarten classroom. Other kids sat on a colorful rug surrounding their teacher seated in a rocking chair. She read a story, showing the pictures to her class. The teacher smiled and used funny voices. Gabe stood to the side of the rug, sidestepping back and forth while swinging his arms, but actually listening and enjoying the story.

His flailing arms hit a little girl near the edge of the rug. She shrieked and started to cry. "He hit me. Gabe hit my head, Ms. Black!"

The teacher looked up from the story book. "Gabe, did you hit her?"

Gabe nodded, but offered, "Not on purpose. It was a accident."

"*An* accident, not *a* accident. One does not accidentally hit another person, Gabe. You know the consequence. Go sit in the Time Out chair until story time is over. I'll talk with you more when you've had time to think about why we should never hit. Go!" His teacher pointed to the little chair in the niche at the end of the loaded bookshelf. There was just enough room for the small chair in the space between the shelving unit and the wall.

Gabe huffed and headed toward the chair. Instead of sitting in it, he threw it toward the rug full of children. He slung books and stuffed animals that filled the shelves, littering the floor with the contents of the lowest shelves in just a few seconds. Children whimpered and wailed.

The teacher pressed the intercom button, declaring, "I need help right now!" She shepherded the rest of her flock out the classroom door and told them to wait against to the corridor wall.

Gabe continued throwing books and book-themed trinkets from the shelves, a frenzied look on his face. When there were no more objects within reach to hurl, he climbed the shelves to the top and stood there, five feet above the floor. His eyes darted around the room.

He saw the principal come in the classroom door. Her face showed she could not believe what she was seeing, a classroom in her building resembling a combat zone. Her stern voice declared, "You need to get down from there, Gabe. We are going to go to my office so you can calm down. Give me your hand so I can help you down."

Instead of giving her his hand, Gabe ran to the other end of the bookcase and leaped to the table a few feet away. He ran the length of that table and leaped to the next table as his principal tried to catch up and grab him. He was fast and scurried out of her reach several times. He finally jumped to the floor and crawled under tables, headed to the door. He was out of the principal's reach when he stood and bolted for the exit. His teacher suddenly appeared in the doorway. He crashed into her. Hands from behind grabbed his shoulders, wrapping him in a stifling hold. His principal asserted, "That's enough. That's more than enough, young man!"

She kept the bear hug hold on him as she carried his stiff body to her office. She set him on a chair and shut her office door, standing in front of it so he couldn't escape.

Gabe pulled his knees to his chest and laid his head on his knees. A flood of tears sprang from the anguished boy. He fell into a deep crevasse of sorrow from which he was never able to free himself.

The screen snapped to black, leaving the viewers stunned and silent. Dina and Jo weren't sure what they'd just seen. Gabe knew exactly what he'd seen, but it was something he didn't want to face or talk about. He hung his head and clutched one of the pillows so tightly his knuckles turned white.

"Gabe, I'm so sorry you went through that. It's incredibly tragic, really, but you have to dissect it and figure it out, even though it's really hard for you." Jo reached over and patted the whitened knuckles. "Tell us what you're thinking."

"This is some really humiliating stuff," Gabe began. "I don't have all of it figured out, but I do know my problems weren't because of my mom's C-section. Two of the other guys in my first group were born by C-section, too, and they weren't anything like me. They weren't weird, or impulsive, or wild. They were just regular kids with regular problems, with occasional big lessons they had to learn from mistakes they made or things that happened to them. Me, though, I was the weirdo who made everyone uncomfortable or angry. I couldn't stop myself, even when I knew what I was doing could hurt me or someone else. I didn't care and my body really wouldn't stop, even if I was telling myself to stop. Everything I did was a big mistake. Everything about me was wrong. I know my dad felt that way."

"Well," Dina offered, "I wouldn't say everything was wrong.

You were quite the athlete from a very young age. You could run faster and jump higher and longer than anyone I ever saw. Those skills weren't mistakes. They were gifts you never got to unwrap and enjoy, learning how to use them in a good way."

The corners of Gabe's mouth turned upward ever so slightly. "You believe I had gifts? Running and jumping and all the other wild crazy things I did were gifts, good things? Really?"

"You reminded me of a wild horse. I've heard people say someone could run like the wind. *You* could run like the wind! You were completely untrained and undisciplined, but you could run at hurricane force speed. You jumped and landed and kept going and going and going. Your stamina and your strength were pretty amazing. So, yeah, they were gifts. Gifts in the rough, but gifts."

Gabe marveled, "I never ever thought of myself that way. No one I knew before did either, but I see what you're saying. I like that way of looking at it. A wild horse, eh, a stallion in the wild!"

Jo added, "You were wily, too. A kindergartener had the principal trying to figure out what was going to happen next! When she got too close to you leaping from table to table, you outsmarted her and crawled under the tables to escape her reach. You probably would've escaped, too, if your teacher hadn't blocked the doorway. Two adults versus one little kid. That's how you lost that battle. One-on-one, you totally had it."

"You guys, er girls, are really something. I mean, no one ever saw anything good in me before. I hated myself as much as anyone else did, except maybe my dad. He hated me more than anyone."

"He hated his own life." The girls gave one another that here-we-go-again look and snickered.

"Don't go getting a big head, Stallion Boy. You were a great athlete and pretty darn smart for a little guy, but you were a big brat. I thought my little brother was a brat, but you run circles around him in the brat department!" Dina chided playfully.

Gabe grinned. "True. I can't deny that. I see the brat, too, but now I see more. I see myself with a body and brain so different from other people's, so different I couldn't control myself. I needed help to learn how to control myself and nobody helped me. My dad certainly didn't help me with all the beatings."

"You have to go deeper looking at your relationship with your father. Can you see your meltdown in kindergarten as a reflection of your experiences at home? Not the climbing, but the frustration and the rage," Dina prodded. "Until you face your relationship with your dad and the rage born from it, you may be stuck."

A dark cloud crossed Gabe's face as he knit his eyebrows and pursed his lips. Several tense moments passed. He finally spoke. "I really do feel my dad hated me. You saw the moments of my life up to kindergarten. Did you ever once see him hug me or kiss me? Did you ever hear him say he loved me, or even say anything nice to me? Who treats their own kid that way? Your dads didn't."

"I know you were a little kid when all of this happened and you needed love and nurturing, but you're here now and you have to learn to look deeper and try to figure things out. You aren't a little kid anymore," Dina pointed out.

Gabe exhaled the longest sigh either of his friends had ever heard, like a pressure relief valve spewing some excess pressurized fluid to keep the whole system from blowing. "I'm not a little kid, but I don't know how to understand or explain anything about my father and what he did to me. I still feel like that terrified kid sitting here just thinking about him. I know we're supposed to be seeking, giving, and receiving forgiveness. I know that much, but I don't know how to forgive him or myself for feeling the way I do. Talk about anger, Jo. You were angry with your dad for leaving and for dying. That anger was born out of love and longing for him. My anger is like a demon, born out of hate. I hated him for staying and taking so much of his fury out on me. I wished he was dead so many times! How am I supposed to understand that and dig deeper and forgive? I just don't know how to go on. I don't. Maybe I really am as stupid and weird as everyone always said I was." A tear ran down his cheek as he stammered, his voice breaking, "Help me. Please, help me." He hung his head like that scared little boy in the principal's office.

As they sat wondering what to do or say next, the swallowtail grew agitated. Its wings' usual slow graceful flapping accelerated so they could see only a yellow blur above the frame.

Dina's monarch flew from her, as did Jo's blue morpho. The two butterflies circled the frantic swallowtail several times before landing on each side of it. Their wings lulled the yellow blur into a slower rhythm. Soon all three sets of wings opened and closed in a perfectly matched ballet of motion. The butterflies' harmony beckoned the winged creatures from high in the boughs toward them. Brilliant colors flooded the area in front of Gabe's Life Board as a multitude of butterflies, dragonflies, and hummingbirds descended. The winged souls gracefully fluttered and pirouetted until they fit together into a blurry jigsaw of vibrant iridescence. The spectacle of color and motion captivated the trio.

"This didn't happen the first time I was here," Gabe whispered, trembling with nervous awe.

The winged creatures' colorful puzzle flashed and the image cleared, showing Gabe's father, a crestfallen man despairing over a cloth wrapped body. The man's sorrowful image flipped to a rushing movie of his life, illustrating every day he lived. Nearly every day mirrored events they had witnessed in Gabe's story up to this point, except Gabe's father wasn't hyper or prone to so many risky behaviors. He was just a regular boy who did regular boy things. He got beaten many, many times. He could do nothing right. The verbal abuse was as bad as the physical.

The horrified teens saw something none of them knew existed, a back-alley dog fight arena. Men cheered and bet as canines viciously battled, until one collapsed in death and the other howled in bloody victory. Gabe's father, then a boy of about eight, hovered near a man's leg and tried to hide his eyes. The man kicked him and told him to stop sniveling or he'd pin a tail on him and throw him in for the next round. The men all around roared as the boy tried to slink away. His father backhanded him in front of everyone, telling him he wasn't going anywhere, that he had to learn to face life like a man, not act like a weak woman.

More and more scenes played, most of them showing a frightened little boy transforming into an angry adolescent and angrier man.

Only when Gabe's father met his mother did the scenes deviate from the theme of violence. He was gentle and kind with her when they met. He beamed at her touch. They were happy together. They fell in love. After about a year, they decided to marry. The couple was happy, but their parents were not, repeatedly lecturing them: their relationship could never work, they came from different worlds, they would lead a life of misery.

Gabe watched his parents' wedding with wonder. He saw the joy on their faces as they gazed at one another. He also saw the gloomy faces on most other people in attendance. It wasn't a celebration to anyone except the bride and groom.

The next images were happy. The young couple went on a trip together, set up their first apartment, and enjoyed being together for everyday moments like meals, errands, and chores.

In the next scene, Gabe's grandfather lectured his father about being the man of the house and not letting his woman take control. Gabe's father changed back to the angry young man after this encounter. He was short-tempered and demanding. Everything had to be done his way. He backhanded Gabe's mother if she questioned anything. When she tried to slink away from him, he backhanded her again.

Gabe's mother found out she was expecting her first child. She was thrilled, but terrified. How would her husband react? Would the news please him or displease him? She had no idea. He was no longer the man she'd married.

She prepared his favorite dinner. The succulent aromas filled their sparkling apartment and soft music filled the air. She did everything she felt would please him. When he came in the door grumbling about his hard day at work, she had him sit in the chair at the head of the table and massaged his tension-filled neck and shoulders. He relaxed a bit. She served dinner; they enjoyed the meal together.

Things were going well. She quavered, "I have something to tell you." He looked at her, his raised eyebrows part curiosity, part warning. She knew she had to continue, even as tension gripped her stomach. "We're going to have a baby."

To Gabe's astonishment, the look on his father's face was pure joy. His father leapt to his feet and gathered Gabe's mother in his arms. He kissed her passionately, gently, lovingly. The news genuinely delighted him. Things were good between husband and wife for the months she carried their child.

The teens had seen Gabe's birth story, but his father was not in it. Now they saw an older man scolding Gabe's father, ranting men did not witness childbirth, such a thing was an abomination. They watched Gabe's father pace in the delivery waiting room, his anxiety showing on his face and in his body language. When the doctor came out and told him he had a son, Gabe's father radiated relief and delight. Because of complications, they'd had to do an emergency C-section, but everything was all right now. Mother and son were both doing well. The picture shifted to a beaming man tapping on a large window murmuring, "There's my boy. There's my fine baby boy."

Things were good for a few weeks, until the sleepless nights and strain of a fussy baby wore on Gabe's father. He came home later and later, often in a foul mood.

Gabe's mother retreated into her survival mode, trying to avoid confrontation. They rarely spent time together. She was guarded in everything she said and did. Exhausted, she resented the life in which she felt trapped. Maybe her parents were right after all. Her life was miserable, more tormented than she'd ever imagined possible.

As Gabe grew, so did his father's emotional distance from his family. He still went to work and put a roof over their heads and food on the table, as he was taught a man must do. Neither wife nor child felt nourished by his presence when he was home. The very active child frustrated him to his breaking point more often than not. Frequent and escalating violence earmarked their existence. The cycle of frustration, rage, and violence was difficult to witness, let alone live through.

The view went back to the opening image of Gabe's father and the cloth-wrapped body. This time they could hear the howling words from his mouth, "My son, my son! I am sorry. Forgive me. I am sorry. Just as my father before me, I was not the father you needed or deserved. Forgive me, my son."

The image dissipated when the horde of butterflies, dragonflies, and hummingbirds ascended to the upper branches of the trees. The trees' faces were serious and concerned. The trio of butterflies on the frame sat completely still.

The silence did not feel tranquil, but unsettled, as waiting often is. No one moved or spoke. When the hush appeared to have no end, the leaves rustled slightly. Gentle wave sounds filled the air and filled the girls with courage.

Dina murmured, "Gabe, you were just given a gift. Open it. Understand your father's life."

"You can do this, Gabe," Jo soothed.

Gabe stammered, "I... I never knew he was excited about having me. I never knew he had those happy times with my mom. I didn't know he was watching me and talking to me through the nursery window. I guess there's a lot of stuff I never knew. I just assumed he always hated me because I was so bad."

"We hope you can see now that he didn't hate you," the girls chorused. The bright orange and black butterfly and the brilliant blue one drifted from the top of the frame and floated to the girls' shoulders, perching motionless except for an intermittent flap of wings.

Gabe continued, "My father's life was hard. It could've been harder than mine. He wasn't doing bad things like I did and he still got beaten so much. His beatings looked worse than mine, more often and more brutal. I didn't expect someone's life could be worse than mine, but now I see it is. My grandfather said and did awful things to him. I can't believe he threatened to throw his own son into that dog fighting arena! My dad never did anything that bad to me.

"He stayed away in the evenings a lot. I know he was frustrated all the time, so maybe when he didn't come home after work, he was trying to avoid hurting me or my mom. Maybe he figured if he wasn't there, he couldn't lose his temper and hurt us. Maybe it was his twisted way to show love. I don't really know, but I do know he didn't force me to watch dog fights or threaten to let a dog maul me. Now that I think about it, maybe my dad didn't know any better. He didn't know any other way because he never saw anything else. He was just raising me the way he'd been raised, but he tried to do better. Now, I'm sure he truly thought he was doing what a man is supposed to do, and he was always trying to live up to his father's expectations and make him proud."

He took a deep breath and exhaled. It was a cleansing breath after the contractions of awakening his soul had just gone through. "He was grieving over my body at the beginning and the end of his life projection. I'm shocked he was grieving over me, and apologizing, and asking for forgiveness. What does it mean?"

"It only matters what you think it means, Gabe. Tell us your thoughts," Dina soothed.

He speculated, "My father did care about me? He loved me in his own way? He was tormented, asking for forgiveness. He actually wants me to forgive him. He was begging for forgiveness and I believe he meant it. It seemed like he meant it. Could that be right?"

Huge smiles crossed both girls' faces as they nodded and cried, "Bullseye!"

The burden that had been on his back his entire life melted, exonerating him from past fears and hatred. "Forgive me for my hatefulness. I didn't understand. I forgive you. I really do. I'm sorry your life has been so hard, Dad. I hope you find some peace and happiness."

All three smiled, smiles of understanding and shared joy treasured friends know.

The board sprang to life with a cascade of colors. Scenes of Gabe's life flooded the board. They saw Gabe growing and trying more and more things, often pestering or bullying his little brother. They observed Gabe in trouble with his parents, living through his mother's scoldings and his father's rages. They also witnessed Gabe getting in trouble at school for impulsive or dangerous things he did and his struggle to finish schoolwork. Gabe running and climbing to the tops of trees and buildings and hills filled other scenes.

Gabe played and giggled with a Jack Russell terrier. He had a dog that could actually keep up with him, his beloved Bruno. He taught the dog to jump hurdles and catch a frisbee. Gabe was most focused when he was teaching his Bruno how to do things. The hyperactive boy found solace when he was with his dog. Except when Gabe was imprisoned in school buildings, boy and dog were inseparable. Those images showed a happy Gabe.

As Gabe grew, he discovered skateboarding, zooming everywhere and perfecting flips. Fearless, nothing stopped him as he grew more and more skilled on his board.

Then Gabe discovered parkour. He was a natural at running, climbing, swinging, jumping, and ricocheting to get from Point A to Point B. As they watched him practice parkour, they thought they were watching a movie with Gabe cast as the superhero. There was no obstacle he couldn't overcome. The board rolled to a stop and went black.

"That was amazing, Gabe. You're amazing."

"I don't know about that. When I saw the moments I pestered and bullied my little brother, I felt really bad. It didn't affect me that way the first time I saw it. Now I realize I was starting to treat him the way our dad treated me. I wasn't beating him or anything like that, but I was mean and I didn't care how I made him feel. I liked feeling superior to him. I thought I was hilarious when I teased him and made up names for him. I knew he didn't like it, but it wasn't a big deal to me. I was just being his funny big brother. The thing is, now I see it wasn't ever funny to him. When I held him down, or put him in a headlock, or punched him hard in the arm, it didn't seem that bad. Now I understand I was hurting him a lot. I'm sorry. I hope he can forgive me some day. I didn't realize what a bully I was becoming until I saw this again. Please, forgive me. I should've been a better brother."

"You just faced something pretty major, Gabe. Most bullies can never acknowledge being bullies. They really see nothing wrong in the things they say and do. They might really feel insecure, but they act all tough and superior," Dina declared.

"Lots of bullies are pretty funny, though. Did you ever notice most bullies have good senses of humor? They're clever and quick-witted, unless you're the victim of their comments," Jo added.

Gabe was processing that exchange when the board flickered and the kaleidoscope once more filled the space.

This time the board showed a jubilant Bruno chasing an air-borne frisbee and vaulting to catch it before it hit the ground. He bounded back to Gabe with the frisbee in his mouth, dropping it at his feet. He was on the run again before Gabe had a chance to pick up the disc. Gabe launched it time after time and Bruno repeated his dash-and-leap response. It was hard to tell which one of them looked more delighted. It was one of those Heaven-on-Earth moments where pure unbridled joy was all you saw, like Dina and Jo's parents' reactions at the girls' births or Gabe's parents' moment when his mom divulged her pregnancy. It was fun watching them have fun together.

Bruno was on the run again, looking over his shoulder for the slab of plastic fun he knew was headed his way. He didn't see the giant dog standing there. He rocketed into the air and clamped down on the frisbee. He landed on the other dog.

The scene became a melee of snarling, yelping, and spewing blood. People in the dog park rushed to the pair. A man pulled the big dog back by the collar, shouting at him. The dog continued to growl and bristle at his foe on the ground. Bruno lay there, a gaping wound in his throat, a glazed look in his eyes. He was silent. Gabe knew before he knelt that his Velcro buddy was gone. His only friend had been taken from him.

The man called, "Sorry, man. My dog's not vicious. He thought he was being attacked. He was just defending himself. Everybody defends themselves when they're attacked. Your dog started it when he crashed into him. You shouldn't let your dog crash into other dogs or people. See what can happen when you don't control your animal? You have to control your animal, man!"

Gabe was incredulous. He knew the melee started again, this time because Gabe himself launched and sprang in the air. He kicked the smart mouthed man in the face so hard that he stumbled and let go of the collar he was clutching.

Profanity filled the air as the enraged man grabbed Gabe's leg and his dog went in full attack mode. Flailing arms and legs, blood curdling shrieks, and gushing blood horrified all onlookers. Gasps, screams, and cries for help elevated the chaos as bystanders tried to pull the boy from the dog. A siren screamed in the background. Someone had called 911.

A pair of police officers ran from their car to the open field where a small dog and boy lay motionless and a crowd of people shouted at a big man who clutched his dog's collar.

"He started it. That boy attacked me. He kicked me in the head while I was just standing here. My dog was just defending me. That's all. He was just defending me from attack."

The two officers called for backup, an ambulance, and animal control. The officers knelt over the boy, applying pressure to the gashes that gushed hardest. One officer clamped his hands over a wound on Gabe's neck, the other officer tried to stanch the blood from his groin and thigh. They ordered the man to hold onto his beast and to sit on the ground a few feet away. They commanded the crowd to back up a few feet from the scene, in the opposite direction from the man and his dog.

More emergency vehicles arrived with sirens blaring just moments after the call. Paramedics rushed to Gabe and tried to stabilize him. Blood sprayed from his carotid artery as the police officer moved out of the paramedics' way. The experienced first responders knew it didn't look good. It doesn't take long to bleed out when the carotid artery is involved.

Other officers moved the crowd farther back and strung police tape around the area. Animal control officers moved toward the man and the dog, explaining that they had no choice but to impound the animal, placing him in isolation. A judge would decide whether the dog would be released back to its owner or be put down.

The man ranted, "But he didn't do anything wrong. The kid's dog attacked him and the kid attacked me. He was just defending himself and me."

"That doesn't matter, sir. This animal viciously attacked and killed a much smaller animal and seriously injured a human being. He must be put in quarantine and the judge will decide where it goes from there."

They approached the now growling animal cautiously, lassoing his neck with the loop at the end of their long pole. The dog went berserk as they pulled him toward their truck. While his partner pulled the dog's head forward with the pole, the other man thrust a needle into the dog's thigh and pushed, dropping him to the ground as the tranquilizer took effect. They slipped a muzzle over his head before releasing the lasso and sliding his still body into the waiting cage. The owner shouted and waved his fist in the air as his dog was hauled away.

Officers interviewed witnesses, getting similar stories from each. The kid and his dog were just playing frisbee. Neither of them had done anything threatening. The big dog went into a frenzied attack when the little one caught the frisbee and landed on him. Yes, the boy had rushed at the man after he saw his dog was dead. Yes, the man had taunted the boy. It was all so fast. No one knew what to do.

Paramedics loaded Gabe on a gurney and into the back of the waiting ambulance. One police officer got in back with a paramedic, applying pressure on the hemostatic gauze that had been packed into the gushing wound on his neck. Hemostatic gauze had been applied to other wounds and was tightly bound with tape. Gabe wore an oxygen mask and blood pressure cuff. An IV pumped fluids into his traumatized body. His lips turned blue. His breathing was shallow. His pulse was weak. Gabe was in hemorrhagic shock.

The ambulance roared from the dog park. Less than a minute in route to the trauma center, Gabe took his last breath. He watched as the paramedic and police officer attempted CPR and shocked his heart. He did not revive. A team of doctors and nurses took over as soon as the ambulance arrived at the emergency door. Nothing worked. Official time of death: 4:17.

A nurse found his middle school ID badge in his pocket with a small bag of dog treats. At least they knew his name, a nurse mumbled.

Gabe watched as nurses cleaned blood from his stained body. They looked sad as they tried to make him look more presentable for his parents. The nurses knew the boy's parents would have to identify the body.

An exuberant Bruno knocked Gabe from his lofty viewing perch, joyfully reunited with his boy. They were together again, just as they were supposed to be, rolling in an embrace so strong it bound them wherever they found themselves. Everything went black. Gabe could remember nothing until he stood in front of Gavreel.

The screen blackened. The swallowtail fluttered from the frame and flitted from tree to tree. The draperies closed again, cuing the friends it was time for more reflection and processing.

"And you thought my passing was intense," Dina whispered. "Yours was beyond intense."

Jo croaked, "That man in the dog park and his brute of an animal were both awful, but you have to analyze their actions and reactions, Gabe. My dad liked to quote Nelson Mandela. One of the quotes he repeated over and over was, 'When a deep injury is done to us, we never heal until we forgive.' Maybe that's part of the reason you're back here facing all this again. This time, you've gained understanding of your father and forgiven him because you understand more about him. You've also gained insight about how you affected others, like with your brother. You admitted how you treated him and wanted forgiveness so you could forgive yourself. Maybe now you have to understand interactions with strangers, like the man in the park."

"I'm thinking violence is passed on in some families," Gabe ventured. "As I've watched this, I see it was in mine. People who've been treated violently themselves react violently because that's all they know. That's what happened with my grandfather and father. I'm ashamed to say it, but I was starting to do some of it to my brother too. Bullying was all I really knew so it seemed natural. My dad tried to be better than his dad, but he just couldn't control his rage all the time. I was a difficult child. I know I frustrated my parents. They didn't understand how frustrated I was with myself until I got Bruno and started burning off energy on my skateboard and by doing parkour."

He paused as if a thought had just occurred to him. "Do you suppose the man in the park had been abused, too? He kept saying his dog was just defending himself and that Bruno'd started it. He repeated his dog was just defending him after I kicked him, that they'd done nothing wrong. Maybe he had that kind of a dog to protect himself. I don't know. They both overreacted to everything. Maybe, they had a violent past. That guy seemed to love his dog like I love Bruno, so he can't be a bad guy. His dog was just standing there when Bruno landed on him. He was startled and attacked poor innocent Bruno. I suppose that dog could've been abused in the past, or been forced to fight, or trained to attack. I hadn't thought of any of this stuff before. I'm supposed to forgive the dog that killed Bruno and me. If they were victims of violence themselves, they deserve forgiveness, too, like my grandfather and father. And me. I can't be forgiven if I can't forgive others. I realize my death by dog attack was probably really hard on my dad now that I know he was terrorized at a dog fight arena."

"So, we have to forgive others and ourselves to move on," the three intoned.

The swallowtail landed on Gabe's shoulder.

The rustling sounds began again, this time a chant: "Forgiveness is the only thing that liberates the soul. Forgiveness is the only thing that liberates the soul...."

All three butterflies rose to the air at the same time and fluttered in front of the trio. They transformed into human forms. A younger version of Dina's great-grandmother, Jo's father, and Gabe's uncle smiled broadly and hugged the young person with whom they were connected. Dina, Jo, and Gabe were too shocked to say anything, but their bright smiles said plenty.

Jo stammered, "Daddy, I'm so glad to see you. I'm so glad to know we're together again."

"I'm glad too, Pumpkin, but you have to continue on this quest of knowledge and I have more work to do, too. We will be together again before you know it. I promise."

The adults chorused, "You have done well. Go in peace. Learn much and help one another along the way." They disappeared in a pink cloud. An elongated octagonal crystal edged in silver, blue, and black dropped into Gabe's hand. Gabe stared at the beautiful object and read the inscription on the top edge of the crystal.

"Forgiveness is the only thing that liberates the soul." Gabe announced.

He turned the crystal to read the next inscriptions. There was one on each side.

Buddha
"To understand everything is to forgive everything."

Mahatma Gandhi
"The weak can never forgive. Forgiveness is the attribute of the strong."

The Quaran (Surat Al-A'raf, 199)
"Make allowances for people, command what is right, and turn away from the ignorant."

The Bible (Colossians 3:13)
"Be tolerant with each other and if someone has a complaint against anyone, forgive each other. As the Lord forgave you, so also forgive each other."

LDS, Doctrine and Covenants, Section 64:10
"I, the Lord, will forgive whom I will forgive, but of you it is required to forgive all men."

The Mahabharata
"...forgiveness is the one supreme peace...."

Native American Wisdom
"When you choose to forgive those who have hurt you, you take away their power."

Time to move on!" the triad trilled as they stood and stretched. The melodious laughter of the young made the trees smile broadly as the three moved away.

ADVANCING...

Dina, Jo, and Gabe climbed the path's steepest incline. Enormous flowers resembling sunflowers lined this section, but these weren't just yellow and orange. They were many different colors with tendrils connecting one plant to another.

The trio climbed, chatting and admiring the rolling fields of sunflowers surrounding the path. As they reached the top of the rise, they spotted Gavreel seated in an ornately carved chair. Elaborate sunflowers adorned the chair's legs and tall back.

She stood and greeted them. "You have reached the top of the first path. You've done well so far. You've mastered the virtues gentleness, patience, trust, and forgiveness. You've learned one another's life stories. Your thoughts, words, and actions are synchronizing well. You are bonding into the team we need. This is your final task on this trail. You must pass this test, too, or you must remain on this trail and continue working on this section. Do you understand?"

All three nodded.

"Do any of you know the spiritual meaning of sunflowers?" Gavreel asked.

"I never even thought about a flower having a spiritual meaning," Gabe replied. "Do they?"

"All creations have spiritual meaning," Gavreel explained. "Sunflowers are gifts of beauty. They're vibrant and strong and gifts of radiant warmth. Many view them as the happiest of all flowers. They represent loyalty and longevity, too. They're unique. They provide oxygen, as all plants do, but they also provide energy in the form of nourishment. Sunflower seeds can be eaten and they produce edible oil for humans. Their vibrance mirrors the sun and the energy provided by its heat and light. Sunflowers do indeed have spiritual meaning."

"Really?" the three chimed.

Gavreel smiled that smile they all loved. "Yes, really. See the strands growing from these sunflowers that wrap around the stalks of those nearby? Those tendrils connect one plant to the next, giving support so all are stronger. It doesn't matter what color or variety the neighboring sunflower is, they're joined and strengthened by joining together. They understand one another's needs and support one another. That's why they've grown so large and spread so far.

"All lessons on this trail are vital in building caring and forging you into a team. You've reached the empathy lesson on the Trail of Caring. Because empathy is a crucial part of caring, you must have empathy to be united as a team."

Gavreel flipped out a long cord filled with loose knots spaced about two feet apart. It fell to the ground in a straight line. Ten knots extended along the length of the cord. "Each of you will be grabbing this cord anywhere you choose with one of your hands. Once you grab the cord with one hand, you cannot let go. Using your free hands, your brains, and your connectedness as a team, you must figure out how to untie each knot. When you untie a knot, I will say a word or phrase from one of your life's stories. The other two must explain the full event, examine the meaning of the event, and explain the feelings you believe your teammate experienced. Reflect on the meaning and purpose of the life event, not just retell it. Some will be easy. Some will not. You must give an acceptable response before moving ahead with the next knot. I'll assess whether or not you've truly learned about one another, how you work together to solve problems, and whether you're ready to train as a true team. Do you understand?"

Jo asked, "So we'll have one hand holding the rope the entire time, but we can use any of the rest of our bodies to untie the knots?

Is that right?"

"Yes, you can use your free hand or any other part as long as your one hand never loses contact with the cord. You can walk or move any way you choose."

"Did you do this task before, Gabe?" the girls asked simultaneously.

"Um, no. Gavreel stopped me as I left the Board of Insights and sent me back."

"We can begin anytime. Remember, once you grab the cord, that's where you'll be until the task is finished," Gavreel declared. "Deliberate and discuss before you start."

"Maybe we should spread out along the rope and work on different parts," Gabe suggested.

"No, that can't be the right way," Dina blurted. "That wouldn't be working as a team. Besides, if one of us is near each end, wouldn't that stop us from pulling the loose end through any knot that is past our bodies toward the center of the rope? Wouldn't our hand holding the rope block the end from being pulled through to untie it?"

"You're right!" Gabe and Jo exclaimed. All three partners chuckled.

"So, maybe we all need to hold the same segment of the rope near the center, between the same two knots. That way we can work from each end toward the middle, untying the knots from the outside in," Jo speculated.

"That's exactly what I was thinking," Gabe announced. "I'm left-handed so I should hold the rope with my right hand so my stronger hand can maneuver the rope to untie knots."

"We're right-handed so we'll hold it with our left hands," the girls chimed, huge grins on their faces.

The three walked near the center of the rope. "This segment is the middle," Gabe declared. "There are five knots going that way and five going the other way from this section. Let's grab it between these two knots. Are you ready?"

Nodding, all three reached for the cord and lifted it.

"Let's walk toward the end near Gavreel," Dina piped. "She can see our team work up-close as we slay the first knot!"

The trio pulled the rope middle toward one end. Dina reached down, picking up the loose end. "The knot is pretty loose. Jo, why don't you hold the rope right below the first knot. Gabe, see if you can pull up that piece at the top of the knot to loosen the knot and make a hole. I'll thread this end into the hole and pull it through. The knot should fall apart when the end section gets pulled all the way through the opening."

They cheered as the first knot fell apart.

Gavreel broke in, "That was outstanding teamwork! You're off to a strong start. Here's your first talking point. Joy."

"That must be one of the easy ones," all three chimed before they erupted in a gale of laughter.

Gavreel sat on the sunflower seat, surveying the scene as the kids celebrated their synchronized speech, barely containing her own amusement as she listened to their laughter. She repeated, "Joy."

The laughter died down. Dina giggled, "That's what we were just showing you." She composed herself and offered, "I'll be serious now. Joy was Jo's cat's name. She was a stray. Jo and her sister found the cat behind the dumpster at the back of the apartment where they lived after they had to move off the base."

Gabe continued, "The cat was a calico and really skinny when Jo and her sister found her. They took her to their apartment and fed her. They played with her with a string. They thought the cat was funny as she tried to catch the string. They were still playing with the cat and laughing when their mom got home. Jo's mom laughed at the cat's antics, too. Their mom let them keep her because it was the first time they'd all laughed like that since her dad died."

Dina added, "Jo said they named the cat Joy because she brought laughter back to all of them after grieving so long for her dad. They saved the cat, but the cat also saved them. The cat showed them that it was all right to go on with their own lives and laugh again. I'm not sure Joy was just some random stray. She might have been sent to Jo's family to help them. Joy saved them from more and more days of sadness. She helped them move on. She also comforted Jo as she was dying, just like the other members of her family."

Everyone stared at Dina. Finally Gavreel prompted, "Go on."

"Well, I know that cat was super important to Jo. She was more than just a pet. Jo adored her. She became happiness and comfort rolled into a furry purring package. She was exactly what the girls, especially Jo, needed. She came to them at exactly the right time."

Gavreel smiled. "Through the ages, cats have been important to many people in many cultures. They've been adored and worshipped. They acted as guardians of homes and were thought of as omens. They're often thought to be messengers. In Muslim lore, the cat is honored for saving Mohammad from an attack by a ferocious snake. Many believe the 'M' marking on many tabby cats' heads is the mark of the prophet, the 'M' standing for Mohammad. Cats are independent and adaptable. They teach us the value of being unique."

"Joy helped Jo's family adapt to their new life. She filled all of them with happiness, but also with gratitude for being together and learning how to go on without her dad," Gabe offered.

"Speaking of going on," Gavreel emphasized, "it's time you moved on to the next knot."

"The way we did the first one worked great," Gabe reasoned. "Let's do the next one on this same end the same way."

The girls nodded their agreement as everyone moved their hands into position. As soon as Gabe loosened the top strand, Dina poked the end through and pulled. Just as before, the knot fell apart.

"Two down!" they chorused.

Gavreel looked pleased as she announced, "I want you to tell me about kindergarten."

Gabe looked sheepish as he remembered the epic tantrum he threw in his kindergarten class. The girls shot him a look that let him know they were thinking about the same kindergarten scene, but with an unspoken reassurance that it would be okay, that they knew tantrum-throwing Gabe had evolved.

Dina began, "Well, kindergarten is the first year of school and all three of us went through it, but you want us to tell you about one day during Gabe's kindergarten year, right?"

Gavreel nodded.

Dina continued, "Gabe told us he was diagnosed with Attention Deficit Hyperactivity Disorder right after he started school. He was impulsive and got into lots of trouble. The doctor recommended some kind of medicine to help him, but his dad wouldn't allow him to take any kind of drugs. So, he just kept being wild and getting into trouble, getting beating after beating from his dad."

Jo interjected, "When we watched his life at the Board of Insights, we saw lots and lots of dangerous and scary things he did when he was little. Because of his ADHD, he was out of control most of the time. Any way, one day in kindergarten he had a total meltdown. It had to be the biggest tantrum any little kid ever had."

"The thing is," Dina continued, "that tantrum started because he was misunderstood. He really was listening to the story his teacher was reading, but he couldn't stop moving. He didn't really hit the little girl, he just bumped into her accidentally. No one would listen to him though. Everyone expected him to be bad all the time. He just couldn't take the unfairness any more when he was sent to Time Out."

Dina added, "The principal came and tried to get Gabe, but he kept escaping."

"The principal finally grabbed him and carried him to the office," Jo explained. "He had another meltdown in her office, but it was a different kind. He was enraged in the classroom; he'd just plain had enough and couldn't bear anymore. He couldn't stop his rage once it started. His uncontrollable crying in the principal's office was something else, though. It was more than sadness about being caught and being in trouble. It was sorrow. He'd just figured out he was different from every other kid in his class, but didn't know why or how to make people understand or like him."

Dina continued, "That sobbing in the principal's office was grief. Gabe was grieving for the little boy who came to school all excited about being there, about making friends and being happy, enjoying things like stories. He discovered, even if he didn't understand it, that he'd never be a little boy like the other ones in his class. Maybe he thought nobody'd ever like him and he'd never be happy. Maybe he'd thought school would be better than home, where maybe he could be happy at least for part of his day. He was grieving the loss of his little boy fantasy about fitting in and being happy."

"That's kind of my opinion, too," Jo agreed, "but I also feel the classroom tantrum mimicked his life at home, with confusion, rage, and wanting to escape. Gabe's behavior was like both of his parents' behavior, his dad's rages and his mom's feelings of being trapped and wanting to escape. The little apple didn't fall far from the tree."

Gavreel studied the young people's faces a minute then spoke. "You've shared some remarkable insights about Gabe during this incident in his life, but I told you before that you must think deeply and try to look at all sides in every situation. That's the only way you'll be successful as we move forward. Did you reflect on all sides of this incident?"

The girls glanced at one another then back at Gavreel. "I guess not. We were just considering Gabe."

Gavreel nodded expectantly. "Go on, then. Think empathetically."

Jo blurted, "Well, I felt sorry for the teacher when all of it happened. She seemed like a good teacher. Every kid, even Gabe, was paying attention and the she had great voices. She seemed to enjoy what she was doing. Then she was interrupted by the little girl crying and accusing Gabe of hitting her. Her whole lesson was disrupted and she had a big situation to handle."

"I never thought of that," Gabe whispered. "I liked Ms. Black and her stories."

"The whole thing was really hard for the teacher," Jo explained. "She had her lesson messed up, a kid crying, then another kid getting out of control and trashing her classroom, causing other kids to get scared and start crying. She stayed pretty calm though. She didn't yell at Gabe or act mean to him. She just reminded him of the consequence for hitting other kids, called for help when he started throwing things, and got the other kids out of the way. I bet she was the one who had to clean up the mess he made, too. It was a really bad day for her."

"I agree," Dina declared. "The teacher might've thought the principal would accuse her of not having good discipline in her classroom or blame her for causing Gabe's behavior. My mom's friend was a teacher and she sometimes talked to Mom about things that happened at her school. She insisted her principal expected her to handle everything that came up in her classroom, but I don't know what the teacher could do if a kid pitches a fit like Gabe did. I mean, she had a lot of kids to take care of, not just Gabe. It was definitely a bad day for the teacher."

Gabe kicked the ground as he listened to their observations. "I didn't mean to make a bad day for my teacher or anyone else," he muttered. "I just couldn't act the right way."

"No one wants you to feel bad, Gabe," Gavreel asserted. "You were made *exactly* as you were supposed to be. You had experiences you had to have to be who you are. We just need to look at this day in your life from different points of view."

Dina offered, "It was a bad day for the principal, too. She was probably shocked when she saw the mess in the classroom, then she had to try to catch this fast, agile kid. She was getting winded and frustrated chasing him from table to table. When she finally caught him, she had to restrain him and carry him to her office. I'm sure it was really hard watching a little kid cry as hard and long as Gabe did. Sometimes I start crying myself when someone around me cries. She probably felt like crying, too. She had to call his parents and deal with them. I bet she had lots of paperwork she had to do about the whole thing, too. I'm sure she worried about the other kids' safety and getting complaints from other parents when they heard about it. She was expected to handle a lot that day."

"The other kids were really upset," Jo declared. "One minute they're enjoying a story, then things were being thrown at them. The next thing they knew, they were being moved out of their classroom. Some of them were scared. They didn't know what was going on and probably got bored standing by the wall in the hallway. I know I didn't like it when other kids caused trouble or got in trouble when I was in school. I felt helpless. Most of them probably felt confused and helpless."

"Gabe's parents probably felt confused and helpless, too," Dina continued. "They didn't know what to do about their own kid or understand why he acted the way he did. They loved him, but they were frustrated and angry with him, and with each other, most of the time. Maybe they hoped things would get better when he went to school, but it wasn't better. Now they were getting calls from the principal about his behavior. It was even more for them to handle. They were probably embarrassed."

"They were always embarrassed by me," Gabe growled. "I wasn't the kid they wanted."

"You were the kid they *needed*, Gabe," Gavreel soothed. "You were an important part of their lives and part of the plan to move them forward on their life paths. You were *always* who you were supposed to be, *exactly* who you were supposed to be."

"Let's continue with the rope now," Gavreel suggested. "You handled the kindergarten topic well."

"Third time's the charm. Ready to tackle the third knot?" Gabe glanced from his team to the next knot.

The teens maneuvered the rope the same way they had for first two, but this time without having to say a word. The knot quickly fell apart and they turned their attention to Gavreel.

She announced, "Sketching."

"Well, Dina's the artist in this group, so you must be referring to her," Gabe offered. "You probably want us to talk about the time she was working on a drawing and her little brother scared her."

Gavreel sat silently, waiting for them to proceed.

Jo continued, "Dina was at home with her dog on the floor next to her. She was concentrating so hard on her drawing that she didn't hear her brother come up behind her. He poked her. She jumped and her pencil made a huge streak across her drawing."

"Dina fell on top of her dog," Gabe continued. "The dog knocked a fancy glass lamp to the floor. Dina was so upset she yelled really mean things at her brother. He ran from the room and she kept yelling at him."

"The lamp was special," Jo recalled. "It was a Tiffany lamp, a family heirloom, that had been Dina's great-grandmother's. Dina was really close to her great-grandmother, so the lamp was a nice reminder of her. Those lamps are works of art, so it was really special to Artist Dina. She was mad about her drawing being ruined, but she was also mad about her dog being scared and getting blamed for breaking the lamp. She was mad about the broken lamp, too, knowing that her mom and the rest of the family would be upset. She probably felt guilty about it because she fell on the dog, causing him to jump and knock the lamp off the table. She shouldn't have said those things to her brother, but too many feelings crashed on her at once, no pun intended."

"I'd say that sums up Dina's feelings and actions, but her brother's feelings were important, too," Gabe murmured. "I'm sorry, Dina, but I have to say this. You were a bully to your little brother, too. You told me I bullied my little brother, and I did. I didn't realize it until I sat through my life the second time at the Board of Insights, but I did bully him. I know I had to admit it and forgive myself. You were more than mean to your brother, Dina. You were a bully. You were his big sister, someone who should've loved and protected him. Instead, you yelled that you hated him and his existence in your family. You made him so sad. I know that feeling. I felt that way as long as I can remember. Your dog went to him and tried to comfort him, but you never did. He ran away because he felt so bad. That's about as drastic a thing a little kid can do. He did that because you bullied him."

"I guess I did bully him," Dina squeaked. "I was sometimes moody and I did take out a lot of my feelings on him. I wish I could take it all back."

"We can't go back," Gavreel soothed, "but we can go forward, using our mistakes to grow and become better and stronger. That's what you should do now. Go forward with this challenge. On to the next knot."

The trio moved to the next knot and expertly loosened the loops until the knot fell away. They addressed the topic Gavreel gave them. They continued the unknotting and discussion of every topic Gavreel threw their way: soccer, parkour, singing, respecting parents, mothers, fathers. Finally, only one knot remained. They knew they could work together to unfasten the last knot easily. They had demonstrated their ability to work as a team and had gotten faster and more efficient with each knot they untied. They'd delved into very personal and painful topics in one another's pasts and had made it to the final knot. The last three topics had been about all three of them. They knew the last topic would probably be about all of them, too, and toughest of all.

"This is it. The last knot," they declared simultaneously, snickering at their synchronicity. They untied the final knot with no effort, just speed and gracefulness as their hands worked together.

Gavreel laughed right along with them, then announced,

"Team."

"Us," Gabe declared matter-of-factly.

"Yes, us," the girls agreed.

Gavreel studied them. "You believe you've formed a team? What does being a team mean?"

Dina began, "I was part of a soccer team since I was five years old. I know it means working with other people to accomplish the same goal. In soccer, it was scoring the most goals and winning each game. The team members have to work together to win. No single player, no matter how good they are, can win games alone. One person can't move the ball alone and it takes a strong goalie to block the other team's shots and keep them from scoring. A team has to train, get strong, and learn about one another to work together. Team members have to figure out each other's strengths, like who can run the longest, who shoots goals the best, who blocks the best. It's all important if you want to win. Believing in yourself, the other people on your team, and your coach is a big part of success, too. You have to listen to your coach and follow directions, but you have to be able to think for yourself and make decisions on the field that help your team. You must be well-trained and well-conditioned, but sometimes you have to react instinctively to situations that come your way."

Gabe and Jo stared at Dina. She was confident as she spoke. Neither Gabe nor Jo had been part of a team before, except within their families. They hadn't really thought of what it meant to be part of a team before this pathway's experiences. "What she said," they both intoned. Laughter filled the air once more.

Gavreel stood silently, patiently, expectantly.

Finally Jo offered, "Dina explained well what it means to be a team, but I bet you're waiting for us to tell you how the three of *us* make a team. Part of it is that we know everything there is to know about one another. Even knowing everything bad we did in our lives and the hard things we faced, we still accept one another. We want to help one another. We're different in lots of ways, but in lots of ways we're the same. We want to be together."

Gabe's shaking head affirmed her comments. "No one before Jo and Dina ever saw anything good in me or wanted to be with me, except my dog Bruno. I never had a friend. I never felt like a member of a family, either. I was just a lost kid, the weirdo everyone tried to avoid. I don't feel lost any more. Dina and Jo are my new family, my team."

Dina and Jo each put an arm around Gabe. They stood together facing Gavreel. It was their turn to wait silently, patiently, expectantly.

Dina once again broke the silence. "WE ARE A TEAM. We know it in our hearts. We know we are linked now. We went through so much together on this path. We learned to be gentle with one another, to trust one another, to be patient and supportive, to forgive and be forgiven, to work together to figure things out, and do whatever needs to be done. It didn't always happen the first time, but it happened every time. We didn't give up on one another or on our goals. If that isn't a team, I don't know what is."

The trio crowed, "WE ARE A TEAM!"

Gavreel boomed, "Yes, I believe you are!" She raised her arms. The three found themselves clothed in matching jumpsuits, with coordinating ultra-springy lightweight boots, protective armor around their feet and ankles. Wide silver, blue and black bracelets edged in gold encircled each wrist. A gold chain with a sparkling pink stone, a rose gold four-leaf clover charm, and an octagonal crystal hung around their necks.

The stretchy fabric of the new clothes, silky soft as the bunny flowers, resembled opalescent silver, blue, and black scales swirled in captivating patterns. The swirls felt alive, full of power. The form-fitting suits felt like another layer of skin. Somehow, the suits made them feel totally free. Just below the left shoulder, a gold insignia adorned each suit: Warrior Team DJG. Below the letters was a pink 1.

"Does this mean we graduated?" Gabe cried. "Cool!"

"Warrior Team? What does that mean?" Jo asked.

Gavreel grinned. "You're about to find out." She raised her arms once more. The new team found itself transported back to the front of the school.

TRAINING BEGINS...

Gavreel smiled at their confused faces as the new team looked around and recognized the school campus. They were a good distance from the top of the hill where they'd just finished the pink trail's challenges.

"You're wondering how we got here," Gavreel mused. "I'll try to explain. You see, everything in this universe is a tessellation, an orderly pattern. When you can see the tessellations and know how to access them, you can achieve many things very quickly. In this case, I accessed the space tessellation. The space tessellation allows one to go from one part of the pattern to another, even all the way across, in a nanosecond. By Earth's time-terms you're used to, a nanosecond, a billionth of a second, doesn't seem like any time at all. Time is relative to where you are. That's what we did when we moved from the top of that hill to the front of the training center. I moved us through a very small section of the space tessellation. I know it seems like magic, but it's really orderly geometry and physics combined."

"I should've paid more attention in math and science," Gabe blurted.

Gavreel chortled, "That wouldn't have helped. Very few people have any idea about time and space travel while they live on Earth. Very few can conceive things beyond the third dimension. Tessellations are cubic prisms, a concept way beyond most people until they enter this part of the vast universe."

"So you're saying that when you know how to get inside a tessellation, or the cubic prism, you can get from one place to another in no time at all? You just move from one part of the pattern to another part of the pattern and you're in a totally new location?" Jo marveled.

"Yes," Gavreel replied. "It's one of the things you'll learn in training. It's easy once you know how and practice."

"It doesn't sound easy, but we'll take your word for it," Dina, Jo, and Gabe exclaimed together, their synchronicity still a source of amusement.

Gavreel enjoyed the youths' amusement almost as much as they did themselves. She had a good feeling about these three. They seemed so well aligned already. They were so different, yet so alike, the combination of their skills and power strong enough to handle what lay ahead.

"You need to meet someone now," Gavreel remarked. "He's one of our best teachers. He'll handle the first phase of your training. He won't let up on you until you've mastered all that you must know. You must become masters of each skill. These skills must become as natural as breathing and blinking were on Earth. You'll need to use them automatically, without thinking. They must become a part of the new you, Warrior Team DJG."

Gavreel made circles in in air with her right index finger. Instantly, a tall, handsome man, who looked to be thirty-something, stood before her. He wore a swirled white, gold, and silver jumpsuit with "Seraph" emblazoned in bright red lettering on the front. So many charms hung on the chain around his neck that Warrior Team DJG couldn't count them. Bracelets of white, silver, gold, and red covered each wrist and lower arm. His boots were solid gold.

"Hello, Kirron. I'd like you to meet the newest team of recruits. You'll be in charge of Phase 1. You'll especially enjoy working with this team."

Kirron nodded. "I always enjoy working with your recruits, Gavreel. There's something invigorating about training our warriors. All the angel groups are important and interesting, but the warriors are my favorite because of their zest and skills. We must prepare them for the important work that lies ahead."

"Kirron, these young warriors are Dina, Jo, and Gabe. They were each thirteen by Earth years when they came to us. Their youthful transitions will help make them very powerful. Dina, Jo, and Gabe, this is Kirron, Master Seraph. He'll begin your training. I know I leave you in good hands."

Gavreel raised her hands and disappeared. The trio stood gawking at Kirron, too stunned to say anything.

UNIFORMS...

Kirron declared, "I've examined each of your lives and your journey on the Trail of Caring. You appear to have the makings of a strong team, but you have much more to accomplish before you can begin elementary missions to fight evil in the world. Let's begin by learning about your warrior uniforms."

Kirron raised his arms and the group found themselves standing on a sports field rather than by the training center.

"Whoa! I guess we just used that tessellation thing again," Gabe cried.

"Yes, we did, but there will be times when you will need to move without accessing the space tessellation. We're going to work on that skill first."

"We know how to move," the trio answered.

"You'll know how to move better when we finish this segment of your training," Kirron claimed. "First, I want you to race one another to the opposite side of the field and back here, going as fast as you can. I'll determine which of you is the fastest runner. When I say 'Go!' race as if your life depended on it. Ready?"

Warrior Team DJG nodded, their eyes set on the fence at the opposite side of the field.

"Go!" Kirron boomed.

All three were fast. They stayed very close to one another the entire distance to the far end. As they turned and began the return run, Dina pulled slightly ahead. Gabe and Jo were head to head, but about one stride behind Dina. The teens finished their race in that formation.

Good natured laughter erupted as they ran past Kirron. Jo and

Gabe high-fived Dina, exclaiming, "You run like someone on fire! You're so fast!"

Kirron interrupted, "You consider that fast? You're going to run the race again and then we'll discuss speed. This time, though, I want each of you to snap your heels together like this before you take off." He demonstrated a quick hard snap of the heels. "Do you understand? You're going to run the same race, but this time with the heel snap before you take off running."

"Are we in Oz? Are we turning into Dorothy in her red slippers?" Jo whispered.

Her friends snickered.

"My slippers aren't red. They aren't slippers either," Gabe sputtered. "In fact, I'd make a terrible Dorothy. She had a cute dog, though."

The friends chuckled as they lined up and waited for Kirron's signal.

"Snap and go!" Kirron bellowed.

They snapped and pushed off to begin the run. To their amazement, the first running stride took them about halfway across the field. With just a few more strides, they'd gone the entire distance out and back. All three stared at their feet.

"If we break the speed limit, can you fix it?" Gabe quipped.

Everyone, including Kirron, roared. Kirron chortled, "No worries. I can fix almost anything."

"That run was seriously crazy," Jo declared. "The heel snap activated the speed, right?"

"That's right, but that's just one feature of your new boots. Are you ready to try more?"

Eager nods answered his question.

"How would you stop suddenly if you were running at boot-boosted speed? Let's say you see an obstacle of some kind or a cliff edge straight ahead?"

"Maybe we could try planting our feet, but sometimes momentum doesn't let you stop instantly," Dina said.

"Let's test that. When I give the signal, snap and run. When I shout 'Stop!', plant your feet and stop."

The three lined up and waited for Kirron's command. They snapped and took off. They tried to stop when he shouted for them to do so, but just as Dina had predicted, momentum carried them farther than expected. They'd have crashed into any object or run off any cliff.

"To stop instantly when running at hyper speed," Kirron explained, "you have to perfect the heel snap in midair. Gabe, with your parkour skills, this skill should be fairly easy for you to master. With practice, the stop becomes as easy as the start. Watch as I demonstrate."

Kirron snapped his heels and took off running. His first stride took him all the way to the opposite side! He turned and sailed back toward them. They watched as he snapped his heels before landing. He landed smoothly, like a talented gymnast finishing an impressive routine.

"I want you to spread apart for this drill. I don't want you crashing into one another, so give yourselves lots of space. You're going to start and stop many times, sometimes stopping quickly and sometimes running longer before stopping. I expect you to snap your heels for every start and stop, so I'll just shout 'Go!' and 'Stop!' Is that clear?"

Nodding, the friends spread apart and waited for Kirron's shout.

They ran as soon as they heard the "go" command and tried to snap in midair when they heard "stop." It wasn't as easy as Kirron made it look. All three bungled the stop-snap several times, resulting in momentum-driven extra steps or tumbles in the grass. They laughed at one another and with one another with each attempt.

"The great thing about falling is you can get up and start over," Jo chuckled.

The team burst into another fit of laughter. Kirron smiled and called, "You're all very humorous, but we need to get back to work and get this skill perfected. Go!"

They sprang into motion. This time Gabe nailed the landing, snapping and landing right before Kirron. The girls tumbled mid-field.

"Again! Go!"

They raced around the field several times before hearing, "Stop!"

Gabe stopped immediately, grinning from ear to ear. "I've got it!"

"Showoff!" the girls taunted playfully when they finally stopped.

"As I predicted, your parkour skills have helped you with this task," Kirron said. "Do you have anything to share with your teammates that might help them gain this skill?"

"Well, Gavreel kept saying to look at things from different points of view, like when we were reviewing the importance of things that happened to each of us. She never let us get away with just stating the obvious. She wanted us to look at how things that had happened affected others as well as us. She expected us to look at the whole picture. So, I started watching your face as I ran. I didn't turn my back on you the last couple of times. As soon as I saw you start to open your mouth, I thought, 'STOP!' I snapped my heels as I thought the word, landing the stop before you'd finished saying stop. That was the difference. I didn't wait till I heard the command, I anticipated it by watching your face and reacting quickly. I put my arms in the air as I snapped my heels, too. I've noticed that raising arms does lots of things here. I don't know if that's part of it, but it didn't hurt."

Kirron replied, "Let's test your theory. You're going to go again. This time, anticipate the stop order by watching for facial or body clues. Concentrate on what you want to do as soon as you pick up on a visual hint that the "stop" command is eminent. Raise your hands above your head as you think and snap."

The recruits followed instructions. All stopped instantly this time. They repeated the start-and-stop maneuvers four more times, with perfect stops every time.

"Yes! Yes! Yes!" Kirron beamed.

"You have this skill level perfected, so we'll advance to the next level. You're going to run with me. I want you to follow me, but not get too far behind. You need to see me at all times. I'll slow down to half-speed, but you need to keep up with that rate. When I stop, you need to stop. If something appears before you, you need to stop so you don't crash into it. I won't be telling you when to start and stop, you'll just have to react to my movements. We'll be going farther than any of you've gone before, so we need to stay together. Understood?"

Kirron didn't wait for a reply. He took off, with Dina, Jo, and Gabe scrambling in pursuit. They zipped past the hills with trails surrounding the school campus. Very quickly they found themselves in an enormous meadow. The glorious expanse welcomed them with waving grasses and a crowd of vibrant dancing wildflowers.

Kirron stopped abruptly. The trio applied their snapping brakes, but not soon enough. Gabe crashed into Kirron and sprawled on the ground. Kirron towered over him, declaring, "That will not do. That won't do at all."

Kirron pulled Gabe to his feet.

Gabe babbled sheepishly, "Sorry. I guess I'm distracted by this place. It's so beautiful. I've never seen so many different things growing together in one place. And it's gigantic! I can't see the edge of the meadow in any direction. The flowers are changing constantly, like we're in a slideshow or something. I thought my attention span had improved since I got here, but this meadow has me looking everywhere at once. I didn't keep my focus on you."

"That's correct. You didn't keep your focus. You must learn to focus everywhere, every time. If you're going to be successful on missions, you must keep your focus on the mission's objectives at all times, regardless of what you encounter."

"Yes, Sir. I'll be better," Gabe murmured.

"Good. You're still at the beginning of training. You won't be perfect at everything immediately, but you must stay focused. This meadow, in addition to being vast and beautiful, is a crucial training ground. You'll soon understand what I mean." With that, Kirron snapped his heels and took off again.

Quicker than the trainees expected, Kirron snapped to a halt. All three managed to stop behind him without a collision, but not as instantaneously as they'd been able to do when they anticipated Kirron's verbal command.

They started and stopped several times, improving slightly each time.

"You're improving, so now we'll change it up a bit. I'm going to stop running and watch each of you closely. I want you to run and stop when you feel you need to stop. You're going to take turns for this part so I can watch each of you individually. Who wants to go first?"

"I'll go," Dina offered.

Kirron nodded. "Begin whenever you're ready."

Dina took several enormous strides away, turned, and strode back, stopping smoothly in front of her teacher.

"Again," was all he said. Dina took off again, this time running farther than she had the first time out.

An enormous wall of fire surged directly in front of her! Flames licked as high and wide as she could see. Without thinking, she snapped to a stop, barely avoiding the blazing obstacle. As suddenly as it had appeared, the fiery wall disappeared, leaving no signs that the meadow had been ablaze.

She did an about-face, running back to her team and Kirron. "That was intense!" she cried.

Jo and Gabe cheered, "That was great, Dina! You beat the heat!"

"That stop was adequate, but not great. The flames almost caught you," Kirron declared. "You'll need to react faster in the future."

"Well, excuse me," Dina grumbled defiantly. "Maybe if you gave us some idea about what we're really doing, we could react faster. I did my best. That fire came out of nowhere and I stopped before I ran into it."

"You're missing the whole point," Kirron admonished. "On missions, you won't know what lies ahead of you. You must be trained to expect anything. As a warrior, you must anticipate what you'll need to do to survive and accomplish your objective. No one will tell you ahead of time what to expect. You'll only have your training, your senses, your instincts, and your team. You'll be facing evil and danger that makes that inferno look like a ride at an amusement park. You must be ready!"

Dina hung her head. "I guess it's my turn to say sorry. Thank you for helping us become warriors. I'll try to do better."

"Your apology is accepted, but you need to do more than try. You'll have to do better. Lose the attitude, too," Kirron scolded. "You're no longer an adolescent on Earth. You're a warrior-in-training. That kind of behavior is not acceptable here. If you feel you can't handle the demands of a warrior angel, there are many lesser capacities where you may be reassigned. You wouldn't be answering your calling, and I doubt you'd feel as fulfilled as a warrior fighting evil in the universe, but reassignment can be arranged. Your team would be negatively impacted at losing a member, too, but we'll overcome that if we have to do so. If that's clear, let's get back to work."

With that, he barked, "Jo, go!"

Jo glanced around, turned to her right, and ran a great distance in that direction. She circled around and headed back where the others stood. She stopped smoothly next to her teammates.

"Keep going," Kirron instructed.

Jo took off again, this time in the opposite direction. She ran away, pivoted, and returned to her starting point, stopping in front of Kirron. Nothing had sprung up on her runs. She'd just bolted away and returned.

Kirron told her to keep going. Time after time, Jo departed in different directions and returned. Every start and stop was smooth and quick.

Jo loved running, but she wondered why she had to go out so often while Dina and Gabe stood there watching. Why was she running so much more than they were? It didn't make sense. They were about the same speed and they could start and stop when they ran at hyper speed.

As these thoughts filled her head, Jo found herself surrounded by house-size boxes on three sides. Hideous creatures sprang from the top of each box, like strange monster jack-in-the-boxes. She hadn't turned a crank to open the boxes and make them pop out, but they popped out any way, snarling and reaching for her!

Jo snapped to a stop, but too close to one box. The creature on her left grabbed her by the hair, swinging her while growling and chanting, "My first meal in oh so long! My first meal in oh so long!" Black saliva dripped from its mouth.

Jo flailed and screamed, her terror permeating the air. She kicked and punched the creature, but it didn't loosen its grip nor stop chanting. The other creatures paced back and forth on top of their boxes, snatching at Jo as her captor swung her higher and higher.

With a quick glance at one another but no words spoken, Dina and Gabe raced to Jo. Dina jumped and grabbed Jo's feet as she swung, pulling her downward, battling the demon's grasp. The snarling intensified. Gabe leapt and sprang off the box on the right. His ricochet landed a two-footed kick squarely on the side of the creature's head. Startled shrieks shook the meadow as the creature released Jo and turned to face whatever had just slammed his head.

Team DJG found themselves in a tangled heap on a grassy mound. They unwound themselves and lay back, looking up.

They saw nothing but Kirron's face looking down on them. "That was unexpected and really rather impressive. Gavreel's right. You are a powerful team." His expression radiated admiration.

"You s-saved me," Jo bleated. "You rushed in and saved me from that thing, whatever it was. Thank you, guys. Thank you."

"We didn't even think about it," her partners declared simultaneously. "It was as if that thing had a hold on all of us. It was instinct. We had to work together to free the part of us that was being held."

Peals of laughter filled the meadow as the trio realized their synchronicity now included thoughts and reactions, as well as words. One team had been forged. One incredibly powerful team had been forged.

TRAINING CONTINUES...

"We need to discuss what just happened," Kirron told the group.

"Tell me your thoughts."

"If we weren't in Heaven, I'd swear you're trying to kill us," Jo ranted. "That demon thing wanted to eat me. It wanted to eat me!"

"Why do you believe that?" Kirron prodded.

"Why? It grabbed me and chanted about its first meal in a long time! It was drooling that disgusting black spit, too! Its mouth watered as it swung me!"

"As. It. Swung. You." Kirron punched out those four words slowly. "If it was starved and planned to devour you, why would it spend time swinging you? Why wouldn't it just pounce on you and start chomping?"

"It didn't have time. Dina and Gabe rushed in and saved me!" Jo insisted.

"Really? And the other two on the other boxes? Why didn't they attack? Why'd they stay up on their own crates?"

"I don't know. Maybe they're afraid of the one that had me. Maybe that one is the leader or something and the others don't go against it," Jo suggested.

"You're reacting emotionally. You need to really think. All of you need to think," Kirron announced.

Dina speculated, "I'm under the impression that this meadow, this training course, is a simulator of some kind. It's like we're in a video game, but we don't know the rules or what to expect. Things like the fire wall and those giant monster boxes appear. We're supposed to react and handle whatever comes at us, but none of it's real. It feels real and we've reacted as if it is, but that's the point. We're supposed learn how to react and respond to everything as if it was a true enemy. Or maybe the things are real, but they aren't supposed to hurt us, just be part of training us."

Gabe added, "That makes sense. Remember when I was so distracted by the changing scenery here? I noticed everything growing in the meadow seemed like a slideshow, constantly changing. It's like we're in a place of holograms or some other kind of virtual reality, or in a place where there are real things we've never seen before and know nothing about."

"Th-that thing actually swung me," Jo stuttered. "That wasn't in my mind. I wasn't playing a game. It lifted me off the ground and swung me. You saw it."

"Yes, but it didn't do anything other than growl and swing you," Dina reminded her. "I was terrified the first time the guard tree at the boulder swung me like a rag doll, but it didn't hurt me. It just moved me to the trampoline thing. Maybe that creature was doing what it's programmed to do to train you, or all of us. Does it mean we're supposed to learn how to react if we see something similar that's real?"

"You're partly right, Dina," Kirron interrupted. "This is a training course and there are some components that are simulations, like the fire. But, many things are very real here. You won't know which is which when you face them. You'll need to react and handle each situation you encounter as if it was real."

"We'll practice one more skill using your boots, then call it a day. Whether you realize it or not, you've spent a great deal of time completing the Trail of Caring and this first training module. You need time to refresh. Up on your feet again, warriors."

They pushed up from the grassy mound and faced Kirron.

"You're all strong runners without the boots, but the boots enhance a skill you already have. You now know how to activate the speed boost when you need it and how to safely stop from hyper speed. You'll need to keep practicing, but you have the basics. Your boots can also enhance jumping ability so you jump higher and farther than you would ever be able to do without them. There will be times when this skill will be vital."

Kirron moved in front of his charges. "We're going to run back toward the training center, but we'll stop before we get there. Follow me." He clicked his heels and sprinted away with Dina, Jo, and Gabe right on his heels.

Kirron stopped by a sparkling pond surrounded by tall trees and many sizes of rocks, including gigantic boulders like the one that'd blocked the Trail of Caring. "Here we are."

"We're going to practice enhanced leaps. Before we start, I want you to show me how high and how far you can jump on your own. We're going to use this group of rocks." He pointed to a series of flattop rocks that were arranged like a set of stairs, with the first one about a foot higher than the surrounding ground and the each rock increasing in height by about a foot. There seemed to be about twenty of them in neat, ascending height. Each rock was smooth on top and several feet wide.

"Let's see what you can do," Kirron commented. "One at a time, let's see if you can all jump on that first step."

The three easily bounded onto the lowest boulder and jumped back down.

"Just as I expected. Now, let's see if any of you can make the second boulder in one leap. One at a time."

Each of them got a bit of a running start and jumped. Again, the three all made the leap successfully.

The third boulder stood about a yard high. Dina, then Jo, attempted landing on top, but missed by a few inches. Their shins slammed the edge of the rocky step rather than their feet landing on top. Each stumbled backwards as they missed the landing.

"That one's too high for me to make in one jump, obviously, but I hit it hard and it didn't hurt like it would've if I'd done that on

Earth," Jo marveled.

"That's another feature of your uniform," Kirron informed her. "The jumpsuit and boots are made to protect you when you battle evil forces. They're lightweight and flexible, but very strong."

"Awesome!" the friends cried.

Gabe backed up a few feet and ran toward the target. He easily landed on top of the third step. He jumped back down, grinning broadly. "Piece of cake!" he crowed.

"Well, let's find the top of the cake, to use your idiom, Gabe."

Gabe scanned the scene before taking his fourth leap, his attempt to land on a chest high boulder. He backed up a bit further this time. To everyone's surprise, he ran toward a nearby tree rather than the fourth step. His vault slammed his feet against the tree trunk. An upward arched bounce landed him on the fourth step. He raised his arms joyfully, flashing the V for victory sign and a self-satisfied smile.

The girls clapped and cheered his success.

"Stallion Boy is a jumper!" Dina bellowed. "A racehorse and a jumper all rolled into one!"

Gabe's smile widened.

Kirron congratulated him. "Very few can land the fourth boulder. You're well-conditioned for this kind of task. The ricochet was an interesting twist, but you did just jump once and you made it to that level. Your parkour skills are impressive. Come on down here, Gabe."

Gabe landed on the ground near the others, the trio beaming at his success.

"That fifth boulder comes about to your chin, Gabe. Do you suppose you can land that one?"

He affirmed his faith in his skills with a head shake. He raced at the tree again, but this time launched himself from the lowest limb, which stretched toward his true target. Touchdown, boulder five!

The girls cheered as Kirron studied him appreciatively.

"Frosting on the cake!"

Everyone groaned good naturally. Gabe sprinted down the boulder staircase and joined his team.

"Now, for the real challenge, Gabe. The next step is about your height. Few can jump as high as their height. Do you believe you can?" Kirron asked.

"I'm pretty sure I can," Gabe replied. "I used to do lots of jumps off the sides of buildings. Some were pretty high."

Remarkable runs, leaps, and ricochets landed him on the sixth and seventh boulders. He landed to the sound of wild cheering and clapping each time, Kirron joining the girls in congratulatory applause and cheers.

Gabe missed the eighth boulder and crashed back to the ground. He sprang to his feet immediately declaring, "I know I can make it. Let me try it again."

"That won't be necessary, Gabe. You've already impressed all of us with your skills in this area. We need to move on with the training. We're going to try long jumps now instead of high jumps."

Kirron took a coiled wire from his pocket and flipped it out on the ground. "This wire is the starting line. You'll start your jumps behind this line. It will measure each one and let us know how far you jumped. You may back up a bit if you want a running start. All of you can go at the same time. My device can make precise measurements no matter how many people cross over it to activate the measurement. It will accurately track each of you from where you cross to where you land."

The team jumped time after time, until Kirron told them to stop. He scooped up the wire and snapped it in the air. Bright red lights flashed and each of their names and jump averages appeared in the sky in front of them:

Dina: average jump 3 meters / 9 feet 10.11 inches

Jo: average jump 2.95 meters / 9 feet 8.142 inches

Gabe: average jump 3.6 meters / 11 feet 9.732 inches

"These are good averages all around," Kirron noted. "It's apparent you're all athletic."

Warrior Team DJG watched Kirron as he snapped the wire again. The red lights that had displayed their jump averages disappeared and the cord wound itself into a tight tiny coil. Kirron slipped it back in his pocket.

"Your boots are designed to protect your feet and lower legs as well as aid your running and jumping. I'll show you how to improve your jumping now."

He stepped away so they could clearly see his feet. "You know that you snap the heels together one time on the ground to start the hyper speed run enhancement and you snap the heels together in midair to stop the hyper speed enhancement and land safely. If you want to jump higher than you can on your own, tap the heel of the right boot on the ground. One ground tap helps you with one high jump. Two quick taps of your right heel gives multiple high leaps. You need to look where you want to land. Let me demonstrate."

Kirron tapped his right heel once on the ground and leaped to the top boulder in the staircase, about twenty feet above their heads. He waved at them from the top of the plateau. "Try it!"

They eagerly tapped their heels, jumped, and found themselves next to Kirron on the highest level of the rocky formation. Four of them nearly filled the space. The view was spectacular. Far in the distance they saw tiny buildings. It felt surreal, like they were looking at a Monopoly board rather than real buildings. "We'll be headed back there shortly," Kirron told them, "but first we have to practice a bit more in this area."

He descended the boulder stairs, hurtling down two or three at a time until he was back on the ground. Dina, Jo, and Gabe followed him.

"Practice the one tap jumps a few times," Kirron told them. "See how high you can go with one leap, but remember to keep your eye on the desired target. That's important."

The teens chortled as they made it to one high place after another. They scaled treetops and hilltops, sometimes chasing one another in a new version of tag.

Kirron called, "Come back here now, Team!"

They descended from their lofty perches and landed near their trainer.

"You clearly know how to use the one-tap single high jumps. We're going to practice the two-tap feature now. There's a lot of momentum force when the multiple jump feature is activated. You have to pay close attention to what you're doing. You must plan everywhere you want to land before you start and look at your next landing point as soon as you touch down. Your boots will help you get there, but you're in charge. Only you can activate the mode and show it where you want to go by visual cues. Drag your right foot backwards like this to disengage the multiple leap mode." Kirron dragged his right foot back to show them what he meant.

"Watch me as I demonstrate the multiple jump. I'm going to jump from here to the top of the tree that Gabe used to ricochet, then to the top of that pine tree over there, and finally to the top of that hill, which looked to be at least several hundred feet high. I'll return momentarily."

Kirron tapped his right foot twice and smoothly bounded to the swaying treetop nearest them, then to the higher boughs of the stately pine tree, and finally to the top of the hill. He waved to them, then reversed his route. He swiped his right foot backwards as soon as he touched the ground.

"You can use multiple jumps to come down as well as go up, as you saw. You have to learn your own skill level and how high you can leap using the boots. Everyone is different, but most trainees find that they can jump ten to twenty times higher than they could on their own. Don't try to do leaps that are too high before you understand what you're capable of when using the boost. Each of you, choose three targets in ascending heights. You're going to go to them and return. Remember you must immediately look at your next destination as soon as you land. Deactivate the feature as soon as you get back here. Have you chosen your routes? You'll go one at a time so we can all watch. Jo, please start."

She tapped twice and leaped to the top of the stone staircase. She then vaulted to the top of a fifty-foot pine tree growing next to the one Kirron had used. Her third jump landed atop a mesa, behind the stand of pines. She reversed and returned safely, dragging her right foot back as soon as she landed; her face showed her delight at this latest feat.

"Well done, Jo!" Kirron called. "Dina, you're next."

Dina showed clear understanding of the task as she sprang from a nearby tree to the top of a mushroom-shaped rock, then to a crystal outcropping on the side of a cliff wall. An uneventful return and landing garnered a compliment from Kirron.

"Nicely done, Dina! Gabe, you're up. No pun intended."

"This should be something," the girls whispered, elbowing one another in acknowledgment of their latest synchronized thought and words.

Gabe's first leap took him to the pine tree Jo had used for her second leap, his second to the crystal ledge that'd been Dina's final landing place. For his third leap, he launched toward the top of the hill Kirron had used in his demonstration. In midair, Gabe did a double somersault before touching down on the hilltop. As he reversed to the outcropping, flames shot from the toes of each boot, scorching the cliff face in a double line. Vertical lines shifted into diagonal lines as he neared his landing. His boot flame throwers continued burning the rock as he landed, creating circles that grew larger and larger at the end of each diagonal line. The crystals below his boots scorched black.

"Gabe, don't jump to the trees!" Kirron screamed. "Leap back to the ground and deactivate your boots!" He tapped one of the bracelets on his right wrist and opened his right hand in a flinging motion toward Dina and Jo. A shimmering wall encased them. They could still see what was happening, though it was like looking at something underwater, with shimmers and wavy lines slightly distorting the view.

Gabe landed next to the girls. The ground instantly blackened on his side of the shimmering barrier, but not on theirs.

"Deactivate!" Kirron shouted.

Gabe dragged his right foot backwards. Instantly the flames went out. The ground was charred around the girls' encasement, but the original colors inside the circle of protection still showed.

Kirron tapped a bracelet and made a gesture with his right hand that resembled "come here" or "give me." His open hand flicked the fingers closed a couple of times. The barrier around Dina and Jo vanished.

"I didn't expect that," Kirron stormed. "Why would you try something like that, Gabe? You have no idea what you've done or what could've happened because you felt compelled to show off."

Gabe stammered, "I always loved doing twists and flips when I was skateboarding. Doing tricks is just natural to me. They're easy and make me feel good. Actually, skateboard tricks were about the only things I ever did that made me feel proud. Since I was getting so much air when I jumped with these boots, I just reacted and flipped. I didn't even think about it, I just did it. I was in the moment and I felt compelled to flip. I'm sorry. I had no idea my boots would turn into flame throwers."

"You have no idea what just happened, do you?" Kirron interrupted. "You have no idea what you are, do you?"

"What I am?" Gabe gulped. "I'm Gabe. I am part of Warrior Team DJG. I'm just a guy trying to fit in here and learn what I'm supposed to do."

Kirron lectured, "What you are *supposed* to do is follow directions and learn what I'm teaching you in the order I teach it to you.

There are good reasons when and why everything is done here. You're not supposed to do your own thing, regardless of how *compelled* you feel. You are chosen ones. You're special. *All three of you* are special and have been chosen. You're powerful, but untrained and dangerous because of your lack of training."

"I'm sorry. I just didn't realize what could happen. This is all pretty exciting. I know I got carried away," Gabe mumbled.

"That was quite a show! Gabe's a real ripper!" the girls chorused, pride dripping in their voices.

"He didn't mean to cause a problem. He's just being Gabe. He just did what came natural to him," Jo added.

Kirron looked from one team member to the next. "I'm going to tell you some things now, much earlier than I normally would. I'm not sure if you're ready for them, but I don't see any way to avoid it after this incident. I need reinforcements." He raised his right hand in the air and made a circling motion with his index finger.

Gavreel materialized at his side.

"Have you been watching the training?" Kirron asked.

"Most of it. I got summoned to another team for a while, but I've flash-watched your maneuvers," she disclosed.

"Clearly, this team requires more information before training continues," Kirron proclaimed.

"Yes, it appears they do," Gavreel acknowledged, "at least Gabe does. But, they're a team now, so that means they all do."

IMPORTANT INFORMATION...

Kirron looked at Gavreel. "Would you like to begin, or should I?"

"Oh, I'll begin, but you jump in anytime you have something to add." Gavreel said, turning to the three youths who stood in silent anticipation.

"Dina, Jo, Gabe, have you found yourself wondering why you three thirteen-year-olds all died? I mean, have you wondered why your earthly life ended so quickly? Why you and not others?"

"We've been so busy since we got here. I haven't thought about anything like that," Jo conceded.

"Me, either," Dina admitted. "At first, when I was in my house, I was so busy watching below and practicing my hobbies I didn't do any real thinking. Since going on the Trail of Caring, getting this uniform, and doing this training stuff, I've been too busy to think about anything else."

Gabe added, "Everything always seemed unfair to me. I guess I figured death wouldn't be any different for me."

"We don't usually share this information until we're further along in training, but in your case, we believe you need to know some things before we proceed. Take a seat on that lowest step of the jumping staircase." Gavreel pointed.

"First, it's crucial that you understand everyone's major life events are always part of a larger plan. Everything is interconnected. You're needed for a very important role, that of warriors for good. You transitioned young, when you were physically fit, energetic, curious, somewhat self-absorbed, and spiritually pure. Your earthly parents, in their own ways, worked to instill strong senses of right and wrong. You have these characteristics in common. These attributes help build strong warriors. Your interests, earthly faiths, families, home lives, and manners of death are different. Those things aren't crucial when training warriors, but they're often useful on missions. Your manners of death affect those connected *to* you, but *not* to your calling to be warriors. How you died is more important in shaping those left behind than your transition to this life."

Kirron continued, "There are many, many things in the universe you know nothing about. Boundless evil, which takes many forms, is one of those things. Angels have fought the forces of evil for eons. We perpetually add new warriors to our ranks because evil abounds. More fighters are needed as Earth's population balloons. Evil balloons along with it. Evil is rampant across this universe, not just on Earth. The darkness perpetually tries to overpower the light, but warriors fight it. Our ranks of warriors are mostly made from the young. I don't mean just children and teens, but young adults, too. We need warriors who never give up. There are many types of angels with different roles to fulfill, but you are chosen to be warriors. You must understand the demands and responsibilities of the role. By providence you are here."

Gavreel nodded her agreement with Kirron, as she picked up the conversation. "You died, or transitioned, at a young age because you were selected as warriors. People say they don't know why young people die, but there's no greater calling than saving humankind, or other life forms, from evil. The calling to be a warrior angel is a great honor, but wrought with danger and grave responsibilities."

"How do warrior angels actually do that?" Gabe asked.

Kirron announced, "There are many ways, but we're sent where there are crises and evil is about to gain more souls for the dark side. We're trained to fight and slay demons when necessary. That's why youthfulness is an asset for warriors. Properly trained, youth are intense fighters and have great stamina and inventiveness for battle."

Gavreel said, "But getting youthful warriors is only part of the reason the young are called. Losing a young person is a terrible loss for those left behind, but there's a reason for that as well. Parents who lose a child, or siblings who lose their beloved brother or sister at a young age, develop great understanding of grief and others' feelings. People with debilitating injuries or diseases suffer greatly, too, and develop keen senses of empathy and perception. These are very hard circumstances to live through, but these circumstances form the strongest angels of comfort. Because they've lost so much, those left behind understand living with pain and grief. It's training for their future roles as comforting angels. Much of the training for that role happens on Earth, before they transition, as they figure out how to keep going. *Your* deaths are the foundation on which *their* training is built. Without realizing it, they themselves are often comforted by angels sent to them. Your parents and siblings will likely become comforting angels, except your father, Jo. He's a mighty warrior himself."

"Are comforting angels always in human form?" Jo asked.

"No, trained angels can take many forms, as you should recall from the Board of Insights. Each of you had an angel come to you as a butterfly. They take different forms on Earth as well."

"Like cats?" Jo squeaked.

"Yes, like cats," Gavreel confirmed with a gentle smile, "or other animals. Like anything that's needed to bring comfort or to aid some other kind of mission."

Kirron began again. "This training session convinced me that you're a powerful team. "Several things happened that are out of the ordinary for novice recruits. The first occurred when Dina and Gabe rushed in to save Jo, believing she was in danger. Without planning or talking, you two sprang into a concerted effort to save your teammate. You didn't consider any potential danger to yourselves, you just thought of saving someone else. Although foolhardy at this level of training, the heart and gusto are admirable."

"They're quick to jump to one another's defense verbally, too, aren't they?" Gavreel asked Kirron.

"Yes, they are. That's also part of being a strong team, as long as it doesn't blind you to errors that could destroy your team," Kirron asserted. "We really need to discuss Gabe's departure from my instructions during the multiple jumps drill."

"Do you have any thoughts about the line art you created on that cliff wall, Gabe?" Gavreel inquired.

"I wasn't creating art. I was just jumping with a crazy inferno flaring from my toes."

"But you did create a message, Gabe," Gavreel and Kirron intoned simultaneously. "It *is* a message to those who can read its meaning. Everything happens for a reason."

"I know something about line art," Dina offered. "We studied it in my art class. I always tried to add some of it to whatever picture I was creating, like a hidden message in my art. Lots of great artists did that."

"Go on," Gavreel encouraged her. "Tell us what you feel Gabe's line art is saying."

"Vertical lines usually indicate energy that could be released if they fell over. Diagonal lines seem unbalanced, like they're either rising or falling, but you don't know which. They're filled with restless uncontrolled energy. Curved lines, like those that make the two circles, bend and change directions. All of Gabe's lines are thick. Thick lines are hard to break, implying strength. This line art may reflect Gabe himself. He has more energy than anyone I've ever known, but sometimes he's unbalanced in releasing his energy. He's difficult to break because he survived so much in his short life. He's stronger than he knows. His lines could be a statement about himself, or our whole team, or even a statement about all warriors. I'm not sure about the exact meaning, but I'm pretty sure that's what the lines mean." Dina's voice trailed off.

"Very astute," Gavreel acknowledged. "Your understanding of art is a great asset."

"Thanks," Dina murmured as she studied Gabe's face.

"Look what he did to that crystal outcropping where he landed." Kirron pointed to the charred ledge butting against the two black circles. "His flames instantaneously transformed them into black crystals, hematite perhaps. That's never happened to the best of my knowledge. Do you have any idea what that means?"

"That I'm hot?" Gabe offered, a slight smirk on his face.

In spite of the serious atmosphere, the girls grinned and playfully swatted his arms. "You're so bad!" they chided.

Kirron and Gavreel exchanged one of those knowing glances.

"This is a rare phenomenon," Gavreel asserted. "Black is a protective color that actually gives a sense of power. It's interesting that black is Gabe's favorite color and one of your team's colors. Black makes one feel daring, secure, and physically powerful. Black crystals, like hematite, are power crystals. They can relieve fear of physical harm. Many carry black crystals for protection and a feeling of safety."

"We should harvest some of those crystals for all of us," Kirron announced. "If we're going to be working closely training them, there's no doubt we could benefit from adding the crystal power. I'll go and get some good specimens."

Gavreel nodded. Kirron tapped his heel one time and bounded to the now black ledge. He bent over, grasping the edge with one hand, and sliding it along until he felt what he wanted. Still grasping the blackened rock, he tapped with his other hand several times. A fist-sized chunk broke off. He stood up and tapped the chunk seven times with the heel of his hand. Particles of black dust floated downward. He closed both hands around the crystals in his hand. He tapped his heel one time and landed next to his trainees.

"Look at these crystals, then we'll add them to your chains along with your other charms. No other recruits will have them.

You must not divulge what they are, where they came from, or why you have them. Is that clear? This pact will be between the five of us and Michael right now."

"Yes, sir," Warrior Team DJG affirmed.

Kirron placed a charm in each of their hands. The shiny black crystals seemed to wink at them. Each received their initial in fancy script. Dina's *D*, Jo's *J*, and Gabe's *G* pulsed in their hands while they examined them, suggesting a life force embedded in them. When they flipped their charms over, they discovered a message winding along the letter's shape: "The human soul on fire is the most powerful weapon." The initials snapped on each of their chains when Gavreel waved her hand.

Gavreel's and Kirron's charms were stars, not letters. They, too, snapped in place on their chains the moment Gavreel waved her hand. They stood out among the uncountable charms that formed a lei around each of their necks. The new black stars were bigger and centered. They hung slightly below the others. The top point of the star connected to the chain and the outward stretching points nestled below several charms on each side, seeming to buoy them. The 'human soul on fire' inscription was clearly readable on the exposed side. Gavreel slipped the extra black star and another crystal in her pocket.

"Now it's time these young ones head home. They've done more in this session than they realize. They need to time to rest, refresh, and reflect before their training continues," Gavreel commented.

"I said something very similar before the last training maneuvers," Kirron agreed. "They do need rest, as do we if we are tasked with training super seraphim."

RETURNING HOME...

Gavreel raised her arms and the five found themselves standing in front of the training center.

"Thank you for your hard work today, Kirron. You handled everything admirably. I'll send for you when it's time to continue training. Until then, rest and refresh," Gavreel praised.

Kirron nodded once, raised his arms, and disappeared.

Gavreel turned to her young charges. "We will walk from here. It's a very short walk to your home, and I want to talk to you on the way."

The four strolled away from the school's campus. Gavreel told them, "You're now a confirmed team. You successfully completed your first challenges on the Trail of Caring, where you learned much, and bonded as a team. You received your uniforms and began training using their features. Something else is coming your way."

"What?" the young warriors warbled wearily.

"Your homes are now connected. You each have the same personal space you had before you left, but now you have shared common areas. You must always be close to one another when your team is called. You can spend as much or as little time together as you desire when you're not on duty, training or performing missions. Your new home has a very large shared porch, stretching the width of your three homes' facades. You will find your porch an enjoyable space for relaxing. The front doors open to a shared lounge. You'll find it comfortable for hanging out together. Three doors across the back wall of this room lead to each of your chambers. Your private chambers should be pretty much as you remember them from your earlier time there. The three wings of your home stretch out behind the porch and lounge. Oh, here we are."

Gavreel pointed to a structure featuring a massive porch, adorned with porch swings on each end and comfy furniture arranged in groups along its length. Pots of magnificent blooms hung along the roof edge and among the seating areas. Matching pots flanked the double front doors. Each pot's simple curves formed the sculpted stage for the flower show. Bold flowers took center stage as the sparkling stars of the decor, their vibrancy bursting from every pot. The porch looked like a picture out of a home and garden magazine.

They climbed three steps and surveyed the porch from one end to the other.

"It's beautiful," they chimed.

"Yes, it is. Go ahead, check it out."

Gabe headed for one of the swings and plopped down, one arm on the armrest and the other flung along the back of the swing. He swung back and forth rhythmically, closing his eyes after a couple of swings. He appeared to be in a world of his own, a world of pleasure.

The girls sniffed some flowers before settling on a sofa's impossibly soft pillows. They glanced from Gabe to Gavreel to one another. "This day just got even better," they sighed.

Gavreel smiled at her girls. She delighted in their delight. "I need to show you a couple of things before I leave you to rest and reflect. Shall we go inside now?"

The girls scrambled up as Gabe jumped from the swing. They joined Gavreel as she swung open the double doors and stepped inside, the others right on her heels.

"Welcome home, Team DJG!" Gavreel exclaimed.

They scanned the room, incredulous at its size and splendor. None of them had ever lived anywhere so beautiful. They saw a marble-topped island with a refrigerator and stove behind it. Next to the island, a glossy black table with stuffed chairs tucked around it caught their eyes. The chairs' upholstery fabric resembled their jumpsuits, with black legs that matched the table. A floor-to-ceiling fireplace adorned with lustrous tiles beckoned them. Comfortable chairs and a huge sectional sofa, covered in a luxurious blue fabric, surrounded the fireplace. Soft throw pillows congregated on the sofa, some made from the same fabric as their uniforms. Black tables filled in spaces at the ends of the sofa and by the chairs. Shiny silver lamps and other decorative pieces embellished the tables. Striking art was everywhere. Along the back wall, they spotted three doors. The one to the left was silver with an ornate D, the center door was blue and featured a large J, and right one was black with the letter G. The wall surrounding the doors featured graphic art, blue and black lines on a silver background. The design connected the doors, affirming their unity.

"As you see, the entrances to your individual chambers are clearly marked. You're welcome to go into one another's spaces if that's your choice, but only when you're in agreement. I recommend it sometimes, especially for viewing below. You'll gain great insights by observing one another's families and others left behind. It will make you a stronger team and aid the synchronization process. You shouldn't worry about that until you have refreshed though."

Gavreel continued, "I need to show you one more thing before I depart. We'll need to go into one of your chambers for me to show you this thing. Dina, since we're here by your door, may we all enter your chamber so I can demonstrate the care of your uniforms?"

"I guess so," Dina replied.

"We have to do something special with our uniforms?" the three asked, chuckling at the same question voiced at the same time.

"Yes, you do, but it's easy," Gavreel answered. "You'll be intrigued by what I'm about to show you."

"More intrigue. I can hardly wait," Gabe quipped.

"Follow me to Dina's closet," Gavreel instructed. "It will only take a minute, but you need to know this."

The group paraded through Dina's space, Gavreel in the lead. Jo and Gabe looked all around as they passed through Dina's open kitchen, dining area, and living room. It had a cozy homey feel. From the living room, they walked down a short hall with three doors. The open door to the left revealed an art studio stuffed with easels and a plethora of art supplies. Solid windows on the far wall brightened the room. The open door to the right showed a spa-like bathroom with a fancy sink and faucet as well as a huge tub and shower. The door at the end of the hall opened to Dina's bedroom, simple and lovely, a soothing retreat for rejuvenating.

"Here we are," Gavreel announced as she opened the walk-in closet door.

"Please, step in here."

Dina, Jo, and Gabe crowded into the closet. Folded shirts, pants, and shorts filled the space, as well as a few hanging pieces and a rack of shoes. They gathered around Gavreel, who stood next to a circular platform at the far end of the closet. The platform was some kind of polished stone edged in metal, about six inches higher than the floor. Something resembling heat shimmers rose from the platform.

"Changing clothes is different now. You cannot remove your uniform anywhere but on your platform in your own chamber. You cannot pull them off as with other clothing. They're like a second skin and do not pull off. This is a safeguard so no entity can ever take your suit and use it for evil purposes. These uniforms are capable of more than you can imagine and are highly coveted. Your regalia can be stored only on this platform when not in use. This platform is the *only* place you can take them off and put them on. Your spiritual essence is programmed into the platform and the uniform. Only you can activate the robing and disrobing feature."

Dina, Jo, and Gabe stared at the shimmering platform.

"Dina, step up on the platform," Gavreel urged. "I'll explain what to do as soon as you're in position."

Dina stepped up and faced her friends. "I'm not going to get naked right now, am I?"

Gavreel snickered, "Getting naked is one option, but dressing in other clothes is another option. Let's go for the second option for this demonstration."

"If you want to remove the uniform and not put on other clothes, simply swipe both hands down both thighs to your knees, like this. That's what you'd do if you were headed to the shower or tub." Gavreel demonstrated the motion.

"If you want to change into other clothes to be worn at home, select your outfit, visualize it, then swipe your hands down to your knees and back up to the top of your thighs." She again demonstrated the needed motion.

"Dina, look at your clothes on the shelves or hanging up and decide what you want to wear. Visualize those clothes. If you want your striped t-shirt and jeans, visualize that pair together. If you want those black shorts and that red tank top, visualize that pair. Have you selected your outfit?"

Dina nodded.

"Visualize the clothes and swipe your hands down your thighs and back up like I showed you," Gavreel urged.

To everyone's amazement, Dina stood before them in a bright yellow shirt and pair of cut-off shorts, barefooted and wiggling her toes. Her uniform stood behind her, as if hanging by some invisible hanger, the boots to the side of each leg of her jumpsuit. Her bracelets and collection of amulets on the chain were resting on the platform with her boots. It seemed like magic, just as the space travel using tessellations had seemed.

"Step down here a minute, Dina. I want you to see your uniform. Turn and look where you were standing."

Dina gawked at her uniform hovering on the platform, the legs barely skimming the surface with the boots propped up against each leg. The shimmers surrounded the suit. "What's happening?"

"The uniform is being refreshed and secured. It's in a forcefield vault. Only you can remove it, Dina."

"How do I do that?" Dina asked.

"Exactly the same way you changed into the clothes you're wearing. The platform will refresh the outfit and place it back where it belongs in your closet. You never have to do laundry. One of the many perks of this place!"

"We have platforms in our closets, too? Ours work the same way?" Gabe and Jo asked. Chuckles filled Dina's closet.

"Yes, you do," Gavreel assured them. "They all work exactly the same, but you can only use your own platform because it's programmed with your essence."

"Dina, if you want to take a bath or a shower when we leave, step on the platform and swipe your hands down, but not up. Your clothes will drop to the platform and you'll have accessed nude mode. You can go to your tub or shower then come back here to dress in whatever suits you."

"I can hardly wait to try out this closet platform thing," Gabe said, "but I'm starving. Do we ever eat around here?"

Gavreel roared. "We don't *have* to eat, but many still enjoy it. You don't process food the same way and never have to void, but you may eat and drink for pleasurable tastes, that filled-up feeling, and camaraderie. All of your refrigerators and pantry cupboards are filled with things you loved on Earth. Everything is ready to eat. Another one of those perks I mentioned earlier. If you want something heated simply set it on the stovetop. It will heat to the perfect temperature and texture instantly. You're welcome to share one another's food and eat together, or you may eat separately in your own home if you need some alone time. It's up to you. The food never spoils or runs out. It's automatically resupplied after use."

"Hey, Dina, what've you got to eat? I don't think I can make it back to my wing without some sustenance. I really feel famished after the workout we had today," Gabe announced.

"I have no idea, but we can find out. I feel like I could eat, too. How about you, Jo? Join us?"

The three teens skipped back to Dina's kitchen and threw open the fridge and pantry doors.

Gavreel followed them this time, smiling at their exuberance. "I'll leave you now. Rest and refresh. Your training has barely begun. I'll come for you when we're ready to commence your training." She waved as she went out the door.

They waved distractedly as they pulled out a platter of fried chicken, a second platter heaped with French fries, and a huge bowl of fruit salad from Dina's fridge. They set the platters on the stovetop. Instantly steam rose from each one.

When the three turned toward the table, each carrying a loaded platter or bowl, they found it set and waiting for them. A loaf of steaming bread sat on a cutting board with butter and an assortment of jams next to it. A full glass of icy lemonade set at each place setting, with a full pitcher ready for refills. A tray of delectable looking cakes and cookies filled one end of the table.

"Aren't Gavreel's waving hands are just wonderful?" they exclaimed. Uproarious laughter filled Dina's home as the team settled down for their first meal together.

TEAM TIME...

The three friends sat contently at Dina's table surveying the dents they'd made in each platter and bowl.

"I've never eaten so much before," Gabe sighed as he leaned back in his chair rubbing his belly. "That was the best food I ever tasted."

"It was heavenly," the girls chimed, before erupting in another round of hilarity.

"We seem to think and say the same things more and more often," Jo observed. "I know we're getting synchronized because we're a team, but is there more to it than just being a strong team?"

"Maybe," Dina and Gabe chuckled.

"We don't know nearly enough about how things work here to say," Gabe continued. "I mean who would've thought anyone could develop flaming feet by doing a couple of midair flips?"

Dina studied him. "Do you remember I told you I loved everything about art?"

Gabe and Jo nodded.

"You showed it when you talked about Gabe's line art, too," Jo praised.

"Thank you, but I wasn't fishing for a compliment. I loved reading about artists and techniques. I consumed anything about art. Gabe's flames made me remember a quote I memorized because it seemed so strange to me at the time. I kept reading it over and over and saying it over and over because I was trying to understand what it meant."

"What was it?" Gabe asked.

"Well, it's a quote from Vincent van Gogh," Dina answered.

"People thought he was crazy, and he probably was, but he was also gifted. I believe he was completely misunderstood, too, like you, Gabe. He said, 'There must be a great fire in our soul, yet no one ever comes to warm himself at it and passersbys see only a wisp of smoke.'."

"What do you think it means?" Jo and Gabe asked together.

Dina reasoned, "Well, maybe van Gogh meant everyone's soul has potential to ignite something. Maybe not literally, like your feet did, Gabe, but figuratively. Perhaps he felt there's a burning in everyone, a passion for something, that has to be discovered and developed. Very few people develop their gifts because they aren't nurtured. No one celebrates their budding talent or gifts because they don't understand what they're seeing. I think he was saying that even if *others* don't see the soul's raging fire, one should keep pursuing one's own passion, feeding one's own fire. That spark is what drives everyone to create or do. Maybe van Gogh was just talking about himself and people not appreciating him and his creations, but he might have actually been talking about everyone. Maybe he was part philosopher as well as an artist."

"What does all that have to do with my flame thrower tootsies?" Gabe asked.

"What if people who discover their talents and use their sparks to create, really do have embers within their souls? What if those flames can be called out, literally, like your flips called out the flames from inside you?"

"So you're saying you really do think I'm hot," Gabe teased.

"Oh, Gabe, you have no idea how hot you are," Dina countered. "I don't mean it the way you're implying, but, yes, you're like a volcano, with much more deep inside than what we see on the outside."

"I still don't understand why my toes shot out those flames when I did those flips. I am passionate about moving. I used to be unable to stop moving, even when I wanted to stop. I loved practicing skateboarding tricks and parkour, but why would I turn into a flame thrower by flipping over a couple of times?"

Jo offered, "It might've happened because you didn't even think about the flips when you jumped. It was second nature to you so you just did it. But, you jumped with enhancement from your boots. Maybe your passion for the movement and your flips ignited more of the enhancement, like sprinkling gasoline on a smoldering fire."

"That sort of makes sense. If I really have embers inside my soul, I guess extra moves could do something with the uniform's power. I guess I'll have to try to just follow Kirron's and Gavreel's instructions without adding my own touch."

"That's probably for the best," the girls teased.

"Do you think we still need to sleep?" Jo asked.

"I was thinking about that, too," Dina replied.

"It might be like eating. We can sleep if we get pleasure from it, but we don't really need sleep. Teenagers like to sleep and we have beds, but we only go to sleep if we want to sleep, not because we need it. Gavreel used the expression 'Rest and refresh.' She said that to Kirron and to us. She never said to sleep. I mean, do we have any idea how long we've been here? I know I watched below for a while before I walked to the school. I started on the trail with one team and had to stay until I joined you. We did all the challenges, then started the training. How long did all of that take, by Earth time? It must've been a pretty long time."

"I have no idea how long we were actually out there," Dina remarked, "but I'm certain time is very different here than on Earth. I noticed it went from daylight to nighttime several times when I watched below, but it seemed like just a few minutes to me."

"Same here," Jo agreed. "I watched my family and saw nighttime come several times, but it didn't seem as if days had passed to me."

"My parents have a calendar hanging on the wall in the kitchen. Maybe we could look through the crack into my parents' house. We could at least see what month is showing on the calendar," Dina suggested.

"Let's do it!" Gabe and Jo snickered.

The trio stood and stretched a bit, then followed Dina to a spot near her bed. She plopped on the floor. "This part of the crack showed the kitchen when I looked before."

Her friends joined her on the floor. They lay with their eyes near the narrow fissure that had opened for them. Sure enough, a kitchen came into view.

"The calendar's on the bulletin board right above that small desk," Dina told them.

"November? We've already been here like three months?" they marveled.

"No wonder I was starved," Gabe joked.

They burst into another fit of laughter, until they saw a boy they knew must be Dina's little brother. Looking sad, he talked soothingly to a little dog. "Come on, Yodels, I'll get you a treat. You'll feel better when you've had one of your special bones. Come on, boy."

A little dog slinked into the room, his tail hanging listlessly behind him. "I know you're sad, Yodels. We're all sad, but you can't just lay on Dina's bed all the time. Let's get you a treat and go outside for a while. I'll throw your ball for you."

The little boy stuck his hand into a jar on the counter and pulled out a bone shaped dog biscuit. "Here you go, boy. Here's your treat."

He held the biscuit out to the dog, who sniffed it and slowly took it in his mouth. "That's a good boy. Eat your treat and we'll go outside for a while." Boy and dog locked sad eyes, as if searching for a spark of joy in one another's souls.

Jo and Gabe glanced at one another and then at Dina, frozen in place, watching her little brother and her dog.

Yodels laid down and dropped the bone between his outstretched front legs. He pressed his head against the boy's knee. It was impossible to tell if their touch was an attempt to siphon sadness away from one another, or an attempt to find a spark of something besides sadness in their souls. Maybe sharing their sadness would lighten the load enough so that they'd find that spark for life again.

"There's nothing like the love of family," Jo whispered.

"There's nothing like the love of a good dog," Gabe added.

"No, there's not," Dina murmured as she sat up, then stood. "That's all I want to watch for a while. November, huh? I guess we'll have to visualize a turkey dinner for our next feast."

AT HOME...

Jo and Gabe pushed up from Dina's floor and looked around. "You have some cool things," they remarked.

"Thanks. It's amazing how this place is filled with things I love, things that are *so me* even though I didn't pick any of them. Things you love make a place home, that and your family, of course. I'm looking forward to seeing both of your chambers, too, but not right now. I actually do need to 'rest and refresh'. Maybe I'll check out that platform's naked mode, take a long bubble bath, and check out that bed. I haven't tried my spa soaker tub or my bed yet."

"Maybe we should have a signal that we're in the lounge or on the porch, in case either of the other two want to join us," Gabe suggested. "How about one knock on the door? We'll know it's nothing important, just a hang-out signal? If any of us are sleeping or busy doing something we don't want to stop doing, we can just ignore the knock. What do you think?"

"Sounds good. I'd say 'See you in the morning,' but I have no idea what that means around here," the girls chorused.

The three laughed all the way to Dina's door, giving quick hugs as Gabe and Jo headed to their own spaces.

When Dina returned from her door, she saw that the table'd been cleared. No dirty dishes or leftover food littered the table or kitchen. She opened her fridge and saw the platters and bowl back in their places, refilled with a golden-brown turkey, buttery mashed potatoes, and stuffing, ready for another meal. Flipping open a cupboard door, she saw clean neatly stacked dishes and glasses. "Cool! Have a feast and no clean-up. Heavenly!"

She danced back to her closet, humming happily. She stepped

on the platform, swiped her hands down her thighs, and stared at her tank top and cut-offs laying by her feet. "Naked mode works, I see. Now for that soak."

She walked through the bedroom door entrance to her bathroom and saw a steaming tub brimming with bubbles. "Ah, ask and you shall receive," she murmured as she slipped into the warm tub. She dozed immediately, soothed by the warm water and relaxing scent of the bubbles.

Jo and Gabe moved toward their own doors, eager to check out their platforms and relax in their private zones. "See you soon!" they called, turning their own doorknobs as they broke into another round of laughter.

Jo heard excited barking as Gabe threw open his door. An adorable Jack Russell terrier threw himself into the boy's arms, licking his face with such vigor that Gabe stumbled backwards. "Okay, Bruno. I missed you, too. How's my good boy?"

He noticed Jo standing in her doorway, enjoying the Gabe-and-Bruno-Meet-and-Greet Show. "Um, this is my dog, Bruno," Gabe squeaked as Bruno continued washing his face. "He's glad to see me."

"I'd say so," Jo conceded. "I didn't know we had pets here. Is Bruno friendly with other people?"

"Bruno loves everyone," Gabe answered. "Bruno, settle down. There's someone I want you to meet." He set his dog on the floor by his feet. He commanded, "Sit!" and pointed to the floor. Bruno immediately sat.

"Jo, this is Bruno. Bruno, this is Jo. She's a cat person, but we won't hold that against her." Gabe grinned. "She's part of our family now. I know you're going to love her."

Jo knelt by the little dog and let him sniff her hand. He slurped it one time and looked into her eyes, assessing every particle of her being. Jo stroked his head gently and scratched behind his ears. Bruno's enthusiasm vibrated through him, sounding remarkably like a purr. "Your dog purrs? You have a dog that purrs?"

"I guess I do," Gabe responded. "He's never purred for me before, but maybe he's gained a new skill or maybe he just knew you'd like it. He's a very special dog."

"His purring is pretty adorable. You're an adorable fellow, aren't you, Bruno? Yes, you are. You're stinking adorable!" Jo continued to stroke the purring dog, who rubbed his head on her hand, much as Joy used to do.

Jo stood up. "Seriously, I didn't know we had animals here. I haven't seen any other dogs or cats. Why do you suppose Bruno's here with you?"

"It might be because we died together. We transitioned together so we're staying together. At least I hope so. It wouldn't be Heaven for me without him. He was the most important thing in my life. He saved me from total misery. I was only happy when we were together."

"I never had a pet before Joy. I hope she comes to me when it's her time to transition, that is, if she's really a cat and not a comforting angel in a cat's body."

"I guess I'll head in now. See you soon. Come on, Bruno. Let's get you a nice big bone to chew on while I check out my new platform thing." The door clicked shut behind them.

Jo headed in her own door, still pondering whether she'd have Joy with her sometime in the future. She sang, "Pussycat, pussycat, I love you," as she danced her way to her closet. She inspected all the clothes and shoes that stuffed the shelves and hangers, then stepped on her platform. She swiped her hands down her thighs muttering, "Hot shower, here I come!"

Jo's jumpsuit hovered behind her with shimmering waves encasing it, her boots, necklace of charms, and bracelets. "This is totally amazing," she whispered.

She scampered to the shower stall, finding a steamy spray waiting for her. An assortment of bottled soaps lined the shower shelf. She sniffed one labeled Celestial Scent Hair and Body Wash. The divine scent wafted through the room as she poured some on her hair and the fluffy washcloth she found rolled next to the bottles. She scrubbed her hair, enjoying the squeaky-clean feel and glorious aroma. "I don't know what's in this stuff, but it sure smells good."

She sang a medley of her favorite tunes while she finished her shower, enjoying the soothing patter of the warm spray. The acoustics of her shower lifted her voice to new heights.

She stepped from her shower, reaching for one of the fluffy blue towels hanging on the bar. She wrapped her wet hair in the towel and reached for the other one. She dried and wrapped the second towel around her body. "These towels are so soft. They feel like Mom's angora sweater. I didn't know towels could be so soft."

She returned to her closet and chose her outfit. She stepped on the platform visualizing the red, white, and blue striped t-shirt and blue shorts that were folded next to one another on a shelf. She swiped her hands down and up. She wore the t-shirt and shorts and the towels were heaped at her feet. She felt her hair, finding it dry and feeling soft and smooth, like it was already styled. "Awesome! No such thing as a bad hair day around here. I have to check this out."

Jo strode to the mirror hanging above her sink and looked at herself. Startled by the beautiful reflection that stared back, Jo glowed with sleek shiny hair beautifully styled to frame her face. "That is some good hair and body wash," she chuckled.

She tore herself away from the mirror and headed back to her bedroom. "That bed is calling me," she announced as she headed toward it. Sounds of rhythmic breathing indicated sleep had come.

In the next chamber, Gabe and Bruno checked out their kitchen.

"Look, Bruno, we have cheese sticks. You love cheese sticks. Want one?"

The wagging tail and happy yip answered his question.

"Okay, but you have to earn it. Sit!"

Bruno sat, never taking his eyes off the cheese stick in Gabe's hand. "Good boy. Good sit, now shake." Bruno pawed the air until Gabe took it and pumped it up and down a few times. "Good boy. Good shake. Jump!" Bruno leaped through the hoop Gabe made with his arms. He sat again, looking expectantly at the cheese.

"Good boy! You earned it." Gabe handed him the cheese and stroked the dog's head. "You are such a good dog." A thumping tail showed how much he relished the simple pleasures.

Gabe rummaged in his pantry. "I found your bones. Here you go. Chewy bone for you and chips for me, my favorite kind." He pulled open the big bag and munched on a handful of his salty snack. "For some reason, I'm hungry again. I bet I can eat this whole bag."

Plopping on his sofa, he requested, "Play the Olympics skateboard competition." Athletes catching air and doing flips filled the huge screen on the wall. The audience oohed and ahhed at each performance as the announcers critiqued each run. Gabe sat watching the top skaters as he munched his way through the bag. A contented pooch stretched out next to him, gnawing his bone.

"Time to get out of this suit. I should take a shower, too. Want to see something cool, Bruno? Come with me. Come on, boy. You can bring your bone."

Gabe and Bruno padded to Gabe's closet.

"Sit!" Gabe ordered. He scanned his clothing choices before stepping on the platform as Bruno watched and chewed. Gabe slid his hands down each thigh and his ensemble was shimmering on the platform behind him.

Bruno barked.

"I know. It's freaking amazing, isn't it?" Gabe stepped from the platform and darted to his shower.

The water from several shower heads filled his massive shower. He let the water pound his body before lathering and letting the warm water carry away the foam. The fresh scent of body wash filled the room. As soon as he stepped from the shower, the water turned off. He toweled off from head to toe and wrapped the towel around his waist.

Bruno lay at the foot of the bed, still intently chewing his bone. "You look pretty happy there." Tail thumps affirmed Gabe's assertion. "I'll join you in a minute."

Gabe stepped in his closet and onto the platform, visualizing a pair of black athletic pants and matching shirt. He swiped his hands down and up. The towel lay at his feet and the stretchy shirt and pants clad his body. "Freaking amazing!" he cried.

As soon as he stretched out on the bed, Bruno abandoned the bone and snuggled at Gabe's side, resting his head on Gabe's chest. "Good dog," barely escaped Gabe's lips before soft snores from both of the bed's occupants filled the air.

Dina, Jo, Gabe, and Bruno had no trouble with rest and refresh mode. The pleasure of sleep filled each of their chambers.

REFRESHED...

After who knows how long, the teammates and a little dog stirred from slumber. Dressed in comfortable clothes, they milled around their own areas, happily doing whatever they felt like doing.

Dina worked in her studio on a painting of Gabe with flaming feet creating line art on the cliffside. Jo played the piano and sang in her music room, trying her hand at writing a new song. Gabe swooped up and down on skateboard ramps in his section of their shared backyard, flipping and twisting in different ways with each run. Bruno ran around the outside edge of the ramps, determined to keep up with Gabe.

Jo wandered to their shared lounge first. She knocked once on Dina's door and once on Gabe's door before settling on the sectional with a huge music history book. Dina entered and found Jo admiring illustrations as she thumbed through the pages.

"Hey, girl!" they both called. Grins crossed their faces. Their break from one another hadn't affected their unity of thought.

Dina plopped on the couch near her friend, "Have you seen Gabe yet?"

"No, I knocked on his door once, just like I did yours, but he hasn't come out yet. I guess he'll come when he's ready. I met Bruno last night."

"What? His dog is here?" Dina asked.

"He sure is. He's a cute little guy. He was thrilled to see Gabe," Jo told her.

"I didn't know pets were here," Dina mumbled. "I wonder if everyone can have a pet if they want one."

"I have no idea. I guess that's a question for Gavreel. Gabe believes Bruno might be here with him because they transitioned together. I never had a pet before Joy, though, so I wouldn't have a pet here waiting for me, if that's what they do. How about you? Did you ever have a pet before Yodels, one that died?"

"No, Yodels was my only pet. I love him so much. I hated seeing him so sad with my little brother. I hated seeing my brother so sad, too."

"Yeah, that was tough to watch," Jo validated. "They miss you a lot."

"I know they have to grieve and it takes time for things to get better, but I wish I could do something to help them," Dina murmured. "I bet you feel the same way."

Jo nodded. "I do. It's hard seeing my mom, sister, and grandparents going through it all again."

Gabe's door opened. An exuberant Bruno bounded into the room, with Gabe following. Bruno ran a partial circle around the perimeter until he spotted the girls on the sofa. He launched himself near one end and ran up the cushions until he reached Jo. He landed a slobbery kiss on her cheek and jumped over her to greet Dina. Tail wagging, he planted a kiss on her cheek, too.

The girls giggled as Gabe shouted, "Bruno, no flirting. Sit!"

Bruno sat on the couch between Jo and Dina with tail wagging and a big grin on his face.

"Sorry, he's just being overly friendly. I hope you can live with dog kisses from time to time," Gabe blurted.

"He's so cute!" both girls cried as they petted the joyful little dog.

"Dina, this is Bruno. He already introduced himself, but I'll make it official."

Gabe called, "Come here, Bruno. Leave the girls alone."

Bruno glanced at Gabe but didn't move. He looked from Dina to

Jo and pushed his head against each of their hands, cajoling them into more pats and scratches.

Everyone laughed. "Well, I guess we know what he feels about that suggestion!"

Gabe joined them on the couch. "My dog approves of both of you. That's obvious. So, what are we talking about?"

Dina replied, "We were just talking about pets here. Neither of us had a pet before Yodels and Joy, so we've never had a pet that died. We're wondering if they'd come to be with us when they die, like Bruno's with you. What do you think?"

"Honestly, I have no idea," Gabe told her. "I thought Bruno might be with me because we transitioned together. I have no idea if it works the same way if the person and the pet don't transition at the same time. We should ask Gavreel."

"That's what I said," Jo volunteered. "Great minds think alike."

"Speaking of that, have you noticed how many times we say the same thing at the same time now? It's funny, but kind of freaky, too. Gavreel keeps saying we need to be synchronized with one another, but we won't eventually lose all free thought, will we?" Gabe looked from Dina to Jo as he voiced his concern.

"We do say the same thing pretty often," Dina confirmed, "but we're certainly not losing our identities. We're supposed to spend so much time together that we really know and understand one another. My mom always said you really get to understand others when you laugh and cry with them. Synching with each other and sharing so many emotions will help us know how we'll react when things happen on our missions, whatever those are."

"Yeah, what are these missions they keep talking about? Why would we, thirteen-year-old kids, be warriors?" Jo put in. "If I'm remembering correctly, our lessons on the first path were about gentleness, patience, trust, forgiveness, cooperation, and empathy. Those don't exactly sound like warrior traits to me."

"More questions for Gavreel, or maybe Kirron," Dina and Gabe announced before peals of laughter sent Bruno zooming around the room.

GAVREEL RETURNS...

Excited barks and peals of laughter greeted Gavreel as she climbed the stairs to Team DJG's porch. She smiled to herself as she knocked on their door.

Gabe threw open the door saying, "Hi! Come on in."

As she stepped over the threshold, Bruno approached and dropped to the floor near Gavreel's feet. He put his head between his front legs, raised it, and lowered it again, as if bowing. He repeated the motion three times before he rolled over to show his belly. He flipped back over, placing his head between his front legs once more. He looked up at Gavreel but didn't move.

"What's he doing?" the girls called.

"I have no idea. I never saw him do that before. Bruno, come here, Boy."

Bruno remained motionless at Gavreel's feet, refusing to take his eyes off her.

She flicked her finger at the dog. Bruno rose and went to Gabe, sitting next to him while watching Gavreel.

"What's going on? Why's he acting this way?" Gabe questioned.

"He's showing respect and acknowledging my dominance. He's been in training, too, while you were in yours. There are times when his speed and enthusiasm are good things and times when he must be very still and controlled. He has learned that well. He's a quick learner. He should be an asset on some of your missions."

"He's being trained to go on missions?" the three asked incredulously.

"Yes, he is. He's a very special dog, capable of many things. You'll soon see some of those things. He'll need these though." She reached in her pocket and pulled out a garment, a miniature jump-suit, four matching booties with treaded black soles, and a chain with a shiny black B dangling from it. The garment and boots were made of the same fabric as Warrior Team DJG's uniforms.

"He's supposed to wear this stuff?" Gabe asked. "He's never worn anything but a collar."

"He'll like these things," Gavreel assured him. "He must be trained well though. By all of you."

"If you say so."

Gavreel announced, "You all need to suit up. You look and sound ready to continue training. I'll put these things on Bruno while you get yourselves ready."

Gavreel knelt down next to the dog who still had not moved nor dropped his gaze from her. Gavreel did some hand motions; the dog was suddenly clad in a uniform and four boots. The shiny B hung just below his chin. Bruno remained motionless.

"He looks so cute!" the girls bubbled.

"He looks ready," Gavreel rebuffed, "which is how all of you need to look. Go suit up and come right back." She flicked her finger again and Bruno released his spellbound stare at her.

He looked up at Gabe and wagged his tail. He walked to the silver door, turned and looked at Dina. He proceeded to the blue door, giving Jo a long look as he paused there. Finally, he sauntered to the black door and sat next to it, turning and looking at Gabe, as if summoning him to come.

"I guess we've been told twice we need to get ready," they chimed as they headed to their closets, laughter trailing each of them into their separate chambers.

"Come, Bruno," Gavreel called. Instantly he was at her feet. "Good boy, Bruno," She beamed as she stroked the dog's head. "You've remembered all that you learned. Your communication skills are so improved. You certainly told them what to do, didn't you? I appreciate the backup."

MORE TRAINING...

"We're meeting Kirron at a new section of the training grounds," Gavreel told them. "I hope you'll master every uniform feature during this session."

She raised her arms. They found themselves facing Kirron next to what looked like part race track and part gigantic obstacle course.

"Kirron, this is the dog I told you about. He's been Gabe's pet, Bruno. He seems quite trainable and tireless, so he'll do well in mission training," Gavreel commented.

She turned to face Dina, Jo, and Gabe. "It's important that all three of you learn the signals and commands for Bruno and practice with him. He must be conditioned and comfortable taking commands given by any of you, or by Kirron, or me." With a raised arm, Gavreel vanished.

"We'll start with a quick review," Kirron announced. "This is not a quarter mile track like you were used to at your schools. It's a twenty-five-mile track, a hundred times bigger than the kind you used to run. It is small by standards here, but will serve our training purposes. Are you ready to run? Line up side by side on the track. Do one full lap in boot-boosted mode and stop right where you started. Bruno, come. Sit!" Bruno sat next to Kirron's feet as Gabe, Dina, and Jo lined up on the track.

Kirron watched as all three took off, rounded the track, and snapped their heels in mid-air to land gracefully right in front of him. Bruno yipped one time and wagged his tail in greeting.

"Well done. You were fast and efficient at starting and stopping in boosted mode," Kirron congratulated the trainees. "Now you must figure out how to train Bruno to access the assist mode in his boots so he can keep up with you. He'll need to know how to start and stop."

"He has to snap his paws together on the ground to start and in the air to stop?" Gabe inquired. "Does it matter if he snaps his front or hind legs together?"

"No. Since he has four boots instead of two, giving the signal from either pair will work. You must have a clear hand signal that he understands and possibly a short verbal command."

Dina offered, "We could snap our hands together like this and command, 'Hyper speed!', snapping his front paws together every time we give the command until he figures out how to do it by himself."

"That might work," Gabe agreed. "He learned to shake and give five with his front paws so chances are he'll understand the motion after a few tries. What about stopping, though? How will we get him to stop hyper speed?"

"Hmmm, that'll be harder. Maybe the stop mode signal could be snapping our hands together twice instead of once. I'm not sure we need a word. Gavreel didn't use words when she mesmerized him in our lounge. She just flicked her finger one time."

"But he didn't have to watch where he was going when Gavreel used just a hand signal. He never took his eyes off her. He might not be able to watch us as carefully if he's running. That means we probably do need a word he'll understand if he doesn't see the hand motion," Gabe explained.

"I guess that makes sense. How about shouting, 'End!' as the hand signal is made?" Jo suggested.

"I like 'End!'" Gabe and Dina chorused.

"Well, let's see your demonstration," Kirron called.

"You should give the signals first, Gabe," Dina offered. "Bruno's used to you and you've trained him to do other things. I'll lean over him and snap his front paws together every time you give the signal. Jo, would you mind sitting on the ground next to Gabe's feet and snap your hands together every time the command is given? If he notices you doing the same thing to the command, he might process what we want faster."

"Do we have treats?" Gabe asked. "I always had training treats in my pockets. Bruno loves to eat."

Kirron snapped his fingers and handed Gabe a pouch. "This should be helpful."

Gabe poured several dime-sized, meat-smelling discs into one hand. "These smell so good, I may have to try them myself. Let's see how our plan works."

Jo sat on the ground in her best doggy position. Dina straddled Bruno, leaning over to wrap her hands around each of his front legs.

"Hyper speed!" Gabe cried as he snapped his hands together one time.

Jo snapped her arms, bumping her hands together as Dina snapped Bruno's paws together at the same time. They repeated the motion several times, giving happy Bruno a treat each time.

"Dina, let's see if he'll do the snap by himself now," Gabe said.

Dina let go of his legs and stood up, still straddling Bruno's back.

"Hyper speed!" Gabe ordered as he gave the hand signal. Jo obeyed. Bruno just sat there, eyeing the treat in Gabe's hand.

"No, you don't get another one till you really earn it. You have to snap your paws together when I signal you." Gabe took Bruno's legs and snapped them together.

"Let's try this again. I'm going to give Jo the treat if you don't earn it."

"Hyper speed!" Snap. Jo obeyed. Bruno did not.

Gabe pretended to put one of the treats in Jo's mouth. She pretended to chew and savor the morsel.

"See, Jo got the treat because she did as she was told. She did her hyper speed."

Bruno stood up, whining softly.

"You have to earn it. Sit!"

Bruno sat immediately. "Hyper speed!" Jo and Bruno both snapped on the command.

"Good dog, Bruno! I knew you could do it!" Gabe praised as he handed over a treat. The group burst out laughing when Bruno looked at Jo with a gloating expression, as if declaring, "I got the treat this time. No more for you!"

Gabe repeated the start command several times. Bruno snapped his front legs together every time and relished his treat every time.

"Let's see if he'll do it for everyone else. Gavreel says he has to follow commands from all of us. Give me a couple of those treats, Gabe. I'll try it next," Dina announced.

Bruno did exactly as she commanded and scarfed down the treats, exactly as they expected. Smiles spread across their faces as Dina verbally praised and stroked the happy terrier. Jo and Kirron took turns giving the command and rewarding the successful obeys by Bruno. He definitely had this new action down.

"Now we have to get him running and know how to stop the mode," Gabe observed. "Any ideas?"

"I don't know if this'll work, but maybe one of us could give the command while you hold him stretched out in front of you, Gabe. If he's off the ground and learns to snap his front legs together, then we could show him how we do it while running," Jo suggested.

Bruno wagged his tail, enjoying his view of the new game his friends were playing from Gabe's arms.

"I'll stand up and jog in place. I'll do the snapping motion to the command," Dina added. "Jo can give the signal this time."

Kirron observed as the team took their positions to work on the next step of Bruno's training.

"You have to do it too, Bruno." Dina walked over to him and took his front legs in her hands. She snapped his legs together twice as she commanded, "End!" She repeated the double snaps with the command several times.

"Let's do it with me jogging and you giving the commands, Jo."

Jo called, "End!" as she smacked her hands together. Dina immediately copied the gesture and stopped jogging. Bruno also snapped his legs together.

Jo handed him a treat, crying, "Good boy, Bruno! That was so good!"

The girls lined up opposite the boys to practice again. As soon as Dina began jogging in place, Bruno pumped his legs, as if swimming or running.

Jo blurted, "End!" Dina and Bruno snapped and stopped their legs.

Gabe, Dina, and Jo exploded into cheers as they hugged and petted the very good little dog. Bruno sniffed Jo's hand. "I agree. You earned it. As a matter of fact, I believe you earned two," she told him as she stroked his head.

Kirron snickered, too. "Impressive work, team. Let's see if he'll do that again, then see how he does when really running."

"Since he's learning so fast, let's demonstrate fast running for him. Gabe, why don't you give the commands and we'll run a lap around the track in hyper speed mode," Dina suggested.

Bruno wagged his tail in greeting as the girls returned.

"I'll run with him," Gabe offered. "He's used to running and playing with me. He always watches everything I do. One of you give the commands this time."

Dina moved onto the track. "I'll run, too, if Jo gives the command. That way one of us will be on each side of him. He should see one of us snap our heels when Jo orders us to stop."

Bruno and Gabe moved out onto the track next to her, with Dina on the inside and Gabe on the outside. Bruno stood between them, looking expectantly from one face to the other, sensing something fun was about to begin.

Jo and Kirron stood side by side, eyes fixed on the runners. Jo shouted the command and watched as Gabe and Dina snapped and took off. Bruno stood still. She quickly repeated the command. This time he, too, snapped his front legs together and took off after the others. When she saw them returning, she stretched her arms in front of her, snapped her hands together, and yelled, "End!"

Gabe and Dina halted right next to her. Bruno blasted right past them.

They took off in hyper speed after the bolting terrier. They trailed him around the track, getting close but not catching up. He ignored or didn't understand the repeated shouts of "End!"

"Everybody stop," Gabe called. "I have an idea."

The girls pulled up next to him.

"We don't have much time until he's around here again. One of Bruno's tricks is to leap through my arms when I make a hoop like this," Gabe explained as he demonstrated his arm hoop. "I'm going to stand here making the hoop and you guys stand behind me and catch him if he sails through my arms. You can snap his legs together to stop him."

They moved into position as they spotted Bruno charging toward them. Gabe's arms made the hoop. The girls were right behind him, prepared to grab the zooming pooch.

Bruno leapt through Gabe's arms. The girls scrambled to snatch him in midair and slam his legs together. His momentum knocked them flat on the ground.

A euphoric dog bounced from one girl to the other, licking their faces. He ricocheted off Gabe, turned a couple of circles, and returned to licking the girls. His tail wagged fast enough to stir up a breeze as he jumped around with unbridled enthusiasm.

"Bruno, sit!" Gabe blurted after a couple of rounds of Bruno bumps.

Bruno sat, looking from one teammate to the other with the happiest, goofiest look on his face any of them had ever seen.

The team's peals of laughter spread to Kirron, who joined them in a long laugh before gasping, "That is the funniest animal I've ever seen. He looks like he's laughing, too. He seems to love hyper speed."

"We have to figure out how to get him to end his fast running," Gabe finally remarked. "I don't want him to get hurt."

Kirron replied, "He won't get hurt, but he might get away from you. If you're running somewhere besides this track, he has to know how to follow your commands and stop when you stop or when you tell him to stop. He has to be completely controlled if he's going to accompany you anywhere."

"Gabe, can you hold him and control him if you're running in hyper speed?" Jo asked.

"I'm pretty sure I can," Gabe responded. "Why?"

"Maybe he'll get the idea if you hold him in front of you, clicking his legs together when you do your heels and say the commands. He likes to run so much he might resent being held rather that getting to run himself. He might get it if he doesn't get put down until he starts doing the snapping motion himself while being held."

Dina added, "Start and stop in all different places, too, not just here at this spot. Maybe you should stop right away, after just a few bounds, then resume. Try going around more than once so he gets the idea that it's the running that's linked to the snapping motion, not this place on the track."

"It's worth a try." Gabe scooped up Bruno.

"Look at me, boy," Gabe murmured as he locked eyes with his dog. "You have to learn how to start and stop the fast running. You have to mind when you hear the command. I won't put you down and you won't get to run yourself until you show me you will snap your legs together *every* time you hear the commands."

He tucked Bruno like a football, one arm cradling the dog next to his body. He held one front leg in each hand.

Gabe called, "Hyper speed!" as he snapped his heels together while simultaneously snapping Bruno's front legs together. He took off running, circling the track three times before giving the end signal and pulling up to a stop.

Bruno squirmed to get down, but Gabe calmly and firmly told him, "No, not until you show me the snaps with every command." He then snapped his heels and Bruno's legs as he shouted the command. He took off again, but stopped right away this time, clicking the squirmy dog's legs together.

Gabe rounded the track over and over, starting and stopping many times. He finally stopped next to Kirron, Dina, and Jo. "We're not getting through to him," Gabe complained.

"Give him to me," Kirron ordered. "Perhaps he needs a new perspective. I want the three of you to run together while I give the commands. Line up right here."

Gabe handed Bruno to Kirron as he stepped between Dina and Jo.

Kirron murmured, "Now for that fresh perspective." He pointed upward with his index finger and made several circles in the air. He floated above their heads several feet with Bruno looking down from his arms. "This should do."

Dina, Jo, and Gabe gawked at their teacher, not sure they were really seeing what they thought they were seeing. There was no time to say anything because Kirron called, "Hyper speed!"

The trio pushed themselves into hyper speed running mode. Kirron kept up with them, hovering above their heads, calling out the start and stop commands over and over as Bruno watched intently.

Kirron landed next to the runners. "Let's see if you're ready to try this the right way, Bruno."

He set Bruno on the track a short distance behind Gabe, keeping one hand on his back. "We'll see whether he really wants to run with you now. If he doesn't stop when told, he may run right into your legs, Gabe. Be ready for that. Hyper speed!"

The four runners snapped themselves into hyper mode and hurtled away around the track. After two laps Kirron hollered, "End!" All snapped to a complete stop. Team DJG swarmed Bruno, petting him and gleefully voicing their praise. Gabe handed a couple of treats to the grinning dog.

"Again," Kirron barked. "Take your positions."

They lined up, Bruno right behind Gabe. They took off together when they heard the signal and stopped together when Kirron ordered them to end. They repeated the process several times, showering Bruno with praise, pets, and treats each time.

"Time to see if he'll do it without the treats," Kirron announced. "When you stop next time, give him a quick pat and verbal reinforcement, then be ready to take off again. We're going to start and stop quickly now, without lots of reinforcement."

The team did exactly as they were told. Bruno performed perfectly every time. The look on his face told everyone that he not only loved running for the joy of running, but that he also fully understood how to run and stop with his team.

SO MUCH TO LEARN...

"**L**et's review enhanced jumps now," Kirron directed. "Each of you show me one enhanced jump. Pick your target, go to it, and return."

The trio each tapped a heel on the ground, sprang to a lofty spot, then returned to Kirron's side.

A curious Bruno sat watching, cocking his head over and over as Gabe, Dina, and Jo disappeared and suddenly reappeared. They couldn't help laughing as they watched the confused dog trying to figure out what was going on.

"You're going to do it again, Gabe, but this time, I want you to call Bruno's name from your perch. Wave to him and call to him. Get his attention before you return. Make sure he's watching you."

"Bruno, sit! Watch me," Gabe ordered. "Tap! Jump!" he called as he tapped his foot and leaped to a raised platform built in the center of the track. As soon as he landed, he waved his arms all around. "Hi, Bruno! Are you watching me? Bruno, look where I am! Bruno!"

Bruno's cocking head and gyrating tail confirmed his view of Gabe on the platform.

"That's my good boy! Watch, Bruno! Tap! Jump!" Gabe again tapped his heel and leapt back down, kneeling to stroke Bruno after landing.

"Did you see how I made that big jump, boy?" Gabe asked the wiggling dog. "Do you want to jump with me? Do you?"

"Let's get him to tap the ground with one of his paws," Gabe told his friends. "He knows to jump when I make a hoop with my arms, so I'm pretty sure he will know how to do that part. We just have to get him to understand that tapping down his foot before he jumps will let him make big jumps."

Dina tapped Bruno's paw down, repeating the motion until Bruno pulled his paw out of Dina's hand. "He's tired of me slapping his paw down on the ground," Dina remarked.

"Let's see if he'll do it on his own now," Gabe suggested. "Tap!"

Bruno tapped his foot and looked expectantly at Gabe. A daffy grin of pride spread across his face communicating his treat desire for a job well done.

Several successful repetitions of the tap maneuver convinced the team Bruno had mastered the needed motion to activate enhanced jumps. Now to see if he could pair that motion with actual jumping.

"I'm going to jump to the platform again," Gabe announced. "I'll make a hoop with my arms and give the command. Why don't you two jump up there when I give the command. We'll see if Bruno will tap and jump up to us."

"Will do." A look of amusement flashed between them.

Gabe tapped his heel and bounded to the platform. He held up his arms, showing Bruno the arm hoop before calling, "Tap! Jump!"

Dina and Jo landed next to Gabe on the platform. Bruno watched from below, his head cocking in puzzlement.

"Come on, Boy, You can do it. Come to us. Tap! Jump!" the trio called. Gabe held his arm hoop as the girls clapped and made come-here motions with their hands.

To everyone's surprise, Kirron joined them on the platform, cajoling Bruno to come up.

As if declaring, "Well, I'm not going to sit here all by myself if you're all going to hang out up there," Bruno tapped his paw and launched himself toward Gabe's arms. His arc took him smoothly through the hoop, landing just behind the waiting group.

Cheers and loving pats filled the little dog with as much joy as the treat he gulped down. He liked these new games with these new people.

"Let's go back down now," Kirron insisted. "We still have a great deal to do." He leapt to the ground and looked up at the others.

"Yes, sir," the team whispered in unison, partly sincere and partly sarcastic. Their grins communicated their shared acknowledgment of the shared response.

Bewildered, Bruno looked around the platform. The group was suddenly gone again.

"Tap! Jump!" they called. "Come on, Bruno. Tap! Jump!"

He hesitated at the edge of the platform, staring at everyone who had just been with him and was now far below.

Bruno heard, "Tap! Jump!" again. He gathered his courage, tapped his paw, and leaped into Gabe's arms, knocking him backwards. They sprawled on the ground together, rolling and laughing. Their delight was contagious. The team's howls echoed around the training field.

"We really need to continue," Kirron told them after allowing them a bit of time for merriment.

They composed themselves and faced their instructor. "We're ready," they babbled as they fought another round of cackling.

"I want you to jump to the platform and back down a couple of times. We'll see if Bruno will come to you each time. If he does, we'll try jumping to other places and see if he understands he can jump anywhere."

They trio did as they were instructed. Bruno followed them with each bound to the platform and back to the ground, and then every other spot they jumped. The group moved to the other side of the track and, again, Bruno followed all of them no matter where they leapt. Without specific commands, Bruno leapt with each team member to every boulder and rooftop. He knew what to do to go with each of them or all of them.

Kirron said nothing, just observed how the team proceeded.

"I don't think he can learn multiple jump mode and how to stop it," Kirron declared, "but it appears he can use the single jump and keep up with all of you. Let's test that. Gabe, make a three-jump run and return, but don't add any twists or flips. Just point to your targets, make the jumps, and see if Bruno follows you each time."

Gabe grinned sheepishly. "No flips. Got it. Just jumps."

Bruno kept up with Gabe and each girl as they made multiple jumps to different locations. He kept up with all three of them when they leaped together.

Kirron acknowledged, "You've mastered two divine powers, enhanced speed and agility. Your proficient use of enhanced running and jumping, as well as your ability to quickly teach the skills to Bruno, assures me you're ready to move on with your training. Your boots will aid you more times than you can imagine."

Kirron centered himself in front of the group. "At times, you need a fresh perspective, especially from above. Just as your spirit hovered before you transitioned, you'll be able to levitate to any height you choose. I used this feature so Bruno could watch you from above, remember? I'll explain it now and then have you practice a few times."

He backed up two steps saying, "You activate levitation mode by running the index finger of your left hand around the first bracelet on your right wrist, raising your right index finger and making clockwise circles in the air. The more circles you make, the higher you levitate. To come back down, make counterclockwise circles with your index finger. To deactivate levitation mode, tap the bracelet five times quickly. Watch as I demonstrate."

Kirron circled his bracelet and made three circles in the air with his index finger. He rose about fifteen feet above them. "Three circles take you about this high," he explained before floating back to them by making three counterclockwise circles with the same finger.

"If you're indoors and want to hover at the ceiling, most of the time you'd only make two circles. In some very big buildings like old cathedrals, it may be four or five circles. You have to judge the space and adjust sometimes. I'll go higher this time. I didn't disengage the levitation mode by tapping on my bracelet so I only have to make the circles with my finger."

Kirron made five clockwise circles and immediately hovered way above their heads. "The view's great!" he called before returning. He tapped his bracelet five times.

"You're going to practice this skill now, but I must point out that Bruno does not have bracelets and will not be able to levitate. Sometimes he'll stay on the ground, but sometimes one of you will need to hold him as you levitate. He needs to be comfortable being on the ground when you rise, not barking or giving away your presence by staring at you. He also has to be calm and controlled in any of your arms as you levitate to any height. Let's try the three circles' height first. Leave Bruno on the ground so we can observe his reaction."

Kirron prompted, "Circle your bracelet and make three clockwise circles in the air with your index finger."

Dina, Jo, and Gabe followed his instructions and found themselves hovering. "This is so cool," they marveled just before they burst into a fit of laughter. Bruno started barking and running back and forth near Kirron.

"Return!" Kirron ordered.

With three counterclockwise turns of their fingers, the three found themselves on the ground by Kirron. Bruno barked wildly and ran around them until Gabe commanded, "Sit, Bruno."

"He might get used to you levitating and not react like he just did, but you might have to train him to be quiet when he's on the ground and you're floating. His barking and running around might be a problem in some situations," Kirron observed. "Go six circles elevation this time."

The team did as they were told and looked around from a height of about thirty feet. "The view *is* great!" they called in unison. Bruno stayed on sit command, but never took his eyes off the team. His whole body shook with excitement as he watched.

"Return!" Kirron bellowed. Dina, Jo, and Gabe reversed their circle gesture and returned.

"I'm going to let you practice a few times now. You decide how high you levitate. Go up and come back down multiple times. Gabe, hold Bruno next time. Make sure you have a good grip on him. You don't want him hurtling from your arms if he's not in enhanced jump mode."

"Come here, Bruno," Gabe called as he clapped his hands. Bruno leaped in Gabe's waiting arms, who tucked him football-style on his left side. Gabe stretched his right arm across his body and circled the bracelet on his right wrist. He made four circles, lifting Bruno about twice as high as Kirron had. Tail thumping, he looked all around, then upward at Gabe's face. His expression declared his feeling about this new trick, thrilled.

"It's pretty cool, isn't it, boy?" Gabe asked just before he went back down.

"Want to go up again?" he asked as he activated the next levitation. They ascended and descended several times to different elevations. Bruno never squirmed or indicated he was nervous or wanted to stop. He just nestled next to Gabe's side and enjoyed the ride.

"Let's see how he does if one of the girls takes him up and he's separated from you, Gabe."

"I'll take him," Dina lifted him from Gabe's arm and tucked him along her left side. "We're going to levitate together now, Bruno. Are you ready to go up? Here we go," she cooed as she quickly traced her bracelet and made circles with her index finger. They rose and hovered. Gabe and Jo rose to the same height.

Bruno greeted them with tail thumps, but he made no noise, nor did he try to leave Dina's arm.

"Good boy," they murmured before counterclockwise circles took them back down.

Up and down the team went, taking turns holding Bruno.

He was happy and secure with all of them. After several ascents and descents, they set Bruno on the ground. "Sit!" they ordered together. Bruno sat, watching as they left him and levitated to different heights. He stayed on the sit command for several risings and returns.

Kirron called, "Great! You have levitation mastered. Let's move on to the next divine power you will need to practice. You must listen carefully and follow directions exactly. We must start slowly, am I clear?"

"Yes, sir," the group pronounced solemnly.

"Invisibility is a tool we use frequently on missions, but it's not a game. You must use it seriously and only to do good, *never* to pull pranks or frighten others. Use it only when absolutely necessary. If one ever misuses the power, the power is stripped from that warrior *forever*. There are no exceptions. Heed my words: take this gift with great appreciation and respect. It can never be returned to you if you lose it. Do you understand the seriousness of what I'm telling you?"

Bobbing heads answered his question.

Kirron continued, "To engage and disengage invisibility mode, the action is exactly the same. If you're visible and you do what I am about to show you, you will become invisible. If you're invisible and do it, you'll become visible. It's another power activated by the bracelets, so Bruno won't be able to do it. However, if any of you are clutching him tightly to you, he'll be shrouded by your invisibility. It's crucial that he's still when he's being held. He mustn't bark or squirm or he can give away your position, even with invisibility engaged."

"This is so exciting!" Jo beamed. "Being invisible is every kid's dream!"

"Perhaps, but this is not a dream. You must respect the power and use it sparingly and earnestly."

"What do we have to do?" Dina asked softly.

"You cross the underside of your wrists forming a T shape, making sure all three bracelets of your right side touch all three bracelets of your left side. Like this," Kirron showed them as he continued talking. "Then you rub the bracelets together three times like this." Kirron moved his right wrist upward, downward, and upward again as they watched.

Kirron disappeared, but they could still hear his voice. "To return to visible mode, cross your bracelets again and rub then together three times." He was standing before them.

"I want each of you to try it individually so I can observe, then do it until you feel confident with the action.

Dina, Jo, and Gabe easily vanished and reappeared.

"You understand how to activate invisibility and return to visibility. I want all three of you to become invisible at the same time and take a few steps while you're invisible. Pay attention to the way motion feels when you're invisible. Give me your observations when you rematerialize. Go."

"Become visible!" Kirron called.

They reappeared, scattered long distances from one another.

"Walk back to me," Kirron instructed.

"That was strange," Gabe observed. "Walking felt like floating, almost like flying. I only took three steps when I was invisible, but it took like twenty steps to get back here to you when I became visible again."

"It was the same for me," Dina noted. "How come we go so much farther when we're invisible?"

"You're weightless when you become invisible," Kirron explained. "Even though this is not a flesh-and-blood body like you had on Earth, there's more substance to it than when you become invisible. Being visible here is your soul mode. Your soul can be seen by everyone here and by some on Earth. When you become invisible, you are disengaging your spiritual self and operating as just your spirit. Your soul and spirit are connected, but separable.

Your soul is your essence as a human. Your spirit is the immaterial part of your being that connects you with God."

"That's why you stressed taking it completely seriously, because we're learning to maneuver through our souls and spirits. Right?" Dina asked.

"That's exactly right. You must always revere your total being as you were created."

"Why can Bruno become invisible if one of us is holding him?" Gabe asked.

"A purely loving spirit can spread that love to others. You'll cover him with your spirit, protecting him with your love, if you find yourselves in a situation where invisibility is needed. You'll know. Your spiritual sense will tell you." Kirron told them. "Let's practice invisibility with Bruno now. Gabe, you take him first."

"You have to be completely quiet while I hold you," Gabe whispered to his best friend. "Completely calm." Gabe made a quiet sign to the little dog by tapping his index finger against his lips. He lifted Bruno and held him tightly against his body before crossing his wrists and engaging the bracelets' power. Boy and dog disappeared, then reappeared. The pair vanished and reappeared again, this time several steps away. "I moved with him in my arms and he stayed completely still just like I told him to do," Gabe beamed. "He completely understands everything expected of him."

The girls took turns holding Bruno, disappearing and reappearing. He willingly cuddled against each of them. He made no movements or noise that would give them away, whether they stood still, walked, or ran while holding him.

"You've mastered levitation and invisibility easily. While you have many powers yet to develop, you must master one more before your visits, which will be your first mission. I'm going to ask Gavreel and a guest trainer to join us for this part," Kirron announced. He raised his right hand and made a half circle gesture with his finger.

Standing before the trio of young warriors stood another trio.

They knew that they were gazing at seasoned warriors.

"Daddy!" Jo shrieked as she threw herself into his arms.

The others watched raptly as father and daughter, warriors now bound by more than their prior biological relationship, embraced one another. They knew they were seeing another power emanating from the pair, the power of pure love. That power took no training.

METAMORPHOSIS...

“We must continue," Gavreel declared. "This section of your training requires individual attention. I cannot stress strongly enough how important it is that you listen and do exactly as we instruct. Do not add extra actions. Do not delete any actions either. The consequences could mean permanent change to your very being."

"That's right," Kirron insisted. "You must be very exacting when morphing from one creature's shape to another. It becomes easy with practice, but the first few shifts can be challenging. That's why each of you will have one of us with you at all times. We'll shift with you and we'll be able to speak into your minds; no matter what physical form you find your shape, your mind will still be accessible to us through telepathy."

"We're going to be shapeshifting? Is that what you're telling us?" Dina, Jo, and Gabe asked together, incredulous.

"That's exactly what we're telling you," Jo's father confirmed. "You saw me morphed into a butterfly at the Board of Insights. You saw thousands of other angels morphed into butterflies, dragonflies, and hummingbirds, too."

"All of them were angels? Why would they take those forms?" Gabe wondered.

"Do you remember when I told you that all creations have spiritual meaning?" Gavreel quizzed her trainees. "We talked about sunflowers, as you might recall."

They shook their heads, assuring Gavreel they remembered.

"I also told you a bit about cats and their spirits, which have caused humans to feel certain ways about felines over the course of the human race,"

Gavreel continued.

"Butterflies, dragonflies, and hummingbirds," Kirron interjected, "have been mentioned frequently and portrayed in many cultures as having unique spiritual meanings. Some humans have actually figured out their connection with the afterlife and the meaning of their presence."

Gavreel prompted, "Michael, why don't you tell your daughter and her teammates about butterflies since they saw you in that form already."

He looked from Dina to Gabe to Jo before speaking. "Butterflies are very special creations with very special spiritual meaning. They're powerful representations of life. Many cultures associate butterflies with our human souls. As a matter of fact, Aristotle named these creatures *psyche*, the Greek word for soul. In the Christian faith, the butterfly is believed to be a symbol of resurrection. In Islam, butterflies symbolize rebirth. In many belief systems worldwide, butterflies are thought to represent endurance, change, hope, life, and life after death. That's why angel supporters take butterfly form when new arrivals must navigate the Board of Insights. Everyone must face transformation, or resurrection, into full spiritual life, facing everything that formed them to this point. As you found out, it takes endurance and hope to face yourself as you were and begin the change into your new self. The soothing presence of a butterfly helps each individual face what must be faced before fully transitioning. The presence of a butterfly can aid transitions in other ways, too. In dreams, a butterfly's appearance can trigger the return of spirit and soul if the mind has fallen into a deep morass from grief or trauma. We can visit during dreams and help the person find a way out of the darkness, but only when the time is right. Sometimes lessons have to be learned in those dark places. A butterfly is non-threatening. It helps the person calm and begin the self-healing process, if healing and moving on is part of the life journey."

"Wow," Dina, Jo, and Gabe whispered.

"Wow, indeed," Michael continued. "Visiting as a butterfly during wakefulness can also be done. Over the ages and across cultures, some people have figured out that a butterfly suddenly appearing and disappearing may be a visitor giving comfort and reassurance that a departed relative or friend is alive in another plane of existence. One who's taken butterfly form cannot speak during such a visit, but can communicate comfort by landing on a certain object or person, or staying while a certain task is being done."

"Are all butterflies visiting angels?" Dina asked.

"No, usually a butterfly is just a butterfly, one of God's beautiful creations," Michael replied. "But those that come in dreams, or those who suddenly appear and disappear after being seen by someone grieving, those are often visitors."

"Thank you for that excellent explanation about butterflies and why that form is so vital in our work," Gavreel complimented. "Kirron, would you like to tell this talented team about dragonflies or hummingbirds next?"

"Both are important and interesting, but I'll tell them a bit about dragonflies and leave the hummingbirds for you, Gavreel, since you love that form so much yourself," Kirron smiled.

The trio noticed the slight upturn of Gavreel's lips as she nodded in acknowledgment.

Kirron addressed them seriously. "Dragonflies are truly fascinating creations. They live most of their lives as nymphs, not fully mature, in the water. They only fly for a fraction of their lives, but they were formed with four wings that can move independently of one another. They're comfortable on land, on water, or in the air, which places them in a category with very few other creatures. They're graceful, swift, agile, and capable of rapid directional changes. Dragonflies have been revered and feared throughout time by humans. While some believed they were creations of the devil and represented bad luck, death, or evil, many indigenous people have embraced dragonflies throughout time and recognized them as spiritual signs. The Hopi Indians credit dragonflies with saving their tribe from starvation while they migrated in search of a permanent home. They believe dragonflies grew corn supernaturally in just four days, saving their people. Their belief is accurate, but many scoff at such miracles because they don't understand or accept all the forces at work. The prairie Indians of North America believe dragonflies are spiritual helpers. Japan is known as the Island of the Dragonfly. In fact, dragonflies are prominent in art, songs, and poetry in Japan, and they're widely accepted as ancestors who have come back to visit loved ones. Dragonflies are prominent in many other Asian beliefs as well. Although some don't accept the idea of visits through dragonflies, most cultures do believe they are spiritual signs of change and maturity."

"Dragonflies were at the Board of Insights, too," Gabe commented. "Lots of them came down from the trees when my father's life was being shown to us."

"Yes, dragonflies are emblems of change and maturity. Their iridescence is part of their importance. They help one see through illusions that bind. They help one see things that enliven and enrich the soul. Dragonflies allow one to see how light and color penetrate perceptions. They helped you understand your father because you saw him in a different light when you saw his whole life, Gabe. They were crucial in transforming your perception of your father and helping you reach a level of maturity where you could understand many difficult things and forgive."

"Thank you, Kirron," Gavreel interjected. "Excellent explanation of dragonflies. The last creature we'll discuss for early metamorphosis is the hummingbird, which as you probably guessed, is one of my personal favorites."

"Here she goes," Kirron and Michael whispered as they nudged one another, trying to hold back grins.

Gavreel began, "Hummingbirds are also fascinating creations with important spiritual meanings. There are more than 300 species of these birds some have called God's tiny miracle. Hummingbirds' wings flutter twelve to eighty times per second and actually make a humming sound. Did you know their wings flap in the pattern of the infinity symbol, or a figure eight? They're found in North America, Central America, South America, and the Caribbean. Beliefs about them come from the ancient civilizations of these areas. The Mayans believed they were created by the Great God from leftover bits from the other birds he'd created. Because they were made so tiny, they were endowed with superior flight skills. Hummingbird flight skills are truly incredible. They're the only birds that can fly backwards, sideways, or upside down. They're also the only birds that can hover up and down and go from high speed flight to an instant stop. Some migrate over 2000 miles. The Aztecs believed hummingbirds were symbols of rebirth and that if a warrior died in battle he would be reincarnated as a hummingbird. As a result, they saw humming-birds as messengers between themselves, their ancestors, and the gods. They thought a hummingbird's appearance was a sign that a loved one had made it to the other side and was doing fine. Many groups of indigenous people in North and South America held strong beliefs about hummingbirds. There are many stories in these cultures about them. Their spiritual meanings include tenacity, endurance, love, joy, good fortune, and healing."

Gavreel paused and shot a look at Kirron and Michael, who were doing their best to stay straight-faced. "Do either of you have anything to add?"

"You didn't tell them about hummingbirds' mating rituals, the shuttle-flights, and dive displays. I also didn't hear you tell them the belief that just seeing a hummingbird is thought to bring love and romance to the person that spots one," Kirron teased.

Gavreel retorted, "I mentioned love and good fortune. I think that is quite sufficient."

Uproarious laughter erupted, Gavreel's loudest of all.

When they collected themselves, Gavreel went on. "We really must move forward in this stage of training. Bruno will be unable to do this, so he must always be in a safe place if he's with you when you transform. Most of the time, he'll need to be left at home if you're doing a mission where morphing is required. Right now, he needs to be on a sit-stay."

"Bruno, come," Gavreel called softly. He was instantly in front of her. "You need to stay here for this part, Bruno. You must sit and stay. Sit. Stay." She pointed to the ground then held her hand flat in front of him. He planted himself at her feet. "Good boy. Sit. Stay."

"Jo, you'll be paired with Michael. Gabe, you'll train directly with Kirron; and, Dina you'll be with me. We'll do butterflies first. Move next to your partner and spread apart from the other pairs."

They separated as Gavreel continued. "We *never*, and I mean *never*, take the form of another human being. You were created perfectly by our Creator in your human form, to be who you are, with the gifts that were bestowed upon you. When we take another form, it's only to aid us in doing good. Dark forces abound. Some dark forces do take the human form of another, transforming to look like a living human and wreak havoc in their form. Others, those with the blackest souls, enter the bodies of living people and take over their lives. Helping those possessed by an evil soul is one of the most difficult battles we ever wage, especially when more than one evil entity has found a human host that can be invaded and controlled. We have been given this gift of transformation by God to use for good, so I must repeat, we *never* shift into the form of another person."

"Kirron, you're the primary trainer, so why don't you take over?" Gavreel suggested.

"I, too, must stress that we never take the form of another human. The human form is the greatest creation of all. We must honor our own being and our relationship with God by never assuming the form of another person," Kirron told them. "To transition to any other life form, you must do several things. First, cross your arms at your wrists, tightly against your chest." He demonstrated the position. "All of you, put your arms in this position. Next, recite these words:

'Great creator of all creatures, from mini beasts to massive, you who created me and sustain me, hear my prayer today. I beseech your help to take another form. I know you see the image in my mind and know what's in my heart. I trust you, God, with all my heart, and do not lean on my own understanding. Help me take this form so I can serve you well.'

"Part of that prayer is like the Proverbs quote on our Trust charm," Jo murmured.

"Yes, it is. Trusting in God and being willing to do things beyond your understanding is critical in many things we do, but especially when transforming," Kirron told the group. "We need to practice until you have it memorized. Put your hands down for the time-being. We'll say it together a few times, then each of us will have you say it to us individually, making sure you have every word memorized."

Soon all were able to say the five-sentence invocation perfectly.

"Also critical in this process is visualizing the form you wish to take. You must see the image clearly in your mind's eye. You must concentrate on that mental image. We're all going to shift into butterfly form so each of us will visualize the butterfly we wish to become. You'll really need to concentrate on that image as you cross your wrists over your heart and recite the words we learned. Don't do it quite yet, though."

Wondering stares told him he had their full attention.

"When you're shifted into another form, you must know how to return to your true self," Kirron told them. "You won't be able to recite the invocation as an animal or plant, but your mind will be with you in the form you take. You may not be able to cross your arms over your chest either, so to return to your human form, you must visualize yourself and concentrate on these words, saying them over and over in your mind:

'Those who trust in themselves are fools, but those who walk in wisdom are kept safe.'

"That's the other Proverbs quote on our Trust charm," the team cried.

Michael smiled at Jo as he declared, "Proverbs 28:26. I knew I didn't raise a fool!"

"All of you make sure they have this important sentence memorized," Gavreel added. "Practice it a few times so you know you can think it when the time is right for your return to self."

Bruno watched the gesturing and talking by Gabe and the others, never moving a muscle. Gavreel's sit-stay command had him calmly waiting for whatever came next.

"I feel they're ready, do you?" Kirron asked.

Gavreel and Michael affirmed their agreement.

"Let's go, team. Cross your arms like I showed you, visualize your butterfly form, and recite the transformation invocation."

Within seconds, six winged beauties fluttered in pairs around the training grounds. Up and down they went, landing on tree branches, flowers, and boulders, then flitting off again. Their butterfly ballet filled the sky with swoops and cabrioles.

Gabe, as a black swallowtail, landed on Bruno's nose and gazed into his eyes. Bruno never flinched. He recognized his best friend and held the gaze until Gabe fluttered above his head and flapped away.

In synch, Kirron, Gavreel, and Michael telepathically sent the message to each trainee to return to human form.

One yip from Bruno greeted them.

"That was awesome!" Team DJG shouted. "We were flying!" They shared a good laugh until Gavreel pulled their attention back to training.

"You were magnificent butterflies on your first transformation. Let's do it again, but we'll return sooner this time. All of you accomplished taking off, flying, and landing like you'd done it many times," Gavreel complimented.

"Okay, team, go to butterfly!" Kirron called.

Whirling, zipping flecks of color held Bruno's attention until the six human forms were once again standing near him, with the youngest three laughing and excitedly talking.

"These three have no side effects from shifting," Kirron observed. "No shaky legs or any other ill feelings. Quite remarkable how quickly they mastered this power."

"I told you this is a remarkable group," Gavreel reminded him.

"Let's do dragonflies next," Michael proposed. "From the looks of it, they'll transform into that form just as easily."

"Dragonflies will be next," Kirron announced to quiet the chattering teammates and refocus their attention. "Cross your arms, visualize a dragonfly, and invoke the change."

Six sets of iridescent wings darted around, chasing one another, and quickly changing directions. The antics looked like a frantic game of tag, where no one was *it* for long.

The telepathic command to return to human form was once more given. Dina, Jo, Gabe, and their trainers stood together near the obedient little dog who greeted their return with happy tail thumps.

"Bruno, did you see me, boy? I was flying up and down and all around!" Gabe gushed as he patted the dog's head. "You're being such a good boy."

"Let's have them shift between butterfly form and dragonfly form without returning to their original form," Michael suggested. "I know it will be harder for them to recite the invocation prayer mentally and make the transformation, but I believe we should practice it."

"I couldn't agree more," Gavreel concurred. "Why don't you explain this step, Michael?"

"Certainly. If you've transformed into one form and need to shift to a different form, other than your human form, you must mentally recite the five-sentence prayer while visualizing the new form you wish to take. If you're moving, especially flying, when you do this, it can feel very strange and you may feel like you're falling. That feeling won't last. It's with you just for the shift."

"Are you ready to try?" Kirron asked. "We'll start as butterflies and shift to dragonflies. Listen to our messages about when to transform. Remember to say all five sentences in your minds as you visualize the dragonfly you wish to become."

Bruno cocked his head as he listened to the six repeating the prayer he'd now heard several times. Like before, they disappeared. Colorful wings flapped above his head and all around, eventually disappearing as they flew farther than he could see.

Very shortly, round two of the tag game started. Bruno watched flashes of iridescence zip by time and time again. He wanted to chase them and be part of the game, but he knew not to move from Gavreel's sit-stay.

The sound of laughter came from behind him this time. Bruno turned his head and saw the six walking his way. Joyous tail thumps and a single yip let them know how happy he was to see them again.

"The last transformation we will be doing before visits is the hummingbird," Kirron told them. "The transformation is invoked the same way, but the transformation may feel different than to butterfly or dragonfly. That's because a bird's physical make-up is more complicated than an insect's. There are bones and feathers in addition to wings and basic parts your bodies shifted to as butterflies and dragonflies. Don't worry if you feel a funny feeling as you transform."

"Remember, hummingbirds can fly every direction, frontwards, backwards, and sideways, and they can hover. Try all those moves when you're in that form," Gavreel told them. "It really is delightful to take hummingbird form for a while."

"Hummingbirds expend a lot of energy with their rapid wing flaps and fast flying so you may want to snack on some mosquitoes or spiders, or perhaps sip some nectar from that clump of flowers over there," Michael suggested with a wink. "It's pretty cool to experience sucking natural nectar through a pointed beak. Most of it's very sweet and tasty."

"I never, ever, thought anyone would tell me to snack on mosquitoes or spiders, or suck nectar for that matter," Gabe whispered. "I'm definitely not going to nibble on any bugs, but I'm always up for something sweet, so nectar, here I come."

Giggling girls elbowed him before beginning the invocation.

Just as he had before, Bruno sat and stared as enchanting darts of iridescence dipped and pivoted before him. One tiny bird hovered near his face before zipping away to an array of brilliant flowers. It scrutinized the blooms before hovering at a red one for a long drink. Bruno watched intently as the irrepressible bird backed up and whisked away, flipping and zooming in all directions. The tiny creature celebrated being purely and intensely alive, reveling in the beauty of motion its body allowed.

Six human forms were once again standing near a tail-wagging delighted dog.

"That was the most amazing thing yet!" Gabe cried. "I could do anything I wanted to do while I flew as a hummingbird! I see why you like it so much, Gavreel. That red flower nectar was pretty good, too."

The girls chimed, "Being a hummingbird for a while was very, very cool. Flying is so much fun."

Dina, Jo, and Gabe smiled, savoring the joy of learning something new and doing it well. Gavreel, Kirron, and Michael smiled at the enthusiasm of their young charges. Sharing this special power had been delightful.

"I'd like us all to have a seat here by Bruno," Gavreel directed. "Let's discuss transformations and what the experience really means. You must understand the essence of this power."

They sank to the ground, all of them patting Bruno and telling him what a good boy he'd been.

Gavreel said, "Bruno, you can get up now. You were a very good dog." She clapped her hands once. Bruno sprang to her for a pat before he darted to the cluster of flowers, sniffed the red one, spun around, flipped in the air several times, and sped back to the laughing humans. He plopped on Gabe's lap, looking up at him adoringly.

"He wants to move like a hummingbird, too," Gabe snickered. "That was a very good impersonation of me as hummingbird, Bruno. You knew it was me even in that form, didn't you?" He petted and hugged his beloved friend.

"Bruno did seem to recognize which one was you," Dina alleged. "His antics were just about like yours when you were flying."

"It's time to discuss what the power of shapeshifting really means," Kirron said. "You must really understand it before you will be allowed to do it anywhere except this training ground under our close supervision. Tell us what you believe."

The team glanced at one another, none of them eager to be the first to respond.

Michael simplified the question by asking, "Why do you think you're able to take different forms?"

Jo gulped and suggested, "Maybe because we asked for it in prayer and believed?"

Gavreel commented, "That's true. 'Ask and ye shall receive' is always important to believe and remember, but you need to dig deeper, just as you did on the Trail of Caring. Dig deeper."

Gabe continued, "Well, it takes the prayer and believing it's possible, but maybe part of it is we didn't try to figure it out with logic. We trusted you and what you were leading us to do. And we trusted God to give the power. We had faith."

"Also true and very important," Gavreel responded, "but there's more to this gift than asking with belief, or having trust and faith without trying to figure it out intellectually. What did the experience show you?"

Dina looked from Kirron to Michael to Gavreel before she spoke. "I know this may sound weird, but possibly we experienced our true selves as we changed forms. I feel that each of us is really life energy, pure life. That probably sounds weird since we all died before coming here, but it may be part of what's meant by everlasting life, why we could transition here when our human bodies died, and why we can transition into different forms now. As humans, our very being, our life force, can pass through a body, our human one or ones we visualize. It can pass through a mind or a soul. I could feel my life force as I was in hummingbird form. I was still me with the capabilities and instincts of a different body, but I am the force as a butterfly, a dragonfly, or a hummingbird. It doesn't matter what the body is, the force that moves it is life. That life force can be part of any other living thing, maybe even nonliving things, because we're all part of everything God created in the universe. I am life. You are life. We are life."

Jo and Gabe stared at Dina before chorusing, "When did you get so profound?"

"Profound indeed. Insightful," Gavreel echoed.

"Bruno's life force was created as a dog so he can't transition to different forms because he wasn't created as a human. Right?" Jo asked.

"Yes," Michael explained. "He's a smart and easily trained animal, but he was not created as a human with this power within."

"Can all humans transition to other forms when they get here?" Dina asked.

"It's a special gift, a power, that was bestowed upon you. Just as your art is a special gift, Dina, or your music, Jo, or your physical prowess, Gabe. This is a gift you share even though there are some gifts you do not share equally. Everyone is unique," Kirron reminded them.

"Okay, but can all humans transform when they get here?" Dina asked again.

For the first time, their trainers seemed hesitant to answer one of their direct questions.

Gavreel declared, "We really don't know about everyone. We train warriors most of the time, but we sometimes work with those who've been selected as comfort-giving angels and guardian angels. These classes of angels can morph to other forms when needed. Many are needed at the Board of Insights when someone else's life story has to be shown. Some are much better at shifting than others. Some prefer to avoid using the power and do it only when absolutely necessary."

"Why?" Dina, Jo, and Gabe inquired.

"The power carries risks. Many have reported feeling shaky and unsettled after shapeshifting, but none of you have any side effects at all. Morphing seems as natural to you as breathing did on Earth. It appears you three have been bestowed a much higher level of this power than some have received. As I said before, everyone is unique," Kirron remarked.

"Is it possible to get stuck in the form you've shifted into?" Jo asked.

"Yes, that's another risk. If something traumatic happens to the creature or plant into which you've morphed, the instinct of survival may overcome the memory of the sentence to return to your true form. It's rare, but it's happened," Gavreel told them. "That's why we use the power only to do good and only when absolutely necessary. It's fun to fly and have other animal powers for a while, but it's not a game and should never be taken lightly. It's a tool for completing missions."

Jo stammered, "If something happens and you're stuck in another form, how long are you stuck?"

"Until the physical body dies and the spirit is released, as it was when your human body died and your spirit transitioned here," Kirron told her. "Life spans of some creatures are very short, but some creatures and trees can live many years by Earth time. Butterflies and dragonflies have short lifespans, which is part of why they're popular morphing forms. Besides being beautiful nonthreatening creatures with great flying abilities, their short life spans are a real plus for morphing needs. Hummingbirds live somewhat longer, but their flying skills often make them creatures of choice for shapeshifting."

"Getting stuck in morphed form is rare," Michael reassured. "This gift is very much worth the minuscule risk of being stuck in a different form. Time here is very different, so the time in another form is really quite short, if it was to happen. It really isn't anything any of you need to worry about. We're being very thorough in your training. You'll be ready to handle whatever comes your way when you're fully trained. Until then, you'll always have one of us, or all of us, with you."

"You've had enough for today's training session," Kirron announced. "We'll take time to rest, reflect and refresh before starting visits to your family members next time."

He raised his arms and the team found themselves standing in their front yard, with none of the trainers with them.

HOME AGAIN...

Bruno yipped and pawed on Gabe's leg.

"He's asking you how we got here," Jo speculated.

"Nope. He's asking when he'll get his chewy bone," Gabe grinned. "He wants to relax and refresh with a big bone."

"Do you guys want to hang out in our shared space or go into your own chambers?" Dina asked as they climbed the steps to their porch.

"How about we all go clean up and change out of these suits, then come back to our shared space? I'd like to talk about what we did today," Jo piped, opening the front door.

"Sounds good to me. A nice shower and some different clothes would partially take care of that refresh part of our homework. I'll get Bruno his bone. I feel like I want to eat, too. That flower nectar didn't hold me."

"Refreshing with pizza and more of that delicious fruit salad should follow our showers and clothing changes," Dina declared. "A nice big cheese pizza with sweet juicy fruit on the side. I know Gavreel told us we didn't need to eat here, but I'm famished."

"Cheese pizza's okay, but I love pepperoni," Jo shared.

"I've never eaten meat and cheese together," Dina told her. "I've never eaten pork either. My family always followed certain diet guidelines, so I guess I like what I got used to having. We always had cheese or veggie pizzas."

"I bet we'll have whatever kind of pizza we like when we open our fridges," Gabe told them. "Let's clean up, then heat the pizzas on that stove behind the island in our lounge. Okay?"

They headed to their own chamber doors, Bruno still jumping

on Gabe's leg as they headed across the shared lounge. "See you soon."

"I'll get you a bone before I get in the shower, Bruno. You can chew on it while I'm showering. I bet I need to put you on the circle thing in the closet to take off your uniform before you start chomping on your bone, though. You don't need any clothes while we're here, so I think I just need to swipe your front paws down your hind legs to take it off. No one told us how to do it, but that makes sense to me. Let's go try it. Okay, boy?"

They bounced together to Gabe's closet, headed to the circular pedestal where Gabe told Bruno to sit. The little dog sat immediately, looking proud of himself.

"Good boy, Bruno," Gabe crooned as he patted his pal's head. "Now let's see if this works for you like it does for me." He swiped Bruno's front paws down along his hind legs.

The boots, collar, and suit settled around Bruno's feet as he looked up at Gabe.

"Yep. Works the same way. Let's go get a bone for such a good dog," Gabe called as he headed to his pantry.

A freed Bruno bounded ahead of him, zooming in circles around the living room and kitchen before landing next to Gabe at the pantry door.

"It looks like you're glad to be free of that stuff," Gabe chuckled. "You only have to wear it when we go out, not here. I have your bone, boy. Do you want to chew on it on the bed or out here? I'm headed to the shower, so you go wherever you want."

Bruno zipped to the sofa with his prize as Gabe headed back to the closet to shed his uniform.

He emerged with wet hair, wearing black shorts and blue shirt emblazoned with a silver and black graphic design of a skateboarder. "Ready to go see the girls again, Bruno?"

Tail whirling, Bruno leaped from the sofa and ran to the door.

"I'll take that as a yes," Gabe hooted as he followed his dog to the door, stopping by his fridge to pull out his favorite pizza, ground beef with chopped onions and lots of cheese. "I'm sure they'll be glad to see you, too," he added as he turned the knob, balancing his pizza carefully.

Gabe set his pizza on the instant-heat stove as Bruno bounded to Dina seated at their shared table, already set with large plates, glasses of fruit punch, bowls of fruit salad, a platter of garlic bread sticks, and a large cheese pizza.

Bruno jumped in her lap and licked her chin. "Well, I'm happy to see you, too, Bruno!" she snickered as she stroked and scratched him.

Bruno jumped down and ran to greet Jo as she entered carrying a large pepperoni pizza. "Hey!"

Everyone laughed as Bruno sat in front of Jo, looking up at her expectantly, grinning as only happy dogs can do.

"Can't you see you're supposed to pet a certain canine?" Gabe laughed.

"Let me put this pizza on the stove to heat, Bruno, then I'll gladly pet you," Jo cooed.

Bruno followed her, sitting at her feet as she set down her pizza pan. As soon as her hands were free, he stood on his hind legs and put his front paws on her knee. She leaned over and stroked the dog's head and back. "You are such a sweet boy, Bruno. Yes, you are."

Gabe and Jo carried their pizzas to the table and sat down with Dina. "This looks and smells so good!" the team exclaimed. Giggles punctuated their synchronized comment.

"For not having to eat here, I sure feel hungry," Gabe declared as he reached for his first slice of cheeseburger pizza.

The girls reached for slices of their favorites, too.

"Mmmm. Best pizza ever!" the trio sighed before bursting into another round of laughter.

"I wonder if we'll ever get used to synchronized comments,"

Dina speculated before scooping a spoonful of fruit salad into her mouth. "This fruit is heaven in my mouth!"

"That makes sense," Gabe teased, "considering where we are."

"What do you think about the training we had today?" Jo asked her teammates.

"I loved it!" Gabe proclaimed. "What's not to love about shape-shifting and being able to fly?"

"It was very cool," Dina affirmed. "It's kind of scary that you could get stuck in another form, though."

"They said it's really rare," Jo stressed. "The natural lifespans for butterflies, dragonflies, and even hummingbirds are so short it wouldn't be a big deal even if it happened when we're morphed into those forms. Now a giant tortoise or an elephant, that would be a different matter."

"I wonder if we're going to shape shift in dreams or waking life when we go to visit," Dina brooded. "The trainers told us that visits can be in dreams or flying around when the person is awake. I'd like to be able to talk to my parents and brothers. I really want to let them know I'm all right and the reason I had to leave them. I want them to know I'll always love them and I'll try to make them proud, even if we aren't together every day."

"Sure, we all have things we want to say to our families," Jo professed. "I want to tell my mom and sister I'm okay, too, and that Dad is helping train me to be a warrior. I don't really understand what a warrior from here does, but I want to let them know I have a purpose. I died young because I'm a strong warrior. They know I battled cancer and my body was very weak when I transitioned, but I'm not weak any more. Maybe I had to get as weak as I did to grow this strong. I want my mom to see me as her strong, healthy daughter who's fulfilling her destiny."

"I'm not sure what I'd say to my family," Gabe murmured, "maybe just let them know I'm not a weirdo here and that I'm happy. I'm happy I have Bruno and both of you with me so I'm not lonely or lost any more. I'm happy I can do so many amazing things and I have a purpose. I never thought I had a purpose before coming here."

"Here's to purpose and being the best warrior angels we can be!" Dina toasted as she lifted her glass of punch.

Jo and Gabe raised their glasses in a toast, "To families, to purpose, and to strong warriors!"

The trio finished their meal, sharing relaxed conversation. Joyful laughter echoed through the halls and every room of their home.

IT'S TIME...

After Dina, Jo, and Gabe had spent alone time in their own chambers, one by one they wandered back to their shared lounge. After lovingly greeting the girls, Bruno positioned himself by the front door, staring at it intently.

"What's he doing?" Dina asked.

"I have no idea," Gabe replied. "Maybe he thinks someone's out there."

Rapid-fire taps sounded at the door.

"It sounds like he was right," Dina exclaimed as she stood to answer the door.

Gavreel, Kirron, and Michael stood on the opposite side of the door.

"Greetings, young warriors. We hope you're refreshed and ready to continue with your training missions," Kirron proclaimed as he stepped inside, followed closely by Gavreel and Michael.

"Please, go suit up quickly," Kirron continued. "Bruno does not need his uniform. Please, change and come back here for instructions."

Dina, Jo, and Gabe departed to their own chambers as Bruno sat at Gavreel's feet, his eyes locked like magnets on her face.

"Greetings to you, too, Bruno," Gavreel soothed as she knelt to pet the adoring canine. "I guess we'll have to tell Gabe sometime that you used to be my dog, too, many, many years ago. You've been such a good boy fulfilling the mission to save him. You're exactly what he needed. You've done well, sweet boy. He loves you as much as I do."

"You have such a connection with that dog," Kirron commented.

"Look at the adoration on his face."

"It's mutual adoration on our faces," Gavreel murmured. "He's a truly remarkable creature."

"You weren't a kid like Gabe when he was sent to you on Earth," Michael remarked, "yet your bond is as strong as those forged by the young with their pets."

"I was as fragile as a child when I found him. It was just a few weeks after the incident. I guess he needed me physically as much as I needed him emotionally. He was so tiny, so vulnerable. I still can't believe or understand how some people can be so cruel to animals, especially helpless babies. He was starved and hurt so badly by someone or something in that alley, just a whimpering mess when I found him."

"You were his guardian angel, even then," Kirron murmured.

"More like he was my guardian angel, put there to save me from myself. His needs became my focus, rather than my own wallowing in self-pity for what had happened to me."

"You're a loving woman," Michael affirmed. "Your care of that weak abandoned pup is testament to that. A strong woman, too, one who overcame great trauma to help others."

"Great trauma. Yes, being beaten and left for dead is terrible trauma, but out of that abyss, emerged a woman with resolve to survive. This little dog and his need of me is what gave me the resolve to fight evil in the world. What was done to both of us was pure evil."

"It was indeed," Kirron and Michael agreed, "but from those experiences a powerful warrior was forged."

Three doors flew open and enthusiastic trainees in full uniforms bounded back in the room. "Ready!" they declared as their laughter punctuated the air.

Kirron motioned toward the comfy sectional. "Let's have a seat on the sofa while I explain a few things about visiting those on Earth."

All six arranged themselves comfortably. Bruno jumped up,

nestling between Gabe and Gavreel. He grinned as they both put a hand on his back.

"Today, we'll be visiting each of your families," Kirron told them. "Each of you will be accompanied by one of us. We'll make the transport and take you with us as we move to where your families are. You haven't been taught how to manage the space tessellation yet, and we don't want you trying it on your own. You'll learn this skill soon, but you're not ready yet. You'll be visiting only with a trainer guide. Is that clear?"

Nodding heads answered his question.

"Good. The first visit will be a comfort visit in morphed form. We may make dream visits if your messages are not clearly understood during your first visit. Dream visits are harder so we'll see how the first visits go," Kirron explained.

"You'll have to pick the family member you want to visit," Michael inserted. "It's fine if there's more than one person in the place we visit, but you must focus on one."

"You'll have to decide if you wish to visit in butterfly, dragonfly, or hummingbird form," Gavreel added. "Each form has benefits. Consider which form the person you're visiting would notice and respond to best, not the form you most enjoy being. This visit's purpose is to give comfort during their grief."

"Isn't it winter where my home was?" Dina asked. "Wouldn't any of those forms suddenly appearing seem really weird in winter?"

"That only adds to the mystique," Gavreel told her. "Imagine seeing a pair of butterflies in your house or outside the window when snow is flying. It actually helps one know that a something special is happening."

"Hmmm, I see that," Dina murmured. "A scene like that might make a captivating painting. I can visualize a bright butterfly on a snowy window sill, bare trees in the background and a wonder-filled face inside the window, gazing at the winged visitor."

"Sounds like you have an idea for your next creation," Jo

remarked.

"Maybe," Dina whispered.

Kirron cleared his throat. "We'll make one visit at a time and the others will observe. We'll move to each of your chambers to view scenes below and allow you to choose whom you'll visit. After you've chosen, you need to declare which form you'll be morphing into during the visit. One of us will perform a space tessellation to transport you to the place of visitation. Your trainer will become invisible first, then hold your upper arm as you cross your bracelets and make yourself invisible. When that step is done, you'll be taken to your site of visitation. When you're there, you'll morph into the decided-upon form and make yourself known to the person you're visiting. You won't be able to speak, but you may be able to communicate with thoughts or actions. Do you understand?"

Three head bobs affirmed.

"Good. It's appropriate for Michael to accompany Jo for her visit, but we'll change the pairings for Dina and Gabe from our last session. This time I'll take Dina and Gavreel will take Gabe. If it's not your time for visiting, you'll observe through the crack in your teammate's floor. You can learn a great deal by watching the visits of others. Watch closely and learn about your teammate and how they handle themselves on this expedition."

"Let's start it off. What do you say, Pumpkin?" Michael asked Jo. "Are you ready to go visit Mom or your sister?"

"I believe so," Jo squeaked. "I'm pretty sure I can do anything if you're with me, Dad."

"Well, let's go then." Michael took his daughter's hand and led the way into her chamber. The others followed like a parade of eager ducks headed to the pond.

Jo and Michael knelt near a tiny fissure that opened in the bedroom's floor. They watched below as the others gathered near them on both sides of the crack.

A woman and teenage girl sat at a table frosting and decorating cookies shaped like stars, trees, and snowmen.

"These frosted sugar cookies were always Jo's favorites. Dad's, too," the woman choked as she spread green frosting on a cookie triangle.

"I know, Mom," Jo's sister whispered. "They know we're making them and remembering them." A tear trickled down her cheek. "They'd be happy we're taking these to the shelter downtown. Those homeless kids will love them."

A weary smile crossed both their faces as they continued spreading frosting and adding decorations, transforming the bare basic cookies into decorated works of art.

JO'S VISIT...

"**W**ell, it looks like we can visit your mom and sister at the same time," Michael declared. "What form have you decided to take for the visit?"

Jo answered, "A butterfly's the only thing that won't freak them out. Mom would go nuts with dragonflies or hummingbirds flying around her cookies. She'll be astounded by butterflies, too, but she won't freak out about them being inside or near her food."

"Butterfly it is. Do you still favor the blue morpho?" Michael asked. "You know they aren't found in North America."

"Being blue morphos will just add to our mystique." Jo chuckled as she glanced at Gavreel. Gavreel winked at her.

"Then it's settled. Blue morpho butterflies ready to visit," Michael declared as he stood, pulling Jo to her feet before they vanished.

The remaining four kept vigil at the crack, watching as a pair of beautiful blue butterflies circled the room where Jo's mother and sister continued their cookie art project.

One butterfly, then the other, landed on the far side of the table, sitting on each side of a sparkling yellow star cookie. They gently opened and closed their wings while staring at the cookie decorators.

"Mom, do you see that?" Jo's sister whispered. "Butterflies in the winter? This can't be real."

"It's real, or we're having the same hallucination," her mother returned. "I've never seen such beautiful butterflies. I wonder how they got in our apartment."

"Mom, those are blue morpho butterflies. They live in Central and South America, not North America. Jo featured them on the cover of her report on Brazil, the one her homeroom teacher gave me after she passed. In her report, Jo noted there are over 2.5 million species of insects in the Amazon, but said the blue morpho butterfly was her favorite."

"This is unbelievable. What do you think it means?" the grief-stricken woman asked her remaining daughter.

"I don't know. What do you think, Mom?"

"They might be messengers from your dad and Jo. I know that sounds really crazy, but it might be true."

One butterfly fluttered to the living room, landing on the table near a family portrait. The picture captured a smiling happy family, featuring a beaming young Jo perched on her father's shoulders. In the picture, Mom had one arm draped over her older daughter's shoulder and one wrapped around Dad's waist. She was nestled at his side. One of Dad's arms circled Mom's shoulders. The other hand reached up and held Jo's dangling leg. Jo's sister held Mom's hand with both hands. The picture showcased connectedness, one to the other, by physical contact and undeniable love. Grandma had taken the picture at the beach. That day, encapsulated in this picture, had become a family treasure. The butterfly studied the picture before landing on the frame, gently opening and closing its wings while gazing back at the table.

The second butterfly flitted across the room and landed on the frame next to the first one. They perched calmly right above the heads of Dad and Jo in the portrait.

Mother and daughter sat speechless, afraid to move or say anything that might interrupt the personal miracle they were sharing. They stared at the pair of winged beauties.

Mom sang Stevie Wonder's song, the one she had sung so often to her girls.

"Isn't she lovely?
Isn't she wonderful?...."

Both butterflies flew back, landing on the singing woman's arm.

"It is you, isn't it?" she squeaked. "You're together. You're both all right and you're together." Tears flowed down her cheeks as she spoke to the pair settled on her arm. She stared at them, filled with wonder and gratitude that they'd come to her and that she understood their message. Somehow loving connectedness crossed between the different worlds in which they now lived.

One butterfly, then the other, took wing, brushing her cheeks with their wings before fluttering over and doing the same to her daughter who sat next to her at the table. They circled the room several times, chasing one another in a playful game of tag. Mother and daughter sat in rapt attention watching the ephemeral meanderings of the winged beauties. Their graceful frolicking had a hypnotic effect. The pair suddenly darted from the kitchen-living room area into a bedroom, where they quickly morphed into human form before becoming invisible. When mother and daughter reached the bedroom door, the butterflies had disappeared.

They were already back in Jo's new bedroom, being greeted by those who'd watched the entire visit.

"That was really something," Dina and Gabe told Jo. "You were amazing communicating with your mom and sister."

"Thanks. It seemed like they really understood," Jo responded.

Michael and Jo settled themselves on the floor and peered through the crack, observing the people they loved.

"Where did they go?" Jo's sister cried. "They couldn't just disappear into thin air."

"Yes, they could," Mom whispered, "because they weren't just butterflies."

"You really believe it was Dad and Jo, or something spiritual sent by them, don't you?"

"I don't just believe it was Dad and Jo. I'm sure of it. Do you have any other explanation?"

"Maybe too much sugar from all the frosting and cookies we've sampled?" she teased.

"Sugar highs don't trigger hallucinations. We both saw the same thing, too," Mom rebutted. "We've just been given a gift. I choose to accept it for what it is."

"It was surreal those butterflies appeared by a star cookie. Dad and Jo both liked to perform and be singing stars. Flying to our family picture and perching right above Dad's and Jo's heads was surreal, too. Of all the places they could land, they chose that picture of the family."

"Yes, they did. The picture your grandmother snapped that captured our happy family, our family before it was torn apart by losing Dad, then Jo. That made it crystal clear to me who they really were. I don't know why they came as butterflies, but I'm sure it was them. I feel like I've been buoyed up by waves of sustaining love, by love and the power of more than we know, but can choose to accept."

"I see what you're saying, but I'm more skeptical, I guess. It just seems too crazy."

"Many thought the greatest ideas and inventions were crazy at first. That's why some people called them mad scientists. Great scientists, artists, inventors all had to endure the scoffing of doubters, but those who persevered proved many ideas were not crazy," Mom retorted. "Spiritual encounters, like the one we just had, are not crazy if you're open to them."

"My science teacher told us everything we know about the universe makes up only about four percent of whatever's out there. The rest is dark matter and dark energy. He explained that 'dark' really means unknown stuff. I guess there's plenty of space in the universe for unknown things like mysterious blue morpho butterflies which suddenly appear in an apartment in North America, thousands of miles from their natural habitat. In winter, no less."

"We can believe what we choose to believe, but we must answer for what we choose. I choose to believe the Lord sent us this experience. I choose to say, 'Thank you, Lord. Thank you, Michael. Thank you, Jo. I praise you for the effort and love I know it took to return from the other side. You know where I am and where I've been.' I won't deny this experience or try to explain it with logic. My heart roars acceptance. No proof is necessary. No proof is possible. Only faith. Faith and that feeling deep inside that we've been given this gift to help us move forward."

"Mom, do you remember that song Dad liked to sing to Jo and me? He sang the first part of it every day."

"Of course, I remember. I can still hear him singing *'Butterfly Kisses'*."

"Dad and Jo gave us butterfly kisses before they left, didn't they?"

"I believe they did," Mom whispered as the tears flowed down her cheeks. These were not the tears of unimaginable grief, but tears of personal faith and joy, buoying her with strength to go on.

Michael and Jo rose from the floor and high-fived one another. The others clambered to their feet, marveling at the successful visit they'd just witnessed.

"Michael, you knew exactly what to do to guarantee this visit's success," Kirron raved.

"This success was all Jo. All I did was follow her. She landed by the star cookie so I followed her there. She chose to go to the picture and stare at it before perching on top, right above her own image. I just perched above my image, next to my clever girl. When Jo headed back to her mother as she sang 'Isn't she lovely,' I thought I might have to stop her from doing something too overt, but she just gently landed on her mom's arm, so I landed next to her. I have to admit, it felt good to touch that woman again. That move was as much for the two of us as it was for her. The butterfly kisses were brilliant. I can't imagine anything that would've brought more comfort and affirmation that it was us than those cheek caresses with our wings. I don't know how Jo knew her mother and sister would be mesmerized watching us chase one another around the ceiling, but they were. That gave us time enough to dart out of sight and depart. She even had that move figured out. Her instincts and closeness to her mother and sister guided her like an experienced visitor."

Jo's smile told everyone how much her father's praise meant.

"Well done, Jo," Gavreel and Kirron commended, as they smiled, flashing one another one of those knowing looks.

"So, Dina, are you ready to make your visit?" Kirron asked as the parade of trainers and trainees filed out of Jo's chambers.

DINA'S VISIT...

"Have you decided whom to visit?" Kirron asked as the group stood in Dina's bedroom.

"I want to watch my parents' house for a while, if that's all right. I'll decide when I see where they are and what they're doing."

"Very well, we'll watch for a bit," Kirron allowed as he knelt beside Dina. The others gathered around, peering through the tiny fissure that had opened.

Dina watched her big brother stretched out on his bed with his iPad. He appeared distracted, not really focused on his tablet, but lost in thought.

She shifted a bit to her right and watched her little brother on the floor of the family room. He rolled a ball across the room for Yodels. Her dog chased the ball and brought it back several times, no enthusiasm in his fetches, just robotic motion as he did what he thought he was supposed to do. He stretched out and put his head on her brother's leg. The boy gently stroked the dog's head. "You did great, Yodels. You played a few minutes. You're getting better every day."

She shifted again and saw her parents sitting in the breakfast nook, looking out the window at swirling snow piling up on the patio and window sill. They had mugs of tea and one of her sketch pads. An old fairy garden sketch, one she'd forgotten about, was on the open page. She'd drawn it after going to the ballet with Grandma and Grandpa. Her dancers were fireflies and dragonflies, flitting above and through a garden of many flowers. The fireflies' spins spewed ribbons of light, connecting the aerial dancers. The art, clearly created by a younger Dina, still showed great talent and passion.

"I used to sit at the table and show Mom and Dad each drawing when I finished it. I'd have a cup of tea with them, too. Mom and I both liked one spoon of sugar in our tea. Dad liked his plain. He never understood why we liked sweet tea. Neither of my brothers like tea, but I always did. Sitting at the table with my parents, sipping tea and discussing my art, made me feel grown up and special. My parents liked every drawing I ever did. My dad told me I needed to start signing my drawings and paintings when I finished them. He told me most artists sign their work in the bottom right-hand corner. That's one of the first ones I signed. I was about ten when I drew that one."

Dina stood up. "Okay, I've decided. I'll visit my parents as a dragonfly. Maybe they'll get the connection since they've been looking at that old drawing of dragonflies swooping with fireflies."

Kirron stood next to her and touched her arm. Both disappeared.

The four watchers saw two dragonflies appear in the Lerners' kitchen. The dragonflies sat motionless on top of the window blind. One flew downward, darting back and forth in front of the window where Dina's parents stared. The other perched statue-like on the window blind casing.

"Will you look at that?" Dina's father marveled. "How on earth did we get a dragonfly in the house? It's December. There's snow everywhere. How can there be any insects at all?"

"I don't know, but this one's beautiful. Look at those silvery and blue shiny wings," her mother replied. "It likes flying back and forth by the window. It's so beautiful to watch."

"Maybe it's looking for a way out," Dad suggested. "It will die right away out in that freezing weather though."

"I don't want it to die," her mother cried. "It isn't hurting anything flying in here by the window."

The couple watched their visitor as it circled the table and

202

floated to the rim of Mom's tea cup. It opened and closed its mouth along the rim of the cup.

"It looks as if it's tasting my tea," Mom whispered. "How odd."

The dragonfly settled on the sketch pad, landing on top of a dragonfly in the drawing. It sat there, slowly moving its wings, before walking to the bottom right hand corner. Its slender body covered the rudimentary cursive writing that formed two words, *Dina Lerner*.

"That dragonfly is right on top of Dina's signature. Why's it sitting there?" her mother asked.

"It almost seems to be telling us something, doesn't it?" her father suggested. "I don't know what, but it seems like a message."

Her fascinated parents watched the dragonfly resting on Dina's name. No one moved as the spellbound couple studied the dragonfly that had come to call.

Dragonfly Dina finally broke the reverie of motionlessness. She flitted to her father's hand, landed there, sat motionless for a short time, then returned to the signature corner of the sketch. She repeated the steps, returning to her father's hand a second time, then back to the corner of the sketch.

"That insect is definitely trying to tell us something," her mother declared. "Could it be something about Dina?"

"It may *be* Dina," her father murmured. "Do you remember when she was ten and I told her about artists signing their work? We sat at this table and looked at this very drawing. She got one of her pencils and signed the corner with her usual flair. She promised to sign every drawing and painting in the future because she was an artist, too."

"I do remember that," her mother drawled. "This dragonfly seemed to taste my tea, too, not yours. Dina always liked a little sugar in her tea, just like me. Oh my, has our daughter come to tell us something?"

"I believe so," her dad uttered. "She's telling us she's still with us. She knew we were looking through her sketch pad and feeling blue. She's telling us her life has changed, but she isn't really gone."

Mr. Lerner took Mrs. Lerner's hand, holding it on the table top near the quiet dragonfly. The dragonfly crawled on top of the joined hands, resting on both, gazing up at their faces before gliding to the top of the window blind.

Amazed that a second dragonfly sat there, the couple watched as it leaned forward, as if bowing, before the pair flew into the living room together.

The couple stood and followed the flying pair, but found no sign of them in the living room, or anywhere else in the house.

"Where did they go?" Dina's mother whimpered. "I want more time. I want my baby girl."

Her father wrapped his arms around his wife, who clutched her husband as another flood of tears flowed between them. "She couldn't stay any longer," he whispered. "The other dragonfly summoned her back wherever they need to be."

"No one will believe this. I'm not sure I believe it myself and I'm here."

"I believe it and you do, too. We know our daughter and we know the moments we shared. There was nothing random about that dragonfly's actions. Miracles are expressions of love. We love Dina and she loves us. That will never change. The real miracle, the gift, is the love that inspired it."

"So you really believe Dina came to tell us she still loves us and she's still with us?"

"Yes, but she seems to have another message, too. I believe she wants us to go on with our lives. She wants us to enjoy being alive, not just survive after losing her. Her drawing's theme was unrestrained joy, illustrated by fireflies and dragonflies performing a jubilant ballet together. Their movements streamed rays of light, wrapping the winged dancers with ribbons of hope and love. She's telling us to have hope, to know our love doesn't end because we're separated for a while. She wants us to find joy again."

"You are a wonderful and brilliant man, Mr. Lerner," his weary wife proclaimed as she wiped the tears from her face.

"Your father does seem quite astute, Dina. You are very much alike in that regard," Gavreel concurred.

"That was a brilliant communication visit, too, Dina," Kirron added. "Your actions led your parents to some perceptive conclusions. That's rare on a first visit. You figured out exactly what you needed to do and executed your plan effectively. I'm impressed with how well these first two visits have gone. You and Jo are both naturals at communicating messages inconspicuously. It's an important skill."

"Thank you," the girls chimed.

The group watched a bit longer as the couple returned to the table and sat together quietly. Man and woman watched the snow outside their window with no need for words. The quiet between them was comforting, two people bound by love and shared experiences who had no need to fill every minute with words which did not improve the silence they now shared. They could clearly communicate with one another via words and silence. Dina's mother ran her finger over her daughter's name several times before closing the sketch pad's cover and taking the tea mugs to the dishwasher.

"Why don't we see if the boys want to watch a movie with us?" Mom suggested. "It's been quite a while since we did that. I can pop some popcorn and we can snuggle on the sofa together. The boys might like that. Let's watch a comedy though. I feel like I might be able to laugh a little. It's been quite a while for that, too."

Dad smiled at her. "Great idea. I'll gather the boys and get our big blanket while you make the popcorn. I'll scan the list of comedies, too."

Warrior trainers and trainees stood. The small fissure in Dina's bedroom floor closed.

"Your parents are really good together, Dina. You were lucky to have such loving parents," Gabe mused.

"I was. I'm glad they still have one another and my brothers. I know the family isn't the same, but they still have one another to lean on and love."

"I never saw anything like that in my house," Gabe continued. "I'm glad I got to see it in yours."

The elders shot glances at one another. They knew Gabe's visit was going to be harder. It had to be. His early life hadn't had much support or love, but they were asking him to go on a mission to give those things to someone left behind.

Dina surprised them when she piped, "Gabe, you might not have seen it in your former home, but you're part of *this* family now. You have plenty of love and support from Jo and me. Oh, and these three." She gestured with her thumb toward Gavreel, Kirron, and Michael. "We're able to rejoice with our new family as we honor and comfort our old families. You can do this, Gabe, whether you feel you can or not. *I* know you can."

The procession headed back to the lounge from Dina's chambers. Bruno ran to Gabe and jumped on his leg, begging to be picked up.

"We can't forget about you when we're talking about family, can we, Bruno?" Gabe asked as he scooped up his precious pooch.

Enthusiastic doggy kisses wet Gabe's cheek and filled the room with laughter.

GABE'S VISIT...

"We must get on with the visits now. Gabe, have you decided?" Gavreel asked.

"I don't really know what to do. My dad would never acknowledge the visit. His faith doesn't believe in spiritual returns. My mom might acknowledge seeing something unusual, but I don't know if she'd make the connection to me. My brother? I really don't know. I'm not sure he'd understand anything about a visit. He always just tried to stay below the radar, not be seen or heard."

"It's your obligation to communicate comfort to those left behind. You have to figure out a way to do that. You must complete this step before we can move forward with more training or other missions," Gavreel murmured softly.

"Easier said than done in my case," Gabe grumbled.

"No one ever said it would be easy, young man," Michael explained. "Nothing we do on missions is ever easy. You must be willing and able to do anything that's asked of you. You're bright and talented. You need to use your gifts to solve your dilemma. You're bigger than any problem. Believing you can solve the problem is the first and most important step."

"Perhaps watching your family for a short time before deciding will help you, as it did Dina. Why don't we move to your chambers and give that a try?" Kirron coaxed.

"I guess," Gabe mumbled as he trudged toward his chamber door, Bruno still cuddled in his arms.

The others followed, exchanging concerned glances as they walked in silence.

When Gabe set Bruno down and stretched out on his bedroom floor, a tiny crack opened. The others joined him on the floor, peering through the narrow opening at Gabe's family seated at a table. They all looked tense and tired. Bruno's tail wagged wildly as he pawed the floor near the crack. He clearly recognized the people below and was glad to see them.

"Dad, Mom and I baked cupcakes yesterday. We made them for Gabe's birthday today. We're going to take a couple to his grave to let him know we didn't forget. We want you to come with us, if you will," the tired-looking boy pleaded. "Please, Dad."

"My son, that is a futile act and a waste of food," the man responded wearily. "Gabe isn't there and he doesn't eat cupcakes anymore."

"Well, then let's do it for us. *We'll* know that we remembered him on his birthday. We can tell our favorite stories about him and pray that he knows we haven't forgotten him. Please, Dad. Do it for Mom and me."

The man sighed as he ruffled his remaining son's hair. "All right. For you and Mom I will go to the grave of my dead son on his birthday. We will pray for his soul and that he knows we remember him."

They finished their breakfast in silence. When dishes were piled in the sink, the forlorn family filed out to the car. Gabe's brother carried two cupcakes.

"So, today's your birthday, eh?" the girls asked simultaneously.

"I don't know. You know we can't keep track of Earth time very easily here. I guess it is if my mom and brother made cupcakes for me and they're talking about going to my grave on my birthday."

Gabe turned to face Gavreel, Kirron, and Michael. "Can my visit be in the cemetery? Can you take me there? Can the others watch that place instead of my parents' house?"

Gavreel told him, "I can take you there. Kirron and Michael can make a space tessellation from this opening to the grave and hold open the view for the others."

"Well, I guess that's what I'll do then. I'll go to my whole family at my graveside. I'll try to figure out some way to give them comfort."

Kirron and Michael nodded, made some hand gestures, and held their index fingers together above the floor fissure. Their fingers formed a tent or steeple over the opening.

The scene shifted to a neat graveyard with manicured grass and row after row of polished headstones of varied sizes. Winding paths helped visitors navigate the grounds. Some graves had floral tributes and others were bare except for their stone markers. Large scattered trees offered shade to the graves surrounding them. Birds chattered with one another and squirrels raced from one tree to another. It was not winter in this place.

"How can a place be so full and so empty at the same time?" Jo wondered. "It's full of graves and growing things, but feels so empty."

"You'll find that's true of many places, Jo. This place isn't much different from many others. I'm not just talking about other cemeteries with countless headstones but very little life around them. People can be in a crowded room and still be all alone, lost in loneliness or depression. Others can be alone, except for the ideas filling their minds and hearts, driving them to work passionately to bring those ideas to life." Her father smiled as he finished speaking.

As they watched, Gabe's family plodded to his grave. His mother brushed a couple of leaves from her son's marker and set a bouquet from her garden on his grave. She slid to the ground saying, "Happy birthday, Gabe. Mama's here. I love you. I miss you so much."

Gabe stood. "Hummingbird. I'll visit as a hummingbird."

Gavreel nodded as she stood by his side and placed her hand on his upper arm.

Gabe's father and brother settled on the ground, one on each side of the grave. His father was near his mother, but they were not touching. The distance seemed to be a chasm, though it was really only a few inches.

Gabe's brother set the two cupcakes on the grave next to the flowers. "Mom and I made cupcakes for your birthday, Gabe. I know you'll like them. They're your favorites. This one is a strawberry cupcake with white frosting. Mom made this bright red rose out of frosting. Isn't it pretty? Mom told me red roses stand for love, and she wanted you to have the rose from us so you'd know we love you. We should've told you that when you were with us. I hope you know, even though we never said it much. The other one is a vanilla cupcake with strawberry frosting. See the bright orange and black skateboard Mom made out of frosting? It looks cool on the pink background. She made that one because you loved your skateboard. I know you made it known that black was your favorite color when you got to middle school, but Mom says orange used to be your favorite, so she made it orange and black."

Gabe's father looked from his son, to his wife, to the birthday offerings on the grave. "Happy birthday, Gabe. You are with us in our hearts, son. My memory of my first glimpse of you through the nursery window is as sharp today as it was the day you were born. I was proud of my fine son that day. I am proud that I had two strong sons. I should have told you that you made me proud so many times. I pray for your soul every day."

The family hadn't noticed the hummingbird hovering just above and behind the headstone while Gabe's brother and father spoke. They noticed the tiny bird when it settled on the slab of granite marking Gabe's resting place. It studied the boy and his parents as they watched it intently.

"Look at that beautiful hummingbird! It doesn't seem to be afraid of us, does it?" Gabe's mother marveled.

"No, it doesn't. I've never seen one this close," his father admitted. "Maybe the flowers or the sweet frosting smell attracted it. It's a beautiful thing."

Gabe took flight, zipping all around his grave and family, darting this way and that. He flew sideways and backwards, up and down, moving every way a hummingbird can move before landing on the headstone once more.

"This bird is putting on a show for us!" his brother exclaimed. "I didn't know birds could move like that."

"Most can't, but hummingbirds are exceptional flyers," his father announced.

"Why is it staying here by us?"

"I have no idea," his father confessed. "It's very unusual for a wild creature of any kind to approach a human."

The bird hovered directly in front of the words Aslan Gabriel Burakgazi. It appeared to be pointing at the name with its beak. It fluttered to the dates below the name, the date of birth, and the date of death. It hovered there before circling the family again and settling on top of the marker.

"This can't be happening," the man croaked. "It's not possible."

"It is possible," his wife murmured. "Indeed, we are seeing a miracle because Gabe has come back to us on his birthday."

"That can't be," his father chided.

"How else do you explain this bird visiting us *here* on *this day*?"

"Is that you, Gabe?" his brother bluntly asked. "Is it?"

In reply, the bird flew to the boy and hovered near his nose before turning to the skateboard cupcake. He stuck his beak into the frosting as if sucking nectar from a flower. The bird put on an aerial show of dips and dives, spins, and turns, zipping around the awe-struck family time and time again. He hovered before the name on the gravestone once more, pointing at it with his frosting-smeared beak.

"It's pointing at Gabe's name! It really is. Mom's right. I think this is Gabe, too. This bird did stunts just like Gabe did on his skateboard and when he did parkour. I don't know how or why, but it's him."

The bird turned and hovered above the red rose that adorned his other cupcake. He dipped his beak in the red frosting and flew in front of his mother's face. He hovered near her nose, looking deeply into her eyes as she looked into his. He tipped his beak so a speck of red frosting dotted the tip of her nose.

He returned to the frosting rose and dipped his beak once more. This time he flew to his father, hovering there before delivering a frosting kiss to the tip of his nose. Tears streamed down the man's cheeks.

He delivered his third frosting dip to his brother. He'd done all he knew to do to comfort his family.

He circled them once more then flew farther away than he had since they'd noticed him. He flew back, this time with another hummingbird. The pair circled the family three times and darted off, disappearing behind a giant tree.

When Gabe reappeared in his bedroom, Bruno leaped into his arms, licking red frosting from his face as he fanned the air with his tail. Smiles beamed around him.

"Another impressive visit!" Kirron crowed. "This entire team has the best morphing and communication skills I've ever seen in all my centuries as a Seraph."

"Agreed," Gavreel and Michael bellowed.

They turned their attention to Gabe, who'd sunk to the floor, intently surveying the scene below.

Gabe's parents clutched one another as if afraid one of the graves would open up and pull them into depths from which they could not escape. His brother knelt behind his parents, his arms wrapped around both of them, his head resting on his mother's. They sobbed unceasingly, leaning against one another, their clinging hands anchoring them against the waves of pain. Conjoined howls of misery shook their bodies as they shook the silence of this place, echoing off the scattered trees. A tiny lapse allowed some recovering breaths with only stifled sobs. The break was short-lived. A new wave of pain crushed them, hurling them back into the outstretched arms of grief. The family went on like this, in and out of the crushing depths of grief, over and over, until Gabe cried, "What did I do? I messed this up so badly."

"You did not," Gavreel told him. "Your family had not yet hit the deepest part of their grief. They hadn't truly faced losing you or what might have been. They *had* to go this low before they could begin their climb out of misery and back to living. You helped them more than you realize, Gabe. They're a real family now. Look at them. Surely you can see the love and unity through the shared pain. The walls have come tumbling down. They're broken, all of them, but they're together. Now they'll rebuild, brick by brick, as a family, supporting and loving one another through the whole difficult process. Their emotions are no longer walled off behind a facade of coping."

"But I was supposed to bring them comfort, not more pain," Gabe sniffled, near tears himself. "I always seem to mess things up. It's my life story."

"Oh, get over yourself, boy!" Michael snapped. Surprised faces turned his way.

"This may not be the best time," Gavreel insisted.

"It's *exactly* the right time," Michael retorted. "As an experienced parent, I can tell you there are times when young ones have to know they've crossed a line, that as a parent, you'll take no more. We don't have time for his 'I-always-mess-up-poor-me' routine every time something happens that isn't exactly as he expects. Gabe, the Pity Train passed the stop of Woe-Is-Me before it derailed at the intersection of New Life and Move On. Son, *that part* of your training, your earlier life, is over. Everyone, everywhere, has problems. It might sound like a worn-out platitude, but it's true: Your reaction to whatever happens is more important than anything that happens to you. You need an attitude adjustment."

Michael took a deep breath and spoke more softly. "You know

almost nothing, Gabe. You're gifted, but you understand very little. What Gavreel told you is true. She knows far more than you. You need to respect that fact and respect her. Everything she says is truth. Your parents and your brother were forged into a *real* family today because the time was right. God allowed you to be the blacksmith, in the form of a hummingbird. You helped shape them into what they were always supposed to be. They're comforting one another because of your visit. You brought more than a few short minutes' comfort from the other side. You brought them comfort for the rest of their lives through one another."

Gabe stammered, "I... I just feel so bad about what they are going through." He was still watching the scene below, relieved his parents and brother seemed to have calmed the crushing waves of tears as they sat by his grave.

"My son looked me in the eye and kissed me today," his mother mused. "He came back to us and he k-kissed me. He kissed all of us, didn't he?" Her voice was quavering, but with a mother's undeniable strength and certainty.

"I think so, Mom. Gabe came back and performed for us. He showed us who he was and that he knew we brought the cupcakes for his birthday. He pecked us with the red rose frosting to say he loved us, too."

"He gave *us* this gift for h-his birthday," his father sputtered. "I do not know how this thing is possible, but I cannot deny the miracle we experienced today. I wouldn't have believed it if I hadn't been here to see it myself."

"It's one of those things most people would have to see to believe," his wife asserted. "This was the most incredible experience of my life. Thank you, Gabe. Thank you, God. I love you, Gabe. I always have and I always will, my sweet baby boy." She looked to the sky. "Please, come again. We miss you so much."

"We should go now," his father blurted. "We've been here quite a long time." He stood and offered his hand to his wife. "Goodbye,

Gabe. Happy birthday. Know that you were, are, loved."

Gabe's mother took her husband's hand and he pulled her to her feet. He kissed her hand as she stood facing him. "You were wise, my wife, to come here on our son's birthday." She nodded but said nothing as he held her hand and headed toward the winding path that would take them back to their car.

"Bye, Gabe. That was quite a show! You're still my cool big brother. You always will be. Happy birthday, bro. Cupcakes at home are calling me!" He was smiling as he turned and followed his parents.

Kirron and Michael broke the space tessellation they'd created and the crack closed. Everyone stood.

"I guess you were right, Michael," Gabe offered sheepishly. "I did bring comfort when I visited. I didn't understand what was happening until they stopped crying. I'm really glad they seem better now and that they recognized me, even as a hummingbird. I'm sorry, Gavreel, if my words disrespected what you were telling me. I think you're great. I really do."

"Thank you, Gabe. We, all of us, feel you're great, too. You still have a lot to learn, but there's no denying the greatness within you. There's no denying any of this team's greatness." Gavreel led the group through Gabe's home to the shared lounge. "A celebration is in order!"

Gavreel gestured and raised her hand as she passed through the door to the lounge. The table, laden with crystal bowls brimming with mixed nuts and chips, a tiered cupcake tower loaded with fancy decorated cupcakes, and glasses filled with sparkling cider, awaited them. Stacked by the tower of cupcakes, plates and napkins called them to share the offerings.

"Your successful visits in your chosen morphed forms completed the first section of your training, Team DJG. You mastered the virtues' challenges of the first path as you became a team. You mastered the powers of enhanced running, agility, levitation, invisibility, and shape shifting. These tokens will be added to your reminder chain. You earned them admirably with your fine visits to your families."

Gavreel placed a gold charm in each young warrior's hand. The center section was circular with seven triangular pieces encompassing it, the edges filigreed with delicate threads of twisted gold reflecting light in every direction. The charm reminded them of the sun, spreading light and warmth. The center section of the front bore the words: "Never let *your* fear or *your* needs stop you from giving comfort to others." Flipping their charms over, they found words inscribed on each triangular ray:

The Bible, Psalm 34:17-18:
"17 The righteous cry out, and the Lord hears them; he delivers them from all their troubles. 18 The Lord is close to the brokenhearted and saves those who are crushed in spirit."

The Quran, Surah baqarah verse 286:
"Allah does not burden a soul beyond that it can bear."

Hippocrates:
"Cure sometimes, treat often, comfort always."

Buddha:
"Have compassion for all beings, rich and poor alike; each has their suffering...."

Mishnah, About 1.2:
"The world stands upon three things: upon the Law, upon worship, and upon showing kindness."

Yoruba Proverb (Nigeria):
"Gentle character, it is which enables the rope of life to stay unbroken in one's hand."

The Book of Mormon, Mosiah 18:8-9

"...Bear one another's burdens, that they may be light;... mourn with those that mourn; yea, and comfort those that stand in need of comfort..."

As the trio finished reading the newest tokens, Gavreel waved her hand, affixing each charm to their chains. She continued, "You'll begin section two at the training center the next time we gather. After the next full section of training, you'll be ready to go on a mission as warriors. Let's enjoy this celebration of your success thus far, before we leave you to reflect, rest and refresh. Help yourselves. I do have to warn you, my cupcakes are undeniably addictive, the best you'll ever taste, except those made with a mother's love." She winked as she gestured to the table.

The others clamored around the table, filling plates and chatting about the remarkable visits they'd shared.

"Gabe, I believe these are yours," Gavreel proclaimed as she handed him a plate. Two cupcakes, one with a red rose and the other with an orange and black skateboard, sat on the plate. There's nothing sweeter than a mother's love. Happy Earth birthday, Gabe."

AFTER VISITING...

"I really believe I've had a sufficient number of your addictive cupcakes, Gavreel. Perhaps we should take our leave and let these young ones rest and refresh. They'll need to be well-rested and sharp for what lies ahead," Michael announced.

"Dad, you only had six cupcakes," Jo teased. "I bet you can put away a few more."

"I probably could, but that's probably not a good idea. I need to be able to walk out of here, not have to ask Kirron to roll me out and bounce me down the porch steps!"

"Oh, Dad, I could do that for you if you don't want to ask Kirron," she teased right back.

"As generous as that offer sounds, I do believe my sweet tooth has had quite enough for quite a while. You three really need time to reflect, rest, and refresh before your next session with us. Your visits were impressive. You earned those comfort charms. I'm proud of all of you." He hugged his daughter and waved as he headed to the front door.

"Michael's right. It's time for us to part for a while. Gavreel, excellent celebration spread. Thank you. Dina, Jo, and Gabe, truly remarkable visits. Your communication with your families was amazing to behold. The ways each of you let them know, without a shadow of doubt, that you'd come was quite astounding. Refresh. One of us will call for you when we're ready to proceed." Kirron turned and joined Michael near the door.

"I, too, will leave for the time being," Gavreel announced. She handed Bruno the last bite of her cupcake, allowing him to lick her fingers. "You've done well, team. Very, very well. Reflect, rest, and refresh. We'll see you soon." She walked to the others standing by the door, raised her arm, and they were gone.

"What a day!" they chorused the instant the elders were gone. Hearty laughter filled the lounge as the team spread out on their sectional.

"Both of your visits to your families were so cool," Gabe told the girls. "I learned a lot from watching both of you."

"Thanks. Yours was amazing," Dina and Jo snickered as they finished their identical remark.

"Your mom was so sure it was you, Jo. She just knew it was you and your dad. Her faith was so strong. She convinced your sister." As he spoke, Gabe leaned into the corner of the sofa and stretched his legs out. Bruno jumped on top of them. "You have frosting on your nose, buddy."

"My mom's always had a lot of faith. She's had a pretty hard adult life. She's had to have a lot of faith to cope with my dad's deployments, his death, then taking care of my sister and me alone, my sickness and my death. Sometimes I wonder how she keeps going."

Dina asserted, "No doubt, you helped her keep going with your visit. Remember when Gavreel told us why we died at the age we did? She emphasized that *we* were destined to be warriors, but our parents and siblings who suffered such grief were being melded into comforting angels. Your mom's going to be one strong comforting angel when she gets here. Your sister, too. They already are, really. Baking and decorating cookies for kids in a homeless shelter so soon after losing you is pretty impressive."

"They need these comfort sun charms, don't they?" Jo murmured as she ran her finger along hers.

"I bet they get them, when the time's right," Gabe assured her.

"All of our families will get better faster since our visits," Dina added. "I'm so glad my family was going to watch a funny movie together. We always liked family movie nights. I hope they all laughed a lot. They need to find laughter again, to know it's okay to go on and feel happy."

"They will," Jo told her.

"It was a very clear message, that's for sure," Gabe agreed. "I was impressed Kirron just stayed motionless on top of the window blind casing and let you use your judgment about the best way to communicate with your parents. You knew just what to do and he let you do it. They didn't even know he was there until you flew up by him and you left together."

"Your parents were really sweet, comforting each other after you left. You can tell how much they love one another." Jo smiled, remembering the tenderness they'd witnessed.

"I was lucky to live in a loving home with loving parents," Dina affirmed. "Gabe, your visit at the cemetery was spectacular. I really mean that."

"It was," Jo affirmed. "The ways you maneuvered and the way you hovered in front of your name and birth and death dates was so clear and convincing."

"Thanks. I did my best. Mom's frosting was really good. She remembered I love strawberries and strawberry-flavored desserts."

"Of course, she remembered. She's your mom," the girls reassured him as another round of synchronized laughter overtook the group.

"Your parents seemed good together when they left. Your brother was fantastic. He understands so much for one so young. He knew how to talk to both of them and connect with them," Dina said. "You can tell how close he is to your mom by the way he talked to her and rested his head on top of hers when they were riding those waves of grief together."

"You can start feeling better about your family now. It looks as if your dad has softened some and your brother's learned to come out of the shadows. He's braver and stronger than you thought," Jo reassured him.

"*Your* dad is still pretty tough," Gabe insisted, a slight smile crossing his face. "I guess I had it coming, but he really let me have it."

"He's always been tough, but fair. That's partly from his military background," Jo told him. "No one anywhere, is kinder or more loving than my dad, though. Everyone who ever knew him loved him and he loved everyone. If he came down on you, it was done out of love and wanting to help you."

"I hope you've exited the Pity Train now that you know it derailed," Dina chuckled as she tossed a pillow at Gabe.

"That was pretty funny," Gabe admitted as he snatched the pillow and stuffed it behind him. "He has a way with words."

"Especially when he's mad," Jo confided. "He's very patient and he never got mad easily, but when he's had enough of something, you know it."

"I didn't mean to make anyone mad, but I always had talent for that without even trying. It was so hard watching my whole family like that, knowing I'd caused it. I always felt guilty about being the way I was. I always felt as if I caused nothing but problems, but I couldn't help it."

"Now that you know you got off that train at New Life and Move On, you'll have to stop blaming yourself for things that are over," Dina snickered as she tossed another pillow at him. "The past is the past. Everyone thinks you're great, not just Gavreel. New and Improved Gabe needs no pity."

"I'll try to remember that. Thanks."

"So, any guesses about what's coming next?" Jo asked.

"Not a clue," Dina and Gabe exclaimed. Peals of laughter shook the sectional, causing a dozing Bruno to tumble to the floor.

He looked at Gabe with accusing eyes before turning and jumping up between the girls. His grin announced, "This is a safer spot. They won't throw me to the floor. I'll just snuggle with my girls." More laughter shook the sectional as the girls petted and cooed over the snuggled-down dog, beaming happily as he stared at Gabe.

"The next part must be pretty intense if all three trainers told us to rest and refresh," Jo offered as she recovered from her recent spasm of laughter.

"They emphasized a mission will follow this phase of training," Gabe reminded them, "so it must teach us a lot. They keep calling us warriors, but I know I don't feel ready to fight evil, whatever they mean by that."

"I guess we'll find out soon enough," Dina replied. "I believe I'll go board the Refresh Train at the intersection of Shower and Bed." She grinned as she stood and headed toward her door, pumping her right arm in the air. "All aboard!"

Her friends stood and chimed, "Shower and Bed is going to be a pretty busy intersection."

Laughter boomed like thunder as they exited to their own chambers. The team members enjoyed their synchronized words now and the laughter it brought them. Laughter was a small vacation, blessed relief from the things that had happened to them and the demands made on them.

Bruno enjoyed his people's levity as much as they did. He zoomed around the room before following Gabe through the shiny black door.

BEFORE TRAINING RESUMES...

Gabe sauntered into the lounge after a long rest. He munched on a giant sandwich, an enthusiastic Bruno bouncing at his feet, cleaning up the bits that fell as Gabe walked.

"The girls aren't here yet," Gabe observed. He walked to their doors and pounded once on each. "We'll see if they're ready to hang out."

Jo flounced through her door almost instantly. "I wondered if anyone else was up. I've been writing songs in my studio. I have no idea how long we've been apart, but I wrote two songs after I woke up so it's been awhile. You're eating again, I see," Jo teased as she watched Gabe stuff more of his sandwich into his mouth.

"I am a sandwich magician. I make them appear and I make them disappear, with a little help from my assistant," he crooned, watching Bruno gobble a piece of meat that fell to the floor.

"I had an apple and a chunk of cheese when I got up. I know Gavreel explained that we don't *need* to eat here, but everything tastes so good. Why would you resist the urge to put this heavenly food in your mouth?"

"Agreed," Gabe blurted with a full mouth.

Dina burst through her door, a canvas hanging from each hand. "Hi, guys!"

"It looks like you've been busy," Jo and Gabe greeted her. The sound of their laughter tinkled like bells in a breeze.

"I have been busy. Happily busy. I painted these for you. I hope you like them." Dina turned one painting so the front showed. The other one still hung by her leg, the image turned toward her body so it wasn't visible.

She held an oil painting that was so precise and detailed that it resembled a photograph, like something created by old masters of art before photography existed.

"This one's obviously for you, Jo." Dina extended the painting in her right hand to her friend. The canvas was filled with a framed picture of a smiling Moore family with two exquisite blue morpho butterflies perched on top. "I hope you like it. I made it to remind you of your amazing first visit."

"Like it? I love it!" Jo cried as she hugged her smiling friend. She took the canvas and examined it closely. "This is perfect. The picture of my family looks just like the photograph. It's the perfect reminder of how happy we were together before Dad and I had to leave. These butterflies are so detailed and the color is so vibrant. It's a masterpiece. I don't know how you did it, but I love it. Thank you so much."

"You're welcome. I'm glad you like it so much."

"I'm going to hang it in my music studio. I'll see it a lot in there since that's where I am most of the time when we're here. I bet it inspires me when I'm writing songs. It's fabulous. You're the best!" Jo wrapped Dina in another hug.

"It's beyond fabulous," Gabe marveled. "We might have to start calling you Michelangelo or Da Vinci instead of Dina."

Dina's joy flooded the room. Her generosity was an offering of insight, love, and respect. She'd grown to cherish her friends, those who were her team, her new family. These paintings were gifts from her heart to theirs. "This one's for you, Gabe. I hope you like it. You need to see how powerful your first visit was, see it like all of us saw it. I hope this is a good reminder of what happened when you visited your family." Dina turned the second canvas and offered it to her other teammate.

This canvas was a collage of images and words, each scene encircled by black ribbon swirling back to brilliant Hummingbird Gabe, centered on the canvas. The collage showcased scenes from his visit and words his family had spoken. One section showed a hummingbird perched on a headstone. Another featured a hummingbird hovering before the name on the stone, pointing at the name with its beak. They saw the little bird dipping its beak into a decorative red rose atop a cupcake. Three sections featured the hummer near the faces of the mother, father, and brother left behind, tenderly pecking each of their noses. His father kissing his mother's hand filled one enclosure. A ribboned compartment featured close-ups of the skateboard-decorated cupcake the red rose cupcake. Three sections featured words in lovely calligraphy:

"My son looked me in the eye and kissed me today. He came back to us and he kissed me. He kissed all of us, didn't he?"

"He gave us this gift for his birthday. I do not know how this thing is possible, but I cannot deny the miracle we experienced today. I would not have believed it if I had not been here to see it myself."

"Bye, Gabe. That was quite a show! You're still my cool big brother. You always will be. Happy birthday, bro. Cupcakes at home are calling me!"

Gabe took the canvas from Dina's hand, staring at the images and words on it. He finally declared, "I have no words."

Dina told him, "You don't have to say anything. I just hope you like it."

He gulped, practically crushing her in a bear hug, "This is the nicest thing anyone has ever done for me. It's the best present I ever got. You perform miracles with your art, Dina. Thank you. I'm glad I have sisters now. You and Jo are my sisters."

"Lucky boy!" The words tumbled out of both girls' mouth as spontaneous uncontrollable laughter overtook the group.

"We're lucky, too, Gabe," the girls squeaked between their squeals of laughter. "Just one lucky family."

Boisterous laughter abounded as they teased one another, siblings by choice. They didn't hear the knock on door, but Bruno did. His sharp bark alerted them as the second knock came.

"Hey, Michael. Come in." Gabe swung open the door.

"It's time for phase two of your training to begin. I hope you're well-rested and refreshed. This will be a long session."

"Everyone's feeling pretty good. Come look at the paintings Dina did. They're unbelievable."

Michael walked toward the girls seated at the table, stopping to stare at the paintings. "You did these, Dina? They're remarkable."

"Thanks," Dina replied.

"Look at our family picture, Dad. Doesn't it look like the real photograph?"

"It certainly does. Dina is an even more talented artist than I'd imagined. Very few have an artistic gift this great. This collage painting is truly captivating. Your eyes travel from image to image. You become more amazed and moved by each image. The quotes from his parents and brother are perfect accents."

Dina beamed. "Uh, thanks again. I guess it's time for us to suit up and go?"

"It is. Bruno will be staying here. Get ready and come right back here. We have no time to spare."

PHASE TWO TRAINING BEGINS...

Michael walked with Dina, Jo, and Gabe to the training center.

"Dad, can I ask you a question?" Jo inquired.

"Always, Pumpkin."

"Are you on the same team as Kirron and Gavreel, like I am with Dina and Gabe? You guys wear the same white, red, and gold uniforms and your chains are all completely filled."

"Well, you might say that. I work closely with Kirron and Gavreel often. We're trainers of warriors and guardians and we've been on many missions together. So, yes, we're a team, but there are many more of us. You'll see that momentarily."

As the group rounded the corner, the school campus came into view. Just as before, many milled around the grounds. Some wore matching uniforms proclaiming their team membership while others wore regular clothes.

"We'll work inside the center today, not on the learning paths or training grounds. Follow me," Michael instructed.

As they neared the building, massive glass doors spread apart. They stepped inside what appeared to be an enormous solarium. A luminous glow like filtered sunlight welcomed them. Clustered seating areas and innumerable plants of all sizes filled the room. Crystal sculptures and baubles hanging from branches infused the room with dancing specks of colorful light. Soothing scents of healthy growing things filled their nostrils. A serene sound, similar to the one at the Board of Insights, wafted around them. Uniformed teams, studying strange devices, filled some seating areas.

"This is the training center's lounge area. Teams often use it for planning after receiving mission orders. Those you see with the devices have received orders and are planning their courses of action. Notice that at least one trainer sits with each group. Come this way," Michael directed.

Several doors lined the back wall of the immense room they'd just crossed. Michael approached the one on the far-left side. "These doors lead to control centers for different operations at different levels. All operations are important, but some require much more skill than others. Since you're novice warriors and have had limited training, we begin here. You'll get more training for skills you must master before you're given your assignment. I hope you're ready to work. I have clearance to enter all sectors of the training center. Because you have clearance for no sectors yet, you must be accompanied at all times by one of us." Michael pressed his hand flat on the door. It swung open.

As the group stepped inside, Gavreel and Kirron greeted them. "You appear refreshed. That's good."

Kirron continued, "We'll turn that corner, leaving the level-one foyer. You'll see the magnitude of our need for strong, well-trained warriors. This section is exclusively level one needs. Because they're very much needed and appreciated for the work they do at this level, teams displaying particularly strong gentleness and caring traits stay at this level long term. Most teams stay at this level for several missions and help us clear the backlog of needs. Others advance to level two after only one or two post-visit missions. Staying or advancing is determined by need and skills shown during missions. Only the strongest with the widest array of skills advance to the final levels, those of Archangel or Seraph."

"Aren't you a Seraphim?" Jo asked.

"One is referred to as a *Seraph*. *Seraphim* is plural. We all are Seraphim or Archangels," Kirron gestured toward his teammates.

"Let's head around the corner so they can see the level-one area," Gavreel prompted.

The group crossed the foyer and stepped through an open doorway. A short hall led to a gigantic room, expanding farther than they could see. The walls and ceiling resembled a honeycomb, with scenes playing out in each hexagonal cell. A thread of green, yellow, red, or black light outlined each cell. While some flashed, most outlines were solid colored. Uniformed individuals stuffed the vast room. Some sat at a control center in the center of the mammoth room. Others stood or sat in groups throughout the room. Many held the same strange devices Dina, Jo, and Gabe had seen in the lounge. Several held equipment they didn't recognize, while others practiced hand motions. Many groups performed a variety of tasks.

"What are all those scenes on the wall and ceiling?" the teammates wondered simultaneously.

"Those are scenes where a mission is required, where darkness must be fought to help the people who are at risk. The colored light around each cell prioritizes the need," Gavreel told them. "A green light means there's still time. The need is real and is growing, but it's not at the dangerous level yet. Yellow means the danger has built and needs attention. Red is imminent danger. Flashing red is crisis. If the evil is not conquered, the cell goes black. When darkness has overcome someone or something, the need moves to a higher level. It's no longer phase one. It might not even be phase two. It may have jumped all the way to the top. It depends. Needs and missions are very different. That's why we train warriors to think deeply so they can figure things out in any situation."

"I don't see many green lights," Dina observed.

"No, there aren't many," Kirron concurred. "Evil spreads quickly. It's powerful. Situations never stay at green level long. We fight to save as many as possible from turning to evil, but there are many temptations and situations slide to red quickly."

"I don't understand what we're supposed to do to fight evil," Jo confessed. "What kinds of things are you talking about at this level?"

"Many things," Michael disclosed. "Let me give you some examples. Let's say there are young ones who don't get much love or attention at home. Maybe the parents drink a lot or do drugs, which are evils that have to be fought at a higher level. Young children are vulnerable because of their exposure to the parents' actions. Some parents are stressed by daily life and their inability to get ahead, or by demands they feel they can never meet, so they vent rage on the kids. Sometimes a single parent, who tries but just can't do everything solo, leaves kids alone way too much. Some kids never have enough to eat or even a place to call home. Or, maybe the kids have way too much, too many *things*, but not enough time and guidance with caring adults. Kids are neglected in lots and lots of ways, all of which leave them vulnerable to evil. They're particularly vulnerable if they haven't been raised in faith. If they haven't been taken to church, or temple, or mosque and taught about God, they do not have a foundation to resist evil. Evil is always watching and waiting, ready to prey upon the vulnerable, especially young ones."

"I still don't understand," Jo repeated. "What are we supposed to do? How do we stop evil if we don't even know what it is?"

"You will understand. You've earned your gentleness, trust and patience, forgiveness, empathy, and comfort charms. You even have your initials, the souls on fire charm, something most never get or don't get until they are very high ranking. These tokens mean you're champions of these virtues. You understand them well and practice them constantly. These are the keys for phase-one missions. They go a long way in saving others and fighting evil," Gavreel told them.

"Things will get clearer as we go along," Kirron assured them. "You must know how to make the space tessellation. You have to know how to get where your mission leads you and how to get back here when you are done. We will practice it many times together before you'll be allowed to try it alone."

"Let's move over to that empty seating area," Michael suggested.

The group headed to several chairs arranged in a rectangle,

settling there comfortably.

"Gabe, you're very quiet. Is everything all right?" Gavreel asked.

"Yeah. I was just trying to take it all in. I'm trying to figure out why no one ever came to help me all those times I was being beaten or bludgeoned with words, or why no one helped my mom when she tried to help me. I don't understand."

"No, you don't, but you will," Gavreel told him. "Let's focus on learning the space tessellation right now, okay?"

He nodded.

Kirron spoke again. "This is a defining moment. You're learning one of the great secrets of the universe. In this lesson, faith and reason tessellate. When that happens, you'll be allowed to juxtapose locations all over the universe. You must accept the old, but true, fact that with great power comes great responsibility. Are you ready to assume that gift, that responsibility, that power?"

"Yes, sir," three subdued voices intoned.

Each trainer put out a hand, revealing a golden grain, about the size of a grain of rice.

Gavreel told them, "These are the tessellations of the universe. They mark every location on every planet and every location in the heavens. Everywhere. They're literally the map of the universe. They update automatically, constantly, as new places are built, or old places are destroyed. They're the tool that allows space travel. Accepting these grains of knowledge means you'll be able to go any-where instantly. It's a wonder and a great responsibility, one that's used only in service of good for God."

Michael continued, "You must willingly make the Oath of Acceptance and abide by it throughout your eternal life. If you break the oath at any time, the grain will be stripped from you. If that happens, you must begin over in service as a novice of the lowest rank of angels in a lower level of Heaven. Individuals at this level never become warriors so you'd be forsaking your gifts and your true destinies. Do you understand the seriousness and value of this gift?"

"Yes, sir," synched from the trio's lips, but with no accompanying laughter.

"Are you willing to accept the Grain of Space Tessellations?" Kirron asked them.

Without hesitation, "Yes, sir!" rang from mouths of the three young warriors.

"Please, stand," Gavreel instructed. "Face us. Put your hands in praying position in front of your chest. Keep your hands in that position until we tell you that you may put them down."

Dina, Jo, and Gabe did as instructed.

Michael informed them, "We'll now administer the Oath of Acceptance. You must repeat it clearly and exactly. We'll say it one line at a time and you should repeat that line before we proceed to the next line."

Kirron spoke first, "I do solemnly swear, as one of God's chosen angels, that I willingly accept this gift of Space Tessellations."

Three young voices repeated the line.

Gavreel continued, "I solemnly affirm, upon my honor as a warrior angel, that I will use this gift only in service of the greater good for God."

The trio perfectly uttered the second line of the oath.

Michael proceeded, "I further swear that I will safeguard the knowledge of the tessellations with vigilance, never revealing any information about this gift to anyone, anywhere, ever."

Repetition of the line flowed perfectly from Dina, Jo, and Gabe.

Kirron, Michael, and Gavreel recited the final line together, "I promise to uphold the traditions, integrity, and high standards set by the angels that came before me whenever using the Space Tessellation, so help me, God."

When Team DJG had finished their proclamation of the Oath of Acceptance, each trainer stepped forward, pressed the grain between the eyebrows of each trainee, and declared, "In so much as you have spoken the Oath of Acceptance in this company, we now bestow upon you this great gift. Use it wisely and well, remembering always that it is a powerful tool for doing good works and serving God."

Gavreel, Kirron, and Michael beamed as they backed away from their young charges. The three put their hands in praying position and conveyed, "You must touch the spot between your eyebrows where the grain entered your soul with the tips of your fingers, then lower your praying hands to your chest level again. You will tilt your steepled hands down and back up three times, like this, to activate the tessellations grain. When you do this motion, say 'I thank you, God, for this gift and your trust in me as your servant'."

Dina, Jo, and Gabe again did exactly as they were told.

"You can put down your hands now, young space travelers," Gavreel told them.

"Let's take our seats again to discuss the next steps." Kirron pointed to their chairs.

Gavreel stressed, "You must know where your home is so you can return when you've used a tessellation to travel elsewhere. We are in Sector WHL6. That's the entire area where you've been since transitioning. This sector is Warrior Heaven Level 6. There are many sectors in Heaven, but this is yours. It's a vast area. By using that information only, you'd return to your sector, but it could be anywhere in this sector, places you've seen or places you haven't yet seen. To make an efficient return to a specific location, you must visualize more information and the grain will help you move to that specific location. There are two locations, your home and this training center, that I want you to be able to transfer to easily and quickly, no matter where the transfer is beginning. Your home's identification is WHL6TeamDJG+AACB. The center where we are right now is WHL6TCB1. You should memorize those two locations because you'll use them often."

"I get the WHL6 part of the codes, and the TeamDJG, but what does the +AACB and TCB1 mean?" Gabe asked.

Kirron grinned. "The +AACB stands for plus animal angel canine Bruno and the TCB1 acronym stands for Training Center Building 1."

"Let's start by using the space tessellation to go to your home, then back here. Each of you'll make the actual transfer in space, taking one of us with you, in case you make a mistake using it. We can get you back, no matter where we go in the universe. It's easy to make a mistake when you first use the tessellation because you must be very exact every time." Michael pulled Gabe to his feet, "I'll go home with you first."

"What do I have to do?" Gabe asked.

Michael told him, "Right now, since you're new at using the tessellations, visualize the place and the location code. You might see the code on top of a visual image of the place. When you have a good visualization, brush your hand over the spot between your eyebrows and raise that arm in the air above your head. That should take us where you want to go. To take someone with you, you need to be touching or you can look directly at them as you do the visualization. What's the code for your home?"

"WHL6TeamDJG+AACB," Gabe told him.

"That's right. We'll go there momentarily." Michael turned to the others. "We'll wait for you to join us on the porch before transferring back here."

"Here we go, Gabe," Michael encouraged as he lightly held one arm. "Take us to your home, young angel."

The pair disappeared.

"Whoa!" the girls exclaimed. "He did it!"

"Yes, it appears he did," Kirron agreed. "How about we go next, Jo? Are you ready to take me to your home?"

Nodding, she stood and put one hand on Kirron's shoulder. She went through the motions she'd been told to do. The second pair disappeared.

"Your turn, Dina," Gavreel announced. "Let's make that first transfer."

Dina took Gavreel's hand in one of hers as she visualized her home and its code. She brushed the bridge of her nose as she raised the other hand in the air.

They appeared in the front yard, greeted with enthusiastic cheering and chatter from the four who waited.

"Well done, Team DJG! Your first space tessellation travels were successful. We'll transfer back to the training center. Visualize the seating area as you visualize the code for the center. Dina, since we were last coming here, we'll go first returning. Are you ready?"

"Here we go again," Dina proclaimed as she and Gavreel vanished.

The other pairs soon joined them at the seating area where they'd begun this exercise.

"That was very, very cool," Jo attested when she sat down with the group.

"Let's go again," Kirron directed, but this time we'll use the tessellation to go to the first training zone. I'm talking about the area with the stair step boulders on which you first used enhanced jumps. Can all of you visualize that spot?"

Affirmative head shakes assured him they all remembered.

"The code for that area is WHL6EATA1," Kirron told them. "Everybody repeat it."

After a few attempts, the trainees were repeating the new acronym perfectly. Dina asked what the full code stood for this time.

"All acronyms are logical and name the specific area by using the first letter of each word in the name of the place. In this case the letters signify Warrior Heaven Level 6 Enhanced Agility Training Area 1," Gavreel informed them.

"Jo, we haven't gone first yet, so this time why don't we start the transfers?" Kirron prompted as he placed his hand on her shoulder. They vanished instantly.

Pairs of trainees and trainers successfully moved from one location to another all over the training grounds, quickly understanding the logical acronyms for each. They then moved to entire group movement, with one trainee taking the other five to the designated destination.

Gabe announced the next code. Trainers and trainees found themselves atop the stair step stones surveying the surrounding scenery.

"Another excellent group transfer, Gabe. How are you feeling?" Kirron asked again.

"On top of the world," a gleeful Gabe bellowed. The group's giggle morphed into cackling that ricocheted from the surrounding hills and trees, splattering the landscape with merriment.

"Laughter is good for the soul," Gavreel gulped, "but we really need to compose ourselves and get back to the training center. Jo, it's your turn to take the group through the tessellation. Go back to our seating area at the center."

Jo nodded and took the group straight back to the chairs where they'd started tessellation travel training.

"These three appear as adept at tessellation space travel as they are at morphing into different forms. No reactions at all. Remarkable," Kirron noted.

"That might change when we actually leave their home sector," Michael cautioned. "That's the true test of tessellation reaction."

"No better time than the present to find out," Gavreel declared as she held out a device like the ones they'd seen when they first entered the training center foyer. It resembled an old-fashioned pocket watch, but was about the size of a softball sliced in half, one side flat and the other domed. The case appeared to be a mixture of metals, swirls of gold, silver, bronze, rose, and black around the letters DJG.

"Any of your hands will open this case. It's programmed with your essences. Only the three of you, the three of us, and the programmers can open this particular device. You must keep it with you at all times, but it doesn't matter which teammate carries it. I recommend you take turns," Kirron explained.

Michael continued, "It's called a Dynamic Milestoning Device, DMD for short. It holds records about the tessellation, all tessellation use, and your missions. It's the ultimate recording and memorizing device. When you're given a mission, it will show you your destination and give you as much information as possible about the mission itself. This is its full size. It can shrink for easy transport. Gavreel can show you the features since she's holding it."

"Any of you can open it by passing your hand across the rounded side from edge to edge, then back again, like this." Gavreel slid her hand over the domed side as she had described. The case rolled back and seemed to magically tuck inside the flat side that set on her hand. The internal surface was a shiny black screen. "Show Team DJG's next training tessellation destination and code."

Colorful lights twinkled on the screen then a scene appeared. Something resembling a gigantic golden iceberg rose out of a blue and white checkerboard plain. Nothing else was visible in the scene, just the enormous gold whatever-it-is. The code HHCPC1-1 appeared below the image.

"Oh, you're in for a treat!" Gavreel piped. "Michael, the programmers had you and Jo in mind for this destination."

His smiling nod encouraged her to continue. "We'll leave this sector for your next transfer. We will travel in pairs again, this time to Heavenly Host Choir Practice Chambers One for level-1 singers. Before we depart, I want to show you one more thing. This is how you close the device." She ran her hand along the bottom, the flat side of the device that was not the screen, back and forth just as she had done with the domed side to open it. The domed half rolled out and snapped shut, concealing the screen within. "This is how you shrink the device for easy transport." She tapped three times on the dome. It shrunk to the size of a dime. "You do the same three taps to bring it back to full size when it's minimized. You transport it on the top of your bracelets like this." She set the dime-sized dome on top of her bracelet. It was secured there. "It won't come off until you signal it to release. It's held in place by energy more powerful than any magnet you ever heard about on Earth. It won't come off until one of the six of us does this." Gavreel ran her index finger around the edge of the device three times then tapped the top three times. It lifted off into her hand.

"Here, Dina, bring it back to full size." Gavreel placed the tiny disc on Dina's left palm.

Dina tapped it three times. The disc became the size it had been when they'd seen the image of the golden iceberg thing.

"Now open it," Gavreel told her.

Dina rolled her hand across the dome from one side to the other, then back. Once again, the domed top rolled away and tucked into the bottom. The screen was black.

"Give it the same oral command I did when I showed you how to open it," Gavreel told her.

"Um, show me where Team DJG is supposed to go for the next tessellation training stop, and the code."

Even though the command was not worded exactly the same, the message was clearly received. The screen flashed and colors rolled around, showing the image of the golden monolith that they had seen before. HHCPC1-1 was clearly shown below the structure.

"Outstanding! Now close the device and shrink it."

Dina mimicked the moves she had watched Gavreel demonstrate. The device closed and shrank on her command.

"Attach it to one of your bracelets," Gavreel told her. "See how tight it is when you've attached it. See if you can remove it without signaling with the three circles and three taps."

The DMD stuck so tightly to Dina's bracelet, nothing could pry it off.

"Now remove it the right way and hand it to one of your teammates," Gavreel instructed.

Dina marveled at how it easily it came off when she traced its edge three times with her finger and tapped three times on the top. She handed it to Jo.

Jo and Gabe went through all the steps of opening, closing, shrinking, and enlarging the DMD. They discovered how tightly it stuck to their bracelets until their touch in the correct pattern of commands released it.

"These three appear ready to transfer from this sector for the first time," Michael declared. "Shall we begin our transfers to HHCPC1-1?"

All heads bobbed in enthusiastic agreement.

"Very well. Secure your device."

"Gabe, visualize our destination and the code." Michael placed his hand on Gabe's shoulder. They dematerialized as soon as the words were out of his mouth.

The other pairs followed immediately, reuniting next to the enormous golden structure they'd seen on the tiny screen.

They stood on opaque white squares near the center of the golden structure. Looking closely, they saw notes and other musical symbols swirling around inside the white squares. The squares, lit from within, glowed softly.

A couple of steps any direction took them to the edge of a bordering blue square. Looking closely, they discovered more musical notes and symbols gyrating inside these squares, too. The blue squares were also illuminated from within.

The huge golden structure loomed behind them, with alternating white and blue squares stretching as far as they could see in every direction.

"What are these squares?" Jo asked.

"They're song containment cubes," Michael replied. "They're really astounding. The white cubes contain the notes and lyrics of music that's already been created and shared. The blue cubes are containers for songs that haven't been created by some musical mind, on Earth or elsewhere in the universe. There are more cubes than anyone I know could count. The songs themselves are arranged in a tessellation so they can be easily tracked and delivered to whomever needs the song or the song components. Only the correct individual can receive the song components when the time is right. While a musical mind can take those components and put them together to form great music, the components are from God. There's a cube for every musical creation ever, from the simplest lullabies to the greatest symphonies. There are even containers for silly songs created by children and parodies of other songs. Music from every culture and every language is stored here. Music has been around for eons and is part of many cultures so the number of creations throughout time is vast."

"So every song ever is here?" Jo asked. "Even the ones I just wrote?"

"Yes, every song. The ones you just wrote started as blue squares, but shifted to white when the song was created. They're somewhere in the music tessellation. The tessellation is many layers deep as well as stretching widely as you can see."

"Let's take them inside for a little while," Gavreel suggested. "I'm certain the inside of the practice chamber will be of interest."

She turned and walked to the golden structure. She placed her right wrist against the wall so all of the bracelets on that arm touched the wall. Part of the wall slid away, creating an opening about the size of a double door. "Please, remain silent inside the chamber. Listen, but don't talk or make any noise. This way. Follow me."

Gavreel led the group to another door. This one opened automatically and silently as she approached.

Entering a balcony, they looked down on a chamber resembling an immense cave. A multitude of creatures filled the chamber. All wore colorful flowing robes fastened with golden braided belts. Every kind of instrument imaginable and those that played them formed the bottom row. Choir members stood on giant risers arranged in an oval around the director. While some choir members were human, others were creatures Dina, Jo, and Gabe had never seen before. Quite a few had velvety tentacles growing from the sides of their heads. Others had long trunk-like features centered on their faces. Several resembled birds, but were much larger than any bird on Earth. Mixed groups, male and female humans side-by-side with those who were clearly not human, stood or sat together.

Even more striking than the view of the creature assembly, was the sound they created together. Leonard Cohen's "Hallelujah!" rang from the instruments and mouths of the choir. Velvety tentacles swayed with swirling notes through the perfect acoustics of the chamber, magically caressing and enhancing the notes. An ethereal version of the beloved song saturated the space. They'd all heard the song before, but never as spiritually moving and fulfilling as the sounds that now pierced their souls.

When the choir finished the final verse of the song, Gavreel motioned the others to follow her out the doors that had opened for them a short time before. Reluctantly, the group followed, with Jo bringing up the rear, repeatedly glancing back over her shoulder.

As soon as they'd gathered outside the practice hall, the team's enthusiasm overflowed.

"That was unbelievable. What were those other creatures singing in the choir?" Gabe asked.

"There are great musicians of many faiths across the universe," Gavreel maintained. "You just saw humans joined by melodeons, harmonics, and euphonious."

"Huh?" erupted from Dina, Jo, and Gabe.

"The melodeons are the angels that have head tentacles rather than hair. Those tentacles are as soft as the softest fur and strong enough to move boulders. They actually caress musical notes and help spread them into a wider range than just singing the notes. The effect is quite remarkable, as you just heard."

"All of those creatures are angels, too?" Dina asked.

"Of course. We've told you often that you have much to learn. Angels come in many forms and serve many functions. They come from many places, too. Melodeons have always been great musicians, as have harmonics, and euphonious. When the four groups you just saw come together, the music they produce is, shall we say, otherworldly."

"So, melodeons are the ones with tentacles. What's the name of the ones that look like they have long trunks?" Jo asked.

"Those are the harmonics. Their trunks allow their notes to come out with enhanced depth and layering, sounding like they're created by several singers rather than one. They can sing a solo that sounds like it's being sung by a quartet with soprano, alto, tenor, and bass parts produced simultaneously from one creature."

"So the ones that looked like giant birds are the u-somethings?" Gabe asked.

"They're the euphonious." Gavreel smiled. "Their notes are similar to the melodious trilling of songbirds on Earth. They add a honeyed melodiousness that wraps around the notes of other singers and adds to the beauty."

"That song was definitely beautiful," Team DJG announced, grinning at their unified opinion.

"Leonard Cohen, the writer of that beloved song, is an interesting angel," Kirron declared. "He was an interesting person and continues to be interesting in his work here."

"Why do you feel he's so interesting?" Dina asked.

"Oh, for many reasons. Take the song you just heard. The full version now has fifteen verses. Cohen was a perfectionist even on Earth. He claims that song took him two years to write and originally had eighty verses. More than 100 versions of that song have been recorded on Earth. None compare to the one you just heard though, do they?"

"No, they don't," Jo acknowledged, "and it has been beautifully performed by many people. I always thought the song spoke to every person who heard it."

"Maybe Cohen's own words about the meaning of "Hallelujah" explain that better than anything I could offer," Kirron said. "He contends, 'It explains that many kinds of hallelujahs do exist, and all the perfect and broken hallelujahs have equal value.'."

"What does that mean?" Dina, Jo, and Gabe wondered aloud.

Michael told them, "The word 'Hallelujah' is Hebrew. It means *'praise God'*. Cohen is saying that praises from everyone everywhere have equal value with God. Cohen was Jewish by birth and upbringing, but he became a Buddhist monk and lived in a monastery for five years. He says he never stopped considering himself a Jew, but never met a religion he didn't like. He felt knowing other spiritual systems helped enrich his understanding of his own traditions and practices."

"Our transfer to this sector has been very enlightening, but we must head back to the training center in our sector now. We'll return to the area where we began," Gavreel directed. She placed her hand on Dina's shoulder. "Take us back now."

Their departure was swift, followed closely by Michael and Gabe as well as Jo and Kirron.

"Remove and open your device, Gabe," Kirron ordered as they sat in the chairs in the training center.

Gabe traced the edge three times, tapped three times, then ran his fingers over the domed side to open their DMD.

"Request the next tessellation training transfer destination for Team DJG," Kirron commanded.

Gabe called, "Please, give us the next destination and code for Team DJG's training transfer tessellation."

The black screen flashed. A new image and flashing red code appeared.

Kirron, Gavreel, and Michael shot disbelieving looks at one another before Gavreel murmured, "This is a first."

"It certainly is, but it appears there is little time to waste," Kirron pointed out.

"Team DJG, as you can see by the image on the screen, we're needed immediately. The code continuously flashed red. This will be more than a simple visit to observe. Our help is desperately needed. Your mission is at hand. We'll be with you the entire time, but you must follow directions and use your instincts. Those creatures swarming that school bus have hunted that group of children. They'll soon prey upon the injured inside and use their powers to lead them into the legion of darkness. We must stop that from happening. Secure this device. Join hands. We're going now!"

Kirron barked the code and they were gone.

THE MISSION...

The six landed on the edge of a winding road with a deep ravine on one side. Dense trees stretched along the other side of the road. The school bus they'd seen on the DMD screen laid on its side at the bottom of the ravine. A dozen men and women surrounded the bus, attempting to open locked windows that were now the top side of the vehicle. They ran frantically from one end of the bus to the other searching for a cracked window they could pry open.

"Oh, good. Help's already here," Jo blurted as she looked down on the group surrounding the bus. "They can't get in the bus, though. Since it is lying on the side where the main door is, they'll probably need to break a window or pry open the emergency exit at the back of the bus."

"That's *not* help," Kirron growled. "Those are agents of darkness. The DMD shows only truths. The creatures you saw on the screen are what these really are. They've morphed into human form to lull the children into a false sense of security, to make them believe they're here to help them. They cannot access the bus easily because of an electromagnetic power shield generated by our transfer to this location. It's temporarily enhancing the strength of the windows and side of the bus. It won't last much longer because our transfer is complete. We must get down there and save those children and the driver. Just as the young can become powerful warriors for good, the dark side can make them powerful tools for evil. There are too many souls in that bus who haven't fulfilled their roles on Earth and learned the needed lessons to fulfill their true destinies. We must intervene to stop this hunting party from gaining these souls."

Michael added, "We'll activate enhanced speed and agility, as well as invisibility, to battle the dark agents, but they have tools, too. They'll sense our presence and won't be easily defeated. You haven't been trained for physical battle yet, so the three of us will handle the fighting. We need you to remove the children. Remember how you held Bruno against your body, and your invisibility also made him invisible? You need to lift the children one at a time, shroud them with your invisibility, and carry them out of the ravine, across this road, and behind those trees. Tell them to stay there and stay silent. Hopefully none are too badly injured. If these creatures don't see where you're taking them, they'll be safe there for a short time. Safer than they are in that bus. The gas tank might have cracked in the fall. It might be leaking gasoline. We need to use extreme caution and get those kids out of there."

"Remember, you're masters of trust and gentleness. You'll need those gifts to save these children. You may have to let down your invisibility to talk to them and explain that you're taking them to safety. Time is critical. Remove as many as you can as quickly as you can. Be silent when you're outside the bus and keep them silent or the dark agents will pounce upon you, even when you're invisible. Trust your instincts and remember you're a team," Gavreel told Dina, Jo, and Gabe. "We must go now. Activate speed, agility, and invisibility. Get a window open at the front of the bus while we lure the evil ones to the rear end of the bus. Move quickly and get those kids to safety."

Gavreel, Kirron, and Michael drew dollhouse-size knives from compartments in their gold bracelets. Each pulled the mini-blade three times over the gold bracelet where it had been sheathed. A mighty sword replaced the tiny blade in each warrior's hand. "We go forth in service of God!" rang from their mouths before they disappeared.

Dina, Jo, and Gabe quickly activated enhanced skills before following their trainers into the ravine. Just as they'd said, the warriors lured the angry pack to the rear of the bus. Kirron made himself visible, a target for them to attack. With his flaming sword, he slashed the first man who approached. The snarling man-beast morphed into the hideous gargoyle shape they'd seen on the screen before it dissolved into an ashy pile at Kirron's feet.

Leaping, Kirron ricocheted off the back of the bus, bringing his sword down on the top of another man-beast's head. An agonized howl filled the air as the gargoyle surfaced from the manlike body, collapsing to the ground as black ash.

Two more gargoyles wailed as they descended into ashy heaps, but these two were not close to Kirron, but at the back door of the bus where they'd almost gained access. Gavreel and Michael hit their targets just in time.

Dina, Jo, and Gabe managed to pry open the first window behind the driver's seat.

Jo whispered, "One of us is going to have to go inside and become visible. We have to tell the kids what we're doing and why. We have to convince them not to scream or fight us, or try to get out and up the ravine on their own. We can go faster if one of us lifts kids out the window to the other two who get them up and hidden in the trees."

"Dina's the fastest runner, and I can jump the farthest," Gabe replied, "so maybe we should take the kids to the trees and you should go inside, Jo. Besides, you're so gentle. You might be able to soothe and distract them with a song."

Jo slid inside the open window and deactivated her invisibility. She saw a jumbled mess of backpacks, books, and young people, many of whom were crying or whimpering, their terrified eyes fixed on her.

"It's okay. You're going to be okay. My friends and I are here to help. My name's Jo. You might find this hard to believe, but I'm an angel. My friends are angels, too. We're here to get you out of this bus and up to safety. Really we are."

Most whimpering and crying subsided, but bewildered eyes still stared at this person who'd joined them claiming to be an angel.

Jo continued, "You're in danger here, but my friends and I have come to help you. We need to get you out and away from the bus. You have to be completely silent, though. Do you understand?"

Several heads nodded.

"Good. I'm going to lift you one at a time out this open window where I came into the bus. One of my friends will take you, carry you up, and put you behind some trees on the other side of the road. You have to stay silent up in the trees, too. Okay?"

More head nods.

"One more thing. My friends are invisible right now. You won't be able to see them, but you'll feel them lift you from me. Let them hold you tightly, even if you can't see them; you'll be safe. Let's get going."

Jo reached for the closest child, a boy about ten years old. She softly sang, "In the arms of the angel..." as she hoisted him up. His head and shoulders poked out the open window. Something pulled him from her grasp and the boy disappeared.

Jo reached for the next child, a girl who'd joined her in song. Jo put her index finger to her lips in the silent signal just before she lifted the girl into the arms of her invisible angel friend. "Make your way up to me. I'll lift you and one of my friends will carry you up to the trees. More help's coming, but you have to stay quiet and hidden until it gets here. Come on, now. Come up to Jo."

Jo boosted one child after another, soothing them with her voice and gentle reminders that they'd be taken to safety.

Dina and Gabe carried each child to the forest on the opposite side of the road, setting them down behind the largest trees or thickest bushes before bounding back for another passenger.

Like Kirron, Michael and Gavreel dropped their invisibility shields to lure the creatures farther from the bus. They'd slain eight of the disguised gargoyles. Four of the creatures, who no longer took human form, sprang swiftly from boulders and tree limbs, pursuing the interferers who wielded flaming swords. Baring fangs and slashing at the foes who'd cremated eight of their comrades, these four would not relent. They circled and leaped, matching move-for-move every parry the angel warriors made. Because the battle was far enough behind the bus, Dina, Gabe, and Jo had sufficient time to remove most of the children. All but the last five children and the driver, all of whom were injured and unable to walk, now hid in the forest.

Two gargoyles turned their wrists outward, unfurling whips. Each snap of the whips unleashed a puff of black fog. A rancid odor, like rotting flesh, filled the air. Swinging wildly, the gargoyles' whip snaps drew the attention of all three warriors. The warriors tried to get close enough to cut down the evil scourge. They leaped and parried, but the gargoyles stayed just out of their blades' reach. The gargoyle tried to lasso the swords and pull them from their enemy's hands. They circled and dodged, changing directions constantly. The fury of the whip-wielders siphoned the warriors' attention and efforts. The increasing cloud of black fog made them hard to see. Seeing an opportunity, the other two gargoyles headed back to the bus.

Dina and Gabe had returned to the open window. Jo called up to them, "We can't move the rest of them. They're injured, and I can't move them over the stuff thrown everywhere. We're going to need help to get them out. There are five kids and the driver. I know I couldn't lift the driver, even if he was able to move. He's unconscious. He's hurt pretty bad."

"Do you want to come out here or stay in there?" Dina whispered.

"We shouldn't leave these guys alone in here," Jo maintained. "They're hurt and scared. I need to stay with them until we have more help."

A pair of gargoyles pulled on the rear doors, but they wouldn't budge. Snarling viciously, they slashed at the metal around the door with dagger-like claws. They were totally engrossed in their frenzied attack on the bus. The remaining children screamed as they spied the monsters trying to break into the bus. Jo saw them, too. She levitated and somehow managed to pull the child closest to the back of the bus forward. She set her down by the driver and went back to move another sobbing girl.

"It will be all right. I'm here with you. I know it hurts, but I have to move you away from these doors. Okay? Sing with me, will you? 'In the arms of the angels.' Sing it. 'In the arms of the angels...'"

The girl's muffled repetition of that line of the chorus diminished her sobs. Tugged by a floating angel over shifting piles littering the walkway, she, too, made it to the front of the bus.

Jo managed to move all five injured children forward, setting them near the bus driver who was still motionless, strapped in his seat.

"Oh, man!" Gabe cried. "Two of them are trying to slash into the bus! We have to stop them."

He sprang from the bus and ran toward the side of the ravine, throwing himself at it, slamming his feet against the rocky side. As he ricocheted, he flipped and twisted, bouncing from a boulder on the far side of the bus. His boots ignited. Still invisible, the flames were all that could be seen as his feet slammed into the heads of the gargoyles. Shrieking, they flew back about ten feet, fully engulfed in flames. They tumbled to the ground as two smoldering heaps, now nothing but black cinders. Gabe landed between them, ready to kick again if they tried to get back to the bus.

Their shrieks drew the attention of one of the whip-brandishing gargoyles. With one smooth vault and one snap of his whip in the direction of the flames, the gargoyle immobilized the invisible flame-throwing enemy.

Thrown to the ground and completely wound up in the whip's long strap, Gabe's flaming feet gave away his location. Bound by the strap, he was unable to deactivate the flames or escape. The gargoyle stood over him snarling, sensing he'd captured valuable prey, staying far enough from the thrashing flames to avoid being ignited. His reward would be great if he could escape with just this one.

With just one gargoyle and whip lashing at them, Gavreel, Michael, and Kirron confused it by running in opposite directions, staying just far enough away that the lash never met its mark. Michael's sword did, though. As the creature danced around trying to lasso a sword, Michael sneaked in from the rear and slammed his sword on the gargoyle's skull, reducing the creature to a pile of smoldering dust.

The warriors turned and saw the final whip-wielding gargoyle about ten feet behind bus, snapping at something flaming on the ground. Before they could move toward it, something unseen knocked the creature off its feet. The invisible force pulled the whip from the gargoyle's hand and spun the handle several times.

The surprised beast sprang to its feet and lurched toward its whip. Gruesome fangs snapping, the gargoyle grabbed wildly, attempting to retrieve its weapon. Whatever held the handle sashayed sideways, thwarting its retrieval. The flames sprang away in the opposite direction. Before the gargoyle could decide which one to follow, it felt the whip's strap encircle its throat in a death grip. Flames slammed into its head. The incinerated gargoyle formed the twelfth and final ash mound on the ground near the bus.

Gavreel, Kirron, and Michael vaulted to the rear doors of the bus.

Gavreel called, "They're gone. They're all defeated. Make yourselves visible."

Dina stood holding a scorched whip as Gabe shifted on blazing feet.

"That is a weapon of evil, Dina. It may contain more powers than we realize, especially since it destroyed that gargoyle. It may have absorbed the creature's power before it was cremated. That whip must be eradicated. Throw it on the ground. Gabe, stomp on it before you deactivate your enhanced power," Kirron ordered.

As Gabe stomped on the whip, it came to life, writhing on the ground then winding itself around his feet. The effort was in vain. The flames from Gabe's feet were so intense the whip recoiled and collapsed into a black wisp of ash on the ground.

"Deactivate your enhanced powers, Gabe, so you quell those blazing boots," Kirron barked.

As Gabe dragged his right foot backwards, the flames went out.

"Jo is still inside the bus with five injured kids and the driver. None of them can walk. We can't get them out by ourselves, but we got the rest of them up to the trees like you said," Dina told the trainers who stared at her and Gabe. "Will you be able to help us get them out? They need medical help."

Gavreel spoke first. "With a team of six, we'll move them to safety."

Michael moved toward the back of the bus. "Kirron and I'll remove these rear doors and some of the rear seats. We'll be able to carry the injured more easily on the seats. Pairs of us will able to carry the final passengers out of this ravine."

"Go tell Jo what we're doing. See if she needs help inside while we make a bigger opening to get them out," Gavreel told Dina and Gabe. "Stay at the front of the bus while we're working back here."

Dina and Gabe scampered to the open window and peered inside. Jo sat in a cluster of children singing softly. They held hands and hummed along with her.

"Gavreel says we're going to get the rest of you out. Everybody is supposed to stay at the front of the bus while they work at the back. They're going to get those doors open and take out some the rear seats to carry you up. It won't be long," Gabe announced.

"It's almost over," Dina added. "It looks like you're enjoying Jo's singing. She has a really amazing voice, doesn't she?"

Bobbing heads answered her question.

"Her dad's a great singer, too. He's at the back of the bus taking off the doors. Maybe you'll get to hear him sing, too." Dina continued, "They might sing something together for you."

THE MISSION CONTINUES...

The bus shook and light flooded in as the rear doors were set to the side. Michael climbed inside and pulled one of the rear seats free of its bolts. He handed it down to Kirron, who set it to the side. Michael removed seat after seat, handing each one to Kirron and Gavreel.

When he'd removed five seats, Michael turned toward the front of the bus. "We're ready to get you out of here now. Who wants to go first?"

The children clutched one another and Jo. None of them wanted to reach out to the strange man who hovered close to them. Whimpering erupted again.

"Hi, Dad!" Jo greeted her father.

"Hi to you, too, Pumpkin. It looks like you have some new friends."

"I do. They're scared and hurt, but I know they'll be brave now. This is my dad. His name is Michael. He's a really nice man-angel. You can trust him. He won't hurt you. Kirron and Gavreel are also out there at the back of the bus. They're also very, very nice. You can trust them, too. All six of us are here to help you. You'll let us finish our mission to help you, won't you?"

Timid nods signaled readiness.

"Let's sing while we're in the bus together, Dad. The kids might like that."

"Let's do 'My Favorite Things' since it was always one of your favorites, Jo."

"Raindrops on roses and whiskers on kittens," rose from their lips in perfect harmony as Michael gently lifted the first child. Her

254

legs were swollen and bruised, both likely broken. He held her carefully as he levitated over the debris and out the opening at the rear of the bus. He placed her sideways on one of the waiting seats with her legs stretched out on the seat.

"He's floating!" the remaining children marveled.

"I told you we're angels," Jo reminded them. "We can do lots of cool stuff."

Michael floated to the front of the bus humming "My Favorite Things."

"I'll go next," one boy offered as he raised one of his arms. The other dangled loosely at his side.

Michael joked, "Looks like you have an injured wing there, young man. Let's be careful that we don't hurt you anymore. Put your good arm around my neck and I'll scoop you up."

"Okay, but I don't have a wing. I'm not an angel, Mr. Angel Man. It doesn't look like you have wings, either. Are you sure you're a real angel?"

Michael's laughter filled the bus as he floated out with the boy. "Quite sure, young man, quite sure."

Michael settled the boy on the next seat, noticing that he also had a swollen ankle.

"I'll get another one," Kirron offered as he headed in the opening.

Gavreel told the two children who were now out of the bus, "You're being very brave. You've had such an interesting and scary day, haven't you?"

"Something hit the bus over and over. I couldn't see what it was, but I heard it and felt it. Our bus driver told us to hang on. He was trying to get away, but whatever was hitting the bus wouldn't let us go. Then we got pushed off the side of the road. It was so scary," the girl told her.

"I know that was very scary, but you're safe now. We'll get you out of here and get all the help you need before we leave," Gavreel soothed. "You're all going to be just fine."

Kirron and Michael worked together to remove the remaining children.

Kirron reappeared out the back of the bus cradling a little boy. "Where's Jo? I want Jo," he whimpered.

"She's still here. She's in the bus with the driver. She'll be out here soon. Maybe she can help get you out of this deep ditch. Would you like her to help you get out?" Kirron asked as he set the little boy on the last empty seat.

"Uh huh. She sang to me and it made me feel better. She's real nice."

"Michael and I are going back in to get your bus driver out now. I'll send Jo and the others back here with you. Okay?"

The pair of mighty warriors headed back to the bus for the final evacuation. They found Jo holding the bus driver's hand, singing softly near his ear.

"I want the three of you to go out there with Gavreel and the kids while we work on freeing the driver. Help keep the kids calm. We'll work in pairs to transport them up as soon as we have the driver out. He seems to be stirring, so he may be coming out of unconsciousness," Kirron declared.

Cheering children greeted the men as they set the bus driver, still strapped in his seat, down near them. The driver was definitely stirring and trying to open his eyes.

"We need to get these people out of this ravine and get help for them before it gets dark," Michael announced. "If there was a hunting party of gargoyles in this forest, who knows what else lurks nearby. It will only get more dangerous as darkness descends. Let's slide those rear doors inside the bus before we head out of here."

"Working in pairs, we can transport two children at a time. That leaves two of us here with the remaining children," Gavreel announced. "Let's get started. This little boy had a special request. Jo, get on one side of his seat and Michael you lift the other. The two of you can carry him up near the trees where the other kids are hiding." She winked at the little boy. "See, Jo's going to get you out of here."

"Kirron, why don't you and Dina take up another seat? Gabe and I'll watch over the others until you return."

"Whoa!" the boy cried as his seat rose. "This is so cool!"

"Hold on to the back of the seat," Jo advised. "We're going to go high and fast. We don't want you to fall."

Two seats carried by levitating pairs of angels disappeared over the edge of the ravine. Almost instantly, they were back in front of the waiting children.

"Two down, four to go," Jo announced. "Oops, I think I should say two *up,* four to go."

Giggles told her the kids understood her little joke.

"Who's next?"

Two girls waved their arms and called, "Me, me!" The pale girl and driver said nothing.

"I guess you two'll be round two of up-and-out!" Dina and Jo spieled together. Their giggles mixed with the other two girls' giggles, filling everyone with a moment of relief from the stress they'd all experienced.

Jo and Michael hoisted one seat as Dina and Kirron hoisted the other. Giggling girls clutched the back of their seats as they floated upward until they reached the far side of the road where the rest of the children waited.

"We have to go down one more time and bring up the last two people," Jo told the group. "We'll be right back." She and her teammates disappeared over the far edge of the road.

"Michael and I'll lift the driver's seat together. He's heavier than the children. Gavreel, why don't you and Gabe get the last child up? Dina and Jo, you levitate yourselves up and out of here," Kirron announced.

"Let's go. The sun's getting pretty low. The kids are already scared and the dark will make it worse. We need to secure the help they need," Michael voiced as he placed his hands under one side of the driver's seat. Kirron did the same on the opposite side. They were up and over the edge almost instantly.

Gavreel and Gabe set their load near the others. There were forty-three pairs of eyes on them. Only the driver did not stare. His eyes flicked open then closed again. He was not really back with them. His consciousness swirled just below the surface of his eyelids, trying to free itself and come back to the children in his charge.

"We need to get human rescue teams here right away," Gavreel reminded them. "This bus is more than an hour late getting these children home. Surely someone from the bus company or the police will be nearby searching along its route."

"Do any of you have a cell phone?" Jo asked the group of watchful children. "We need to call 911 and get help."

"We're not allowed to have cell phones at our school," one of the girls told her. "If we bring them, they go to the office and our parents have to pick them up from the principal."

"Maybe the driver has one. I'll check his pockets," Michael did a quick pat down of his shirt and pants. He didn't have one, either.

"There's a radio on the bus," one boy offered.

"It won't work from deep in that ravine, especially with the bus on its side and the antenna pointing out rather than up," Kirron replied.

"I could run up the road and see if I can flag down a car. The driver would probably have a cell phone and could call for help," Dina suggested. "I might be able to get them to come here and help."

Kirron stared at her. "You can't go anywhere alone on your first mission. It simply isn't done."

"How about if I go with her?" Gabe offered. "That would leave four of you here with the kids and we'll get help. We'll either flag down the first vehicle we see, or go to the first house we come to down this road. It shouldn't take too long."

"That might work. Usually, no novice would go anywhere alone, or in pairs, on a first mission. But then, no novice has ever been sent on a mission like this before either. We do need as many armed fighters as possible to guard these children until help arrives," Kirron mused.

"Gabe and I can do it," Dina affirmed. "We'll just go find someone to call 911 and come right back."

"Stay together. Get right back here as soon as you have found someone to call for help. Watch out for one another and use your instincts. If something doesn't feel right to you, go invisible and move away together. Hold hands so you stay together when you're invisible. Don't get separated. You saw those gargoyles in human form. There may be more of them or other things nearby. Be careful. Go!" Kirron waved his hand down the road to signal which way they should head.

Gabe and Dina activated enhanced speed and agility once more. They practically flew down the road and were out of sight before anyone could say anything else.

MORE HELP...

Gavreel, Kirron, and Michael herded the children near the ones on bus seats, just a short distance back from the side of the road. They spread themselves along the backside of the group, constantly scanning the woods.

The children were getting restless and fussy. Some were crying again, others whining. "I want to go home!" or "I want my mom!" flowed from one mouth after another.

Jo noticed Gavreel, Kirron and her dad had posted themselves behind the children, placing themselves between the children and the woods that had been their hiding place a short time ago. They guarded the group, watchful and expectant of something. She didn't know what, but she sensed danger lurked nearby. The lengthening shadows added to the uneasiness everyone felt.

Jo settled herself on the ground in front of the group. "I bet all of you know the song 'Old MacDonald Had a Farm'. It's so much fun to sing. You older kids probably think you're too old for this song, but you probably make the best animal sounds. I know you'll help me with the song. I'll bet there's lots of good singers in this group. Let's do it together. The little kids and I'll sing the song and you big kids supply the animal sounds when we get to that part. Okay?"

Jo smiled, "Here we go!" Her angelic voice lifted with the sweet voices of little ones. "Old MacDonald had a farm, e, i, e, i, o...." Hearty cow, pig, and chicken sound effects had everyone laughing. Horse, duck, and sheep sounds added to their distraction and level of laughter. By the time they'd sung the song enough times to add dog, goat, and rooster sounds, everyone had overcome their crankiness and fear.

"That's so good! You guys sound like a choir! I never heard that song sounding so good," Jo oozed. "Let's play a game now. I always like to play I Spy. It makes you look carefully and choose good words to describe the thing you see. I'll start. See if you can figure out what I am describing."

Jo looked around the area then began, "I spy with my very own eyes, something that's green."

Guesses flew at her, but none were right. Not the grass, not the tree leaves, not the clump of weeds, not the boy's jacket or the girl's pants.

"You need another hint," Jo proclaimed. "I spy with my very own eyes something that's green and is usually one place, but is now somewhere else."

More guesses. Not his fluorescent green shoes. Not her shirt stripes.

"Oh, I bet it's the bus seats. They're green and they're usually in the bus, but now they're here," the oldest-looking child suggested.

"You're right! Now you get to choose something else and describe it so the others can try to figure it out," Jo told her.

Jo distracted the children as Gavreel, Kirron, and Michael kept vigilant watch of the woods. Lengthening shadows merged into deepening darkness as the sun sank toward the horizon. Twilight loomed.

Gabe and Dina ran a couple of miles up the winding side road. Dense trees lined both sides of the road after they rounded the first bend, but they saw very little else. They hadn't seen one vehicle or house. Finally, they came to the intersection of a main highway. Vehicles zipped by in each direction.

"Maybe we can get one of these cars or trucks to stop if we wave our arms," Gabe suggested. "Let's stand here before the turn off for the side road and see if someone will stop for us."

They moved a short distance down the shoulder and started waving their arms. Several cars flew by. One blew its horn as it passed.

"This isn't working," Dina cried. "We have to get them to stop somehow. Maybe if we're out in the road and they think they're going to hit us they'll stop. We know we can get out of the way, but they don't know that."

"That might work, but what if the driver loses control and crashes. We'd be the cause of that person's accident, or maybe even death."

Dina cried, "Kirron told us to trust our instincts. Mine are telling me we need to do whatever it takes to stop a car or truck and get help before it's totally dark."

As she finished her statement, Dina strode to the middle of the highway. She straddled the center lane line, waving her arms and shouting, "Stop! Stop!"

Squealing brakes sounded from both directions of the highway. A car heading one direction and a plumbing van headed in the opposite direction jerked to abrupt stops.

"Get out of the road!" an angry voice boomed. "You're going to get hit."

"Help! You have to help," Dina cried. "There's been a school bus accident up this side road about two miles. Kids are hurt and the driver's hurt really bad. He's unconscious. Please, call 911."

Both vehicles pulled onto their respective shoulders and flipped on emergency flashers.

"Get out of the road, girl," the voice called again, a little softer this time. "Come over here. You can tell me why you're in the middle of the road acting like a crazy person. You can sit in my van and rest if you want. I'll drive you wherever you need to go."

Dina moved to the other side, standing in front of the car that had stopped near Gabe. The woman in the car was already on her cell phone. The man in the plumbing van called across the highway, "Tell me again what happened."

"There's been a school bus accident. People are hurt. My friend and I ran down here to get help. The wreck is about two miles up this winding road." Dina pointed to the road that wound into the forest. "Please, call 911!"

The woman lowered her window a few inches. "I'm on the phone with 911. I gave them this location and told them you say there's a wrecked school bus about two miles up this side road. They're sending the highway patrol here."

"Thank you. Thank you so much. We need to get back to the kids. Tell the officer it's about two miles up this road. There are forty-three kids and the driver. They need help right away."

"The 911 dispatcher says for you to wait right here until the officer arrives," the woman relayed. "It should be less than ten minutes."

"We have to get back," Gabe explained. "We said we'd come right back. Just point the officers up that road and tell them to go about two miles. They'll see the children. We got them all out of the ravine. They're right by the side of the road. They'll see them."

"Out of the ravine? You got them out of a ravine?" The woman was not sure she was believing what she was hearing.

Dina and Gabe were already on the run. They rounded the first bend in the side road and disappeared from sight.

"Did you hear what that boy said?" the woman called across the highway to the plumber, who still sat on the opposite shoulder.

"He claims they got the kids and the driver out of a ravine and to the side of the road. Those kids must be on something. So many teenagers are these days," the plumber snorted. "That girl stands in the middle of the road with oncoming traffic, then says things like they got kids out of a wrecked school bus down in a ravine. It's just nuts."

"They seemed serious. They didn't seem high to me," the woman remarked. "Did you see how fast they ran?"

"Maybe they're high school athletes or something. They're wearing matching clothes."

Fiery ribbons of scarlet and gold danced in the sky as the sun dipped to the horizon. Within minutes, the red and gold dancers surrendered to a growing platoon of purple clouds. The clouds had invaded the evening sky slowly from all directions, but had now taken control as the sun disappeared. Only its final glow kept total darkness at bay for a few minutes longer.

"That's a gorgeous sunset," Dina observed. "But that means it's almost dark. I hope the cops get here before it's dark."

"I hope there's nothing else in these trees we have to worry about," Gabe replied. "It's already pretty dim and there are lots of night sounds coming from the trees."

"Is that a bear over by that tree?" Dina whispered.

"That's no bear. It's huge. I don't know what it is, but it's no bear. Take my hand. Go invisible!"

No sooner had Gabe uttered the words and the pair had disappeared, the beast charged from the tree where Dina had spotted it. It snapped and roared. Standing on hind legs in the spot where it had just seen the pair of runners, it towered about ten feet tall. It sniffed the air.

Dina and Gabe were already several enhanced strides down the road away from the beast.

The thing turned circles, checking the scent in every direction, clearly agitated that it had missed its prey. The scent came from both directions, confusing the creature. It was unsure which way to search for the runners who'd evaded it.

"We have to get back and tell the others about that thing," Dina muttered. "We have to go as fast as we can the rest of the way."

"I've been going as fast as I can since we left," Gabe told her. "I'm sorry if I'm slowing you down, but Kirron ordered us to hold hands and stay together if we sensed something and had to go invisible. I'm not letting go of you."

"No, no, I wasn't suggesting that," Dina protested, "but that thing we just saw is really dangerous. We have to get back and warn them. Those kids can't go invisible and we can't shroud all of them. Gavreel, Kirron, and Michael may have to fight it like they did the gargoyles. They have to know."

"We're almost back," Gabe told her. "See that old dead tree that's fallen? That was just around the first bend in the road when we left. We should see them as soon as we to get by it and around the curve."

They rounded the curve in a few more strides. They heard laughing children before they saw them in the near-dark.

"I'll go talk to Kirron and the others as soon as we get back," Dina whispered. "We don't want to tell the kids."

They removed their invisibility as they stepped off the road behind Jo. Dina sidestepped the group of children, headed back to the elders of their team.

"I need to tell you some things," she murmured. "Where the children won't hear." She walked several steps toward the trees.

Gavreel, Kirron, and Michael followed her, exchanging those looks Team DJG had come to know meant their trainers were all thinking the same thing.

Dina told them about the creepy man in the plumber's van, and the woman who called 911, and the beast they'd spotted on their way back.

"It sounds like you saw a bugbear very close to this location," Gavreel told her. "They're very dangerous and very evil creatures. Their favorite prey is children. They're often found near a horde of goblins. We may have more visitors very soon. I hope not, but we need to be ready."

"You did well, Dina. You three need to return to invisibility. One of you should position yourselves on each side of the group and one at the front. One of us will be between each of you forming a ring around the children. Tell Gabe and Jo to go invisible, engage enhanced agility and speed, and spread out. Be watchful," Kirron rasped. "Go now and get them in position."

Dina whispered in Jo's ear, who stood and looked down the road rather than at the children. Dina then whispered in Gabe's ear. He nodded and moved to the side closest to the direction from which they'd just come. Dina moved to the far side of the group.

Jo turned back to the group of children who were now barely visible in the waning light. "Dina and Gabe got a lady to call 911. Police officers should be here soon. Stay completely quiet until you see the police. Okay? You might not see us, but we'll still be here watching over you. You've been very good and very brave. I'm proud of every one of you. Stay quiet just a little longer. Put your hand up over your own mouth as a reminder not to make a sound." Then she joined her teammates in invisibility mode.

Gavreel, Kirron, and Michael moved into position between Dina, Jo, and Gabe. They faced outward, scanning the surrounding tree line and road, full-sized swords in hand. They, too, made themselves invisible.

Their eyes adjusted to the darkness that descended, but they could see very little. The darkness robbed each of them of their best sense. It seemed to have dissolved everything, like it was never there at all. The curtain of blackness blotted out the trees, the road, the waving grasses. Paralyzing fear gripped the children. The warriors felt that fear and heard the children's hearts racing.

Through the blackness came the glow of red eyes, like distant taillights swaying at the road's edge. These glowing eyes were higher than any of the warriors stood, at least two feet higher. They moved with a slight swagger, as if the unseen body prowled with untold confidence, the confidence of a night predator who enjoyed its kills.

Kirron sent a mental message that flashed in their minds: "The bugbear is here. We will fight again to protect these children."

With swift acceleration and a springing motion, the red eyes headed toward the children. The relative quiet of the night forest amplified the sound of clawed feet scraping over the rocky edge of the road.

They all heard that scraping sound. They also heard the rustling in the tall grasses near the trees, the trees and grasses they'd seen before darkness had erased everything visual from their existence.

The bugbear's charge was thwarted just before he reached the closest child. Something unseen slammed into his chest, knocking him backwards onto the ground. The creature rose, untangling limbs to slash at the air and whatever had done this to him. His nascent yelps filled the night air with his rage.

He charged again, roaring, swinging his arms wildly, no longer concerned about a stealthy approach. His enormous fangs snapped with each bellow, a sound even more menacing than his scraping claws or fearsome roar.

Slammed again, from the side this time, the creature landed in a heap. This blow struck the side of his head, knocking him onto the road. He found his feet once more, but his steps were more stagger than swagger now. There was no way he was giving up on this fine crop of children just waiting to be picked. He hadn't had a feast like this in centuries, not since wiping out that village long ago.

The bugbear charged again, this time advancing in a zigzag. Impressively agile for such a large creature, he changed directions quickly and smoothly. Determined to snatch one of the tasty morsels laid out as a banquet for him, he headed to the far side of the group.

As he pounced at his victim, a child stretched out on some kind of seat, he glimpsed a shimmery outline of a tall man holding a sword. This swordsman stood to the side of his prey. The sword burst into flames as the man stepped in front of the child. Sparks and flames blinded him as the swordsman swung his weapon toward his head. The bugbear ducked, trying to save himself from the flaming thrusts. He staggered back a few steps. Something unseen behind him slammed into him once more. The force of the rear blow threw him into the thrusts of the blazing blade. Its sharpness and heat cut through his body. One final wail, this one of surprise and anguish, filled the night air as the beast crashed to the ground. His flaming body became a bizarre campfire, burning quickly and brightly, scattering just enough light to see the rush from the grasses.

The children's screams reverberated from the trees that surrounded them. A horde of small creatures swinging bows and arrows moved toward them chanting, "Human children taste best!" There was no doubt about their intention.

"Pukwudgie!" Gavreel cried as the horde advanced. "We need to put up a shield to block their poison arrows!"

She and Michael tapped the tips of their swords together. Bolts of lightning flashed in all directions. Their blades held the electrical sparks as they backed away from one another, widening the protective shield between the children and the encroaching Pukwudgie.

The chant changed to angry cries as one after another shouted, "Spread out! They can't block all of us!"

Out of nowhere, flamethrowers tore through the Pukwudgie ranks. Several crumpled in flaming heaps. The flamethrowers seemed to be everywhere at once, bouncing from front to rear and from side to side through their horde. Arcs of fire cut down others as they charged. Chaos reigned as more and more fell to blazing ends. No one knew who'd be struck next or from which direction. Their arrows were worthless against these fiery foes. They retreated into the trees as bright lights and wailing sirens screeched up the road. Too many enemies to fight this night.

The children waved and shouted, "Here we are! Here we are!"

Headlights and spotlights pierced the night, revealing the strange roadside encampment. Disbelieving eyes scanned the scene. A fire smoldered at one side of the band of waving children. Six green school bus seats formed an arc behind the waving children, each seat holding an injured person.

An officer spoke into a radio. "Code 8. HP at the scene of the school bus MVA on the park road off highway 12. Two cars have responded. Many juveniles on scene. We need buses. It looks like there are at least six serious injuries."

"Copy that. Buses and back-up en route."

Six invisible angels floated above them, listening and watching, but saying nothing and giving no sign they were there.

THE INVESTIGATION…

Pandemonium reigned as more and more emergency vehicles arrived on the scene. Sirens screamed more than the arrival of police and ambulances, as if sensing there was more here than met the eye. Strobing red and blue lights pulsed hope in the terrifying darkness. They were lighthouses signaling help, beacons pointing the way home. Adult voices shouted directions and asked questions as men and women scurried among the children.

A trooper pulled the oldest looking child over to the side asking, "I'm Trooper Powers. I'd like to talk to you if I might. What happened here? Tell me how you all got out here."

The girl stammered, "We, we were on our way home from school, on the school bus. That's the driver over there on that seat, the man the ambulance people are looking at right now. I'm not usually on this bus, but I went to school with my brother today."

"Can you tell me what happened here?" the trooper asked again.

"We were taking the rangers' kids to their bus stop a little bit farther up this road. Several of them get on and off the bus at that stop every day. The driver turns around at the wide spot where the bus stop is and goes back out to the highway after they get off."

"Where's your bus now?" the trooper prodded.

"It's across the road, at the bottom of the ravine. It's on its side. We were all trapped inside."

"Do you realize what you're saying?" the officer asked gently. "You're telling me that the bus is on its side at the bottom of a ravine, yet all of you are up here on the side of the road."

"Yes, sir, that's right. We'd probably still be there, too, if the angels hadn't come to save us."

270

"Angels? You believe angels saved you?"

"I know they did. There were six of them. Three of them were older, like my parents' age, and three of them were lots younger."

"You've been through a terrible ordeal," Powers responded. "What you're describing isn't possible."

"It is possible. I was there. I saw it all. The angels could make themselves invisible, or they could be seen. They got us out and they protected us from some bad creatures. I don't know what those things were, but they were trying to get at us and the angels fought them. They really did." The girl talked faster and faster, trying to relay what had happened to the disbelieving officer.

"You need a good rest from all of this. You'll think more clearly after a good night's rest," the trooper told her.

"Go look down in the ravine if you don't believe me. The bus is there on its side. The window behind the driver's seat is open. That's where Jo lifted most of the kids out of the bus to Dina or Gabe. They carried us up and out of the ravine. They told us to stay hidden in those trees back there and stay quiet."

"You're not making sense, miss. No one could get you out of that ravine without special equipment. It would take a whole team of emergency workers to lift you out of there."

"I'm telling you, the angels got us out. The older ones fought the beasts with huge swords and fire. I was one of the last ones out. I saw the angels fighting those things. When they killed one, it burned up and fell into a pile of black ash. You'll find a bunch of those piles down there with the bus. Jo told us two of the creatures tried to claw into the back doors of the bus. She stayed inside the bus longer because the driver and the last five kids were hurt. That's when those monsters tried to claw into the bus. I bet there's slash marks from their claws on the back of the bus."

"You should rest. We'll talk more later," the officer suggested.

"Jo told us they took the back doors off the bus and took out those seats to carry the injured people. They set the injured kids on the seats and carried them up. The seats are right there. I know you can see those," the girl continued.

"Yes, I see the seats with the kids and driver. You're right about those people being hurt. The ambulances will take them to the hospital. The paramedics will check all of you. Lots of you probably bumped your heads," Powers replied.

"Dina and Gabe ran down to the main highway to get someone to call for help. They can run really, really fast. That's why you're here now. They went down there and got someone to call 911. When they got back, some other weird things tried to get us. The angels fought them, too."

The first two ambulances pulled out, headed back to the main road. They'd loaded the still-unconscious driver and pale girl who faded in and out of consciousness. Sirens screamed as they streaked out of sight.

"You should let the paramedics check you soon. See, they're checking all the kids."

"I can tell you don't believe me, but I'm telling the truth. The angels got us out of the wrecked bus, and out of the ravine, and they fought off the monsters that tried to get us. The bad creatures up here were different from the ones in the ravine though. The one that showed up right after Dina and Gabe got back was huge. It was hairy and had sharp claws and huge fangs. It burned up when they killed it, too. That's what's left of it over there. It's still burning a little bit." She pointed to the glowing embers.

"Where are these angels now?" the officer asked. "I'd like to talk with them, too."

"I don't know. Maybe they're still here and invisible, or maybe they already left. They told us they'd stay with us until help arrived. You're here now, so they might be gone."

"I see. Angels help only until mortal humans arrive to take over."

"They promised they'd stay until help arrived and they did.

Right before you got here, they fought some little beasts that ran out of the woods. Those creatures had bows and arrows; they tried to shoot us. The angels put up some kind of lightning shield so the arrows couldn't hit us. Those things burned up, too, when the angels' fire killed them. It looked like there were two flamethrowers and some constantly-moving swoosh of flame. I looked away when you got here. When I looked back, the creatures and the flames were gone."

"All right, that's enough for now. Let's get you over to one of the paramedics." The officer herded the girl to the closest ambulance.

Powers went to his car and grabbed the high intensity flashlight used for searches in the woods. Walking to the far side of the road, he shot the beam back and forth into the depths of the ravine. He glimpsed the bright yellow color of a school bus at the end of his finger of light. It was hard to tell in the dark, but it appeared to be about forty or fifty feet below the road. The ravine's rocky, steep sides required experienced rock climbers with proper climbing gear to get in and out using only manpower.

"Hey, Connor, over here," the trooper called.

The other trooper made his way across the road.

"That kid I interviewed told me her school bus was in the ravine and that angels had carried them up and over to those trees."

"The boy I was talking to said the same thing," Connor claimed. "He mentioned a whole lot of weird stuff about fighting with fire and evil monsters trying to get them. He kept talking about someone named Jo who came into the bus with them. Maybe there was a carbon monoxide leak or something and the kids are hallucinating."

"Look down there." The trooper pointed his beam at the marooned school bus.

"Let's have a look at those smoldering logs. The girl said that's where the angels killed some huge monster."

The troopers sauntered over to the still glowing remains of the bugbear. The pile was mostly ash, but they spotted one solid piece on the edge of the pile.

"What do we have here?" Connor pondered as he kicked a gleaming shard out of the cinder mound.

The remnant was too hot to handle, but clearly resembled a fang. A huge fang. A fang the size of a butcher knife's blade.

"What do you make of this?"

"I don't know what to make of it at this point. We have a lot of work ahead of us before we figure out what really happened here. It's going to be an all-nighter, that's for sure. We need to bag that thing and get it to the lab."

Hour after hour passed as the first responders handled the school bus accident. Most children, except those with serious injuries, had been questioned before being transported to town. The bus driver came in and out of consciousness, but could remember nothing. Three children were hospitalized. Most were treated and released to their parents with strict instructions about watching for concussions. The first girl transported to the hospital was still too weak to speak with officers. She was listed in critical condition.

Upon questioning, child after child declared the bus was at the bottom of the ravine because something had pounded on it and pushed it sideways. They all spoke of monsters trying to get them and angels saving them. Every child mentioned the angels' swords and fire. They talked about Jo, how she came on the bus, stayed with them, and sang to them. Most told how Jo lifted them out the window so the other angels could carry them up and out of the ravine. Four children said they were carried up on one of the bus seats by two angels because they couldn't walk. Forty-two children told basically the same story. Children are known for vivid imaginations, but they couldn't all imagine the same thing.

The park access road was closed to traffic. Only police vehicles and an integrated tow truck used to transport buses and large trucks had been allowed up the winding road. Some officers had spent over twelve hours at the scene.

Darkness began surrendering to light. Birds awakened, their calls announcing the start of a new day. Streaks of pink blurred with blue above the silhouetted trees. The treetops to the east donned crowns of gold as the sun inched higher. Sunlight drenched the sky, illuminating some of the crooks and crevices of the land, but not yet returning full vibrancy to the world. Soon, though, everything would be clear. Maybe one of the gifts of this new day would be answers to the questions about what had really happened here.

A highway patrol SUV eased up. It passed the scene and parked along the shoulder, at the head of the row of six cars that has been here for hours. The day brightened quickly as the forensic photographer ambled back to the scene, carrying a camera with a huge lens and other equipment. He wore a helmet and climbing harness with a specialty climbing rope looped over one shoulder.

"We should get clear shots of the scene with the morning light. I'll shoot the ravine first since the tow truck is here to remove the bus. I'll start from the road edge, shooting the bus as seen from the road. I'll rappel down and take close shots before the bus is lifted. I'm assuming you want me to attach the tow truck's cable while I'm down there. I'll do this area after I climb back up." He gestured to the far side of the road.

In a remarkably short time, a voice from the ravine called up, "I'm finished down here. The tow cable is attached and I'm reattaching my gear right now. I'll start the climb up in a minute."

"You won't believe what's down there," he asserted as he freed himself from his climbing rope and detached it from the tree. "You need to see some of the pictures here on my camera," the forensic photographer declared. "A picture's worth a thousand words, as they say."

"See this one?" he asked as he brought a picture up on the small screen. "There are twelve of these black piles of ash down there. Most of them are way behind the bus, a hundred feet or so, but two of them are only ten feet behind the back end of the bus. Every pile is about the same size, twelve inches across and twelve inches high. I took the measurements while I was there. I bagged a sample of each pile, too." He rummaged in his deep pocket and pulled out twelve small bags of black ash, each one labeled and numbered by their distance from the bus. He handed them to Trooper Powers.

"This symbol is also on the ground near the rear of the bus. I have no idea what it is, but it's burned into the ground." He flipped to another picture and showed the image to the surrounding officers. They stared at the symbol he showed on his screen.

He scanned his collection of photos and stopped on another one. "This is burned into the ground farther behind the bus." He turned the screen so the others could see the image he'd captured.

"I've seen that before. My sister-in-law has a tattoo like that on her arm. She says it means God is greater than the highs and lows. She got it after her sister died," one of the female troopers offered. "Why would anyone burn that into the ground down in a ravine?"

"Even more important than why is *who* did it and *when*," Connor murmured.

"There's another one fairly close to the bus." The photographer scrolled through the images in his camera. "Here it is."

"This investigation is getting stranger by the minute. I feel like we have more questions now than when we started," Powers remarked. "Now we have symbols branded into the ground as well as all the witnesses' talk of monsters and angels."

"I'm going to shoot this area between the road and trees now," the photographer announced. Help with measuring would be appreciated. The tow truck can start the removal any time."

They heard the rumble of the tow truck's winch and a crashing noise. One officer shouted that the bus was upright. More grinding noises told them the winch was doing its slow steady job of raising the bus from its resting place. Soon it would bump over the edge of the precipice where it had spent last night. Surely there'd be more answers when they actually got to examine the bus.

The men spread a few feet apart and walked slowly toward the trees, examining the ground with each step. They saw a number of scorch marks just behind the seats. These didn't seem to be a design, more like a burnt barrier of some kind. The photographer recorded the image from several angles. Connors and Powers measured the burn mark, twenty feet long but only about six inches wide. Another mystery.

As they advanced toward the trees, they spotted more burnt ground. Charred lines scattered across the clearing near the trees, as well as many piles of black ash. These piles were smaller than the ones in the ravine or the one by the bus seat, but there were lots of them.

"I'm going to climb up in that tree and try to get some shots of this area from above," the photographer announced.

Powers and Connor stood by the trunk an old maple tree and watched the athletic forensic photographer scale its branches. The maple stood out from the hemlocks and pines that were most prevalent in these woods. A few deciduous trees dotted the landscape in this area, but most were evergreens. Luckily, this old maple had large enough branches to support the weight of a man as he climbed high in its boughs.

"Unbelievable. This is really unbelievable." The comment was accompanied by repeated clicks of the camera's shutter.

He jumped to the ground from a low branch. "There's another

symbol burned into the ground in this area. I don't know what it is, but I zoomed in on it from up there. There are lots of the little black spots, too. It looks like there was an invasion of polka dots in this area. I bet there's at least fifty of the black spots around this symbol." He turned the screen so Powers and Connor could see what he'd seen:

"That symbol's pretty big. I bet it measures eight or ten feet across in every direction. There's a perfect circle in the center with eight burnt spikes feeding out from the circle."

Powers interrupted, "It looks like they have the bus up. Let's have a look at it before the tow truck takes off. We'll finish up this area when the bus has been hauled out."

The men walked back to the road and stared at the maimed bus. The left side looked perfectly fine. The first window behind the driver's area was wide open, but all the others on that side were closed and intact. The right side of the bus was wrinkled and dented along the entire side. Every window was cracked or broken. The rear emergency doors were off, stuffed inside and wedged under some seats. The five seats closest to the rear exit were gone. Holes where bolts used to hold the seats in place clearly marked where they belonged. Deep gashes scarred the back of the bus, surrounding the opening where the doors used to be.

Peering inside, the troopers saw a mountain of jackets, books, backpacks and other kid paraphernalia near the front of the bus, filling the area where the driver's seat should've been. The winching upward had thrown everything on the floorboards to the front. The effect was a sculptural depiction of kid chaos, a reminder of the children who'd been inside this bus a few hours ago, the ones who'd survived whatever-it-was that had happened here.

The photographer shot pictures of the bus, capturing its condition as it arrived at the top of the ravine from every angle. "That's all we need of the bus. Are we going to put those seats over there back in the bus before it's towed off?"

"We shouldn't leave them here, so, yeah, I guess so," Powers agreed.

Working in pairs, the troopers carried the seats and hoisted them into the back of the bus. When all were loaded, they secured the open end of the bus with a tarp and several strong cords. "That should keep anything from flying out as the bus is transported," Connor declared as he inspected the cables that secured the load.

"Let's work in pairs to gather evidence in the area near the trees. We'll flag each small pile of ash so we can count how many there are; then we'll measure each pile and other burn marks while he's taking the photos. Watch for any other evidence you might come across in the grass. Be careful where you step. The sooner we get this last zone thoroughly searched and recorded, the sooner we can get out of here."

"Copy that," the others agreed as they walked toward the grassy area. Little orange flags began to speckle the area. Fifty-three flags marked mounds of black ash. Every measurement was close to the same size, six inches in diameter and six inches high, about the size of a balled-up fist. Most were near the burned symbol in the center, but a few were near the perimeter.

"Hey, look at this," Connor called. "What do you think it is?" He pointed to an object in a clump of tall grass, about a foot from a fist of ash.

"It looks like something we need pictures of where it lies before we tag it," the photographer said as he started clicking pictures.

"It looks like a miniature bow. It's only about a foot long, but you can see the upper limb, the handle with an arrow rest, and the lower limb. There's a string notch and a tight cord. Definitely a bow, but it's so small. I've never seen anything like this. It doesn't look like a toy. It looks like a real weapon, just shrunken. I wonder if there are any arrows in the area? They'll be tough to spot in this tall grass."

"Let's search this area carefully. Everybody, see if we can find any arrows to go with this bow," Powers commanded. "We're about to wrap it up here, but we need to see if there's anything else out of the ordinary."

Troopers fanned out, walking slowly, separating the grass with each step.

"Hey, come here! I found something." The trooper stood next to a feathers-fletched shaft about the size of a pencil embedded in the ground. No one could tell how long it was. The exposed part certainly resembled an arrow.

Multiple pictures recorded the object's location and angle of entry into the ground. When the photographer finished, Powers carefully pulled the shaft free. It was about a foot long. Sinew attached the arrowhead, a razor-sharp shard of flint, expertly chipped into a killing tool, the kind Native Americans used for hunting ages ago.

"This isn't a modern arrow. This bow and arrow only add to the mystery," Powers declared. "I wonder if we'll ever get to the bottom of this. Maybe when we go through all the evidence and pictures, we'll be able to sort it out. Let's gather those markers and load the evidence in my car. We're done here."

WHAT NOW?...

"Come back to visible mode now that they're all gone," Kirron directed the group. "We need to do a few things before we depart."

He stood before the group. "First, let me say that all three of you handled yourselves admirably. I've never been on a mission with novices who've not finished training. It just isn't the way missions are run, but as you saw, we were deployed to a very serious situation very quickly."

"You three really performed incredibly," Gavreel and Michael chorused.

Dina, Jo, and Gabe smiled at their trainers, reveling in the praise and confidence they had in them. "What do we have to do now?" The trio snickered. Their synchronicity still worked on Earth!

"Now we're going to examine the scene," Kirron told them. "We'll start with the ravine. Look at the burned areas from above. Tell me what you see and what you think it means."

The six hovered over the ravine, about halfway down. They could view the ground well from this height, but would not be visible to anyone driving on the road.

"Let's start with that one." He pointed to the symbol closest to the back of the bus. "Dina, you created that one when you freed Gabe from the gargoyle's whip. His flaming boots were your medium, but your spinning motions to free him created this symbol."

From above, they studied the first symbol the photographer had shown the other troopers on his camera screen. A black mound was off to one side.

"It looks like four hearts pushed together, sort of making a four-leaf clover, but with a little shamrock inside each heart. Is a cross formed in the middle where the four hearts press together?" Dina speculated. "I don't know what it is or what it means, though. I wasn't trying to make a design. I was just trying to save Gabe from that thing, just unwinding the whip."

Gavreel imparted, "We've told you that you have much to learn. Symbology is one of those things. Many, many symbols have been used over the ages. You need to learn how to recognize and read signs and interpret the messages they carry. All faiths on Earth use symbols, as do many from other parts of the universe. Some symbols are used by many groups and some by just one group. This symbol is special, a powerful message."

"What is it?" Dina, Jo, and Gabe asked.

Gavreel continued, "This mark is an Adinkra Symbol. Adinkra Symbols are from the Ashanti and Akan cultures of Africa. There are over 400 known symbols and they all mean something different. They're found on rocks and buildings. Now they're popular in art and on fabric. This particular one is called Nyame Dua. It translates as *God's tree*, or *tree of God*, a symbol of God's presence and protection."

"So God was with us?" Dina murmured.

"God is always with us," Gavreel declared. "Always. Sometimes the power of God flows through us in order to intensify our effectiveness through our actions. Your instincts and actions to save Gabe were totally selfless. You haven't been trained for battling nor have you been issued weapons, yet you slew a gargoyle, a powerful and wicked creature from the darkness, an experienced fighter with a powerful weapon. God's presence and protection through you is undeniable. The three of you protected those children."

"Then there's this one." Michael pointed to another black design seared into the ground. It was a few feet from the spot where the bus had been. "Gabe made this one when he killed the two gargoyles clawing the back of the bus. His flaming kick knocked them out here. Those ash heaps just outside the symbol's two curved blades are where the two gargoyles ceased to be."

Everyone stared where Michael pointed.

"Any ideas what this one is?"

Shaking heads confirmed that Team DJG had no idea.

Michael went on, "This was the first symbol Gabe's flaming feet created. It's another Adinkra Symbol. It's actually a funerary message, a message of transitioning. This symbol is called Gye Nyame. It literally means *except for God*. Declaring the supremacy of God, it expresses God is omnipotent, omnipresent, and omniscient. A powerful symbol, it's often worn by warriors declaring, 'I fear none except for God.'."

"So what does all that mean?" Gabe asked.

"It's a warrior symbol acknowledging God is all-knowing and all-powerful, that God is everywhere. God helps warriors sent forth to battle evil. Your ability to ignite fire from within you speaks of God's use of you as a warrior."

"This one is very popular right now," Kirron said as he drew their attention farther out in the clearing. "That trooper was correct when she spoke of it. It's printed on T-shirts and has become a popular tattoo."

They looked at the last symbol in the ravine surrounded by nine ash piles denoting where Kirron's, Michael's, and Gavreel's swords had slain nine gargoyles.

"Our flaming swords created this one," Kirron told them. "It literally means *God is greater than the ups and downs*. We see it often when we do battle. We don't intentionally create the message, but it flows from us nonetheless. The thrusts of our flaming blades make the straight lines."

"Become invisible and move up to the grassy area by the trees on the far side of the road. We need to discuss what you see there, too, but we might be seen by someone if the road is now open. The humans are confused enough without seeing six levitating forms above the place where things happened they can't explain."

Pocked with dots of black ash, the grassy area screamed something serious had happened here. Resembling an eruption of skin lesions announcing some underlying condition, the ground announced the evil that had invaded.

Near the center of the area, they saw the symbol the photographer had captured from the limbs of the old tree that towered nearby.

"Let me guess," Dina remarked. "That's another Adinkra Symbol that Gabe's feet just somehow knew how to burn into the ground."

"Yes, it is," Gavreel confirmed. "Known as Nsoromma, it means *children of the heavens* and represents the guardianship of God."

"So it means God was using us to guard those children, right?" Gabe asked. "We had God's help because there were so many of those Pukwudgie coming out of the trees and so few of us?"

"That's part of it. The children were protected through this whole ordeal. They survived a crash to the bottom of a forty-foot deep ravine, twelve gargoyles, a bugbear, and a horde of Pukwudgie with their poison arrows. God guarded all of us, too, by sending us together. We had one another protecting each member of the team as well as the children. We're all children of the heavens and under the guardianship of God."

"I want to know more about the evil things that were trying to get the kids," Jo whispered. "Are you going to tell us more about gargoyles and bugbears and Pukwudgies?"

Michael answered, "Gargoyles have been carved in stone and used to decorate and act as protectors of buildings for hundreds of years. Some say their use stems from the Legend of the Gargouille in France. A dragon-like creature known as Gargouillle or Goji terrorized the area around Rouen. While several versions of the legend exist, one of them says St. Romanus calmed the creature with a crucifix and captured it with the help of one volunteer, a condemned man. The monster was burned in Rouen, but its head and neck wouldn't burn. Those parts of its body had been tempered by its own flame, many times hotter than what wood produces. They mounted the creature's head on the newly built church to scare away evil spirits. Since then, the Archbishops of Rouen have been allowed to set one prisoner free on that day. There are other examples of gargoyles, like the lion heads on Greek temples and many medieval cathedrals. Often, the heads are used as water spouts to spew water away from the buildings. It's a strange architectural feature since gargoyles are really fierce demons, as you saw. They try to capture souls and take them into the dark service."

"Bugbears are a type of hobgoblin, but they're massive and very strong," Kirron continued. "They were called *bugge*, a frightening thing, in Middle English. They're also known by the old Welsh word *bwg*, meaning evil spirit or goblin. The Germans call them *Bogge*. Bogeyman or *bugaboo are other names*. By whatever name, the creature is a fearsome demonic creature whose purpose is to terrorize children. If a bugbear is around, other kinds of goblins are often nearby."

"Which brings us to the Pukwudgies," Gavreel commented. "Pukwudgie translates as *little wild man of the woods that vanishes*. This creature was originally found in Delaware and Wampanoag folklore, but clearly their habitat has spread. They can appear and disappear. They kidnap people for the dark side, or to feed upon. They're known to use poison arrows as well as spears when they attack. Not only do they like to play nasty tricks, they also like to kill. They've been known to blind people with sand. Even though they're small, they're very dangerous goblins."

"You'll definitely get more instruction about the evil forces that we're charged with fighting, but we should head back to WHL-6TeamDJG+AACB," Kirron told them.

"So we can rest, refresh and EAT," Gabe yelped. "I'm starving." The words were barely out of his mouth when they found themselves on the porch, greeted by Bruno's eager yips.

HOME ONCE MORE...

Kirron announced, "We still have much to discuss and much to do, but it will wait until you've had time to reflect and refresh. One of us will come for you when we're ready to resume training." He nodded and was gone.

"Let me tell you again how well you performed, young warriors," Gavreel told them. "Together, we saved forty-four lives and slew sixty-six evil ones. That's a remarkable tally for experienced warriors, but for beginners like you, it's phenomenal."

"Well, for you guys and Dina and Gabe, maybe," Jo countered. "They fought gargoyles and Pukwudgies with you. All of you were fearless. All I did was kick that bugbear once and stay with some kids, talking and singing. I wasn't a fearless warrior. I was a babysitter."

"You certainly were a warrior, Jo. You fought the hardest battle of all. You battled the terror in those children's hearts and minds. Fear is the greatest enemy of all. You can't see it invading, but you know when it's there. When it takes hold, a person can lose control and do all kinds of foolish things. That's what you battled every minute in that bus and on the ground with those children. You brought them God's peace where there had been only rising fear. Because of you, we saved every single one of those children." Gavreel hugged her. "You are truly a master of gentleness, trust, and caring. Your temperament and voice are gifts, your weapons against evil."

"Every single one of those kids mentioned *you* by name when they told the police what happened, Jo. *You.* You're the angel that had the biggest effect on this mission. None of those children will ever forget you as they continue on their life's journey. The ripple effect of your gentleness and your natural ability to build trust will go on, way beyond that bus. I couldn't be prouder of you." Michael wrapped her in a massive hug.

Gavreel added, "You were very brave, going inside that bus alone, not knowing what you'd find there or what you'd have to handle. You made yourself visible and vulnerable to those children. You helped them be brave by showing your own bravery. Before you arrived, those children were battling fear and losing. For anyone, trying to overcome fear is really warring with your own subconscious. When you let fear be in control, you're basically funneling your energy into battling yourself. Most kids are not capable of overcoming fear alone. You helped them handle the situation they were in, channeling their fear into bravery by concentrating on you. By embracing the fear, you turned it into fuel for bravery. You instinctively knew the difference between being brave and being fearless. You didn't expect them to be fearless. Instead, you helped them be brave."

"You were really great with those kids," Dina and Gabe confirmed simultaneously. Snickering they added, "Here we go again."

"Bruno's going to have a fit if we don't go see him soon. I want to see that wonderful fridge and stove, too. I'm contemplating a big juicy steak, fries, garlic bread, and a salad, with ice cream sundaes for dessert. Let's see if our fridge has all that," Gabe jested. He threw open the door, catching the little dog who launched into his arms and licked his face.

"We'll leave you now, too," Gavreel said as she stroked Bruno's head. "Eat. Refresh. We'll be back before you know it." She raised her hand and was gone.

"Enjoy your meal and time at home," Michael said before he, too, left them. "You were all absolutely fantastic on the mission, all of you. Refresh."

They smelled the steak dinner as they entered their house.

"I do love Gavreel's style!" Gabe exclaimed as he headed to the table. "Her style and her hands!"

Laughing, they sat down together to enjoy the meal Gavreel had set for them. It was all Gabe had wished for and more, and included a bowl of bite-sized pieces of steak for Bruno.

"What do you suppose that machine on the far end of the table is?" Dina wondered as she took her last bite of garlic bread.

"Bowls and spoons are right by it, so it must make for some kind of food," Jo theorized. "Maybe we should look at it from the other side."

"I'll look," Gabe proclaimed as he stood and stretched. "I'm pretty full, but I have a little bit of room left."

"There's a sign on this side," he told the girls. "It says, 'Tell the machine what kind of ice cream treat you'd like. Be specific about the ice cream and toppings. Put your bowl on the flat palette below this sign. Speak into the microphone just above this sign. Your selection will be delivered to your bowl.'."

"Well, this sounds interesting," Gabe declared. "I'll order for Bruno first. He put a bowl on the palette. Sensing the weight of a bowl on the delivery dispenser, the machine came to life. Lights flashed and a whirling sound came from deep inside. "Please, give me half a cup of soft vanilla ice cream with five slices of bananas on top." Instantly the requested portion was in the bowl. "Way cool! Thank you."

Gabe set Bruno's bowl on the table to the side of the machine and got another bowl. He placed it on the empty dispenser plate. "Who's next?"

"Go ahead and order yours," his teammates piped as they walked around the table to stand next to Gabe.

Gabe spoke into the microphone, "Please, give me a full bowl of strawberry and vanilla ice cream swirled together with strawberry syrup and fresh sliced strawberries on top." Like Bruno's dessert, Gabe's instantly appeared in his bowl. Filled to the top, his bowl was close to overflowing. "Whoa! Look at that beauty! Thank you, ice cream dream maker." He lifted his bowl. "Next!"

Jo spoke next. "I'd like half a bowl of fudge swirl ice cream with hot fudge and caramel drizzled over it and toffee bits on top, please." Her order appeared as soon as she'd finished saying what she wanted. "Yum! Thank you, ice cream machine."

Dina was ready with her order as soon as Jo lifted her bowl from the machine. Setting her bowl on the dispenser plate she uttered, "Please, give me half a bowl of rainbow sorbet topped with an assortment of fresh fruit chunks." She gazed on the colorful contents of her bowl as she exclaimed, "Thank you so much! I have never seen such beautiful fruit."

The team relished every bite of their frozen concoctions and reminisced about ice cream experiences in their pasts. They teased one another and shared laugh after laugh as they emptied their bowls.

"I can't eat another bite," Jo and Dina squeaked as they pushed their bowls away.

"I probably could, but I won't," Gabe told them. "I guess we should all go to our chambers to refresh. A shower and time stretched out on the bed sound pretty good now that my hunger beast has been conquered."

"I wouldn't say that particular beast is conquered," the girls chimed through their laughter. "It may be hibernating at the moment, but I bet it isn't conquered."

Their laughter set Bruno into a howling fit, then into a frenzied zooming around the lounge, jumping on furniture and hurtling into twists and turns. His antics fueled their laughter. Their laughter fueled his antics.

"That dog is so much like you, Gabe. I wouldn't be surprised to see his paws burst into flames with all those flips," Dina gasped as her laughter subsided.

"He's on an ice cream and banana high!" Jo added. "He has way more energy than I do right now. I'm going to roll my stuffed body into the shower and then onto my bed for a while. Refresh myself, as they say around here."

"That sounds pretty good for all of us," Dina agreed. "We were out quite a while training to use the Space Tessellation and then that intense mission. I'm feeling a bit droopy myself, now that I'm stuffed and have relaxed with you guys. Is that my tub calling me?" She cupped one hand behind her ear.

"Bruno, the girls are going into their own chambers now, so tell them goodbye before we head into ours, too," Gabe instructed.

Bruno planted himself in front of Dina and pawed at her leg. She bent over and stroked his head. "Good night, sweet boy. You're such a good dog." Bruno's tongue delivered puppy kisses to Dina's cheek.

He moved to Jo, planted himself in front of her and looked expectantly into her eyes. She murmured, "I suppose you feel it's time to slobber on my face now, eh, Bruno?" She leaned down and caressed his head. "I agree. You are a good, good dog." His wet tongue on her cheek expressed his acceptance of and affection for her.

"Okay, Romeo. Enough kissing. Let's go, boy," Gabe called as he headed to his door. "See you soon."

"Yeah, see you soon," the girls parodied as they opened their own doors.

Soon was right. Sooner than they expected.

SUMMONED...

Q uickly, Dina, Jo, and Gabe doffed their uniforms. The still-amazing automatic refreshing of their gear began as each uniform landed on the platform.

As soon as each had bathed, brushed hair and teeth, and put on comfortable clothes, they headed to their beds. Even though they'd been told they didn't require sleep any more, it sounded pretty appealing right now. Thoughts of the things they'd seen and done swirled in their minds as they drifted off.

Dina awoke with a start as Gavreel shook her shoulder. "Dina, Dina. You have to get up. You've been summoned."

"Huh? Summoned? What does that mean?"

"It means you need to get up right now and gear up," Gavreel told her. "I'll meet you in the lounge. Get up and ready yourself immediately."

Michael stroked Jo's head and called, "Jo, you have to get up. Come on, Pumpkin, wake up."

She stirred and mumbled, "Dad? What are you doing here? I'm refreshing."

"I know, but you have to get up. You've been summoned. Get up and put on your uniform. Meet the team in the lounge."

Kirron shook Gabe's foot as he called, "Wake up, Gabe. Gabe, wake up. You've been summoned. Get up and get yourself ready to go."

A groggy voice croaked, "I'm sleeping. Leave me alone."

"I can't leave you alone," Kirron objected. "All three of you have been summoned. You have to answer the summons."

"Summoned?"

"Yes, summoned. Now get up and get yourself in uniform. Meet the team in the lounge. Be quick!" Kirron turned and headed out of the room

Joining Gavreel, Kirron, and Michael in the lounge, Dina, Jo, and Gabe exchanged confused looks. Uniformed and eager to find out what was happening, they walked up to their trainers.

"We're very sorry to waken you and pull you from your respite to refresh," Kirron told them, "but we have no choice. All three of you have been summoned by the Council. Actually, all six of us have been summoned. We must go immediately. A summons is always serious."

"What's the Council? Why would they send for us?" Gabe asked.

"The Council is the supreme overseeing and governing body of the universe. They have direct contact with God. They have the power to see everything happening everywhere in the universe. The Council's made up of the most powerful angels who were once prophets and spiritual leaders from all sectors of the universe. Some were humans on Earth. Some were creatures you've never heard of, from places you know nothing about. The Council not only decides what type of service all angels perform and what their everlasting life will be spent doing in service to God, they also decide which warrior angels go on which missions, where and when. Rarely are teams summoned to the Council. Usually we receive our missions through our DMD or from an individual member of the Council coming to us with instructions and information we need. I've never heard of novices being summoned, but we three and you three have been summoned. We must go."

"Gabe, I see you still have your team's DMD attached to your bracelet. Bring it up to full size and open it," Gavreel ordered.

They clustered around the device. The screen displayed an enormous white marble building with stairs the width of the front leading to immense double doors. The structure, adorned with ornate columns and detailed lifelike sculptures, was breath-taking.

Some statues resembled humans and some were forms they could not name nor describe.

"That's the Council Edifice. The DMD is instructing you to go to that location. We'll go together. Let us address the council. Do not speak unless spoken to by a council member. Make physical contact so we transport together," Kirron pronounced as he put his hand on Gabe's shoulder. Each team member joined hands or placed a hand on someone's shoulder. "Put in the code UH1CE, Gabe."

The team materialized at the bottom of the massive stairs. They stared up at the doors at the top of the stairs. "Shrink and stow the DMD. We'll go up together," Kirron said.

The group mounted the stairs. As soon as they reached the top, Kirron, Gavreel, and Michael held up their right hands, exposing their palms to the door. The doors slid open.

As soon as the team stepped inside, they knew they'd entered a sacred place, place of both peace and power. The ordinary became the extraordinary in this place. The white marble floor and walls reflected uncountable halos of uncountable angels who served. The ethereal light pulsed and beckoned their eyes to scan and observe as much as they could, to learn by looking, really seeing. The glistening sculptures of beings large and small, enraptured them. The walls and ceiling, filled with symbols, icons, and stained-glass scenes, captured their attention. Faint chords of music, perfect tones like those they'd heard at the choir chambers, soothed all who entered. Opaque clouds, so faint they were barely visible, wafted around the room. What was that sweet scent? Were those puffs carrying the divine aroma that added to the joy and serenity they felt? Everything about the Council Edifice was captivating.

"This way," Kirron gestured, walking toward a station at the back of the room manned by human-looking angels and unknown-creature angels. All looked welcoming, but intent on the tasks they were doing.

"Warrior Team GKM1 and novice Team DJG+AACB reporting

for summons," Kirron told the human-looking angel nearest the door.

"Wait right here. I'll announce your arrival." The angel smiled at the group before passing through the door behind him. Upon his return he announced, "The Council is ready for you. Please, follow me."

Behind the door, honeycombed walls stretched as far as they could see. Just like in their sector's training center, scenes played in each cell. This mural of scenes was colossal, many times larger than the one they had seen at the training center. What looked like stems and tendrils of some wild plant, coming together and parting, connecting and disconnecting, shuffling around the scenes in the cells, covered the walls. Just glancing around was overwhelming, like being scooped into a strobing kaleidoscope of continuously-shifting scenes. The images' constant fast-forward changes threw Dina's, Jo's, and Gabe's senses into overload. Even if they hadn't been instructed to remain silent, the novice trio doubted they could have said a word after passing through this shuffling view of the universe.

"Here we are. When you enter the auditorium, please proceed down the stairs to the Chamber floor and face the dais," he directed as he threw open another gigantic door.

Kirron led the way down. Ornate chairs lined every row. Row after row, section after section, they passed beings seated in fancy chairs. Some figures looked human, but many did not. None of them could ever have imagined this collection of souls. Like an orchestra warming up, thousands of voices hummed in a monotone buzz. No words or melody came to the team, just the drone of voices united in communicating a single thought: the ones they awaited had arrived.

When they reached the floor, Teams GKM1 and DJG+AACB stood at attention, facing the dais. The souls in the seats of honor all appeared human. They studied the six angels who stood before them. A single shimmering figure entered and stood behind the center seat on the dais. Sheer authority permeated the air, silencing the room. All fell to their knees until one word rang through the holy hall, "Sit."

FACING THE COUNCIL...

The man seated in the center seat rose and addressed the group. "I am the good shepherd. My life exemplifies God's generosity and love for all creation. I am proof that God can transform any mess made by mankind. Any mess can become a message, a messenger, or a messiah when put into the hands of God."

Smiling, he radiated a glow of euphoria and tranquility. "I call forth faithful servants from different faiths on Earth to assist me. Moses, Mary, and Ishmael, please go to the floor with these two teams."

When the three prophets had moved to the floor, he continued. "You three, Dina, Jophiel, and Gabriel, have been under the Council's watchful eyes. You are among the chosen. We knew you were extraordinary at your creation and through your development on Earth. The gifts you received were not allowed to go dormant. You discovered them and honed them into special skills. These skills have served you well. They continue to serve others as you serve God. The choices you've made on your journeys have intensified your strength and warrior aptitude. Even though you've completed only one of the character virtues mastery trails and completed only phase one of training, you have melded into a strong warrior team."

He continued, "You were sent on a vital mission, accompanying Team GKM1, to save innocent children from the evil that sought to drag them to the dark side. Your divine consciousness has been measured by your actions. You move without conscious decision to move. You simply move, allowing God to guide your movements. You trust your instincts, not needing to be told every answer, but feeling them from within. This trust allows God to work through you, accomplishing what needs to be done. Your selfless acts to save others and protect one another are unprecedented for those so near their arrival here. Your valor in battle has not gone unnoticed. It is our honor, as the High Council, to bestow upon each of you the Angelic Medal of Valor. Prophets, please address each recipient and present the medals."

"Dina, please, step forward. I, Moses, humble servant of God, bearer of the commandments given to mankind, and leader of our people out of Egypt, present to you this Angelic Medal of Valor for your service. Your selfless acts of bravery helped save innocent lives and saved one of your teammates from capture by the evil one. The burning of the Nyame Dua symbol into the ground of that ravine proclaims God's presence and protection through you. Well done, intuitive warrior. Well done."

He placed an ornate charm in her hand. It looked like a shield surrounded by a wreath and featured a dove on top. Religious symbols of many faiths from Earth decorated the shield. She saw a Star of David, a cross, a star and crescent, a lotus, a Wheel of Dharma, and the Alpha and Omega symbols.

"Thank you. I'm overwhelmed," Dina marveled. "Did I really did do anything to deserve this award? I'm grateful for your confidence in me."

"Jophiel, please, step forward. I, Mary, also known as the Blessed Mother, humble servant of our Lord, daughter of Saint Anne and Saint Joachim, mother and disciple of Jesus, present to you this Angelic Medal of Valor for your service. Your selfless acts of bravery and gentleness calmed the fears in those children on the bus. By revealing your true self, by staying with them, talking and singing, you instinctively conquered fear, the greatest enemy one ever has to battle. You showed by example what it means to be brave and be a conduit of God's love. Well done, gentle warrior. Well done."

She laid Jo's charm in her hand and bowed her head as she backed up.

"Like Dina, I'm overwhelmed by this, but I thank you very much," Jo exclaimed. "It's an honor."

"Aslan Gabriel, please, step forward. I, Ishmael, first born son of Abraham and Hagar, ancestor of Arab tribes, and forefather of Muhammad, present to you this Angelic Medal of Valor for your service. Your selfless acts of bravery helped save innocent children from the evil one. You have discovered a natural weapon within your being and have instinctively used it to serve God. You slew several evil creatures using this gift. You branded the ground, first with the Gye Nyame symbol proclaiming God is all-knowing and all-powerful, then with the Nsoromma symbol claiming yourself, your team, and all those children as children of the heavens. Both of your given names, fittingly, mean warrior. Well done, fierce young warrior. Well done."

"I'm humble and grateful. I never felt like I belonged anywhere on Earth, or that I ever deserved anything. Thank you for this award and for allowing me to function better here and find happiness with this team," Gabe responded.

As soon as the charm was laid in Gabe's hand, the voice from the dais called, "Team GKM1, please step forward."

Gavreel, Kirron, and Michael each took a step forward.

"You three are high ranking and highly achieved angels who have served God selflessly for eons. Michael, your return to Earth as a human was an important and noteworthy mission. Few are willing to do it, but you accepted the mission. You handled your role as a warrior on Earth honorably. While there, you trained other warriors and saved many lives. You also shared God's love and touched many hearts, saving them from evil ways. Your seed from that lifetime produced another fine warrior for our ranks. You handled that time on Earth as well as you have handled your role here before and after that lifetime.

"Team GKM1, your service to all creation has not gone unnoticed by this Council. Your training of multitudes of new warriors is exemplary. Your teamwork and skill in battle is second to none. Your last mission, with these three novices accompanying you, is particularly noteworthy. You saved forty-four humans from capture by the evil one and slew sixty-six of the evil one's servants. You've adapted the training of these three to meet their unique needs and foster their skills. For these reasons and countless others, the Council gratefully bestows upon each of you another Angelic Medal of Valor. Gavreel, Kirron, and Michael, words cannot adequately express our gratitude for your selfless service."

The prophets laid the medal in each of their hands, bowed their heads, and returned to their places on the dais. Applause filled the auditorium as the six honorees smiled and humbly bowed their heads.

"Read the inscription, words originally from Chief Seattle, on the back of each of your medals, and they will be attached to your chains."

Michael's voice boomed, "'This we know, all things are connected. Like the blood that unites one family, all things are connected. Our God is the same God, whose compassion is equal for all.'"

The medals snapped on each warrior's chain.

"Now, we must share and discuss the second reason for your summons. It will require *this* team's response. You will understand when you see what we have to show you."

The room darkened and four distinct screens filled sections of the wall behind the dais. The room was silent as they viewed the scenarios that filled the screens.

Solemnity permeated the chambers. Scenes in places they did not recognize with people they did not recognize whizzed before their eyes. When the screens faded to black, a voice in the dark boomed, "You are called forth in service. Go. Prepare. Time is short, but you have some time. You are the best hope."

As the chamber illuminated, the six on the dais bowed their

heads. "We go forth in service of God!" rang from their mouths just before they hurried up the stairs and out of the chambers.

ONWARD...

he group transported back to Team DJG's lounge.

"We have time to plan and prepare, but we must begin soon," Gavreel announced, "but we will allow a bit more time to refresh since your time was cut short by the summons. You four will need to get going on your second training module; you'll need the virtues and lessons of that training before we can depart." They studied their DMD monitor. "This will not be a typical Level-2 mission, as you probably guessed from what you saw on the screens at the Council Chambers. We must all get ready."

"I need to tell you something," Dina fretted.

Turning their attention to Dina, Gavreel, Kirron, and Michael announced,

"Go ahead."

"I'm pretty sure that man we saw on the screen was the same guy in the plumber's van when we went to find help for the kids on the bus. It was getting dark and I was only by him for a minute or so, but that voice was the same voice. He screamed at me. I got the same feeling watching him on that monitor as I did when I saw him in the van. There's something really wrong about him."

Gavreel, Kirron, and Michael exchanged their familiar look of shared thoughts.

"That might mean we're dealing with Aka Manah," Michael uttered.

"I haven't dealt with Aka Manah for centuries," Kirron retorted.

"What's Aka Manah?" Gabe asked.

"He's an evil demon. His name means *mind made evil*. He's the demon of evil intention. He specializes in preventing people from fulfilling their moral duties. He's known by other names, but his mission is always to poison minds against good and push them into serving evil. He corrupts minds, so people cannot discriminate between good and evil," Kirron told them.

"So he's a really bad dude, this Aka Manah," Gabe replied.

"He is evil and serves the dark one. He's come among humans before, but not for a very long time. He is capable of toppling civilizations. If he's surfaced again, his intent is evil," Michael remarked. "He can morph into any form he wishes. Appearing human can help him achieve his goals."

"How can we fight Aka Manah?" Jo asked softly.

"Earthly weapons cannot permanently harm him. Only a Seraph's blade, infused with heavenly fire and angels' spirits, can topple him," Michael warned. "His life force will be cast back to the dark realm if it's pierced by a Seraph's sword."

He glanced at the DMD monitor, now showing the first streaks of light chasing the darkness in the sky. It was not flashing red, though, so there was still time.

"Everything we saw on the mission screens was pretty hard to see," Jo admitted. "How do you get used to all the evil?"

Kirron spoke softly. "You don't ever get used to evil in any form it takes. It's the catalyst that drives us. You know it's lurking and will swallow up every good thing if you don't stand against it. We completed a very successful mission. Dina, Jo, Gabe, you've become enlightened warriors after only one training module. Your instincts and skills are unparalleled by any warriors I have ever trained. I can't even imagine what you'll be capable of when you finish your training. When you finish the character virtues challenges on the other trails and the other training modules, you'll be ready to go anywhere in the universe and fight for God. You've forged into a strong team that will continue to defeat evil in all forms. I'm certain of that."

Gavreel looked lovingly at the trio. "We know that losing each of you was devastating to your families. Losing one's child, or a sibling, is a great loss. That loss creates a hole that can never be patched. It changes the person, but that's part of that person's life journey. Their grief is real and will never go away as they continue their lives on Earth." She paused a moment, reflecting. "They still have things to do there and their own lessons to learn. Until they're reunited with you here and have their own missions to fill their everlasting life, they won't understand. But, we hope you can now see and understand how vital young warriors are in fighting evil. You're fulfilling your purpose."

Michael summed up the elders' feelings. "We're proud of you, young warriors. You continue to amaze us as we watch your enlightenment in service. It matters not that you three came from different families and faiths. Your enlightenment is taking you on the same path, the path to fight the darkness that is a constant threat. You're honoring your calling as chosen ones."

Michael held out his hand. "You absolutely earned these."

He handed Dina, Jo, and Gabe gold sun-shaped charms. The front inscription read:

Lao Tzu
"There are many paths to enlightenment. Be sure to take one with a heart."

The back simply said:
"Every choice leads to the light or to darkness. Will pain be inflicted or alleviated by your actions?"

As soon as they had read their latest charm, it clamped onto their chains, right next to the Angelic Medal of Valor.

"I don't know about any of you, but I'm thinking some food would alleviate some of the pain my stomach's starting to feel. Can anyone do that hand trick for instant food, or do we have to go all the way to the fridge and see what's there?"

Snorting with laughter Gavreel crowed, "Allow me." One flick of her hand and a banquet appeared on the table. Tantalizing aromas filled their lounge. Bruno stood on his hind legs, staring at the feast.

"Now, that's what I'm talking about!" Gabe cried as he headed to the food. "Come on, everybody. Let's eat."

"We'll share a meal another time," Kirron declared. "We still have much to do. You four enjoy your meal and refresh some more. Your training continues the next time we call. We must be ready for the mission we were shown."

Kirron nodded at Gavreel and Michael. They stood shoulder to shoulder and disappeared together.

"That Gavreel sure can cook!" Gabe declared as he stuffed a forkful of spaghetti in his mouth.

ACKNOWLEDGEMENTS

I extend my heartfelt thanks to all who have supported me through the writing and revising phases of this book. I appreciate your words of encouragement and suggestions more than I can adequately express.

Special thanks to my husband Dave and our sons for their support through the process. Extra special thanks to my friend Laura Vidrine and my son Jamie Hobson, both of whom encouraged me to start and were the first readers of the first draft. Your thoughts and suggestions were so valuable. I can't possibly thank you enough. Extreme gratitude to Dorothy Caldwell Minor for her support, encouragement, and editing skills. She spent so much time giving suggestions to tighten the writing.

My other alpha readers, Jonathon Hobson, Becky Aftreth, and Nichole Green, I appreciate the time you devoted to reading this book, giving feedback and praise, and encouraging me to follow through with publishing. As you see, I did it!

Made in the USA
Monee, IL
18 June 2020

34231786R00177